STARW

The STARBROW Series by Tim Ray includes:
Book 1: **STARBROW**
Book 2: **STARWARRIOR**

Music by Tim Ray:
CD-album: **SPIRITUAL POP SONGS**

About the author

Danish-American author Tim Ray is a spiritual seeker and teacher who is not associated with any particular religion or tradition. In his books, Tim seeks to communicate in modern language his understanding of ancient spiritual wisdom and principles—and to point a way out of pain and suffering to peace and harmony.

Tim Ray is also a singer and songwriter. His first CD *Spiritual Pop Songs* contains 12 funky pop songs with positive, consciousness-raising lyrics that you can sing and dance to.

To spread information about spiritual principles and their practical application, Tim Ray and Barbara Berger founded *BeamTeam*, a publishing company and center in Copenhagen, Denmark. For more information about Tim Ray and Barbara Berger's books, music, lectures, and concerts, see www.beamteam.com

About the editor

American author Barbara Berger has worked closely with Tim Ray for many years and is the editor of The *Starbrow* Series. Barbara Berger has written more than 10 self-empowerment books including *Mental Technology*, *Gateway to Grace*, *The Spiritual Pathway* and her bestseller *Fast Food for the Soul*. In her books she describes the same spiritual principles and mental technologies that are presented in Tim Ray's novels.

STARWARRIOR
A Spiritual Thriller

TIM RAY

Edited by Barbara Berger

Book 2 in The Starbrow Series

FINDHORN
Press

STARWARRIOR
© Tim Ray 2002, 2004

British Library Cataloguing-in-Publication Data. A catalogue record for this book is available from the British Library.

Original Danish edition first published in 2002 by BeamTeam Books, Copenhagen, Denmark.

English version by Tim Ray and Barbara Berger.

Cover, book design and maps by BeamTeam Books
Portrait of author by Søren Solkær

Published in 2004 by:
Findhorn Press Ltd
305a The Park, Findhorn
Forres IV36 3TE
Scotland
Tel 01309 690582
Fax 01309 690036
E-mail: info@findhornpress.com
Web site: www.findhornpress.com

Printed in Denmark by AIT Nørhaven A/S, Viborg

ISBN 1-84409-036-1

Thanks Again

Once again I would like to thank my faithful (and long-enduring!) editor, Barbara Berger, who also accompanied me on the second part of the adventure. The Force is with you!

SYNOPSIS

In Book 1, Starbrow and his two friends Jacob (Moncler) and Janus (Telperion) are called upon to help save humanity from total annihilation by learning spiritual truths and how to raise the collective consciousness of humanity.

It all starts one night in Copenhagen, when Starbrow, a young man in his early twenties meets a mysterious woman called Ticha who says she is his Guardian Angel. Ticha says she has come to remind him of his ancient oath to create peace and harmony on Earth.

Confused by this strange experience, Starbrow tells his beloved grandfather Elmar, who is an adventurer, about this mysterious meeting. To Starbrow's great surprise, his grandfather tells about his own spiritual quest and how he met the Tibetan master Djwal Khul in the Himalayas when he was searching for the lost city of Shamballa, half a century ago.

Still shaken and confused, Starbrow, who is just a regular guy, goes out partying with his friends, Jacob and Janus. When he returns home that night, he finds the mysterious woman Ticha in his bedroom. She tells him she has a message for him from Ashtar, the Commander of the Intergalactic Fleet about 'Mission Earth Ascension'. Ticha turns on Starbrow's television set and Ashtar appears and explains that Planet Earth is ascending to the higher dimensions. Ashtar then invites Starbrow to come to the Ashtar Command's Mothership in the higher dimensions to receive training in 5th dimensional living so he can return to Earth to help humanity raise its consciousness and ascend peacefully into the higher dimensions. Starbrow has 24 hours to reply to the invitation.

All this makes Starbrow think he's going crazy. That same night, his beloved grandfather Elmar has a heart attack and Starbrow rushes to the hospital to his grandfather's bedside. Just before he passes over, Elmar says: "Follow your heart, for your heart alone knows the way..." These are the very same words the mysterious woman Ticha just said to him in his bedroom after he heard Ashtar's transmission. Hearing these words triggers something deep in Starbrow and he rushes back and accepts the invitation.

Once in the Mothership in the higher dimensions, Starbrow discovers that his best friends Jacob and Janus have also been called. But now when he meets them he finds them transformed into their True Selves. Jacob is the mighty Wizard Moncler, Janus is the heroic Elven Warrior Telperion, and Starbrow discovers that he is the 'One with the Sight'. Together again, the three are given a past life regression where they learn they lived together in Britain at the time of King Arthur and Merlin—and were also on a mission at that time to establish peace on Earth by raising the collective consciousness. In that incarnation, Starbrow was Dana, a priestess of Avalon, Moncler was Gaius, a Christian priest, and Telperion was Sir Loran, one of King Arthur's Knights of the Round Table. During that lifetime, they failed in their mission and were betrayed and killed by Lord Gavin.

After their past life regression, they meet the 600 other Earth volunteers who were called by Ashtar. Commander Ashtar tells the volunteers that the collective consciousness of humanity has fallen so low that if humanity doesn't raise its consciousness during the next 48 hours, Planet Earth will do a total axis shift and annihilate all of humanity. The mission therefore for Starbrow, his friends, and the 600 is to go back to Earth and raise the collective consciousness of humanity to avert the axis shift. They are to do this by anchoring a positive New Vision in the minds of humanity. Time is short—they have only 48 hours to do the job. But before they go back to Earth, they are given a crash course in Spiritual Principles and the Power of Mind so they can carry out their mission.

The first lesson Starbrow and his friends learn is about the Power of the Force. They learn this when they come to the first Gateway, the Blue Temple, which is guarded by the Ascended Masters Kuthumi and Serapis Bey. Here they learn how to contact the Force and experience it through meditation and prayer. They are then tested by being sent back to hell on Earth and land in the middle of a violent battle on the West Bank of Israel. The three almost get carried away by the anger and violence, but finally calm down and start to meditate on the Force. They are then joined by a group of young Israelis and Arabs, and together they succeed in calming the consciousness of people in the area and the fighting stops. By doing this, they pass the first test and move on to the next lesson which is about the Power of Mind.

At the Second Gateway with its Violet Flames, guarded by the Master Saint Germain, Starbrow and his friends learn about the Power of Mind. Saint Germain teaches them about mind and how thoughts are creating our reality. As a test, they must survive the Manifestation Chamber, where their every thought manifests instantaneously! At first everything goes from bad to worse, until finally they take control of their minds, and in a horrific battle with the Dweller on the Threshold, they pass the second test.

At the Third Gateway, Starbrow and his friends find Archangel Michael and the Pink Clouds. Archangel Michael teaches them that the Will of the Force is Love, the Highest Good of All, and that when they choose Love, they are in harmony with the Force and peace and harmony are the result. Then they are tested again. Starbrow is tested by waking up in what he thinks is his perfect dream life where everything he always wanted is his. Then he is faced with the difficult choice—is he willing to relinquish this dream life in order to choose Love for the Highest Good of All?

After passing this test, Starbrow and his friends face the final test, which is a composite of all they've learned. They find themselves in a vast, barren desert—without food or water and about to die—looking for Shamballa, the City of Light. By using the three lessons they've just mastered, they raise their consciousness and the desert around them is transformed into a lush paradise—and they find themselves in Shamballa, the City of Light!

Once they have learned the lessons and passed the tests associated with them, they are sent back on their mission to save Planet Earth. When they return, they discover that Planet Earth has been thrown into chaos by violent earthquakes, storms and floods. To carry out their mission, Starbrow and his friends must travel from their home in Copenhagen, Denmark to Glastonbury Tor in England to anchor the New Vision because Glastonbury Tor is part of the ancient Light Grid formed by the Earth's Power Spots. Due to the chaos on Earth, getting to England and Glastonbury Tor is a major challenge and they almost don't make it. But by focusing on the Force, they get to England, then to Stonehenge, and even manage to escape death by a huge tornado. When all hope seems lost, they are helped in their desperate race against time to get to Glastonbury Tor by two Star Elves. As they struggle forward on foot, the veils between the dimensions are lifted and they pass through a dream-like landscape of ghosts, temptations and scenes from their past. With their last ounce of strength, they make it to the top of Glastonbury Tor just before midnight and begin the Activation Meditation. They meditate for 24 hours non-stop, reactivating the Earth's Power Spots with the other volunteers who are meditating simultaneously at other Power Spots around the globe. During the Activation Meditation, the New Vision spreads out over the entire Earth, raising the collective consciousness of humanity high enough to save humanity from an axis shift and total annihilation.

The book ends with Starbrow and his friends gazing out from Glastonbury Tor and enjoying the magical new peace that has descended over Planet Earth.

CONTENTS

PART THREE
THE GATHERING OF THE BROTHERHOOD

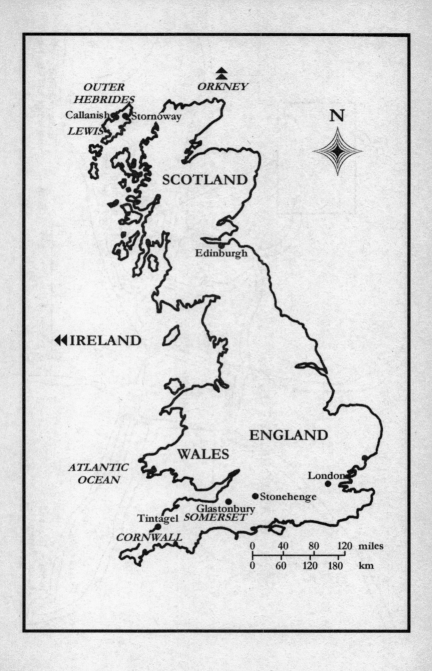

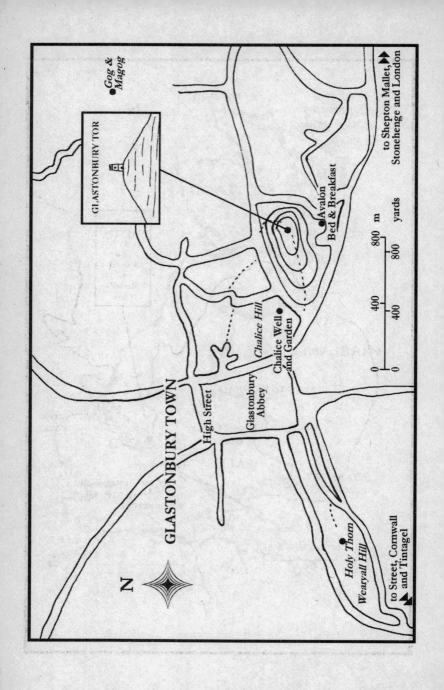

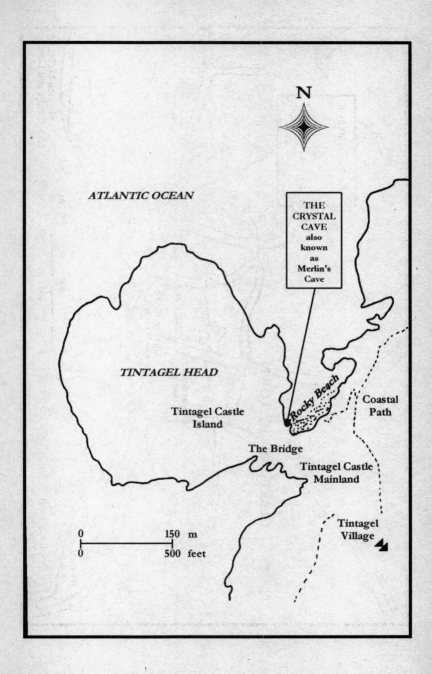

The Prophecy of Starwarrior

When the One with the Sight
is reunited with the Warrior from the Stars
the Perfect Being will be born

From the Perfect Being
will come the Single Eye

From the Single Eye
will come the Perfect World

And then the Angels sing

PROLOGUE

THE HUNT FOR STARBROW

"Ben, I've got something I want you to see."

"Now?" said Ben Nevis, looking at his watch. It was almost midnight.

"Yes, now!"

Ben Nevis realized it must be pretty important or his boss, General Peter Elson, wouldn't be calling him at this hour of the night.

"OK boss, I'll be right over."

"Good… and Ben, you better pack your bags… you'll probably be gone for a couple of days."

Special Agent Ben Nevis knew the drill. He'd been General Peter Elson's right hand man at DETI—the American CIA's Directorate of Extra-Terrestrial Intelligence—for the last five years. So he was used to being sent on all kinds of wild goose chases, hunting down stray satellites and debriefing disoriented civilians who'd seen more than they were supposed to. But a call at midnight was something special. Usually the cranks could wait till morning.

So Ben couldn't help but ask his boss what was up.

"SETI's observatory has picked up a signal," said the General.

"Really? Arecibo in Puerto Rico?"

"No. The Very Large Array in New Mexico."

"And it's that unusual?" asked Nevis.

"Yes, to say the least."

"All right boss, I'll be there as fast as I can."

The drive from Agent Nevis' house in Georgetown to CIA headquarters in Langley, Virginia, where Nevis worked when he wasn't out on one of his secret missions, usually took about 20 minutes. Now since it was almost midnight, it took less than 10. In fact, it was exactly midnight when Agent Nevis drove his dark blue

Jeep Cherokee past the security guards up to the main building. Even at this time of night, CIA headquarters was a hive of activity so there were plenty of people on duty as Nevis strode down the long corridors. He nodded now and again to a familiar face as he moved swiftly down the halls.

DETI was CIA's latest and most hush-hush intelligence operation. To access the section, Nevis had to pass through the tightest security checks including a retinal scan and voice identification.

"Ah Ben, thanks for coming over so fast," said General Elson as Nevis walked through the door into his boss' spacious office. "Come in and have a seat."

General Elson was a heavy-set man in his late fifties. Major Ben Nevis knew him well, having served under him during all his years in the CIA. Their years together had created a deep bond between them, so it made sense for Elson to choose Nevis to head one of his special units. The ones he often dispatched on "sensitive" missions that required the skill of a warrior and maximum discretion. Nevis possessed exactly the right combination of brains and fighting skill to keep a cool head and maintain the right perspective on such missions. It was also to his credit that the agents who served under him had great respect for him, although some of the other squad leaders whispered that Nevis might, on occasion, be just a tad too reckless. Some attributed Ben's icy cool and fearlessness to the fact that unlike many of the other squad leaders, he didn't have a family. No, his job was his love—to him the mission was everything.

So yes, Major Ben Nevis was the perfect man to lead a special unit on highly sensitive, covert operations—which was why General Elson didn't think twice about making Nevis his number one man in the field when he became head of DETI. It took some time for Elson and Nevis to get used to tracking UFOs instead of international terrorists and Russian mobsters, but after a while they both settled into the brave new world of outer space. In fact, they'd become so proficient at the job that they almost always could find a logical, "non-extra-terrestrial" explanation for 95% of the Unidentified Flying Objects and other so-called "Mysterious Events" they investigated during the course of a week. Five percent, however, did remain unexplained.

"So what's up?" said Nevis as he sat down on General Elson's worn brown leather sofa, which was placed strategically in the middle of the room. There was a bottle of whisky and a tray of glasses on the coffee table. There was whisky in one of the glasses.

The General sat down in the armchair across from Nevis. "Have you heard of 'the interdimensional radio'?"

"Yes," answered Nevis. "It's one of SETI's inventions. They tell me it's what they call a 'high-vibrational-frequency-receiver'. They use it to pick up high vibrational frequency signals from outer space, signals that are on a higher frequency than ordinary signals. Some of the SETI astronomers have this theory that intelligent life in the Universe may operate on higher vibrational frequencies—and if that's the case, they may be trying to send us messages using higher vibrational frequencies. As far as I understand, that's why they built this contraption—to pick up these messages if there are any. But last thing I heard, the radio was not living up to their expectations so it was demoted from SETI's main observatory in Arecibo to their observatory in New Mexico… seems it never picked up anything worth listening to!"

"Not anymore," said the General.

"Really… you mean the radio's finally picked up something?"

"Yeah." said Elson and got up and walked across the room to the TV set. He picked up the remote control and turned to Nevis. "At 20:32 Eastern Standard Time—just three and a half hours ago—SETI's high-vibrational-frequency-receiver picked up a signal via the Very Large Array radio observatory in New Mexico. Apparently it came from outside the Earth's atmosphere—and it was crystal clear so the astronomers had no problem converting it to visual images."

"So you're saying it was a TV signal?"

"Exactly. The head of the team out there, one of my old friends from Annapolis, Professor Eric Ross, was so alarmed by the signal that he immediately sent me a copy. Ross thinks… or hopes it's a hoax… but then again… it might not be… so I thought you ought to take a look."

"Was the signal sent to SETI?"

"We don't know who the signal was sent to—or who sent it. That's one of the reasons why I called you in."

The General turned on the television. The screen was blank.

Nevis looked at the blank screen. It stayed blank and Nevis was just about to ask his boss what was going on when he started hearing a faint hum… a sound that was barely discernible… but it was there nevertheless. The sound was a very high-pitched ringing tone that seemed to come from the television set. Then the screen started to flicker. For a few seconds, it seemed to Nevis that he saw patterns on the screen—flickering colors and geometric shapes—pulsating to some unknown beat. For some reason, the tones and patterns made his body tingle all over—or so he thought. But before he could think more about the tingling, the pulsating shapes turned into a face—a man's face. The man had jet-black hair and was dressed in a shining silvery uniform with a military-style badge on his breast. He seemed to be surrounded by a white light.

"Well, it sure looks like somebody really dug up their old Star Trek outfit..." chuckled Nevis.

Elson chuckled too.

"Greetings, Brother in the Light!" said the dark-haired man. He did not open his mouth yet Nevis heard his voice quite clearly—as if he was speaking out loud.

"What's this?" laughed Nevis again. "Science fiction for ventriloquists?"

Elson sent him a half smile. "Just you wait and see."

"I AM Ashtar, Commander of Mission Earth Ascension, speaking on behalf of the Intergalactic Council," said the man on the screen, still without opening his mouth. "The purpose of this special transmission is to ask for your help in this critical phase of humanity's evolution. Planet Earth and all its inhabitants are standing on the brink. On the brink of a new era. And you can help to determine how this transformation will take place. And whether this transformation will bring chaos or harmony to Planet Earth.

"This transmission has been made possible thanks to a special dispensation from the Intergalactic Council. This dispensation may have a profound effect on your role in Planet Earth's ascension into the higher dimensions. But before I go into detail as to your role in these critical events, let me first take a moment to briefly sketch the present situation as I see it..."

"Is this a joke or what?" Nevis turned and looked at Elson.

The General pressed the pause button. "Ben, do you think I would have gotten you out of bed in the middle of the night if I thought we'd gotten a hold of Steven Spielberg's latest home video!"

"So how can this guy speak without opening his mouth?"

"If I knew the answer to that I would know the answer to a whole lot of other things too. But just listen, there's more."

Nevis muttered under his breath and turned back to the TV. General Elson pressed the play button. Then he sat down at the other end of the sofa and picked up his glass of whisky.

"... For many hundreds of thousands of years, Planet Earth has been a designated test zone for soul evolution," continued the glowing man on the screen. "Time and space, birth and rebirth, karma, creativity and free will have all been a part of the curriculum on Planet Earth as souls moved on their way to higher consciousness and the higher dimensions.

"Throughout the ages, only a very few souls have fully mastered the curriculum of the 3rd and 4th dimensions—and ascended into the higher dimensions. This is because the requirements for ascension are very strict and very demanding. And up until now, most of humanity was not even aware that it was possible to ascend to higher dimensions. That is until very recently.

"Now all this is changing rapidly. Here at the dawn of the new Millennium, Planet Earth and all of its inhabitants are faced with the greatest transformation the Planet has ever experienced. A transformation so profound that it makes the events, which took place in Atlantis some 12,000 years ago seem like child's play..."

"Atlantis?" said Nevis.

"And that's not half of it." The General took a swig of whisky.

"... Planet Earth's time as a test zone is now up and the Planet has begun its ascension into the 5th dimension. And this ascension is affecting every human being on Earth. Suddenly, human beings all over the Planet are waking up and beginning to realize that it is possible for them to ascend into the 5th dimension, together with Planet Earth.

"Because of this the old structures on Planet Earth are falling apart, are collapsing. That is why, on the surface at least, it may look as if everything is deteriorating, that things are falling apart. That everything's going from bad to worse. But the many transformations that the Planet and its inhabitants are undergoing at the moment—both on the inner and the outer planes—are in fact the birthing of Planet Earth into the 5th dimension. And this birthing, and the labor pains that go with it, can be heard in the far corners of the universe.

"Many of the souls who are already in the 5th dimension or in even higher dimensions—soul groups such as the Ascended Masters of the Great White Brotherhood—are now actively working to help each individual human being on Planet Earth and the Planet herself make this transition... this ascension into the 5th dimension as smoothly and easily as possible. But my friend, this is a very great task. Indeed, a very, very great task.

"This is also why the Intergalactic Council has appointed me to lead a fleet of starships to Planet Earth to assist the Ascended Masters in their efforts to facilitate the ascension process. My fleet, the Intergalactic Fleet, consists of tens of thousands of starships, manned by millions of ascended beings from near and far in the galaxies. They come from Arcturus, from the Pleiades, from Sirius, Andromeda and Orion, just to name a few..."

Agent Nevis turned again and looked at General Elson, who smiled faintly at him. Whether in jest or not, he couldn't tell.

"... This fleet, which we call the Ashtar Command, has been patrolling around the Earth now for many years as part of our mission to help humanity. Most of you human beings cannot as yet see our starships because they are in the 5th dimension. But there are those among you who have been able to raise their frequencies and their consciousness high enough so that they now are able to see the Ascended Masters and the Ashtar Command. In fact, there are a few among you who are in daily contact with us.

"At this very moment, the entire fleet is about to move from quantum level 4 to quantum level 5. This is because the Planet's birthing into the 5th dimension has now really begun in earnest. All our starships are working to capacity in their efforts to stabilize both the Earth's interior and exterior so that all human beings will have the opportunity to ascend into the 5th dimension with Planet Earth.

"In addition to all this, there is another very important reason why the Intergalactic Council and the Ashtar Command are now working so actively with Planet Earth at this moment. You see, up until just a few short decades ago, Test Zone Planet Earth functioned perfectly as a closed loop—or a closed circuit you could say. The souls that incarnated on the Planet could make their choices, reap their karma, and undergo their learning processes without it disturbing or having any great influence on the rest of the solar system—or on any of the neighboring star systems.

"But in 1945, all this changed. This happened when humanity unleashed the Power of the Atom during what you call the Second World War. And all this happened even though humanity had no idea or understanding of what a mighty power it was dealing with. Since then, humanity has continued to use the Power of the Atom without any real understanding of what it is doing. Humanity does not yet realize the immensity of the Power it has unleashed. Human beings have not understood that in the 3rd dimension, the atom is the fundamental building block of the universe. Nor has it understood that by manipulating the atom—with no spiritual understanding of what you are doing and without true love for all your fellow beings—humanity is in grave danger of destroying itself. And not only of destroying itself, but of destroying its own home planet—and of destroying the entire local solar system. And this is something we cannot—and will not—permit!"

8

Smoke trailed softly past the TV screen and Nevis realized that General Elson was smoking a cigarette, something he rarely did.

"All this means," Ashtar continued in a very serious tone of voice, "that what we call Test Zone Planet Earth is no longer a closed circuit. With the release of atomic energy, humanity's future development and actions are now capable of affecting the entire solar system and the nearby star systems. So this, as I just said, is the other reason why the Ashtar Command is here at this time. Besides assisting humanity in the ascension process, we are here to protect this solar system and the star systems which are your nearest neighbors.

"The Ascended Masters—and we of the Ashtar Command—are not allowed to interfere with the free will of human beings on Planet Earth, except in one instance. And this is in the event of a devastating nuclear war or nuclear catastrophe. If this should happen, then we are empowered to interfere, not so much to save humanity as to protect the actions of humanity from damaging the solar system and your neighboring star systems. We sincerely hope this will not be necessary.

"All of which now brings me to YOU!"

Ashtar paused for a moment as if to make sure that he had his listeners' full attention. He then went on. "In order to give Mission Earth Ascension an added boost at this critical juncture, the Intergalactic Council has issued a special dispensation. This dispensation authorizes us to invite a few, specially selected Earthlings to join us aboard the Ashtar Command's Mothership. The purpose of this invitation and proposed visit to the Mothership is to remind these Earthlings of their True Nature. And to offer them an intensive training program which will teach them the fundamentals of living in the 5th dimension. The knowledge we intend to transmit during this training program is absolutely crucial if humanity wants to ascend into the 5th dimension.

"After this short but very intensive training program in the Mothership, the participants will then be sent back to Earth. Once back on Earth, they will find that they are now fully equipped to work closely with the Ascended Masters and the Ashtar Command to help the rest of humanity pass smoothly and easily through the amazing and all-embracing transformations that are going on on Planet Earth at this very moment.

"During the last 14 days we have been working very closely with your guardian angel to monitor you and your level of consciousness. Based on our observations, we have come to the conclusion that you are ready for ascension in this lifetime! Therefore, on behalf of Sananda, the Supreme Commander of the Ascended Masters, also known as the Most Radiant

One, I would like to invite you to attend the 5th dimensional training program aboard the Mothership.

"We in the higher dimensions sincerely hope you will accept this special invitation. Your personal efforts and your ascension can help bring about a critical mass of enlightened beings that will transform Planet Earth into a new Paradise. So please consider everything I have said very carefully. You have until tomorrow evening at midnight local time to make up your mind.

"This now ends this transmission. In love and peace, I, Ashtar, salute you on behalf of the Ashtar Command and the Great White Brotherhood. Adonai, Brother in the Light! The Force is with you!"

Ashtar's face started to fade. The sound of high-pitched tones returned. For a moment the screen flickered and then went blank. General Elson turned off the TV and squashed his cigarette butt into the ashtray.

Agent Nevis stared at the empty screen for a few seconds. Then he turned to his boss.

The General got up and walked over to the television set. "According to Professor Ross out in New Mexico, there are two things about this 'Ashtar' transmission that he and the SETI astronomers are absolutely certain about. First of all, the signal came from somewhere outside the Earth's atmosphere."

"You mean the signal gradually decreases in strength?"

"Yes. If the source of the signal was located somewhere on Earth, the strength of the signal would remain the same. But because the Earth is rotating, the strength of the signal gradually decreases."

"So the signal could come from a satellite or a space station orbiting Earth," said Nevis.

"That of course is a possibility," answered the General. "The other thing the astronomers are absolutely certain about is that the signal could only come from someone sending on a higher vibrational frequency than usual."

"Well," replied Nevis, "if the SETI astronomers could build a high-vibrational-frequency receiver, I guess someone else could build a high-vibrational-frequency sender..."

"That's a possibility too. But if that's the case, this high-vibrational-frequency transmitter still has to be located somewhere outside the Earth's atmosphere."

"Yeah I see what you mean. So who do you think sent the signal?"

General Elson picked up the remote and looked at it. "As far as I can see there are only two possibilities. The first is that some madman

10

somehow got a hold of a satellite or a space probe or a space station—it could belong to anyone, China, Russia, France—and equipped it with a high-vibrational-frequency sender. And now he's having the time of his life sending us sensational news from outer space..."

"And the other possibility?"

"And the other possibility... well the other possibility..." said the General, hesitating for a moment, "is so far out I haven't dared to think about it yet...."

"Fortunately Professor Ross was smart enough to put a lid on the situation before his two assistants had a chance to call their mothers and tell them that E.T. had just called home," continued Elson, pacing back and forth across his office. "If he hadn't been fast, we'd probably have the place crawling with National Enquirer photographers having a field day by now. And even if it is just some crazy computer hacker who is behind this Ashtar transmission, the newspapers would have a field day—at our expense. They'd like nothing better than to tell the world that someone is playing hide and seek with satellites that are costing the taxpayers billions of dollars.

"Anyway Ben, whatever the case—be it some smart-ass hacker or terrorist who's behind this transmission—I want you to get on it immediately. Take as many men as you need, but go to New Mexico right away. Seal off the whole area and find out what's going on. I don't want anyone in there before we find out what's going on. And I don't want so much as a single e-mail, fax or telephone call leaving that place until we know more. Understood?"

"Yes sir... and once I've secured the area?"

"Make the Professor's people find out what's going on. I just talked to Ross. He knows you are coming and that you are fully authorized to make his people work round the clock. I want to know who sent the transmission—and to whom. And I want to know fast. Check with Wesley and Clark at NORAD and Henderson at NASA. In the meantime, I'll see if I can find out what's going on up in the international space station."

"And if it's not a hacker or terrorist who's behind this?"

"We have to rule out these possibilities first. There's a plane waiting for you at Andrews Air Force Base. I've got you scheduled for take off with

11

your unit in less than an hour, so you better get moving. And Ben, keep me posted."

"Yes, sir," said Agent Nevis, leaving the office fast.

THE PLAINS OF SAN AGUSTIN, NEW MEXICO
TUESDAY MARCH 31, 10:04:37 GMT EARTH TIME

It was still dark when Special Agent Nevis and his unit came charging across the desert of New Mexico in four military helicopters. The dry San Agustin plain below them was surrounded on all sides by mountains, but other than that the area was completely deserted, the perfect place for a high-tech listening post for messages from outer space. The searchlights of the four helicopters lit up the plain below and it wasn't long before the agents onboard could see the outline of the huge antenna dishes in the middle of the plain forming a gigantic Y pattern.

"The Very Large Array radio observatory consists of 27 antenna dishes," said Nevis who was briefing the agents in his chopper about their mission—now baptized "Operation Ashtar". "Each dish has a diameter of 25 meters and weighs 230 tons. The 27 dishes are placed in a Y pattern and they combine electronically to give a resolution that is the equivalent to an antenna dish with a diameter of 36 kilometers. At present, the radio observatory is being leased to a Research Institute called SETI, which stands for the Search for Extra-Terrestrial Intelligence. Anyway SETI has leased this place so they can monitor space. Normally the Very Large Array observatory is open to the public, but right now it's closed… and we are going to keep it that way until we find out exactly what's going on down there."

The choppers were now so close it was easy to see all 27 antenna dishes standing like huge sentinels in the middle of the deserted plain. A dirt road ran along the whole length of the Y formation right up to the observatory's main building, which was situated right next to one of the antenna dishes.

"Right now," continued Nevis, "there are three SETI astronomers working at the Very Large Array. Professor Eric Ross, who's head of the project, and his two assistants, Gene Williams and Barry Duwayne. Professor Ross should be easy enough to deal with—but the other two might be more difficult. So keep a close watch on them. They're the two who invented this high-vibrational-frequency receiver—and at the moment, we don't know exactly what their role is in all of this. So keep your eyes open."

12

The four helicopters landed in front of the observatory and the long row of giant antenna dishes that were pointed towards the heavens and the millions of stars shining brightly in the clear desert sky above.

"Sure is a nice place for stargazing," said Agent Sorvino as he and the other agents jumped out of the helicopter.

"Yup. And not a bad place to start imagining all kinds of far out stuff too," replied Nevis dryly.

Agent Sorvino stared at the starry sky with fascination. "So boss, you don't believe there's life out there?"

"Well, I guess we're going to find out pretty soon Ron," said Nevis as he motioned to the agents to bring their equipment with them.

"Haven't you seen Star Wars?" asked Sorvino, picking up one of the backpacks.

Nevis smiled to himself. Lieutenant Ronald Sorvino was Nevis' trusty right hand man. The two had known each other since they were in military school—and Lieutenant Sorvino had served under Nevis ever since the special unit was established. The Lieutenant was about the same age as Nevis and a formidable soldier. He was stocky, had dark hair and a little moustache—and wasn't much of a thinker. He knew his boss was smarter than he was and he admired him for that. But more importantly, he was extremely loyal; he would follow Nevis into death. But then again, so would most of the other agents in Nevis' unit.

The helicopter propellers slowly came to a halt. All 20 agents in the special unit were lined up in front of Major Nevis with Lieutenant Sorvino at his side.

"All right. You know the drill. Harrison, Daniels, Mitchum… and Jackson," said Nevis, nodding to Agent Jackson to join the other three. She was the only woman in the unit—but she was tough—a short, powerfully built African-American. "Set up your checkpoints. I want this place guarded from all sides—north, south, east and west. I want you to make sure that nothing and no one gets in or out. Elmore, you take the road. Hama, you stay with the helicopters. The rest of you come with me."

The six agents ran to their posts around the observatory while Nevis quickly led the rest of the unit to the main building.

As soon as Nevis walked into the spacious foyer, a gray-haired man in his late forties greeted them. He was wearing a suit—with no tie—and seemed eager to meet them.

13

"Welcome to the Very Large Array," he said, extending his hand towards Nevis. "I'm Eric Ross, head of the SETI space program out here."

"Good morning, Professor. I'm Special Agent Ben Nevis from the Directorate of Extra-Terrestrial Intelligence. As you know, I have been asked to take command of this facility until we determine exactly what's going on here."

"Yes, I know, Peter Elson informed me, but..."

Nevis brushed past the Professor and through the next door. For a moment the Professor looked surprised, but then he turned and followed Nevis as fast as he could. Sorvino and five of his men were right behind them. The rest of the unit spread out through the rest of the building.

Nevis knew where to go. He headed straight for the big room he'd spotted with the impressive array of computers. There were huge screens everywhere and star maps and other strange-looking pieces of equipment.

"Well hello there!" boomed a triumphant voice from the other end of the room, "if it isn't the cavalry themselves!" The voice came from one of the two men who were sitting in front of a very big computer screen. Both seemed deeply engrossed in the diagrams on the screen and in the charts strewn on the tables around them. Nevis headed straight to them. The two men appeared to be in their early thirties—one was black; the other white. The white man was a bit on the chubby side, with shoulder length blond hair and a little goatee. The African American was very fit looking with close-cropped hair. He was wearing a baseball cap turned backwards on his head.

"These are my assistants," called out Professor Ross from behind Nevis, trying to keep pace with him. When he caught up with Nevis he continued, "Gene Williams," he said motioning towards the heavy-set one, "and Barry Duwayne. They're the ones who picked up the transmission."

Nevis studied the two men. It wasn't hard to see that they were the two hopeful young astronomers who'd built the "high-vibrational-frequency receiver" that picked up the Ashtar signal. Who else would dare wear shorts and baseball caps to work? Nevis just hoped they weren't so naive that people of a more unscrupulous nature were exploiting their unconventional invention.

"This is Special Agent Ben Nevis," Ross said to his men. "The CIA has sent him and his unit to help us investigate the transmission."

"Hi," said Gene and extended his hand.

14

Nevis was looking at the silver machine that stood on the table next to the two researchers' computer. Parts of the machine were transparent so you could see something shiny inside, something that looked like clear mountain crystals. In fact, the machine looked like a cross between a large computer and a bunch of glowing stones. Nevis thought he could hear the faint sound of high ringing tones coming from the machine. It was the same sound that he'd heard before and after the Ashtar transmission.

"And this must be the high-vibrational-frequency receiver," he said. "The famous interdimensional radio."

"Yup," said Barry, fondly patting the silver machine. "She's our baby."

"You two built this thing?"

"Yes," said Gene with a big smile.

"Tell me about it."

The two young astronomers looked at Professor Ross, who nodded for them to go ahead. Clearly this was not the heroic reception they'd expected.

"Well, do you know anything about hyperspace?" asked Barry.

"I do!" said Sorvino. He looked with fascination at the two astronomers' invention. "It's like in that book 'Hyperspace' by that Japanese Professor. The one about the higher dimensions that was on the New York Times Bestseller List for several months..."

"Thank you Sorvino." Nevis gave the Lieutenant a cool look. "Please continue, gentlemen."

"Go on, Barry," said Professor Ross.

"According to many leading scientists, the entire physical universe is made up of energy that vibrates at various frequencies," explained Barry. "The 3rd dimensional physical world, for example, is everything that we can see, hear, touch, taste and smell. But what if the 3rd dimensional world is not everything? What if there are worlds that vibrate at much higher frequencies, such as a 4th and 5th dimension?"

"Go on," said Nevis.

"Okay, as you know SETI and other research institutes have been trying to pick up signals—signs of intelligent life—from outer space for decades—with no apparent luck. When Gene and I began our research into the dimension theories, we started wondering if maybe the reason that SETI and others had never picked up any signals from outer space was..."

"Because the signals were coming from a higher vibrational frequency," said Nevis.

"Exactly!" exclaimed Barry.

"So you built this machine," said Nevis, taking a closer look at their invention. "And until a few hours ago, nothing happened. Then suddenly you picked up this transmission with this guy in the silver tights who calls himself Ashtar. What makes you think that you haven't just picked up the latest episode of Star Trek?"

"That's completely impossible!" protested Gene hotly. "Television programs are sent at a frequency that is far too low to be picked up by our receiver!"

"The same goes for radio frequencies," added Barry.

"Okay, let's just say you're right about that," said Nevis. "If you two geniuses have managed to invent a high-vibrational-frequency receiver, couldn't someone else have invented a high-vibrational-frequency sender?"

"Well sure, I guess it's possible," replied Barry with a sullen look on his face.

"But whoever did it still had to send the transmission from someplace outside the Earth's atmosphere," said Gene.

"A place such as?"

"A spaceship of course!" said Gene.

"How about a satellite? Or one of the space shuttles or space stations that are orbiting Earth?"

"The only way anyone could do that would be by taking the high-vibrational-frequency sender with them into space. And why would anyone want to do that?" answered Barry, obviously irritated at this unwanted turn of events.

Nevis was silent for a moment, while he studied the two astronomers' invention. "That's what I'm here to find out," he said. "In the meantime it is your job to find out where that transmission came from—and who it was sent to."

The sun was about to set over the New Mexican desert. Special Agent Nevis was sitting alone in one of the choppers, studying the dry desert landscape. It was completely empty except for the long row of antenna dishes.

It was time for him to report back to General Elson.

But what did he have to report?

The last 14 hours of intense investigation hadn't yielded a single clue as to who the transmission had come from—or who it was sent to. Every possibility that the Ashtar transmission had come from an ordinary sender had been ruled out completely. The transmission could only have come from a high-vibrational-frequency sender—and one that was sending transmissions from somewhere outside the Earth's atmosphere. And what was more, every possibility that someone had somehow smuggled such a machine on board a satellite, a space probe, or space shuttle had also been completely ruled out. Nevis had been in contact with every satellite station and space center around the globe and they all completely ruled out that possibility. Even the Russians had been most helpful, making a thorough search of the international space station.

And now, as far as the other option was concerned—the one Elson hadn't thought about yet... was it time for Nevis to report back to his boss and tell him that every other plausible option had been checked and eliminated?

Nevis sighed and pulled out his mobile phone. He looked at it for a long, hard moment.

His hand was shaking slightly.

He flinched. His hand couldn't shake. "My hands just don't shake," Nevis muttered to himself, "and never have..."

That's when he realized the whole helicopter was shaking.

Then there was a low rumble, like thunder in the distance—but where the sound was coming from he couldn't tell.

Nevis looked back at the observatory. The tremors intensified and he saw the main building and the smaller buildings next to it suddenly swaying like trees in the wind. He was close enough to the buildings to hear the sound of things crashing to the ground inside the main building and breaking.

An earthquake? In New Mexico?

Agent Sorvino appeared in the observatory's main door waving frantically at Nevis as if he wanted him to come inside.

That's when Nevis realized a huge black shadow was descending over the chopper, blocking out the last rays of the evening sun.

Nevis looked around him and saw several of Very Large Array's antenna dishes swaying perilously from side to side. The nearest one was swaying dangerously right over the four helicopters that were parked in front of the observatory. Agent Hama was sitting in the chopper closest to the swaying dish, starring blankly at Sorvino who was now waving at him frantically.

17

In a fraction of a second, Nevis realized what was about to happen.

The huge dish was about to break off and crash down into the choppers—and Hama didn't see what was coming.

At that moment, there was a huge tremor.

Nevis jumped out of his chopper and ran at breakneck speed across the shuddering earth towards Agent Hama. The broad-shouldered Agent was starring at Sorvino completely oblivious of the fact that Nevis was charging straight at him.

Then there was a loud cracking sound as the huge dish broke off its tower, tumbling directly down towards the chopper where the unsuspecting Hama sat.

At that very moment, Nevis leaped up into the chopper and threw himself at Hama with such force that the two men flew right through the chopper and out the door on the other side, landing on the ground a few meters from the machine. The moment they hit the ground, the enormous dish crashed into the chopper, pulverizing it completely.

"Hurry!" yelled Nevis. "Run for the tower!"

Huge pieces of the structure were falling all around the two agents. Their only hope was to seek the shelter of the tower and hope it would not fall on them. As they charged towards the tower, they heard the sound of the other antenna dishes crashing to the ground in the distance.

Just as Nevis and Hama reached the tower, the last huge chunk of the antenna dish landed right behind them completely demolishing the chopper parked next to the one Hama had been sitting in.

The scene was one of utter chaos.

Nevis saw one of the smaller buildings next to the observatory collapse like a deck of cards as Agents Jackson and Daniels ran towards the main building. Another wing of the main building collapsed and he heard shouts coming from inside. Sorvino was no longer standing in the main entrance. The earth continued to shake and Nevis fell, head first toward the warm sand and just lay there. With everything in motion, it was impossible to move anyway. So Nevis did the only thing he could do when up against an enemy of this kind.

He waited…

… until the earthquake subsided… the way earthquakes must do… eventually…

And subside it did, but it took longer than usual. It had been so powerful that more than two minutes passed before the tremors and the tremendous rumbling began to quiet down. Then the earth stopped quaking.

And there was a sudden stillness.

Nevis slowly lifted his head and looked around.

The whole Very Large Array observatory had more or less collapsed. Behind him, only one antenna dish was still standing. All the rest of the 27 had crashed to the ground.

Nevis and Hama got up and ran towards the smoking remains of the main building.

Nevis was still trying to assess the extent of the damage when Sorvino handed him a cell phone. It was General Elson.

"Ben, what's going on out there? I've been trying to get a hold of you for the last 15 minutes?" barked Elson, clearly annoyed.

"I'm sorry boss, but we were just hit by a massive earthquake. It's a good thing we've got this satellite link or you'd never have gotten through to me."

"You mean you were also hit by an earthquake?" asked the General, incredulously.

"What do you mean?"

"Well Ben, the whole world is in chaos! During the last 15 minutes there have been massive earthquakes all over the planet, from Brokdorf to Beijing! They've hit everywhere, Ben! Even Denmark was hit by an earthquake, for Christ's sake!"

"And what about Washington?"

"Fortunately Washington wasn't hit. But they say San Francisco has been practically leveled to the ground. Turn on a television, for God's sake!"

"If we can find one," replied Nevis.

"Have you been hit that hard?" asked the General.

"Several of my men are injured—not seriously—but I think one of the astronomers broke his leg."

"And how about the observatory?"

"The observatory?" Nevis looked at the chaos surrounding him. "All the antenna dishes are down except one. The main building has collapsed, but that's about as far as we've gotten."

"And what about the high-vibrational-frequency receiver?"

"I think it's still intact."

"That's not what I mean. What have you found out?"

Nevis did not answer.

19

"Ben? Are you there?"

"Yes, sir."

"Well... what have you found out?"

"It's completely impossible that the Ashtar transmission could have come from a satellite that is sending at normal frequencies. The transmission could only have come from a high-vibrational-frequency sender that is located somewhere outside the Earth's atmosphere. We've checked everything, General. NASA, the Hubble space telescope, the international space station, Landsat 7, NORAD... the transmission cannot have been sent from any of them."

"So you are saying that all the other options have been ruled out?"

"Yes, sir."

There was silence on the other end of the line.

"All right, Ben. I'll notify the Director of Central Intelligence immediately so he can inform the President and convene the National Security Council."

Nevis looked down at his bleeding hand. The last of the tremors were over, but his hand was still shaking slightly.

"But, sir, if the Director makes his report right now, won't the Security Council think that there is a connection between the Ashtar transmission and the earthquakes?"

General Elson didn't answer.

Twenty minutes later General Elson called him back. "I want those astronomers to find out exactly who the Ashtar transmission was targeted at," barked the General again. "Once I've shown that transmission to the National Security Council all hell is going to break loose."

"What do you think they will do?"

"I have no idea, Ben! But one thing is certain, they will move heaven and earth to find out who that transmission was sent to. So get those boys working on the double! I'm sending you two extra units right now."

"I need more than that. I need a construction team if those astronomers are going to be able to work. We have no electricity."

"I'll send whatever you need. Operation Ashtar is now our number one priority. And for God's sake Ben, don't let word of this leak out to the rest of the world, no matter what... understood?"

After Nevis talked to General Elson the second time, he and his men began the cleanup. Despite the massive damage, the high-vibrational-frequency receiver remained miraculously untouched, and so was most of the equipment the astronomers used to decipher data.

"I just got orders from Washington. I want you two to find out exactly whom the Ashtar transmission was sent to."

"That's easier said than done," said Gene, who was being carried around on a litter by two agents. Agent Jackson had just finished binding up his broken leg.

"But can you do it?" asked Nevis.

The two astronomers looked at each other. "Maybe," said Barry. "But we'll have to go through all the high-vibrational-frequency data that we intercepted during the 20 minutes of the transmission"

"How long is that going to take?"

Barry shrugged. "Hours, days, weeks, maybe even months..."

"Then you better get started. My unit is at your disposal. There will be no sleep until we find out who received that transmission."

It was 5 o'clock in the morning and the dawn's first rays should by now have appeared on the horizon.

But they hadn't.

Instead the sky over the desert of New Mexico remained dark. In the distance, there was the ominous rumble of thunder.

Nevis sat in one of the few rooms in the main building that hadn't collapsed. He was drinking coffee out of a paper cup. In front of him was a TV set they'd hooked up to the observatory's main generator. In the 12 hours since the earthquake, he'd used his loaded gun to persuade the two astronomers to work non-stop to find out who the transmission was sent to. Neither Nevis nor the astronomers had slept that night. Nevis felt the least he could do was stay up with them.

Until morning came.

That was if it was going to come at all.

A few hours after the massive global earthquake, volcanoes had erupted all around the world—in such different places as Iceland, the Philippines, and the Caribbean. These volcanic eruptions were followed by violent storms and hurricanes that were wreaking havoc all over the globe from Asia to the Americas. Even Europe was badly hit. A storm of huge

21

magnitude was pounding most of Ireland, Scotland and Northern England. The latest report from CNN said a violent hurricane had suddenly erupted in the Caribbean and was now moving swiftly towards the southern states of the US. Tens of thousands of people had been killed all over the world and millions more were now homeless. The whole world was in uproar. CNN was already calling the day "Black April".

A frustrated Nevis leafed through the piles of documents and notes that he and the other agents had collected about the Ashtar transmission and the high-vibrational-frequency receiver. Then he got up. It was time to have another word with the astronomers.

Sorvino stood in the half-demolished doorway and watched Nevis. He had a worried look on his face.

"Do you think it's the end of the world, boss?"

"And what if it is!" said Nevis roughly and patted the Lieutenant on the back. "All it means is that we'll be a bit busier than usual!"

Sorvino smiled and walked with his boss through the shattered lobby. Since General Elson had informed the President and the National Security Council about the Ashtar transmission and its possible link to the earthquakes, volcanic eruptions, and storms, Nevis' special unit had been reinforced with two more special units, an entire construction team, 10 helicopters, two military jets, truckloads of emergency supplies, and two large power generators. The entire area for many miles around had been sealed off. No one from the outside world could get in. The official story was that the observatory was now being used to "monitor global seismic and volcanic activity". The only civilian who had been allowed into the base during the past 24 hours was the President's national security advisor, who was accompanied by a four-star general. Nevis had briefed them both about the high-vibrational-frequency receiver.

"What's up boys, how are you doing?" said Nevis, trying to sound cheerful.

The two astronomers were working frantically while the construction team was building an entire little village around them. The astronomers' computers were working on super drive and their desks were strewn with miles of data and printouts. Plastic coffee cups and food trays were everywhere. Both men had dark circles under their eyes and both looked like they were just about to fall apart completely.

"Be quiet, so we can think," yawned Gene as he went through the next pile of printouts.

"We don't have time to think! Just find the people that I'm looking for!" said Nevis as he turned around and started to walk back towards the lobby.

"And what if we don't find them?" said Sorvino in a low voice when he and Nevis were out of earshot of the astronomers and the rest of the men in the unit.

What if we don't find them thought Nevis. Good question...

"I've got it! I've got it!" Gene yelled suddenly, almost leaping up from his makeshift litter. "Barry, I broke the code! Give me the keyboard, man, give me the keyboard!"

The eyes of everyone in the room were riveted on the two astronomers.

Nevis strode back towards the two young men, who were now frantically pounding their keyboards.

"Gene! You're a genius! I love you man!" cried Barry.

"Gentlemen! If you would be so kind as to explain to the rest of us what you have discovered," said Nevis.

"It's so simple, it's so mind-bogglingly simple..." triumphed Gene as he kept on pounding his keyboard. "The sender of the transmission was on a higher vibrational frequency... and the interdimensional radio, the receiver of the transmission, was also on a higher vibrational frequency... but the other receivers... the people who the transmission was addressed to... did they necessarily have to be on the same vibrational frequency... yes, of course... but did they have to have a high-vibrational-frequency receiver... no, not necessarily... what if they were able to simply receive the transmission as they were... in their normal state... perhaps mentally..."

"Would you please be so kind as to tell me what you are talking about in plain English!" thundered Nevis impatiently.

"Yes Major Nevis sir!" Gene triumphantly hit the computer's ENTER button. A long printout whizzed out from the printer on the next table.

Gene handed the printout to the Major. "What this means Major, in plain English, is that the transmission was picked up on channel 75 on a plain old, ordinary television set!"

"But where God damn it? And by whom?"

"By exactly 600 television sets, in 144 locations, located in different areas all around the globe." Gene proudly pointed to the printout. "You can read it all here Major, it tells you exactly where in the world the transmission was received, down to the city, the section of the city, the street, the street number and the apartment!"

"Sorvino! Get me a map of the world! On the double!" yelled Nevis. "And get me General Elson on the phone! Right this minute!"

Six hours later, Special Agent Nevis was standing behind the podium in one of the briefing rooms at CIA's headquarters at Langley, Virginia. At his side were General Elson and the Director of the CIA, plus several other high-ranking officers and government officials. In front of them sat 144 of the CIA and the American military's best and most highly trained agents and soldiers, selected from the cream of the Navy Seals, the Marine Corps, the Rangers, and the US Air Force. Each of the 144 was selected to head a special unit to each of the 144 locations around the world that were home to the 600 receivers of the Ashtar transmission.

"... So your mission is clear," continued Nevis. "When you land at your destination, those of you who are going to NATO or other countries friendly to us will be met by their intelligence people who will by that time have been briefed by us. Together with the local security forces, your unit is to locate the three, four or five people who received the Ashtar transmission in your area and report back to General Elson and myself here in Washington immediately. Those of you who are going to countries that are hostile to the United States will be met by our CIA operatives in those areas who will help you locate those who are wanted."

"What if the people who received the transmission refuse to cooperate?" asked one of the agents.

"Your job is to make them cooperate," said Nevis and looked out of the window next to where he was standing. Even though it was only one o'clock in the afternoon, it was as dark outside as if it was the darkest night. Rain was pelting down and there was the sound of thunder in the distance.

"I believe that the last 18 hours of Earth catastrophes and the growing number of casualties speak for themselves," said Nevis as he leaned forward on the podium and looked intensely at the group. "I know that you have lots of questions, but the reason I am not taking your questions at the moment is because quite frankly we do not yet know a lot more about what is really going on than you do. And this is precisely why it is of the utmost importance that you find the 600 recipients of the transmission as quickly as possible and report back to us immediately. We want to know everything about these 600 people—and I mean everything—the number of hairs on their heads, what they eat for breakfast. Everything. If they have even the slightest connection to the

Ashtar transmission, I want to know all about it. So use every means—except one. I want them alive."

"Another bird's just flown the coup, Major."

Agent Sorvino carefully placed the report from Rio de Janeiro on Nevis' desk, which stood in the middle of the CIA command center. This was now Nevis' operational command post for the manhunt for the 600 recipients of the Ashtar transmission. It was ten in the evening and almost nine hours had now passed since the 144 special units had been sent to the four corners of the globe to track down their prey. Already after a few hours, the first reports had begun to come in. So far, each of the special units had located the premises of the people in each area who had received the Ashtar transmission on channel 75. And so far, not one of these people could be located. Every single one of them had quite simply disappeared into thin air. It was odd, almost spooky. Nobody knew where they were. Not even their family or friends.

Nevis leafed through the report about the four who had disappeared in Rio de Janeiro. Two women and two men. A computer software developer, a nun, a bank clerk, and a carpenter. The two women were friends and had known each other for years. But apart from that, there seemed to be no obvious connection between the four.

They were just four ordinary people.

Just like all the others.

In frustration, Nevis threw the report on top of the fast-growing pile of reports. They were pouring in… from Athens, Tokyo, Montreal, Berlin, Cairo... And everywhere it was the same story. The people who had received the transmission were just regular people. Ordinary men and women. Some young, some old. From every walk of life. Doctors, businesswomen, some scientists and physicists, a few teachers, a couple of nurses—there was even a group of US Air Force pilots from Texas! Five of them! Some of the 600 knew each other well, some did not.

It made no sense.

What was the connection? What was the common denominator? Out of all the people in the world, why these people?

Nevis sat down and gazed blankly at all the activity in the command center around him. It was buzzing—CIA agents bustling about, trying to figure out what these 600 people had in common.

There was a missing link somewhere. There had to be.

Nevis smiled to himself. So far, the only thing these people had in common—as far as he could see—was that all 600 of them seemed to have disappeared from the face of the earth. And nobody, not their family or friends, seemed to have the slightest idea where they were.

The phone rang. It was General Elson.

"Ben, I have a four star general, a Secretary of Defense, and a National Security Advisor chewing my ass. Make me happy, Ben. Tell me you found someone…"

"Sorry boss. Not yet… not a single one. They're all gone. Disappeared without a trace."

"All 600?"

"So far, yes."

"And you have no idea where they are? Our special units must be able to track someone down. Can't you initiate large-scale manhunts—at least in the NATO countries?"

"We're trying boss, but it's very difficult. Most countries have been hit so hard by the earthquakes, volcanoes, tornadoes and storms that they've got more than enough to do just trying to deal with that. So we're not getting much help from local police or military."

"And these 600 who received the transmission—what are they? Para-militants, revolutionaries, terrorists?"

"No, sir. Just ordinary people, most of them with good jobs and regular lives. It's almost spooky. So far the only common denominator we've found is that they've all completely vanished."

"Hmm. Well that anyway indicates some kind of conspiracy."

The General was silent for a moment. Then he said, "Well Ben, we've got to do something. People are talking about the end of the world and when I look out my window I almost believe them. Most of the world is without electricity. Half the countries in the world have declared a state of emergency. People are dying out there by the thousands. Who knows if Washington is going to be the next city to be leveled by an earthquake or a hurricane?"

"And there's nowhere to run to," said Nevis dryly.

"You've got to find these 600 people, Ben. You must. They're the only lead we've got."

"I know, sir." Nevis put down the receiver. The moment he did, a young agent came running hurriedly into the command center. He headed straight for Nevis' desk.

"Sir, I think we've picked up something… I think we've picked up the trail of one of the groups!"

Nevis got up, "Details?"

"It's the group in Copenhagen, sir. Three young guys. A physics student, a bartender, and a copywriter. They've been friends since they were kids. One of the guys left a message on his mother's answering machine saying the three of them were going to England for a couple of days. Apparently, his grandfather just died so he called and left a message."

"England?"

"Yes, sir. Our unit quickly traced the three to Copenhagen Airport. They left on a plane to London Heathrow Airport at 08:00 Greenwich Mean Time. About 19 hours ago."

"And after that?"

"I just got off the phone with the MI6 in London. They say that the three Danes rented a car from Avis right after their arrival at Heathrow."

"Does MI6 know where they're going?"

"No, sir, but we have the car's license number and the unit just faxed us pictures of the three."

"Good work," said Nevis, patting the young agent on the back.

"Why MI6?" asked Sorvino, who was standing next to Nevis. "Didn't our special unit in Denmark follow the three to England?"

"They couldn't and still can't," replied the young man. "A killer storm is on the loose in Northern Europe and tornadoes are devastating huge swaths of territory. No one has ever seen anything like this before. All the airports are closed and no one, not even military aircraft, is able to fly at the moment."

"That means we'll have to send a special unit across the Atlantic to England." Sorvino looked questioningly at Nevis. "And who's going to head the unit boss?"

"I am," said Nevis, already on his way out of the command center. "I'm tired of being cooped up here. We need some action Sorvino. Round up the rest of the crew. We're leaving immediately."

NORTHOLT ROYAL AIR FORCE BASE, LONDON, ENGLAND
TUESDAY APRIL 2, 08:39:17 GMT EARTH TIME

Six hours later, the CIA Special Task Force plane landed at Northolt Royal Air Force Base in England. Several of the agents in Nevis' special unit sighed with relief as the plane touched ground. The five-hour flight

27

from Andrews Air Force Base outside Washington DC to the Northolt base, a few miles outside London, had not been too rough. That is once the plane climbed above the Earth's storm-ridden surface. Once they reached cruising altitude, everything was peaceful and quiet. But landing was more problematic. First of all, the plane was put into a holding pattern for more than half an hour before it was even deemed safe to attempt a landing. Then when the wind finally died down for a moment, they got their chance. But it was all rather hair-raising.

Nevis let out a yawn. He thought he was going to get a chance to sleep during the flight—for the first time in almost three days, but no, he had been on the line almost constantly with either General Elson or the other various leaders of the 144 other special units he'd sent around the world. So far, the three young Danes were the only ones they'd found any trace of.

The Special Task Force plane came to a screeching halt at the end of the wind-swept runway. Nevis checked his watch. Local time in England was 08:43 in the morning. Greenwich Mean Time. It would have been morning in England if it hadn't been for the black storm clouds covering the sun. Outside it was pouring rain. Every once in a while, jagged bolts of lightening lit up the dark sky, followed by loud bursts of thunder.

"Get a load of this weather," said Agent Sorvino, pointing at the gray landscape out his window. The whole air force base was shrouded in thick, gray mist and fog.

"Looks more like soup to me," said Agent Jackson, unbuckling her seat belt.

"And according to the latest reports, the whole country is being devastated by tornadoes," said Agent Hama. "We're lucky we were able to land."

"Tornadoes in England!" muttered Sorvino, "I wonder if all those old medieval castles you see in the movies have been destroyed…"

Nevis was watching the three agents. Not counting Sorvino, Jackson and Hama were the two who had served under him the longest. They were both in their early thirties. Agent Jackson, the only woman in the unit, was small and feisty. A lone black woman in a profession dominated by white males, she had to be more crafty and a whole lot stronger than most of the men in the unit, and she was. Physically speaking, Agent Hama was the opposite of Jackson—a big, broad-shouldered giant of Lebanese descent. Intellectually he was no Einstein, but he was loyal and could always be trusted.

"All right gentlemen—and milady," said Nevis, nodding to Jackson. "Your holiday is officially over! Get your gear and let's get started. You know the drill."

Nevis and his unit left the plane and descended down the stairs to English soil. They were met by a middle-aged man in a long trench coat. Nevis recognized him immediately. He was Commander Henry Holm, head of the British MI6 Special Section for Extra-Terrestrial Intelligence. The CIA and MI6 had been working closely together the last couple of years and Nevis had collaborated with Commander Holm on more than one assignment. Next to Holm stood a British officer, a general.

"Hello, Ben," said Holm crisply, giving Nevis his hand. His English accent was very proper. "Welcome to England."

"Hello, Henry." Nevis shook his hand.

"I'm sorry that I wasn't able to conjure up a bit better weather for your visit," said the Commander.

"The weather's not much better back in the States."

"This is General Nathaniel Hecht." Holm motioned to the General at his side. Nevis saluted—Hecht saluted back and said, "We are at your service, Major Nevis. You can be sure Commander Holm and I will do everything possible to facilitate your mission."

"Thank you," replied Nevis briskly.

Commander Holm and General Hecht turned around and began to lead Nevis and his unit towards the base's main building.

"You must be on to something quite extraordinary this time, Ben," said Commander Holm as they made their way through the fog and rain. "We've been told from the highest level to give your mission absolute top priority, which is quite unusual, to say the least."

"Any news about the three Danes?" asked Nevis.

"I'm afraid not," said Commander Holm. "But let's get you inside first so I can bring you up to date on the situation here in England."

"It's like finding a goddamn needle in a haystack," muttered Sorvino in despair as he threw the latest surveillance updates on to Nevis' desk. "No, not even a haystack, it's like finding a bloody drop of water in the Pacific Ocean!"

Nevis didn't answer. He was leaning back in his chair with his feet on the desk, staring at the king-size map of England he'd just hung up on the wall. Commander Holm and General Hecht had given Nevis and his unit the whole top floor of one of the Northolt buildings to use as their headquarters. Nevis picked the central room for his office while his agents set up shop in the wide hallway outside his door. Every few minutes, Sorvino would go out into the hall and bring back the latest batch of reports for Nevis. His people were funneling in the data from all sorts of sources including the British Secret Service, the armed forces, and the English police.

But so far, there was nothing to report.

Where could those Danes be?

Just getting out of Heathrow would have been a major challenge for them. London and all its surroundings was gridlocked in one enormous traffic jam. As far as anyone could see, you could only get around by helicopter or airplane. And even that was extremely dangerous at the moment because of the fierce storms and the many tornadoes.

"We've been here for almost 10 hours now boss and we still haven't found jack shit!" Sorvino was talking as much to himself as to Nevis. "I mean these guys could have gone anywhere...north, south, east, west. Your guess is as good as mine." He kept pacing back and forth impatiently. "And the other special units haven't found anything either. Most of the unit heads are asking if they should return to Washington. What should I tell them boss?"

Nevis kept staring at the map of England—as if merely by staring he'd be able to find the three Danes.

After a while he said slowly, "No Ron, tell them all to stay put for a while."

"For how long?"

"At least until I get some sleep." Nevis stood up and yawned. He suddenly realized he hadn't slept for three days. He felt strained to the breaking point. Maybe that was why he felt he couldn't think straight...

"Wake me up if there's anything important." He lay down on the military cot in the corner of the room and was fast asleep even before Sorvino closed the door of his office.

Nevis woke with a start and sat up on the cot.

For a moment he didn't know where he was—or even who he was.

He'd been dreaming—something about a light—a warm and peaceful light that lit up the whole horizon.

But where the light came from, he wasn't sure. Was it coming from him or from the horizon? Or from the point between his eyebrows that was tingling with this strange feeling?

Nevis touched the tingly spot between his eyebrows and for a moment the office around him seemed to shimmer with dancing light.

He scanned the room in bewilderment, still wondering where that strong flash of light had come from.

He looked at the door in surprise. It was closed and he was alone in the room.

And what about the strange words he'd just heard?

One Glorious Garden of Goodness... One Heavenly Hymn of Harmony...

Nevis stared at the windows. They were all shut.

So where in the hell did those words come from?

One Glorious Garden of Goodness... One Heavenly Hymn of Harmony...

Nevis shook his head and thought it must have been something he'd been dreaming.

But the words lingered on, crystal clear in his head.

One Glorious Garden of Goodness... One Heavenly Hymn of Harmony...

He shook his head vigorously. All this Ashtar nonsense must be getting to me he thought.

He stood up and looked at the clock on the wall.

The time was exactly 00:00:00 Greenwich Mean Time.

Midnight in England.

He'd slept for more than six hours.

Nevis walked slowly over to the window. It was still dark outside. But at least it had stopped raining.

He opened the window and looked up at the dark storm clouds above.

Something was different, very different. Nevis examined the night sky—and there, for the first time in many days there was a hole in the clouds. And in the open space, he could see stars twinkling, the first stars he'd seen in... It seemed like an eternity. One of them was a large golden star that flickered in the night, far more beautiful than any of the others.

Nevis took a deep breath and felt his whole body relax. A fresh breeze blew into the office—and to his great surprise, it did not feel as fierce or furious as the wind had felt before.

Something had happened.

Something had changed.

More and more patches of the night sky began to appear between the clouds and suddenly he could see the light of the moon reflected on the wet runway just outside his window.

"Major Nevis!" someone cried excitedly from the door.

"Evening, Ron." Nevis turned towards Sorvino.

"Major Nevis!" cried Sorvino again, his voice trembling slightly. "He's on TV again!"

"Who's on TV?"

"That Ashtar guy, sir! He's on every single channel!"

"On every single channel?"

"Yes, sir, on every one!"

Nevis headed for the door. "All over the world?"

"Yes, sir! CNN, BBC, ABC—he's everywhere!"

The two agents ran out of the office. Out in the hallway everyone was gathered around the three television monitors that were mounted on the wall in the lounge area. Everyone was there—every single American agent in Nevis' unit plus all the British agents and several soldiers. And they all had the same slightly glazed look in their eyes, almost of disbelief, as if somebody had just woken them up from a deep sleep and they weren't quite sure if they were awake or still dreaming.

Nobody even noticed Nevis' arrival.

Everyone's eyes were glued to the television sets.

All three sets were showing the same picture. One of the Brits was switching the channels on one of the sets, but no matter what the channel, the picture was still the same—a dark-haired man with a radiant face, dressed in a silver uniform with a military-style badge on his chest.

Nevis pushed his way through the crowd and stood before the largest of the three sets.

"Greetings, Brothers and Sisters in the Light!" The dark-haired man did not open his mouth, but everyone in the hall seemed to know exactly what he was saying. "I AM Ashtar, Commander of Mission Earth Ascension, speaking on behalf of the Intergalactic Council. My mission here today is one of peace—and I am honored to be the one to bring great tidings of joy to all of humankind. I have come here today to announce the dawning of a special intergalactic event of huge magnitude: STARDAY!"

Everyone's eyes were glued to the screens.

Ashtar smiled and continued: "A STARDAY is a momentous intergalactic event that is automatically triggered when the inhabitants of a planetary system reach a higher collective level of consciousness— known by us as quantum level 5. When this happens, Intergalactic Decree requires that the Intergalactic Community make its presence known to the inhabitants of said planet and initiates contact with its inhabitants. The first step in this process is usually what we call a "full-planet" or blanket global transmission such as the one you are now watching.

"In exactly seven Earth days after this transmission, the next phase of this momentous intergalactic event will take place—the Coordinated Mass Landings of the Intergalactic Fleet at all the capitals and major city centers on your planet. We call this "Day of Mass Landing" a STARDAY because on this momentous occasion, you will meet your intergalactic brothers and sisters for the very first time."

Sorvino was about to say something but Ashtar continued.

"Perhaps you are wondering, my dear brothers and sisters, why this is happening right now? You are probably also asking yourselves if this has anything to do with the dramatic Earth changes you have just experienced? The answer to your question about Earth changes is yes.

"But let me explain briefly. Both Planet Earth herself, and every human being on Planet Earth, is evolving towards higher consciousness and the higher dimensions. Right now Planet Earth is about to ascend into the 5th dimension, which is a higher level of consciousness than the one most of you have been experiencing so far. For Mother Earth, this has been problematic because you human beings who live on Planet Earth have not yet attained a high enough level of consciousness to ascend with Mother Earth. That is why during the last 48 hours Mother Earth has been attempting to get rid of you all! Her attempt is the explanation behind the very violent Earth changes you all have been experiencing.

"But so far Mother Earth has not succeeded to expel you from her sphere, thanks mainly to a small group of 600 dedicated Earthlings who have been trained by us in the use of advanced spiritual technologies to prevent the total axis shift that would have eradicated all life on Earth.

"This in fact is what just happened. Just a few minutes ago at exactly 00:00:00 Greenwich Mean Time, these 600 Earthlings anchored a positive New Vision of Life on Planet Earth in the collective

33

consciousness of humanity. I know for a fact, that each one of you, each in your own way, has had a brief glimpse of this positive New Vision during the last few minutes.

"But there is more. Not only was this New Vision anchored in the collective consciousness of humanity by these 600 Earthlings, it also lifted the collective consciousness to such a high level that it has triggered a STARDAY. This happened because the New Vision has collectively raised your consciousness. But my friends, I am happy to say this is only the beginning... the beginning of great and momentous events... of this I can assure you. You can look forward to much, much more."

A beaming smile spread itself across Ashtar's face. His body was surrounded by white light. "At this very moment, the Intergalactic Fleet's starships are putting themselves in position over every capital and major city center on Planet Earth to prepare for STARDAY and our meeting of celebration in seven days time. When this transmission is over, you will all be able to see our starships locked in their positions above your cities. This should be a source of great joy for all of you.

"On STARDAY itself—seven days from now—that is to say—on Friday the 10th of April at 00:00:00 Greenwich Mean Time—all the starships will land. And then on this momentous occasion, we will be raising our glasses and toasting all our new friends with glasses brimming over with that famous intergalactic champagne we of the Ashtar Command fondly call the 'photon brew'!

"After we have celebrated our friendship in suitable intergalactic style, each one of our starships will then invite a team of 144 Earthlings to be the first human beings to set foot inside our starships and learn about the 5th dimension.

"Once the chosen 144 from each city are on board, the starships will take off and once again lock into their positions above your cities while these Earth representatives undergo their training program. The training program, which will last for 40 Earth days, will include specific training modules for the attainment of 5th dimensional consciousness, also known as cosmic consciousness. Besides learning about higher states of consciousness, the various groups of Earth representatives will have access to our advanced spiritual technologies, which among other things can be used to eliminate pollution, make the Earth's deserts bloom, develop environment-friendly and sustainable energy sources, materialize and dematerialize physical objects from the etheric, and of course travel effortlessly through time, space and the dimensions.

"When they have completed their training program, the various groups will then be sent back to Earth to instruct the rest of humanity in these advanced technologies. And this is only the beginning."

Ashtar bowed. "This transmission is now ending. I, Ashtar, send greetings in love and peace to all of humanity on behalf of the Ashtar Command and the Intergalactic Council. I look forward to STARDAY, in seven days time, when I will personally be welcoming the first representatives from Planet Earth aboard the Ashtar Command's Mothership.

"Adonai, Brothers and Sisters in the Light! The Force is with you!"

All the TV screens flickered at the same time and the image of Ashtar began to fade. Once again, Nevis heard that faint hum of those very high-pitched ringing tones he'd first heard in General Elson's office. Ashtar disappeared and all the TVs began broadcasting their regular programs. On the channels that had been sending live news broadcasts, most of the reporters were staring at the cameras looking rather bewildered.

All the men and women at Northolt were also starring blankly at the TV screens.

Then one of the agents pointed at the TV that was broadcasting BBC World News.

"Look!" he cried.

Everyone's eyes turned to the TV he was pointing at. An excited reporter was standing in front of the Tower Bridge in London, pointing at the dark clouds above the city. About half a mile above Tower Bridge floated an enormous, four-sided pyramid.

The pyramid was several hundred meters long. It glimmered as if it was made of golden, almost translucent light.

"Oh my God!" said Sorvino, "then it's true after all..."

"There's another one!" cried an English police officer, pointing towards the TV that was showing CNN.

CNN was filming the gray sky above Atlanta, Georgia There too an enormous golden pyramid of light floated about half a mile above the city center—right above Peachtree Center.

CNN then switched to New York City. Another golden pyramid was floating right above Central Park. Thousands and thousands of people were pouring into the park, all looking up at the pyramid with the same eyes of wonderment. One could even see some people falling to their knees, obviously praying.

"Jesus Christ..." said one of the English agents.

Once the agents and soldiers began to digest what was happening, the shocked silence turned into complete bedlam. Many were grabbing their mobile phones, trying to get a hold of their families and loved ones. One of the Brits kept flicking from channel to channel. It was the same story on every channel…golden pyramids everywhere, hovering above Washington DC, Rome, Tokyo, Delhi, Copenhagen, Buenos Aires, Oslo…

The only ones who did not move were Nevis and Sorvino.

Nevis turned up the volume on the set broadcasting BBC World. "Approximately 10 minutes ago," the reporter said, "at exactly the same time as the mysterious so-called "full-planet" or blanket global transmission from Ashtar, this enormous golden pyramid of light suddenly became visible above London's Tower Bridge…" He was obviously struggling to hold his ground as crowds of people surged past him, running madly towards the Tower Bridge for a closer look at the pyramid."… I cannot say what the pyramid is made of… So far it does not seem to be moving…"

Sorvino turned towards Nevis. "Well boss, what do we do now?"

An hour later, US Senator Alexander Waters from Arkansas was being interviewed live on CNN. Since Senator Waters was a member of the National Security Council, it was relevant to ask him about the US government's reaction to the worldwide Ashtar transmission and to outline what he believed would be the US position vis-à-vis these extraordinary events.

Nevis turned up the volume and then pulled up a chair and sat down. It was now almost two o'clock in the morning in England and the storms and the rain had actually stopped—not just in England, but all over the world. In fact all the Earth changes—the volcanic eruptions, hurricanes, tornadoes and storms—had all stopped at precisely the same time. 00:00:00 Greenwich Mean Time.

And not only that, something else had happened too. Someone turned on the electricity again, everywhere. So all around the world, people were rejoicing because the lights were on again. It was amazing. Not only had Ashtar, the Commander of the Intergalactic Fleet spoken to all of humanity, but everyone's refrigerator, TV and computer started working at precisely the same time. And now, huge golden pyramids were floating serenely over every major city on Earth. And even though these strange-looking golden pyramids seemed to make no noise, many people were already saying they could hear faint, high-pitched tones coming from the pyramids. And now, millions of people were flocking to city centers everywhere to see the starships with their very own eyes. But so far, none of the world's governments had officially responded to events or made any comments. That was, until Waters went on the air…

"Mr. Senator," asked the CNN anchorman, obviously trying to stay calm, "what do you believe will be the President's response to the worldwide Ashtar transmission and to the hundreds of pyramids that are now floating above all the major cities in the world?"

"I have not spoken to the President yet," replied Senator Waters. "We expect him to return from his visit to those areas in the South that were devastated by the latest storms and hurricanes in about half an hour. I will then join him at the White House where we will be discussing the situation with the Secretary of Defense, the Joint Chiefs of Staff, and the National Security Council."

"But what do you believe the Government's reaction will be?"

"It's too early to tell."

The anchorman smiled. "Well, I guess you were just as surprised as everyone else when all this happened."

"No, as a matter of fact, I wasn't," the Senator answered. "The Central Intelligence Agency has been aware of the Ashtar Command's presence for the last three days and has been closely monitoring their movements."

Nevis sat up in his chair, wondering who authorized the Senator to suddenly divulge such highly classified information. Obviously the anchorman was surprised too. "But how could the CIA have detected their presence, since no one could see them before now?"

"Our people have developed a so-called high-vibrational-frequency receiver," replied the Senator, "that is able to pick up messages from higher vibrational frequencies—and since our intergalactic guests are operating on a higher frequency, we were able to pick up signals from them several days ago."

"Really?"

"Yes," said Waters, "as I said, we've known about them for a while."

The anchorman cleared his throat, trying not to show he'd been caught off guard. "Then can you tell our viewers what conclusions our intelligence forces have come to about our intergalactic guests so far?"

"It's still too early to tell, we're still in the process of analyzing our data."

"Well whatever the case, I guess we can say we are fortunate that our intergalactic guests have stopped the last 48 hours of catastrophic Earth changes..."

"I'm not so sure that this is the truth of the matter," said the Senator.

"What do you mean?"

"Many things indicate that it is the Ashtar Command itself that is behind all these so-called Earth catastrophes."

A look of disbelief passed across the anchorman's face. "But ... Ashtar just said that their intentions are peaceful..."

"That may very well be," said the Senator. "But what people—or space beings—say is one thing, what they actually do can be quite another thing."

"But... why on Earth would they want to do something like that?" The anchorman was so shaken that it almost seemed as if he'd forgotten he was on TV.

"Well it's very simple, " said the Senator. "If these space beings have the technology to construct gigantic floating pyramids and transmit whatever they want over every TV channel on the planet—then why shouldn't they possess the technology to create chaos below and above the surface of the Earth and cause volcanoes, earthquakes and storms?"

"But..." gasped the anchorman in horror.

"If you think about, it's one hell of a clever strategy," continued the Senator, leaning ever closer to the pale-faced anchorman. "While these space beings mesmerize the entire world with their platitudes of love and peace, they are systematically destroying the entire planet's infrastructure and communications networks—and preventing us from defending ourselves. Why? Because the military forces in every country are now so busy trying to clean up the mess, restore order, and save the lives of millions of people who are homeless—that they have precious little time to think about their primary job, which is national security. Humanity has never been as vulnerable as it is now. All I can say is Planet Earth has never before been such an easy victim."

For a long moment there was silence.

Finally the anchorman said, "But what will the United States do? Go to war against the Ashtar Command?"

Senator Waters did not answer.

And that was more than enough of an answer.

38

"Damn Senator Waters and his low-down politicking," roared General Elson at the other end of the line. "You should be thankful you're not in Washington right now, Ben. The President and his staff are furious at Waters for letting himself be interviewed like that without consulting them first. There's going to be heads to roll for this, that's for sure! But it won't be Water's, unfortunately. No that would only make matters worse. But it could easily be the head of the Director of Intelligence or mine!"

"How are the world's other governments reacting?" asked Nevis.

"They've all been taken by surprise—every single one of them. But at least all the NATO countries have promised to cooperate with us."

"How is the man in the street reacting to all of this?"

"Does 'global chaos' mean anything to you?" replied the General. "After Senator Waters' statements millions of people are fleeing the cities because they think the pyramids are some kind of intergalactic death machine."

"So people are afraid?"

"Well not everyone, no. Almost as many people are heading straight for the cities to welcome these space beings."

"What do you mean?"

"Just what I said. Hundreds of thousands of people are sitting in various kinds of group meditations under the pyramids in San Francisco and Los Angeles for example. I'm not quite sure what they're trying to do. Our people tell us it's something about raising the collective consciousness. And then there's that rock singer with insect glasses—well he's already arranging a welcome concert under the pyramid in Dublin. We're seeing different spins of this taking place all around the world."

"Has any country tried to contact or attack the pyramids?" asked Nevis.

"So far no," replied Elson. "You must remember things were really chaotic to begin with—even before the space beings arrived. So now everything has practically come to a standstill. Apparently there's nothing like a mass landing of space beings to get people to do some soul-searching and reevaluate their lives."

"And what about you Peter?"

"Ben, I'm too bloody old for soul-searching, I'm just trying to do my job. Which means keeping a cool head while the rest of the world either goes into collective panic or jubilation."

"What do you want me to do?"

"I want you to find the 600 people who received the first transmission Ben. They are our only hope. We've got to find out what's going on and what their connection to the Ashtar Command is before all hell breaks loose!"

Three hours after Senator Waters' dramatic interview on CNN, the President of the United States addressed the Nation in a direct transmission from the White House Briefing Room. In his short statement, the President appealed to the nation for calm and tried to strike an even balance between cautious concern and optimism in relation to the events of the past few hours. At the end of his statement, the President said he was in touch with the heads of all the world's governments and that all necessary measures were being taken to ensure the security of the nation and the peoples of the world.

After his brief address, the floor was opened to questions from reporters. It quickly became clear that irrevocable damage had already been done by Senator Water's off-the-cuff remarks on CNN. When asked about what the Senator said—that the Ashtar Command was probably behind the last 48 hours' dramatic Earth catastrophes—the President skated carefully over the matter, saying it was all just "speculation" at this point.

But obviously the idea that the hundreds of pyramids floating above Earth's cities might be behind the violent Earth changes and catastrophes was already creating havoc in many people's minds. Reports were coming from all corners of the globe of panic in the cities... millions were packing up and leaving and the panic was spreading like wildfire. And it quickly became apparent that it was already too late to turn the tide, despite the fact that leaving the cities made no sense whatsoever. After all, as many were saying, if the world was about to be invaded by space beings with such highly advanced technology, where could you run to anyway? The countryside would be just as unsafe as the cities.

But panic in the streets was not the whole story. Reports were also coming in confirming the fact that millions of people—obviously the more optimistic ones—were going on pilgrimages to the cities to welcome the space beings and to join in global welcoming committees. Still others were participating in the massive group meditations and ecstatic dancing that were taking place in many cities right beneath the pyramids.

Still others were joining together to pray and seek guidance and comfort in churches, mosques and temples all around the world.

But even as all this was happening, every TV set in the world was telling the same story—of golden pyramids floating silently and serenely above all the major cities of the world.

Nevis turned off the TV and walked over to the window. It was five o'clock in the morning and dawn could not be far away. A dawn that perhaps would come for the first time in many days.

Then he went back to his office and stood in front of the large map of England for the hundredth time.

Where could those three Danish lads be?

And why had they gone to England in the first place? What was their link to the Ashtar Command? Were they working together? Maybe every one of the 600 they were hunting had already been "beamed up" to the starships. If that was the case, Nevis and the 144 other units were probably looking in vain for people who were no longer on Earth.

Nevis banged his head against the wall.

For God's sake, Ben, get a grip.

You can't give up now.

A few moments later, Nevis raised his head, walked back over to his desk, strapped his pistol holster around his shoulder, and put on his jacket.

He had to do something.

He couldn't stand being holed up here in Northolt for another minute. He had to get out or bust.

Nevis opened the door to his office and walked quickly down the hallway.

Everyone's eyes were on him as he went past.

He was almost at the end of the hallway when an English police officer seemed to appear from nowhere.

"Excuse me, sir?"

Nevis stopped.

The officer looked nervous.

"What is it?" grumbled Nevis.

"My name is Sergeant Woodhouse, sir and I've found something that might interest to you."

"Well, get on with it then! I haven't got all day."

Sergeant Woodhouse cleared his throat and pulled out a bunch of reports. "As you know, every day the police get lots of crank calls from people who claim they've seen UFOs or angels and all kinds of loony stuff."

Nevis nodded.

"Under normal circumstances sir, I'd never mention a report like this to you sir, but considering what's been going on during the last couple of hours sir..."

"Get to the point, man."

The Sergeant cleared his throat again and opened one of the reports. "On Wednesday, April 1st, at 17:15 hours—almost 36 hours ago, when the storms and tornadoes were just starting—Scotland Yard received an unusual call from an Englishman named John Grey and his partner a Belgian named Jean-Paul Belois. They said they were Ley Line researchers."

"Ley Line researchers?"

"Yes, sir. I'm not quite sure what it is. Apparently it's got to do with the Earth's Power Spots and crop circles..."

"Crop circles! There's nothing new about crop circles. You're going to have to come up with something more interesting than that, Sergeant Woodhouse."

Nevis turned towards the door.

"But sir!" Again the Sergeant stepped in front of Nevis. "The report says the two researchers claimed that they could predict the exact movements of the tornadoes that just wreaked havoc in England!"

Nevis shook his head. "Yeah sure and Agent Sorvino was Cleopatra in a past life!"

Nevis walked past the Sergeant and opened the door.

"But sir!" said the Sergeant stubbornly. "I have checked the predictions of these men and they were correct 95% of the time!"

Nevis stopped.

"95% of the time?"

"Yes, sir." The Sergeant motioned to a nearby table. He unfolded a map and spread it out on the table. "These are the places that the Ley Line researchers reported would be ravaged by tornadoes," said the Sergeant pointing to the map. "Carmarthen, Avebury, Stratford, Glastonbury..."

Nevis looked at the map that was covered with the Sergeant's lines and dots.

"How can you be sure their predictions were correct?"

"I went and checked with the meteorological experts at the Yard who have been tracking the tornadoes," replied the Sergeant, "and in 95% of the cases the tornadoes occurred exactly where the researchers predicted they would *after* they'd called the Yard with their predictions."

"You say after they had called?"

"Yes, sir."

Nevis was still looking at the Sergeant's map.

"Did the researchers say how they were able to predict the movements of the tornadoes?"

"I don't quite understand it, sir, but they said it's got something to do with the tornadoes moving along these so-called Ley Lines and around and towards the Earth's Power Spots."

"Power Spots?"

"Yes, sir. Here is the transcript of their call to the Yard."

Nevis leafed through the transcript. Then he looked again at the places on the map where the Sergeant had drawn his lines. That was when he realized that the movement of the tornadoes was not quite as haphazard as he thought. In fact, he could see that many of the "Power Spots" and the "Ley Lines" that the tornadoes were following formed patterns on the map.

Perfect patterns.

Spirals, triangles, ellipses...

The patterns were almost too perfect to be true.

"Are you sure that these drawings are correct?"

"Yes, sir, I have checked every single one of them with the Yard's meteorological experts."

Nevis stared at the map again.

Spirals, triangles, ellipses...

The movement of the tornadoes formed a perfect pattern. A perfect pattern that covered all of England, Scotland and Ireland.

It was almost too perfect to be true.

Nevis looked over at a group of agents who were sitting in front of a computer screen analyzing the data from the golden pyramid that was hovering above London City.

It might be farfetched, but the events of the last few days had certainly convinced Nevis that many of the things that he'd previously thought were impossible might very well be possible...

"Do you know where the two researchers are now?"

"Yes, sir. They're at Stonehenge where they're studying a crop circle. I spoke to them on the phone last night."

Nevis folded up the transcript and put it in his jacket pocket.

"Get those two on the line and tell them to stay put. I want to talk to them face to face."

He turned and walked back to the lounge area where the other agents were passing time. "Sorvino, round up our unit! And get me some choppers. It's time we get some fresh air!"

Fifteen minutes later, seven heavily armed military helicopters were carrying Agent Nevis and his unit plus several handpicked British agents and soldiers westward towards Stonehenge. Behind them in the east, the sun was slowly rising—the first real sign of daylight in many days. Nevis sat in the lead helicopter with Sorvino, Jackson and Hama plus two other agents from the British MI6 and Sergeant Woodhouse.

A few minutes later, the choppers soared over the M3 motorway that went all the way from London to southwest England where Stonehenge was.

The whole motorway was one gigantic traffic jam.

On the side of the motorway heading away from London, the road was jammed with tens of thousands of cars, buses and trucks trying to get out of London and away from the golden pyramid that floated over the city center. On the other side of the motorway, heading towards London, tens of thousands of vehicles were trying to get to London to welcome the intergalactic guests.

But regardless of the direction, nobody on either side of the five-lane motorway seemed to be moving at all.

Whether this was due to all the debris caused by the storms—the wrecked cars, trees, bushes and other debris that was scattered across the motorway—or just because there were too many cars, was hard to tell. In many places the most panicky (or eager) had left their cars and were wandering in both directions alongside the motorway. In other places, groups of people were working together to clear the debris.

"So not everyone is leaving the city in a panic," remarked one of the British agents looking down from the chopper.

"Definitely not," said Agent Jackson. "According to our reports, there are many places in the world where people are working diligently together to clean up the mess. The Red Cross and the other humanitarian

44

organizations report that they are receiving thousands and thousands of calls."

"Those people over there are definitely not working very hard," smiled Sorvino. He pointed towards a field where a group of buses were parked in a circle. On the side of one of the buses, big letters proclaimed, "Planet Earth welcomes the Ashtar Command". Inside the circle, about a hundred blissful-looking people were sitting cross-legged in meditation with their heads turned upwards toward the sky.

"Don't be so sure about that," continued Jackson. "According to what they and millions of other people are saying, by meditating like that they are raising the collective consciousness so that Mother Earth will be able to ascend into the higher dimensions."

"Don't tell me you believe that mumbo-jumbo do you?" asked Sorvino, giving Jackson that look.

Jackson just shrugged.

"What do you think Major?" asked Sorvino, turning towards his boss.

Nevis was looking straight ahead and nodding. "All I can say is that if the Ashtar Command is behind the Earth changes, they've sure done one hell of a job."

The other agents in the chopper were looking straight ahead.

"Holy Mother..." gasped Sergeant Woodhouse.

A little further ahead, the cause of the gigantic traffic jam became obvious. The M3 was cut in half by an enormous swath of devastation that must have been several hundred meters wide. It seemed that a giant tornado had simply ploughed right through the motorway, cutting it in half. Trees, bushes, rocks—and cars were strewn everywhere.

"That tornado must have been one mother," whistled Agent Hama.

On either side of the belt of destruction there were thousands of abandoned cars.

The choppers speed over the destruction and zoomed westward along the motorway. As far as the eye could see, there were lines of people wandering either towards or away from London.

"It looks to me like most people are trying to get away from London," said Hama.

"That's probably because of Independence Day," said Sorvino.

"Independence Day?"

"You know, the movie that was such a big hit in the late nineties Remember? The one where all these enormous spaceships suddenly appeared over all the world's big cities and sent down these death beams, completely destroying the cities and everyone in them."

45

"And you mean people think that these pyramids are going to do the same?"

"Well, the thought does come to mind, doesn't it?"

STONEHENGE, ENGLAND
FRIDAY APRIL 3, 06:34:00 GMT EARTH TIME

The sun was up now, sending its clear light over the English landscape as the seven military choppers landed a few yards from the huge ancient circle of standing stones called Stonehenge.

There wasn't a soul in sight. Not in the parking lot situated across the road from Stonehenge or by the stone circle itself, which was surrounded by a wire fence. No one was there except two men in functional rain gear who were standing inside the stone circle. They seemed to have some kind of measuring equipment with them.

Nevis jumped out of the lead chopper and headed straight towards the two men, followed by his agents and Sergeant Woodhouse.

The two men inside the stone circle started walking towards Nevis and his men. When they reached each other, it was the eldest of the two who said, "Good morning gentlemen!" He looked as if he was in his late 40s, a robust man with large, bushy eyebrows. "My name is John Grey, I am a Ley Line researcher and this is my colleague, Jean-Paul Belois, one of the foremost experts in our field."

Nevis did not reply but merely studied the two.

Sergeant Woodhouse cleared his throat. "This is Special Agent Ben Nevis from the United States—he is working with the British Intelligence service. Nevis would like to hear how you were able to predict the movements of the tornadoes."

The two researchers looked curiously at Nevis.

Then Grey said rather pretentiously, "If you are familiar with my dissertation on "Personal, Planetary and Universal Energy Centers and Energy Lines and their influence on..."

"Well I'm not," said Nevis. "So please give me the short version."

Grey was ruffled, but one look at the expression on Nevis' face made him continue calmly. "Okay," he said, sucking in his breath, "The short version... the short version... let me see... the human body and the body of Planet Earth both have energy centers and energy lines that circulate what we call the 'Universal Life Force'. This Life Force is a kind of invisible, etheric energy that flows through all bodies—both the body of the Earth and the bodies of human beings. In the human body, these

46

energy centers and energy lines are called chakras and meridians—in Planet Earth's body they are called Power Spots and Ley Lines. When the circulation of Life Force through the energy centers and energy lines is blocked, the result is disharmony, sickness and disease—whether it is in the human body or in the planetary body."

"What's this got to do with the tornadoes?"

"When the human body is ill, it usually gets a fever. The fever is the body's way of cleansing its energy centers and energy lines. The same applies to Planet Earth. The tornadoes are Planet Earth's way of cleansing its energy centers and energy lines."

"Do you have any proof of all this?"

"I most certainly do," said John. "Show him the map, Jean-Paul!"

The Belgian pulled a world map out of his pocket. He and John spread it out on the wet grass in front of the agents.

"This map shows all the Earth's major Power Spots," said Jean-Paul, "as well as the Ley Lines that connect the Power Spots and make up the planetary network or grid of energy circulation."

"You have probably already heard about many of the Power Spots," said John and pointed out some of the most famous spots on the world map. "Machu Pichu in Peru, Mount Shasta in California, Delphi in Greece, the Giza Pyramid..."

"How many Power Spots are there in all?" asked Sorvino, thinking hard.

"There are 144 main Power Spots," replied John.

"144!" cried Sorvino. "Major Nevis, the 600 people who received the Ashtar transmission were located in a total of 144 areas all over the world!"

Nevis grabbed the map, scanning the 144 Power Spots that the Ley Line researchers had marked on the world map.

But of course!

The pilots they were looking for from Texas were not far from the Power Spot in New Mexico, the business women from Tokyo were not far from the Power Spot at Mount Fiji... each and every one of the 144 groups of people who had received Ashtar's first transmission were located in the same country or in a country that was near one of the 144 Power Spots!

It all made perfect sense!

"Sorvino! Get me General Elson on the phone this minute! Jackson! Send a top-priority order to our 144 special units and tell them to go to the Power Spot nearest them on the map. You know the drill. On the double!

I want each and every one of these 600 people in our custody before breakfast!"

"Wait, you can't just take our map..." protested John.

"Just one last question," said Nevis pulling out a fax that had pictures of the three wanted Danes on it. "Have you seen these guys?"

John and Jean-Paul looked at the fax.

"Sure we've seen them," they both nodded. "The three of them were right here at Stonehenge about two days ago," said John.

"They knew quite a bit about Power Spots," added Jean-Paul.

"Did they tell you where they were going?" asked Nevis.

"Yes," said John. "They were heading for Glastonbury Tor. I tried to warn them that all the roads to the Tor would be blocked by the destructive path of the tornadoes."

Nevis turned towards Sergeant Woodhouse. "How far is it to Glastonbury Tor, Sergeant?"

"About an hour's drive," said the Sergeant. "Not far by chopper..."

"All right people! Let's get a move on it! Hama, take Mr. Grey and Mr. Belois in helicopter 4."

"Wait, you have no right to..." protested John as the agents grabbed them and rushed them into the waiting choppers. All the time, Nevis was barking orders to his men.

"Sorvino," he said as he sat down in the lead chopper. "Get a hold of Commander Holm and General Hecht. Tell them that I need the works... troops, helicopters, tanks, I want a whole goddamn army."

"Sent to Glastonbury Tor?" said Sorvino with a smile.

"Yup. On the double. It's time we had a little chat with our three Danish friends."

GLASTONBURY, ENGLAND
FRIDAY APRIL 3, 07:29:38 GMT EARTH TIME

The seven military helicopters were swiftly approaching the mysterious hill that towered up in the middle of the green English countryside. The sun was up, casting bright beams down on the scene from a clear blue sky.

Agent Nevis looked away from that strange hill bathed in the sunlight, barking out his final orders. Underneath the choppers, they'd all seen the paths of destruction that had ravaged much of the countryside surrounding the little town of Glastonbury and its famous hill.

"General Hecht is sending a company of soldiers from a nearby crisis center with orders to completely surround the town and set up road blocks on all roads entering the town," said Sorvino as he finished his latest call. "The General has helicopters with instructions to fan out in the surrounding area and monitor every movement. If you want, he'll send you two fighter planes from the coast guard."

"Good," said Nevis, "you never know who they're working with. And the local police force?"

"They have been notified by Commander Holm," said Agent Jackson. "At this moment, the Glastonbury police are surrounding the hill. They will be backed by the two units General Hecht is sending over. No one is going to be able to get away from that hill now."

The choppers were closing in on Glastonbury Tor very fast now. Right behind the hill, they could see the town—the inroads to the town already blocked by trucks and jeeps. But there was no sign of police or military on the hill itself.

Good, thought Nevis, I want these boys for myself.

"I see them, Major!" cried Jackson, who was studying the hill through a pair of binoculars. "The three of them are standing on top of the hill!"

"Are they armed?" asked Nevis.

"It doesn't look like it..." said Jackson as she studied the three. "But..."

"But what?"

"They're all wearing these weird outfits..."

"Weird outfits?"

"Yeah, like they've just been to a carnival or something."

"A carnival? Let me see."

Nevis grabbed the binoculars. On top of the hill stood the ruins of an old medieval tower.

In front of the tower were the three young Danes they'd been hunting for so many days.

Nevis adjusted the powerful binoculars for a closer look at them. Agent Jackson was right, they looked as if they'd just been to a carnival or been extras in some kind of adventure movie. One of the Danes was wearing a dark blue cloak that went down to his ankles. On his back he had a backpack. The second Dane was a broad-shouldered guy with long, blond hair. He was dressed in what looked like chain mail armor. The third was wearing a long white robe. He too had long hair. They didn't seem to be armed.

"What are they doing?" asked Sorvino.

"They just started walking down the hill..."

Nevis gave the binoculars to Sorvino and called the other choppers over the radio.

"All units ready. We have identified the three males on top of the hill as the Danes we're looking for. They're wearing funny outfits, so you can't miss them. Units 2, 3 and 4 put down at the agreed coordinates around the hill with us. Units 5, 6 and 7 maintain surveillance mode and stay airborne in case there's anybody else around. And remember, no matter what happens, I want these guys alive!"

Nevis grabbed the binoculars again. His chopper was so close that he could clearly see the faces of the three Danes.

They looked radiantly happy—as if they didn't have a care in the world.

"I hope you boys have one hell of a good explanation for all this," said Agent Nevis, patting his machine gun.

PART ONE

THE END
OF THE WORLD
AS WE KNOW IT

1

A Warm Welcome

Jacob and Janus and I stood in silence enjoying the morning sunshine. As far as the eye could see, everything was bathed in a deep, deep peace. We sighed contently and feasted our eyes upon the lovely green hills and valleys that surrounded the Tor. It was beautiful beyond words.

Then we turned and began walking down the narrow path, which wound its way down the hill.

We'd only taken a few steps when Jacob stopped and pointed eastward.

Seven black dots on the horizon were flying towards Glastonbury at great speed.

"Helicopters," said Jacob.

"It looks as if they're headed for this hill," I said.

"Yeah," laughed Janus, "Here comes the cavalry! Maybe it's finally dawned on them that we've just saved all humankind from total annihilation!"

"But how could they even know what we've been up to?" said Jacob.

"You think too much, Master Wizard," said Janus. "I told you the military would give us a helping hand sooner or later!"

We all burst out laughing—it was difficult to wipe the grins off our faces after all we'd been through. Jacob had taken off his worn Fashion Flash trench coat and was now dressed in his long, dark blue wizard's cloak. He'd thrown back the hood and the morning breeze playfully rustled his thick mane of curly red hair. His backpack with Moncler's book of secret spells was slung across his shoulder. In his hand, he held his exquisitely carved oak staff covered with runes and symbols.

Janus had also taken off his trench coat making it hard to tell what glinted more in the morning sun, his golden chain mail or his long, golden elvish locks. Telperion's mighty two-handed sword, the one set with precious gems, was sheathed in its scabbard, hanging on the belt that was strapped around his incredibly muscular body.

"Way to go, Starbro'!" said Janus, gesturing towards the star on my brow.

Our hands met and we gave each other our secret Dungeons & Dragons handshake. But our happy musings were interrupted by the approaching helicopters, which were now so close that it was obvious they were headed straight for the Tor.

"Janus is right, those are military helicopters," I said.

"Well, perhaps they can give us a lift down to town so we can finally get ourselves a decent breakfast!" said Janus.

"Sounds good to me, let's get off this hill," I said.

We looked away from the choppers and continued our descent. Now that the ominous clouds and mist of the night before had vanished; we could clearly see the countryside that surrounded Glastonbury Tor. About a mile from the hill was the small town of Glastonbury and at the foot of the Tor we could see a garden, surrounded by stone walls.

Chalice Well I thought to myself with a sudden knowingness that came from deep within.

"What are those ruins?" said Janus, pointing towards the remains of what must have been several very large structures that stood in the middle of the town.

"Those must be the ruins of Glastonbury Abbey—or what's left of it," said Jacob thoughtfully.

"Where you lived once when you were Gaius the monk," said Janus, munching contentedly on a blade of grass. "I must say the two of you sure picked a beautiful spot to live back then."

As we neared the foot of the hill, we got a closer look at the huge belt of tornado destruction south of the Tor. It looked much like the many other tornado pathways we'd seen during the past few days. Obviously, the tornado had ploughed its way straight through the road that ran past Glastonbury Tor. Trees, bushes, rocks and the remains of houses and cars were scattered everywhere—over the fields and nearby roads and lanes. Even by Chalice Well, we could see traces of the past few days of Earth changes. Many of the trees were down and a few had been flung all the way out onto the road in front of the garden. A section of the stone wall surrounding the garden had been destroyed.

Just as we reached the foot of the hill, the seven military helicopters flew over us and divided themselves up. Three of the choppers flew off to the hilltop, while the other four stayed in formation right over our heads. We looked up at them curiously.

"Look!" said Jacob, pointing at the trees surrounding the field at the foot of the hill where we were standing. We could see men running between the trees.

They were soldiers.

Soldiers with machine guns, which were all aimed straight at us.

I turned around. It was the same at the other end of the grassy field. There too the place was crawling with soldiers with machine guns, all aimed at us. There must have been at least a hundred soldiers.

The four helicopters above us slowly began to descend. We were surrounded on all sides.

"This does seem a bit intense for someone who wants to give us a helping hand..." I said.

A voice boomed from a megaphone from one of the helicopters above us.

"Lay down your weapons! And place your hands behind your heads!"

We looked at each other in surprise.

"Are they talking to us?" said Janus in disbelief.

From all sides, the soldiers began closing in on us.

In the clearing between the trees, we saw two jeeps, a military truck, and a police car tearing towards us.

I stared at the faces of the soldiers. They all looked deadly serious, as if they were facing a mighty foe.

The noise from the choppers above us was deafening.

"Lay down your weapons!" boomed the voice again from the helicopter above us. "And place your hands behind your heads!"

"Are you sure they're talking to us?" I said, looking to see if there was anybody else around.

But there was no one else in sight. No one but us and the soldiers.

And we were surrounded on all sides.

"This is your last warning," said the voice from above. "Lay down your weapons and place your hands behind your heads!"

We looked at each other, not knowing whether to laugh or cry.

A moment later, the grass in front of us was ripped apart by machine gun fire. We jumped back.

"Hey! These guys are really serious!" I shouted.

All the soldiers were pointing their machine guns straight at us. When I looked up, I saw a small arsenal of machine guns and pistols pointing at us from the choppers above us.

"What the hell's going on?" shouted Janus.

Another barrage of machine gun fire ripped through the grass in front of us.

"This has got to be a mistake!" cried Jacob.

"We just saved the whole world for Christ's sake!" shouted Janus.

"We stopped the Earth changes!" I cried, waving my arms wildly.

Another barrage of machine gun fire—this time dangerously close.

We looked at each other in total bewilderment.

"I guess we'd better do what they want until they've calmed down a bit," said Jacob.

We placed our hands behind our heads.

Quickly the solders surrounded us and the choppers began to descend.

"Lay your weapons down!" boomed the voice from above.

"Do you mean my sword?" cried Janus, trying to make himself heard above the din of the propellers.

"I thought regular people couldn't see our interdimensional weapons!" I shouted.

"Let's just keep our hands behind our heads until they've calmed down!" cried Jacob.

The soldiers had now formed a tight ring around us. Then the front ring of soldiers charged towards us and hurled us brutally to the ground.

I landed face first on the wet morning grass and felt my hands being wrenched behind my back as cold steel was locked around my wrists.

"Hey, hey! What the hell do you think you're doing?" protested Janus.

Several hands rolled me onto my back.

The four helicopters had landed, but out of the corner of my eye, I could see the other three choppers were still circling around the Tor.

"Get 'em up!" shouted one of the soldiers.

We were pulled to our feet again.

"Search them!" he ordered.

Many hands quickly searched us from head to toe.

"They're unarmed, sir!" cried one of the soldiers.

None of them seemed to have noticed Janus' great two-handed sword or Jacob's staff—or the star on my brow for that matter.

"Let me through!" we heard a voice of authority cry from the direction of one of the helicopters.

The ring of soldiers around us parted.

About twenty men and one woman wearing civilian clothes came charging towards us. Even though they were dressed like civilians, it was obvious they weren't. They moved with a cool precision that elicited a sense of respect from the British soldiers who had surrounded us.

"Let me through!" shouted the man at the head of the group.

He was very fit and looked as if he was in his late thirties. He was above average height, had short dark hair, and a hawk-like face. He moved with the ease and authority of one who was used to being in charge.

He walked right up to us and stood still for a moment, sizing us up.

"Finding you boys has been one hell of a job." I could tell from his accent he was an American.

"Why are you looking for us?" Jacob asked.

"Oh I just wanted to ask you a few questions," he replied coldly.

"About what?" I asked.

"About what the three of you have been doing the last couple of days."

"No problem," said Janus. "But why the whole Blues Brothers chase? And why the handcuffs?"

"Let's just say it's a small safety precaution to make sure that we don't lose you again."

"Again?" said Jacob.

Again...

Just as the word passed over Jacob lips, I felt a strong tingling at the point between my eyebrows. The star on my forehead was throbbing.

But instead of seeing light with my inner Sight, I saw only darkness.

It was as if a dark cloud had passed in front of the sun.

Everything seemed to flicker and fade and for a moment I saw someone else standing there where the American stood. Someone who was wearing a heavy, richly adorned suit of chain mail. Someone who had a helmet on his head with a nose guard, the kind that knights of old wore.

In his hand, he held a sword—a sword that was covered with blood.

Dazed, I blinked.

The strange vision disappeared.

The sun returned and once again the American was standing there.

"Who are you?" asked Jacob.

"Special Agent Ben Nevis from DETI," answered the man.

"DETI?"

"Directorate of Extra-Terrestrial Intelligence. We've been looking all over the planet for the three of you."

"Extra-Terrestrial Intelligence?" asked Janus. "You mean UFOs and stuff like that? Why were you looking for us?"

"I'm hoping you'll be able to answer that question for me," said the Agent.

I was just about to say something when the point between my eyebrows began to throb again.

The vision returned. A man in armor in full battle dress was now standing where the American Agent had stood. He was black-haired, with sharp features, and a short, dark beard.

He raised his bloody sword towards my chest...

Again I blinked, utterly confused, and the vision disappeared.

What was I seeing?

Who was this man... this warrior in medieval armor who I suddenly saw right where the American Special Agent was standing?

I tried to shake off the vision and concentrate on what was going on around me.

That was when I realized that the American was looking straight at me.

His eyes were cold and grayish-green.

I felt a shiver run up my spine.

Where had I seen those eyes before?

Once again, the vision returned. But this time it was as if the vision of the medieval warrior and Special Agent Ben Nevis blended into one. In a flash, I realized they both had the same eyes.

Exactly the same cold, gray-green eyes.

The warrior touched my chest with the tip of his bloody sword.

Horrified, I stepped back.

Now I knew who the warrior in the vision was.

Lord Gavin.

The Lord Gavin who had betrayed Loran and Gaius and me more than 1,500 years ago in our past life in England. The Lord Gavin who had murdered the three of us, right here, at the foot of Glastonbury Tor. The same Lord Gavin who stopped us from activating our Power Spot and establishing the Light Grid.

Agent Nevis took a step towards me.

At that very same moment, the Lord Gavin in my vision took a step towards me—and with one swift stroke penetrated my heart with his sword.

The vision was so real that I tried to lift my hands to ward off the blow, but couldn't because I was handcuffed.

My sudden movement made everyone jump. The soldiers raised their machine guns and the Americans pulled out their guns.

Jacob and Janus looked at me in surprise.

"What's wrong, Starbrow?" asked Janus. "You look as if you've seen a ghost!"

Agent Nevis and the vision of Lord Gavin merged and became one.

60

The same face, the same eyes, the same strong hand that had driven the sword into Dana's breast.

And then I knew—with an awful knowingness that gripped my heart like ice.

Agent Nevis *was* Lord Gavin.

Lord Gavin *was* Agent Nevis.

Our old murderer was back.

2

Greetings From the Ashtar Command

"What's wrong, Starbrow?" asked Janus again.

The alarming vision that darkened my inner Sight began to fade. I opened my eyes and discovered, somewhat to my surprise, that the field we were standing in was bathed in blinding sunlight.

Special Agent Nevis was barking out orders. With amazing speed, the American DETI agents and the British soldiers began to set up tents, right there in the field where we stood.

"It's Agent Nevis," I said.

"So…what about him?" asked Jacob.

Before I had time to answer, a bunch of soldiers brutally separated us so we couldn't talk to each other. More military vehicles drove onto the field. Nevis kept on barking out orders and talking on his portable military phone. In just a few minutes, the field below Glastonbury Tor was transformed into an army base.

My eyes met Jacob's. He was standing about fifty yards away surrounded by soldiers. He nodded towards one of the helicopters where some DETI agents were pulling out two men wearing handcuffs. As they were led to one of the tents, I realized that they were the two Ley Line experts we'd met at Stonehenge two days ago, on our way to Glastonbury.

Nevis signaled to our guards. Jacob and Janus and I were taken into the largest of the tents. There was a table in the middle of the tent and chairs were already set up around it.

They removed our handcuffs and motioned for us to sit down in the three chairs on the far side of the table. Four agents stood guard in each corner of the tent. The British soldiers left.

"So what's with Agent Nevis?" Janus whispered to me.

"Agent Nevis is Lord Gavin," I said.

"Lord Gavin?" said Janus surprised. "You mean…"

"Yes," I said. "The same Lord Gavin who killed us in our past life."

"Are you sure?" asked Jacob.

"Positive," I nodded.

"But what's he doing..."

Before I could say more the tent door was pulled aside and Nevis walked into the tent. At his side was another agent, a stocky, heavy-set man. Nevis called him Sorvino. The two sat down across from us.

Jacob and Janus looked at Nevis suspiciously.

I stared into his cold, gray-green eyes.

There was no doubt that Agent Nevis and Lord Gavin were one and the same.

"What right do you have to..." Jacob began.

"You just leave the questions to me," said Nevis coolly. "What is your connection to the Ashtar Command?"

We looked at each other in complete surprise.

"Don't tell me you know about the Ashtar Command?" said Janus.

"After Ashtar's little speech last night, I'd be pretty damned surprised if there's a single soul on Planet Earth who doesn't know about the Ashtar Command," said Nevis.

Jacob, Janus and I looked at each other in surprise.

"What speech?" I asked.

Now it was the agents' turn to look surprised.

Nevis turned his cold gaze upon us again.

"Now listen up, boys, I have very little time and the three of you are already up shit creek to say the least. So please don't waste my time trying to deny something we already know about."

"But... we're not denying anything," said Jacob. "We do know about the Ashtar Command, we just didn't know that anyone else on Earth knew about them."

"So where have the three of you been for the last eight hours?"

"The last eight hours..." I said, looking questioningly at my two friends, "... we were sleeping inside the old tower on top of the hill," I said slowly.

"So you're telling me you didn't hear Ashtar's speech to the whole world last night at midnight?" said Nevis.

"He spoke to the whole world...? But no! I mean, what did he say?" I realized I was so surprised that my mouth was open.

Nevis looked at us in silence for a few seconds.

Then he got up and left the tent. Agent Sorvino followed him. I could see their silhouettes on the other side of the tent. It looked like Nevis was talking on the phone again.

Janus looked first at Jacob and then at me. "Do you realize how wild this is guys! They know about the Ashtar Command!"

"According to them, the whole world knows about the Ashtar Command!" exclaimed Jacob. Then he asked the four agents who were still standing guarding us if they'd seen Ashtar. "Did Ashtar really speak to the whole world? What did he say?"

But the agents didn't answer—they just stood motionless at their posts.

The tent door was pulled aside and once again Nevis and Sorvino entered the tent. Nevis placed a laptop on the table and adjusted the screen so the three of us could see it.

"At exactly midnight—00:00:00 Greenwich Mean Time—a little over eight hours ago, the electricity was mysteriously turned on again all over the world," said Nevis. "And at that very moment, this transmission was broadcast on every single television channel on every single television set in the whole world."

Nevis pressed one of the keys. For a moment the screen flickered.

Then the familiar face appeared on the screen.

"Ashtar!" the three of us exclaimed at the same time.

"Greetings, my Brothers and Sisters in the Light!" said the Commander of the Intergalactic Fleet in his familiar voice of authority. "I AM Ashtar, speaking on behalf of the Intergalactic Council and Commander of the Intergalactic Fleet. My mission today is peaceful and I bring good news to humanity. I have come to announce a special intergalactic event of momentous importance: STARDAY!"

"STARDAY!" the three of us cried in unison.

Nevis paused the recording. "And you're telling me you really haven't seen this?"

"Are you crazy, no?" cried Jacob with a big grin on his face. "Was this really transmitted at midnight on every television set in the whole world?"

Nevis nodded.

"Coolness!" I said. "What more did he say?"

Nevis pressed a key.

"... A STARDAY is a momentous intergalactic event that is automatically triggered when the inhabitants of a planetary system reach a higher collective level of consciousness—known by us as quantum level 5…"

Jacob, Janus and I just stared at the screen in disbelief. Ashtar was talking about the Intergalactic Fleet's upcoming Mass Landing of starships at all the Earth's capitals and major population centers.

"STARDAY! Holy Testicle Tuesday!" cried Janus. "He didn't say anything about that up in the Mothership!"

"The Mothership!" Nevis stopped the recording again. "Have you been up in their Mothership?"

"Yes, yes," said Jacob, "but let us hear the rest of it!"

The two agents looked at each other again. Nevis pressed the start key.

"... You may be asking yourselves, my dear brothers and sisters, why this is happening right now. And if this has something to do with the dramatic Earth changes you just experienced. The answer is yes..."

We listened intensely while Ashtar talked about the Earth's ascension into the 5th dimension, about the Earth changes, and the threat of a total axis shift—and about how the 600 volunteers' anchoring of the positive New Vision had lifted the collective consciousness of humanity to such a high level that the axis shift had been postponed.

As Ashtar spoke, I remembered the glorious New Vision and the blissful world of light I had experienced during that fateful moment when the New Vision flowed from the minds of the volunteers and spilled over and flooded into the minds of all humanity... *One Glorious Garden of Goodness... One Heavenly Hymn of Harmony...*

"... But there is more," the Commander continued. "Not only was this New Vision anchored in the collective consciousness by these 600 Earthlings, it also lifted humanity's consciousness to such a high level that it has triggered a STARDAY. This happened because the New Vision has collectively raised your consciousness. But my friends, this is only the beginning... the beginning of great and momentous events... of this I can assure you. You can look forward to much, much more."

"Ha ha!" laughed Jacob. "This is too cool."

"Way to go friends!" Janus gave Jacob and me a high five.

Nevis sent us an icy stare.

We were so overjoyed to see Ashtar and hear the news that we paid no attention whatsoever to the agents. We hung on Ashtar's every word.

"... On STARDAY itself—seven days from now –that is to say—on Friday the 10th of April at 00:00:00 Greenwich Mean Time—all the starships will land. And then on this momentous occasion we will be raising our glasses and toasting all our new friends with glasses brimming over with the famous intergalactic champagne that we of the Ashtar Command fondly call the 'photon brew'!"

"Groovy!" said Janus. "Intergalactic champagne!"

After telling a bit more about the consequences of STARDAY for humanity and about the upcoming stellar party and intergalactic champagne, the Commander bowed. "This transmission is now ending. I, Ashtar, send greetings in love and peace to all of humanity on behalf of the Ashtar Command and the Intergalactic Council. I look forward to STARDAY, in seven days time, where I will personally be welcoming the first representatives from Planet Earth aboard the Ashtar Command's Mothership.

"Adonai, my Brothers and Sisters in the Light! The Force is with you!"

The screen began to flicker and Ashtar's face disappeared.

Jacob, Janus and I turned to each other and laughed loudly. We were so overjoyed that we jumped up from our chairs and started to dance around the table.

"Hallelujah!" cried Janus.

Nevis watched us for a moment and then signaled to the guards. They immediately grabbed us and firmly pushed us back in our seats.

"Sit down!" ordered Nevis. "This is dead serious business—not some kind of carnival!"

After the Ashtar transmission, the agents showed us pictures of the huge golden pyramid of light hovering in the sky above Central Park in New York.

It was one of the starships that we had seen so many of during our visit to the Ashtar Command's Mothership.

The starship hung motionless in the sky. Down below, a huge swarm of people—it looked as if there were several hundred thousand—were all mashed together as everyone tried to position themselves as close to the golden pyramid as possible.

According to the agents, similar pyramids were now floating over all the major cities and capitals of the world—just as Ashtar had said they would.

Nevis turned off his laptop and closed the screen.

"So that's what the three of you missed while you were having your beauty sleep on top of the hill last night," he said. "Now I want to know all about your connection with the Ashtar Command. How you got into contact with them. What kind of work you are doing for them. Everything."

I looked questioningly at my two friends. The fantastic news about STARDAY had almost made me forget Nevis' dubious past.

Should we tell him about our adventures?

"Now, gentlemen," the Agent said. "I don't have all day."

Jacob shrugged.

"Okay, Mr. Special Agent," he said, "if it will make you happy. Where would you like us to begin?"

"At the beginning, please."

"At the beginning..." said Jacob. "Well, that must be..."

"That Sunday night almost two weeks ago, when we met our Guardian Angels," said Janus.

"Guardian Angels?" said Nevis.

We nodded.

Nevis shook his head. He then signaled to Sorvino to start taking notes.

"So it was Sunday, the 22nd of March?" he asked.

We nodded again.

"Go on," said Nevis.

Backed by Janus and me, Jacob proceeded to tell how we met our Guardian Angels in Copenhagen and were invited to participate in a training program on the Mothership. Then he told how we were transubstantiated to the Mothership, met the Ashtar Command, and had various unusual adventures, including our past life regression to England.

None of us said anything about my vision of Agent Nevis being Lord Gavin.

Jacob then told them about the imminent threat of an axis shift that would destroy all life on Planet Earth, about our journey to Shamballa, and last but not least, about our desperate race against time to reach Glastonbury Tor in time for the Activation Meditation.

As Jacob was telling them about the Activation Meditation, I suddenly realized that our shiny silver Ashtar Command watches had disappeared.

Finally Jacob explained how the New Vision had spread all around the globe and about how we had then fallen into a deep sleep only to wake up the next morning and walk down the hill to be captured by DETI and the British army.

When Jacob finished his tale, there was complete silence.

Then Nevis looked at us coldly and said, "Do you really expect me to believe a cock-and-bull story like that? If you do, you guys are crazier than I thought."

"What do you mean?"

"First of all, the three of you come waltzing down the hill all dressed up in these godforsaken pirate costumes and then you tell us that you're the only three people in the whole wide world who know absolutely nothing about what's been going on during the past eight hours..."

"But we told you we were sleeping..."

"... And then you tell me some cock-a-mania story about the 5th dimension and Guardian Angels and pink clouds in Wormholes..."

"But..."

"... you boys are a lot stupider than I thought, if you think I'm going to buy a story like that!"

"But it happens to be the truth," I said hotly.

"Why on Earth would we want to lie to you?" asked Janus.

"That's exactly what I'd like to know," said Nevis.

He got up and walked out of the tent, followed by Sorvino.

"Hey!" called Janus after him. "What about a little breakfast?"

When they didn't reply Janus mumbled, "Cheerful fellas..."

Right after Nevis and Sorvino left the tent, a team of American DETI agents walked in carrying some big boxes and two huge sacks. They immediately started unpacking what looked like some kind of advanced electronic equipment. While they were assembling the equipment, two other agents came over to us and ordered us to take off our clothes.

"What for?" asked Jacob.

"It's time for a little health check," replied one of them.

"My health is just fine, thank you," I said.

When none of us showed any sign of taking our clothes off, he signaled to several of the other agents who then grabbed us.

"Hey, hey, get your hands off me!" cried Janus, pushing the agents away.

At once a slew of guns were pointed at him.

"OK. OK...What's with the paranoia?" asked Janus.

They didn't answer, but just kept pointing their guns towards us.

"All right Janus," muttered Jacob, "let's just do what they want."

Janus shrugged. "Okay... if it makes you guys happy."

So we took off our clothes. Telperion's golden chain mail, Moncler's dark blue wizard's robe, my white robe—but the agents weren't satisfied until we'd taken everything off.

"Did the Ashtar Command dress you up in all this carnival gear?" asked one of them, shaking his head while he examined our stuff.

Apparently the agents could see everything—all our clothes and gear—except the staff, the sword and the star because no one made any reference to them.

While we were undressing, the agents finished assembling a weird looking machine that was about two and a half meters long. It looked like a cross between a tanning bed and a huge scanner. Then they hooked up a powerful computer to the machine.

"So what's the gizmo?" asked Jacob.

"We call it a DETI detector."

Then two of the agents grabbed Janus' arm and pulled him none too gently towards the machine.

"What now?" asked Janus.

"Just what the name implies," said the agent. "The purpose of a DETI detector is 'to detect extra-terrestrial intelligence'. So this detector will scan your body to determine whether you're human—or something else."

"Something else?" grinned Janus, "Like what?"

"That remains to be seen. Now lie down on your back inside the detector."

"I'm getting sick and tired of all this!" muttered Janus as he climbed into the machine. "What kind of welcoming committee are you guys? I mean we just saved all of humanity from total annihilation and triggered an intergalactic event of cosmic proportions—and this is the thanks we get!"

"Lie still please."

One of the agents sat by the computer as the DETI detector started, which did in fact hum slightly just like a scanner. A pale blue light moved along Janus' body, from the top of his head and down to the soles of his feet. After about two minutes, the light went off.

"You're next." The agents signaled for Jacob to lie down in the machine.

"How was it?" I asked Janus as he climbed out of the detector.

"Kind of weird. Like getting your teeth x-rayed or something."

After Jacob, it was my turn.

I lay down on my back in the detector and looked up. The metal bed underneath me was cold and above me bright lights were blinking. The machine began to hum and the pale blue light moved across my body. After a couple of minutes, the light went off and I was allowed to get out of the detector again.

"OK you can put your clothes back on," they said, "and sit down."

Then they dismantled the detector, packed up their equipment and left the tent. The four agents who were standing guard in each corner of the tent remained.

"This is beginning to seriously bore me," said Janus. "Why can't these Men In Black just be happy that it's STARDAY and let us go down to town and have a bit of breakfast and party on with everyone else?"

"You think everyone else is partying?" I asked.

"Well, the people we saw on TV in Central Park looked pretty happy to me."

Nevis and Sorvino walked into the tent again. They sat down and placed a bunch of documents on the table before us.

"So, what does the alien detector have to say?" asked Janus. "Am I human or an E.T.?"

"You're humans all right," replied Nevis, leafing through the documents. "But according to the detector, actually more like super-humans. It's very interesting…perfect cells, perfect organs, perfect pulse, perfect circulation… with the skin of newborn babies. According to the detector, you boys are almost supermen. Is that what the Ashtar Command gave you in return for your cooperation? Eternal life? Perfect health?"

"The detector is just seeing our True Selves… it's just like we told you," explained Jacob. "After we arrived in the Mothership we were reunited with our True Selves—Starbrow, Moncler and Telperion—who all have perfect health, strength, and intelligence."

"Perfect intelligence? Then perhaps you can start giving me some intelligent answers to my questions?"

"What do you mean?"

"What is your real connection to the Ashtar Command for one? And how are these space beings using the 144 Power Spots to cause earthquakes, volcanic eruptions, and tornadoes?"

"Hey man, you've got it all wrong," I objected. "That's not the way it hangs together at all!"

"Well how does it hang together then?" continued Nevis. "How does the Ashtar Command control the world's electricity for example? And what are their real intentions?"

"We already told you—the Ashtar Command's real intentions are peaceful," I said. "How many times do we have to tell you? They're here to help humanity and Mother Earth ascend into the higher dimensions—and to celebrate STARDAY with us—you heard what Ashtar said."

"The American government doesn't think the Ashtar Command's intentions are peaceful. On the contrary, we believe the Ashtar Command is behind the present chaos on Earth and in fact created it by manipulating the deeper layers of the Earth's crust and our weather systems in ways we do not yet understand."

"Oh come on guys!" groaned Janus. "When are you going to get over your paranoia trip? If it wasn't for the Ashtar Command, none of us would be sitting here at all!"

"Let me repeat my question," said Nevis. "How do the Ashtar Command and you and the other 451 volunteers use the 144 Power Spots to control the deeper layers of the Earth's crust and weather systems?"

"451 volunteers?" said Jacob. "Have you caught all the others too?"

"We have taken into custody groups of volunteers at 126 of the 144 Power Spots," replied Nevis.

"126..." I said. "Well, I can tell you that you won't find five of the groups... they never returned from the Wormhole."

"The Wormhole?" said Nevis, unable to hide his growing irritation, "the same Wormhole that took you to the angels on the pink clouds?"

"No," I said. "The Wormhole is an interdimensional gateway that leads you to the Crystal Stair."

"The Crystal Stair? Listen, folks, I have just about had enough of your Dungeons & Dragons role-playing for one day!" Nevis leaned across the table and peered down at us. "Thousands upon thousands of people have lost their lives, millions of people are homeless, and the entire world is in a state of emergency. Do you have any idea of what it's like out there? Well I'll tell you what it's like... it's total chaos. "

"Listen," said Jacob staring right back at Nevis. "You've misunderstood everything. It's us human beings who have totally messed things up. The Ashtar Command and all the other beings in the higher dimensions are trying to help humanity—and they've been doing that for thousands of years. We should thank our lucky stars that they are here at all! And now the time has finally come when we're all going to get to meet them—and you guys are scared!"

An agent stuck his head inside the tent flap. "Major Nevis, General Elson wants to speak with you on line 1."

Nevis got up. "We might as well forget it, Ron. We're not going to get anything out of them."

Sorvino looked at us in disgust.

Nevis left the tent. I could see him pacing back and forth outside the tent while he talked on the phone. After a couple of minutes he returned.

"Bring them outside."

71

"I have a real bad feeling," I mumbled to Jacob and Janus as the DETI agents escorted us out of the tent.

Outside the sun was shining and everything seemed so peaceful.

Except of course for the lively hum of activity at the foot of the hill. There were agents and military personnel everywhere—talking on phones, pounding on laptops, and just generally marching around looking important. In the center of all this activity stood Agent Nevis, like a spider in his web, barking out orders.

Agent Nevis. Lord Gavin. What was he up to this time?

I turned and looked over at Glastonbury Tor and discovered there was also hectic activity on top of the hill. A military chopper was parked next to the old medieval tower. I could see a team of DETI agents working furiously up there, placing something around the top of the hill and around its uppermost flanks.

"I wonder what they're up to?" said Jacob, pointing to the Tor.

"I don't know, but whatever it is, I've got a real bad feeling about it," I said.

"Maybe it's time we got ourselves out of here," Janus whispered.

"How would you do that?" whispered Jacob. "We're surrounded on all sides."

"We could use the staff, the sword and the star," whispered Janus, patting his trusty two-handed sword. "Nobody seems to have noticed our interdimensional weapons."

"But do you think we can use our weapons for violent purposes?" I asked.

"Good question," said Jacob. "And should we use violence at all?"

"I think it might be better if we focused on the Force, the way the Masters taught us..." I said.

Our little exchange was interrupted by a group of agents who escorted us over to the foot of the hill where Nevis was now standing with a group of his people. Most of them were talking on their mobile phones. Sorvino was adjusting a piece of equipment that had a red button on it. Nevis signaled for the agents to bring us over to him.

"Yes, General, we have the go-ahead from the British government," Nevis said into his phone. "The same goes for all the Power Spots in the NATO countries... as a matter of fact there are only 14 Power Spots where we have no presence as yet... yes... mostly in Asia... Yes, sir...OK... we'll go ahead anyway..."

The propellers of the helicopter on top of the Tor began to turn as the agents on the hilltop jumped in. Then the chopper took off and moved away from the Tor.

Sorvino gave the other agents the thumbs up sign.

Nevis finished his conversation with the General and put his phone in his pocket.

"Sir, we're in radio contact with all the other 143 units," said Agent Jackson to Nevis. "They are all ready and waiting for your signal."

"Good," said Nevis.

Then he turned to us.

"On the top of that hill," he said pointing to the top of Glastonbury Tor, "my agents have placed enough explosives to completely obliterate the top of the Tor from the face of the Earth."

We looked at him with horror.

"Why would you want to do that?" I protested. "You must be out of your mind, man! Glastonbury Tor is one of the most important Power Spots on Earth—the very Heart Chakra of Mother Earth!"

Nevis went on coldly, "We have placed similar amounts of high explosives on and around all the other 143 so-called Power Spots that the Ashtar Command is using including the Pyramid of Giza, the Great Barrier Reef in Australia and Machu Pichu in Peru. My people are just waiting for the go-sign from me and they will blow your entire Light Grid to kingdom come."

3

Deactivation

We looked at Nevis in horror.

"You don't realize what you're about to do!" cried Jacob. "If the Light Grid is destroyed, the effect on Mother Earth may be catastrophic!"

"The collective consciousness of humanity will fall drastically!" I exclaimed.

"And Mother Earth might make another axis shift!" cried Janus, the veins standing out in his neck.

"Then tell me how the Ashtar Command uses the Power Spots to create havoc in the Earth's crust and weather systems!" Nevis said slowly. "That's all I want to know."

"But we already told you!" I cried in exasperation. "The Power Spots are Mother Earth's Energy Centers and they circulate the Universal Life Force."

Nevis shook his head. "So you insist on maintaining your interdimensional fairy tale, eh?"

"It's not a fairy tale!" I cried, almost yelling. "It's the truth!"

"You boys leave me no choice."

Nevis turned towards Sorvino. "Are we ready?"

"Yes, sir." Sorvino turned the dial on the panel of the piece of equipment he was still holding. The red button started flashing.

"No!" the three of us cried in unison. "Stop! You can't do this!"

"Jackson." Nevis turned towards Jackson. "Are the other units ready?"

"Yes, sir. They're all waiting for your signal."

I tried to throw myself at Nevis, but several agents held me back.

"You don't know what you're doing!" I shouted.

"I'm asking you for the very last time. How does the Ashtar Command use the Power Spots to control the deeper layers of the Earth's crust and weather systems?"

We looked at him in horror.

The man was completely insane.

And there was nothing we could do.

We were surrounded on all sides by agents and soldiers.

"Okay then, we will continue."

Nevis signaled to Jackson who handed him her phone.

"All units ready," he said into the phone. "5 seconds to deactivation. 5... 4... 3..."

You must focus on the Force, I thought to myself, focus on the Force...

Before I could even begin, Janus let out a huge roar and charged like an enraged animal at Nevis.

Four agents threw themselves at him but he swept them aside and lunged straight for Nevis.

"2..."

"Stop!" bellowed Janus, pulling his mighty two-handed sword from its sheath.

"No, Janus!" I cried. "We cannot use violence!"

"Focus on the Force, Janus!" Jacob cried.

"1..."

Janus hurled his two-handed sword right at Nevis.

Nevis turned towards Janus, but didn't seem to notice the glowing sword, which passed right through Nevis and came out on the other side—just as if Nevis or the sword was made of thin air. The sword landed in the grass a few yards from Nevis.

"Now!" said Nevis in a loud voice.

Sorvino pushed the flashing red button.

A moment later, a blinding flash of light lit up the top of Glastonbury Tor followed by a deafening roar and a huge explosion. The upper part of the hill erupted in flames and smoke.

"No!" I cried in horror.

Enormous clouds of fire shot up in the air. The old medieval tower could no longer be seen. Earth, stone and fire came cascading down the hillside.

Everything grew dark before my eyes and I fell to my knees on the grass.

I hardly noticed that Janus had knocked Nevis to the ground or that he was now fighting the dozens of agents and soldiers who had come to Nevis' rescue—nor did I notice the fact that Jacob was roaring furiously as he tried to come to Janus' aid.

No, I remained on my knees in the soft grass as if someone had just dealt me a deadly blow—right to the heart.

Deadly to Avalon, Mother Earth's bleeding Heart Chakra.

"Oh my God!" I heard someone cry on the edge of my consciousness. "Look, the explosion is spreading!"

Amidst the darkness and ash, I realized the earth underneath me was shaking—like a dying heart in its last death throes. I lifted my head and saw the top of Glastonbury Tor explode once again.

But this time the explosion was ten times bigger than the first.

Then this new explosion triggered a chain reaction and more explosions spread with lightning speed down the sides of the hill as if the Heart of Avalon was now truly bursting. And not just the Heart of Avalon. With the Sight that was given me, I saw the explosions that were also taking place at all the other 143 main Power Spots on Earth—and it all happened at the speed of light.

The Light Grid was in its death throes.

"Everybody run!" someone shouted. Then in panic, the soldiers and agents began running away from the exploding hill.

But it was too late.

We were already engulfed by the flames. Three helicopters and a jeep exploded in a giant cloud of fire and smoke right before my eyes. Then everything everywhere blew up in a whirlwind of black smoke, flying earth, rocks, tents, helicopters, and people. Then amid the screams and shouts, I felt an enormous pressure rise up from the Earth and hurl me into the air. A hot, burning pain seared through my body.

Then I remembered no more.

I opened my eyes, only to find everything was still black. And then, for what seemed like endless minutes, all I saw was blackness. Then slowly the blackness turned into a gray mist and specks of gold and red danced before my eyes.

Breathing was painful and I coughed—and with that first cough, the world came back into focus.

Above me billowed huge black clouds of smoke and the heat from the many fires was beating against me from all sides. Even the ground beneath me seemed to be on fire.

I coughed again. Everything smelt like burnt flesh and metal. Slowly I raised my head, only to discover that I was lying on my side, entangled in the burnt remains of a tent and…. a body. The body was blackened and burnt and I tried to disentangle myself from the corpse, but my first movement sent a sharp wave of pain right through me.

For a moment I thought I was going to pass out, but then I felt something cool on my face.

I looked up.

It was raindrops.

Cool, wet raindrops that were beginning to fall from the dark sky above me.

I tried to push the burnt corpse away from me—and a new wave of pain shot through me, but I managed. I could see from his uniform that the man had been one of the British soldiers.

But now he was dead.

Then I took a few deep breaths and slowly untangled myself from the charred remains of the tent.

I sat up and looked around. The whole field looked like one huge bomb crater. Fires were smoldering and the charred remains of the soldiers, helicopters, jeeps, and tents were strewn everywhere. No one seemed to be moving or breathing.

I couldn't see Jacob or Janus anywhere.

I looked up to where Glastonbury Tor once was. The whole hill was draped in black smoke. Or maybe the hill was not even there anymore? Perhaps all that was left of Avalon, the Heart Chakra of the Earth, was a gaping hole...

I turned away from the hill and looked at the lifeless bodies strewn all over the place. Many of them were covered with earth or buried under twisted pieces of machinery.

"Jacob! Janus!" I coughed.

But there was no answer—and no movement anywhere.

"Jacob! Janus!" I croaked hoarsely. "Where are you?"

Still no answer.

I looked around in despair, trying to remember where Jacob and Janus had been right before the explosion. At the foot of the hill, straight ahead...

I tried to get up, but my legs refused to obey me. Instead I dug my hands into the burnt ground and began to crawl towards the foot of the hill, to the spot where I'd last seen Jacob and Janus.

As I slowly inched my way forwards, I felt some small measure of strength returning to my body—but also more pain. Every fiber of my body seemed to be on fire. But I clamped my teeth and continued my slow crawl. I came to the first heap of bodies. One was an American

DETI agent. I couldn't see who the other was because he was lying face down under a pile rocks and earth. I scraped away the rocks and stones and turned him over. It turned out he was the captain who had captured us earlier that day.

I crawled around the two bodies and continued my search.

"Jacob! Janus!" I cried gruffly. "Can you hear me…? Where are you?"

Still no answer.

I continued to inch my way forward until I came to the next heap of bodies. I was just about to turn over another body when I heard a noise behind me.

I looked around.

It was the sound of voices.

And vehicles.

Through the dying flames and the black clouds of smoke, I could see figures in the distance, in the opening between the trees that led down into the town. Soldiers were on their way up to the burning field.

I turned over the bodies and found they too were all DETI agents. Then I crawled on and examined the two bodies that were crushed under a charred helicopter—another agent and a soldier.

But no Jacob and Janus.

Where were they?

The sound of voices and vehicles grew louder. I could see the soldiers making their way through the burning field—turning over bodies, looking for survivors. They weren't very far from me now.

I crawled behind a burnt-out helicopter and started crawling away from the soldiers towards the west side of Glastonbury Tor. Every time I crawled past a body, I checked to see if it was one of my friends—and each time, I sighed with relief. My friends were nowhere to be found.

What could have happened to them? Maybe Jacob and Janus hadn't been knocked unconscious by the explosion like me, but had escaped? Maybe they had tried to find me but couldn't because I was half-buried under the tent and that corpse.

I reached the line of trees that once stood along the edge of the field. The explosion had knocked most of them over or had ripped them right out of the ground.

The soldiers were getting ever closer and had now reached the foot of the hill. I could hear the sound of a helicopter approaching in the distance.

I began to crawl faster through the fallen trees. After about a minute, I spotted the remains of a hedge a bit further on and then an opening in the hedge, where the explosion had blown away the iron bars. I crawled over

78

and crawled through. On the other side was a road, which looked like it was deserted.

I tried to stand up, but my legs still wouldn't really do what I wanted them to so I half crawled and half hobbled across the road. On the other side was another field, much of which was covered in smoldering ash and the burning remains of the many explosions. Heavy clouds of smoke hung low. The iron gate of the fence around the field was bolted shut. I heaved myself over the gate and fell down on the other side.

It wasn't until I landed on the other side that I really took a look at myself. My white robe—or what was left of it—was in tatters. I had burns almost everywhere, on my arms, shoulders, chest and legs. Plus I was cut and bruised almost everywhere and it seemed like every inch of my body was crying out in pain. I held my throbbing head and groaned.

Then I lay down on my back for a while and stared blankly up at the sky—or what should have been the sky. After a while, I heard the sound of vehicles coming up the road fast. They came to a screeching halt right near the opening in the hedge where I lay.

I stiffened and didn't move.

"Holy Mother of God!" said a voice, "There's nothing left. What on Earth could have caused an explosion like that?"

"We're going to need water and hoses over here on the double!" someone shouted from the burning field.

"The fire brigade and water is on its way! Are there any survivors?"

The shouting was interrupted by the sound of an explosion.

"Watch out for that fire! It's still spreading!" I heard someone shout from the field.

"Give us a hand over here!"

"What are those helicopters doing?"

I could hear the sound of more vehicles coming up the road. More men appeared and began to shout.

I turned over on my stomach and began to crawl slowly along a ditch that looked like it would take me across the field. I was just about to inch my way forward when I heard two of the men on the road talking.

"What about the three Danes?" asked the Englishman who was standing closest to the opening in the hedge. "Any sign of them?"

"We've found two of them, Commander Holm," answered the other man.

I froze.

"Are they alive?" asked the first voice.

"No, sir. They're both dead."

When I heard those words, a second darkness seemed to descend upon me.

"Are you sure that they're the ones we want?"

"Yes, sir, positive. They were both dressed in funny costumes. A chain mail and a long robe."

"Damn!" answered the Commander, "they were our only lead. What about the third one, the one with the long hair?"

"We haven't found him yet, sir. Watch out sir, the fire is spreading."

"Find him!" shouted Commander Holm. "If he's alive, I want him alive."

"No one could survive an explosion like that, sir. They're all dead. He's probably buried somewhere in the wreckage."

The Commander paid him no heed, but turned and barked out orders to the men gathering around him... not that it mattered to me. I dug my hands into the ground and crawled on. I could hear the sound of more vehicles approaching, this time from both directions—and more helicopters were heading toward the hill. Men were yelling, but I no longer listened to what they were saying. I crawled away like a zombie while the Commander's words kept running through my head.

No one could survive an explosion like that. They're all dead.

No one...

I forced myself onward until I reached the other side of the field. Then I heaved myself over another iron gate and landed in a muddy puddle on the other side. There was a path and on the other side of the path there were fields. In the distance I could make out the rooftops of Glastonbury town.

No one could survive an explosion like that. They're all dead.

I crawled along the muddy path for a few minutes until I could drag myself no further. Then I looked up and saw that I was lying underneath two huge ancient oak trees. Their mighty branches creaked in the wind and it almost looked as if they were bending down over me.

Gog and Magog said a voice inside me, a voice that had known these giants, once in a distant past...

But now it was all gone.

I rolled over in the mud and closed my eyes. Tears were streaming down my face.

I could not bear to look back.

My beloved Avalon had been totally wiped out. The Light Grid was destroyed. And Jacob and Janus were dead.

4

Rebecca

"Wake up, Mr. Starbrow. Wake up."

Someone was tugging at my arm.

"Wake up, Mr. Starbrow."

I opened my eyes slowly.

"Wake up," said the voice again.

I looked up. The person was not very tall.

"Wake up, Mr. Starbrow. Grandma is waiting for you."

It was a little boy.

"Grandma is waiting for you." He kept on tugging my arm.

Then I recognized him—the shock of dark hair, the clear face, the big, wise eyes. It was the little boy in the car. Lance, the son of the woman who had given us a ride to Glastonbury in her battered blue Volkswagen van the day when Jacob and Janus and I had...

"Leave me alone, Lance," I mumbled and sank back in the mud.

"No! You have to come with me," said the little boy still tugging on my arm. "Grandma sent me."

"Lance go home, " I moaned, "please…!"

"No, no, the bad men are coming and they're going to find you very soon."

"I don't care. Leave me alone."

"No, no, you can't lie here. The bad men are coming. Grandma said you *must* come! *You must!*""

The little bugger just wouldn't give up. He kept on pushing and pulling me. He was so persistent that he almost managed to push me into an upright position.

"You can't stay here Mr. Starbrow. Grandma says you have to come! She said the bad men would come and get you!" Lance pointed excitedly down the path that I had just dragged myself along—fear in his eyes.

"You have to come with me. Mum is waiting in her car. She'll drive you to Grandma's."

I looked back. All I could see was black smoke where Glastonbury Tor should have been. There was the sound of helicopters and vehicles coming from the direction of the hill. The boy was right, some of the vehicles were heading towards us.

"Come on, Mr. Starbrow. Grandma will help you and put the star back on your brow."

"Put the star back on my brow?"

"Come on!"

Lance ran down the path, which wound its way down towards the town. Then he turned and motioned eagerly for me to follow him.

I looked back. I could hear the sound of cars approaching. The little boy was right. It wouldn't be long now before they found me.

I tried to get up, but my legs still refused to do what I wanted them to. For a moment I felt like I was going to black out again. I swayed and fell to my knees.

"Come on, Mr. Starbrow! Hurry up!"

I clenched my teeth and got up again. This time I stayed on my feet and hobbled forward slowly.

"This way, Mr. Starbrow!"

The little boy eagerly led me down the path. After I half hobbled and half ran a couple of hundred yards, we came to a grassy slope. Lance sat down on the grass and began to slide down the slope. I stood for a moment, watching him slide down and then I sat down and followed him. I landed at the bottom right smack in the middle of a thorn bush not far from my expert little guide.

"Quick, Starbrow! This way! Mum is over there!"

The spunky little kid ran on, heading towards the end of the little dale. At the end of the little dale there was yet another slope—and at the end of that slope, a road. We'd come to the outskirts of town. The battered blue Volkswagen van was parked on the road and in the driver's seat was the young woman with long, curly red hair whom I'd met before. Lance's mother Gail.

Once again, Lance glided down the slope while I half crawled, half rolled my way to the bottom. When I rolled out onto the road, Gail got out of the car and came running towards us.

"He's hurt, Mum!" cried the little boy.

"Oh my God, what's happened to you?" cried Gail in horror.

"The bad men have taken his star!"

I tried to get up, but everything went black again.

Gail put her right arm around my shoulder and helped me to my feet. "Where are your friends?"

"Dead... They're all dead..." I mumbled.

I was losing it, but knew she was somehow getting me into the car and onto the back seat and putting a blanket around me. The car began to move. The last thing I heard was Lance asking:

"Mom... is he going to die?"

It was like being in the Manifestation Chamber again.

The same bloody visions kept repeating themselves.

And each bloody vision led to yet another bloody vision, which led to yet another bloody vision...

First there were visions of my past life as Dana in England... with Loran lying lifeless on the ground with a sword in his belly... and Gaius lying next to him with two arrows in his back... Lord Gavin the traitor piercing Dana's heart... my heart... with his sword...

Then the visions changed and Lord Gavin reappeared as Agent Nevis... the Agent Nevis who blew Avalon, the Heart Chakra of the Earth, to kingdom come... the Agent Nevis who blew the Light Grid to bits and wrapped Earth in a second darkness...

Everywhere there was blood, fire and destruction... There was blood from Dana's pierced heart, blood from Jacob and Janus' charred bodies, blood from Glastonbury Tor, blood from hundreds and thousands of burnt bodies and faces... that all seemed to blend together and became one giant monster, the mother of all monsters... with countless grotesque and distorted faces...

I don't know how long I was stuck there, trapped... about to be snuffed out by the Dweller on the Threshold... and that horrible nightmare of blood. All I know is that it was a voice that brought me back. Back to life and the world. A soft, gentle voice... a voice that reminded me of love and friendship a long, long time ago...

Who will solve the riddle?
Who will tell the tale?
Who will ride on after us?
After we set sail?

Who will know the magic sign?
Who will find the gate?
Who will wake up to their fate,
Before it is too late?

I knew you when the mystery was still untold
I knew you in your younger days, before you grew old
I knew you in your sunny days, the days of wine and mirth
I knew you in the summertime, way before your birth

The Dweller on the Threshold and the bloody nightmare were washed away, dissolved, slowly and gently, by the waves... the waves of the Western Sea... by the great waves with their huge white crests that crashed onto the shores of Planet Earth... pounding to a rhythm that was eternal and everlasting.

The sound of the great ocean filled me with deep peace and a knowingness.

A peace, which I knew I was sharing with precious loved ones…

And then I saw them… the six shining figures.

Six shining figures who were standing together on the shores of Planet Earth, listening to the rhythm of the sea... six shining figures with the wind in their hair... six shining souls who knew each other as well as it was possible for one being to know another... six friends who had been together... since the beginning...

Who will solve the riddle?
Who will tell the tale?
Who will ride on after us?
After we set sail?

Who will know the magic sign?
Who will find the gate?
Who will wake up to their fate,
Before it is too late?

I knew you when the world was young and meadows still were fair
I knew you when you hid the secret in your golden hair
I knew you in your younger days, the days of silver song
I knew you, yes I knew you, before the days grew long

The song and the vision of the six shining figures were like sweet music to my soul, a potent magic spell that gently brought me back to life.

I soared on the wings of the song, back over the windswept coasts of Planet Earth, back to the one who was singing me back to life.

Slowly I opened my eyes.

I was lying on a white bed.

Someone was sitting beside me, singing that soft, familiar melody.

There was very little light in the room, so I could not see the person clearly. All I could make out was the golden ring that glinted on the singer's right hand.

Who will solve the riddle?
Who will tell the tale?
Who will ride on after us?
After we set sail?

Who will know the magic sign?
Who will find the gate?
Who will wake up to their fate,
Before it is too late?

The song ended and the room was completely still.

I lay there for a while without saying a word, almost afraid to break the magical peace the song had wrapped me in.

Then, in a hoarse voice full of hope, I heard myself whisper the great question that was now taking shape within me.

"Elmar?"

"Greetings, Starbrow."

The figure turned towards me.

But it wasn't Elmar who had sung the familiar song.

It was a woman, with a kind, finely chiseled face and deep wise eyes.

She had long silver gray hair and looked as if she was about 60.

I studied her kind, beautiful face.

"But how... do you know that song?" I asked in amazement.

85

The woman smiled gently. "Elmar taught it to me many years ago. It was just one of many things your grandfather taught me."

"You knew Elmar?"

"Yes, I know Elmar."

"You know Elmar? But how... who...?"

"Easy now, Starbrow," she said gently. "You have been through fire and darkness, and have only just returned."

Fire and darkness?

For a moment, the bloody visions of the Dweller on the Threshold raced past my inner eye again.

The woman took my hand. Her hand was warm and comforting. "There now, Starbrow, don't think about it," she said. "It was only a bad dream."

Only a bad dream? Was it really true?

No! Glastonbury Tor really had been blown to pieces, the Light Grid really had been destroyed, and Jacob and Janus really were...

"Don't think about it, Starbrow," she said again and looked into my eyes. There was something very comforting about the sound of her voice—like the sound of a mother's voice.

I gazed into her warm, comforting eyes until the bloody visions faded.

Then I looked around the room and discovered I was lying in a bed in a sparsely furnished room with white walls. The curtains had been drawn. Outside it was dark and only a single candle lit up the room.

I looked down at my body and discovered that my hands and arms were wrapped in bandages. My body seemed to tingle all over. I was wearing pajamas.

The woman kept smiling at me, while she held my hand in hers. Her hand was warm, her fingers long and delicate, but there was no ring on any of her fingers.

So the golden ring I had seen was just a dream? Like the vision of the six shining figures who had stood together on the windswept shores of Planet Earth...

"How did you know Elmar?" I asked.

"Elmar and I have known each other since the beginning."

"Since the beginning?"

The woman smiled. "Yes. Just like you have."

I looked at her questioningly.

"In this life, Elmar and I met each other many years ago."

"When?"

"It was right after the war. In 1948."

"1948?"

"Yes."

"Where did you meet each other?"

"As a matter of fact we met each other right here, in this very house."

"In this house?" I looked around me in wonder. "But where am I?"

"You are still in Glastonbury."

As I looked at the woman, I remembered that Elmar told me that he had been in Glastonbury many times on his countless travels around the world.

"But who are you?"

"I am Rebecca. Rebecca Randall. Lance's grandmother and Gail's mother."

Rebecca... Randall. Where had I heard that name before?

"My father was Gareth Randall," she said.

"Gareth Randall?"

"Yes."

"The Gareth Randall who led the first expedition Elmar went on to the Himalayas?"

"Yes. Exactly."

"But how..."

"My father died on the expedition. But before my father passed over, Elmar promised him that he would return to Glastonbury and take care of me. I was very young then."

Elmar! The thought of my fearless grandfather and his amazing adventures sent new life and courage coursing through my veins. I tried to sit up in the bed, but the movement sent a sharp jolt of pain through my body. Moving was far more painful than I expected it to be.

"Easy, my friend." Rebecca helped me sit up and placed two soft white pillows behind my back. Then she gave me a cup with something that looked like lukewarm tea. "Drink this. It will give you strength."

I took a sip of the drink—and coughed. If this was tea, it was extremely strong. So strong it made tears come to my eyes.

"You met Elmar right here, in this house?" I asked, slowly sipping the strong brew she'd given me.

"Yes. After the expedition, Elmar came here… just as he promised my father he would. Elmar and I lived together in this house for many years as man and wife."

"Were you married?"

"No, but we lived together…"

"You and Elmar lived together? He never told me about you."

"There are a great many things your grandfather never told you, Starbrow."

"I can see that," I muttered, smiling for the first time in a long time. The more I found out about my grandfather, the more I realized how much more there was to find out!

"How long were you together?"

"We lived here together for a couple of years. But in his heart, Elmar was a wanderer... he loved to travel and thrived on adventure. And besides, he had an important mission to carry out, which meant that he could not stay in any one place for too long anyway."

"What mission was that?"

"The mission we're all on," said Rebecca with a glint in her eye.

"You mean...?"

She nodded. "Yes. Mission: Earth Ascension. So in the end, Elmar had to go and continue his wandering. But he always returned to me."

"Yes, Elmar was always on the move," I chuckled.

It felt good to think about my adventurous grandfather. And to think that this kind woman had known him for more than half a century!

"Elmar's first journey—after his Himalayan expedition and his long stay with me here in Glastonbury—was to Greenland."

"Greenland?"

"Yes. He was a member of one of the first expeditions across the inland ice. And it was on that expedition that he met Freja, your grandmother. Siri, your mother came from that meeting. And now the circle is complete. You are here with me, back where it all started."

I nodded. My mother Siri had told me about Elmar's short relationship with my grandmother Freja.

I took another sip of Rebecca's strong brew. "But how did you know that I would be lying under the two old oak trees?" I asked.

"Sooner or later, all roads from Glastonbury Tor lead to Gog and Magog, those old giants," said Rebecca, sighing. "But I also had some help from the other side. With the Sight that is given me, I saw Elmar."

"You saw Elmar?"

"Yes. When they blew up Glastonbury Tor, I felt a terrible tremor pass through Mother Earth."

"Yes," I said. "The military has destroyed the Power Spots and the Light Grid."

Rebecca sighed again. "The entire house shook and I knew that something terrible had happened. So I immediately sat down to meditate.

But before I could close my eyes, Elmar suddenly appeared right in the middle of the room."

"Here in this house?"

"Yes."

"That certainly must have been the Sight..." I said and stopped, realizing that Rebecca might not even know that Elmar was dead.

"Rebecca..." I said slowly. "Elmar is no longer on the Earth plane. He died of a heart attack a few days ago."

Rebecca was gazing at the window. The news of Elmar's death did not seem to surprise her. "Whatever the doctors choose to call the reason for a soul's passing matters little to me," she said. "It was time for Elmar to pass over. He died fully conscious that his mission on the Earth plane was over."

And to awaken me....

"But when Elmar appeared in this room after the explosion, he did not look like he looked just before he left his earthly body," Rebecca continued and turned towards me again. "No, he looked 30-40 years younger and was surrounded by a bright white light."

"That was how he looked in Shamballa," I said.

"Yes, I have heard of you and your two friends' adventures in the higher dimensions."

"How did you hear that?"

"Elmar told me a little when he showed himself to me in this room. You told me more in your delirium."

"What did Elmar say?"

"He told me you were close to dying at the foot of Glastonbury Tor and said only I could help you."

"Did he really say that?" I took another swig of her strong brew. It was heartening to think that Elmar had been right here in this house, thinking about me.

"Right after Elmar showed himself to me, I went to work. The Sight is also very strong in my little Lance. He knows every nook and byway here in Glastonbury and can move in and out of hedges like a little fox. So I asked Gail to drive to Wick Hollow near Glastonbury Tor and send Lance up to the two old oak trees. I had a feeling that you would be there. And so you were."

Suddenly a great weariness swept over me.

I leaned back in the bed and sighed, "The Power Spot has been blown to bits, Rebecca. The two other Guardians of the Power Spot, my best friends, have been killed. The Light Grid has been destroyed."

89

"I know," she said comfortingly and put her hand on my arm.

"The military thinks the Ashtar Command wants to take over the whole world..."

"I'm afraid there are a lot of people who think that, my friend."

"I mean what's going to happen when the Ashtar Command lands in seven days, if everyone on Earth is as hostile..."

Rebecca sighed. "It doesn't look as if the Ashtar Command is going to land in seven days time after all."

"What do you mean?"

"The moment the military destroyed all the Power Spots and deactivated the Light Grid, I felt an awful tremor pass through our entire planet. A moment later all the starships that were hovering over the Earth's cities disappeared."

I looked at her in disbelief.

"All the starships disappeared?"

She nodded.

"You can't be serious!"

"I'm afraid it's true."

I bowed my head.

"Then it's all really over now."

"Don't think about it at the moment," she said. "Rest, Starbrow. You have to regain your strength."

"But if the starships are gone, it means that STARDAY has been canceled."

"Don't think about it right now. You can think about it tomorrow when you wake up."

I turned my head to the wall and sighed, "But there's nothing for me to wake up to anymore."

5

Bed & Breakfast

Even though I was dead tired, I couldn't sleep. After Rebecca left, I just lay in her white bed and stared blankly up at the ceiling, thinking about my two dead friends and all we had lost.

Jacob and Janus.

Moncler and Telperion.

Gaius and Loran.

My friends since the beginning.

My friends through lifetime after lifetime.

And now they were dead, killed once again—murdered—betrayed—by our eternal pursuer, the demon Lord Gavin.

I was so immersed in my own despair that I did not notice the sound of helicopters in the distance or hear the sound of cars on the street outside. Suddenly Rebecca was standing at my bedside holding a candle.

"Shh!" she put her finger to her lips. "Not a sound. Get up quick and follow me."

I sat up in bed dazed—and realized I was hearing the sound of cars and loud voices on the street outside.

"It's soldiers," she said, motioning me to follow her. "I know they are looking for you—searching every house in Glastonbury. We must hurry and hide you."

I got out of bed. My whole body hurt, but I had no problem standing up.

Rebecca had already left the room. I followed her in a daze, like one who is not quite sure if he is dreaming or awake.

She led me down a long hallway and then down two flights of stairs. Rebecca's house was big, white and very clean. We entered a spacious living room. The only light in the living room came from some candles on the coffee table. Gail stood in the foyer with Lance in her hand. She looked frightened.

"Hurry!" Gail whispered. "They're already at the Wellington's house!"

Rebecca led me to the kitchen, through the kitchen door, and into something that looked like a pantry. The pantry was filled with boxes, bookcases and old furniture.

"Quick! Help me move these boxes!"

I looked at her, uncomprehendingly.

"Wake up, Starbrow!" Rebecca said sharply and snapped her fingers. "Do you want to end up like your friends?"

I bent over and together we pushed some large boxes to the side. Beneath the boxes, there was a trap door in the floor. Rebecca bent down and opened it. From the light of her candle I could see that the trap door opened into a small underground bunker. It was about two yards deep and one and a half yards wide.

"My father built this when I was a child," Rebecca said. "He was a Royal Air Force pilot during the war and he always said it was important to have a least one secret hiding place."

I stared down into the dark hole. There was just enough room for three or four people to stand upright down there.

Suddenly someone started knocking loudly on the front door.

"Hurry up!" Rebecca whispered. "Get down there."

I lowered myself down into the bunker. Rebecca threw down a warm woolen blanket.

"Don't make a sound till we come back for you."

Then she closed the trap door and I was alone in the dark.

I heard her push the boxes back over the trap door. Then everything went quiet above me.

It was cold in Gareth's hideaway so I wrapped myself in the blanket and sat down.

The minutes ticked by. I listened for sounds from above but all I could hear was my own breathing.

The moment I focused on my breathing, I felt a faint tingling between my eyebrows. I looked up hoping I could penetrate the dark ceiling with my Sight.

Then I knew *he was there*.

Agent Nevis.

Lord Gavin.

In my mind's eye I saw his sharp hawk-like face, his cold, gray-green eyes.

Searching, searching, always searching for me.

Why?

I got up frantically and put my hands on the cold earthen walls. I felt like a trapped animal.

Then I heard the sound of feet above me... thud... thud... thud. And voices.

I froze and held my breath.

I knew that *he was there*.

Agent Nevis.

He was standing right above me.

He too had survived the explosion.

And he knew that I was still alive.

But how could he possibly know I was right here?

I tried to hold my breath as long as possible. Down in the darkness, I thought the beating of my heart was as loud as an express train. Although it was icy cold, the sweat began to trickle down me.

Suddenly I recognized the sound of Rebecca Randall's nervous voice above me, "... What on earth are you looking for? I dare say, whatever it is, you can't honestly expect to find it here, among my old apple crates...?"

I couldn't make out what the other voices were saying, but it sounded like Rebecca was chattering away, trying her best to distract them.

My heart pounded in my chest.

Every second felt like a century.

What were they doing now? Would they move the boxes and discover the trap door?

I strained to hear every sound, but it was difficult.

Then there was a change in the air. Was it just my imagination or were they actually leaving the pantry?

Yes, they were leaving! Suddenly it was quiet above me again.

Nevis and his men had left!

I took a deep breath and wiped the sweat off my forehead. Then I leaned against the cold earthen wall and tried to calm down.

After several minutes, I again heard sounds above me. Were they coming back? I froze again and listened. How many were they? It sounded like just one person. Was it Rebecca or one of my pursuers?

Whoever it was, they were moving the boxes. I pressed myself against the wall. The trap door opened and a faint light streamed down.

"Starbrow?"

Rebecca was standing above me with a candle in her hand.

"Rebecca," I said, sighing with relief.

"They're gone now."

She reached down and helped me out.

"That was really touch and go," Rebecca said, shaking her head.

"I thought it was game over for me," I said.

"Me too," said Rebecca. "But suddenly his phone rang and he had to leave."

"He?"

"The leader of the American agents. Apparently he survived the explosion just like you did."

"I know."

Rebecca looked at me gravely.

"He is looking for you, Starbrow."

"Yes, I know," I said again.

"The two of you are connected in some way that I do not quite understand. It is no longer safe for you to be in this house. We have got to get you out of Glastonbury as fast as possible."

Rebecca led me back into the kitchen. Gail was standing there with a worried look on her face. Lance was sitting by the kitchen table. The first faint rays of daylight were beginning to peep in through the windows.

"That was very close," Gail said.

I nodded. "I'm sorry I brought danger to your house."

"Nonsense," said Rebecca. "You just sit down and let me make you a nice breakfast. You must be starving."

"But..."

"Sit down. I've got a plan."

"A plan?"

"Do you like your eggs scrambled or boiled?"

"Eh... scrambled please."

Gail gave me a bathrobe to put on and then motioned me to sit down by the kitchen table. While Rebecca was making scrambled eggs and fried tomatoes on a gas burner, Gail and Lance set the table. There were breakfast delicacies of every kind from bread and marmalade to tea and orange juice.

"After the explosion at Glastonbury Tor, all the power went off so I'm afraid we can't toast your bread," said Gail.

I looked at the sumptuous breakfast before me.

"Eat! It will do you good!" Rebecca ordered.

I took a bite of bread and started to chew. That was when I realized I was starving. It must have been days since I had eaten anything. I took another bite of bread and was soon busy eating away. Rebecca was right—eating did me good. I felt new life and strength spreading through my body. It was as if the daze I was in began to lift. Rebecca, Gail and Lance sat down at the kitchen table and watched me stuff myself.

"Yummy! This is better than the best Bed & Breakfast!" I said.

"But this is a Bed & Breakfast!" laughed Rebecca, putting more bread on my already bursting plate. "'Avalon Bed & Breakfast' is what we call this house. Normally this place is filled with pilgrims visiting Glastonbury. But since the Earth changes began three or four days ago, the place has been completely deserted."

Gail stood up. "I'm just going to go and have a look at the road. Come on, Lance, let's go for a walk."

The two left. Rebecca poured herself a cup of tea.

"Your American agent friend and the whole British army it seems are busy searching for you with a fine-toothed comb in every single house in Glastonbury. They've blocked all the roads so no one can get in or out of Glastonbury—and the skies above us are swarming with helicopters."

"Which means that I'm stuck here," I said and stopped eating.

"I didn't say that. I've got an idea… a plan to get you out of here so you can tell the Ashtar Command not to cancel STARDAY."

I looked at her in surprise.

"You want me to tell the Ashtar Command not to cancel STARDAY?"

"Yes."

"You can't be serious."

"Oh yes I am."

"Come on Rebecca. What do you want me to say to the Ashtar Command? That I'm sorry that we human beings are such barbarians? That blowing up all the Power Spots and the Light Grid was just an accident!"

"Not all humans beings are hostile to our intergalactic guests."

"Maybe not you, me, Gail and Lance—but we're just a drop in the bucket! I doubt very much if the Ashtar Command will think the four of us are reason enough to come back to this insane Planet!"

"That's not true Starbrow. We're not the only ones who are open to meeting our intergalactic brothers and sisters. There are many more besides us!" replied Rebecca, her eyes flashing.

"But the American agents told me that people are fleeing the cities by the millions because they think the starships are some kind of intergalactic death machine!" I said in disgust.

Rebecca shook her head.

"That is only half the truth Starbrow. Just as many people are pouring into the cities to welcome the Ashtar Command. Starbrow, you should know about all the good things that have happened since Ashtar's transmission yesterday night."

"But how can you know anything like this Rebecca? The whole world is blacked out."

"No it isn't Starbrow. While Ashtar was announcing STARDAY— suddenly the electricity went on all around the world. That meant everybody could watch TV again and that's exactly what we've all been doing—non-stop. So we've seen great and wondrous things on TV, reports from almost every major city of thousands and thousands of people joining together in group meditations to lift the collective consciousness. The New Vision and the thought of STARDAY have given so many people new hope—the hope of something higher and better to look forward to. There are also many reports Starbrow... of awe-inspiring deeds of heroism and of ordinary people who are exhibiting unusually high levels of compassion and kindness... and even of people who previously were not especially interested in so-called 'spiritual' things, who are now behaving with unheard of generosity and helping their neighbors and other people in distress... Aid organizations like the Red Cross and Save the Children have been flooded with applications. Humanity is so close now. So close Starbrow... to the consciousness revolution... to the ascension to something higher and better that we have all been longing for and working for and dreaming of for so long."

I didn't say anything but suddenly I wasn't hungry anymore. I got up and walked over to the kitchen window. Rebecca's house was situated right at the foot of Glastonbury Tor. The huge blast on the Tor had knocked down most of the trees in front of her house. One of them had landed right on top of her little greenhouse, crushing everything inside. In between the few trees that had not been knocked down, I could barely make out the old hill—or what was left of it. In the misty morning light, I could see that the hill had been reduced to almost half its original size. There was this huge crater... as if the hill had been hit by a meteor from outer space or something. Two helicopters were circling the hill.

Rebecca got up and walked over to my side.

"Starbrow, there is more going on than meets the eye. The events that we are witnessing today are not a coincidence. They are the result, the fruits, of many years of hard work. Work that began long before your time, but which—for reasons I do not understand—it seems to be your destiny to carry on."

"What on earth are you talking about?"

"Do you remember what I told you last night? That even though Elmar and I loved each other and lived together, there came a time when he had to leave me... because he had an important mission to fulfill?"

I nodded.

"Well I think it's time for me to tell you about Elmar's mission. Because it is your destiny to continue the work your grandfather began."

6

Elmar's Mission

Rebecca took an old black and white photograph in a wooden frame down from the wall. The first soft rays of the morning sunshine fell gently on to the picture. It was a faded photograph of 17 men standing in two rows. They were all dressed in rugged outdoor clothes. On the ground before them was an assortment of mountaineering gear including backpacks, ropes and ice axes. The oldest of the men looked as if he was in his late 40s and the youngest of them...

"Is that...?" I began, pointing at the picture.

"Yes," said Rebecca and handed me the photograph. "That's Elmar and the original Shamballa expedition. The picture was taken in northern India in 1948, just before they began their expedition to the Himalayas."

The old photo was fascinating to look at. Elmar must have been my age when the picture was taken, or even younger. Already then there was no mistaking his determination and the power of his clear blue eyes.

"The man in the far right-hand corner is my father, Gareth Randall, the leader of the expedition." Said Rebecca pointing to the stocky, pipe-smoking Englishman with the strong jaw and muscular arms.

I stared curiously at the Englishman. "What made your father decide to organize the Shamballa expedition in the first place?"

"As far back as I can remember, my father had always been keenly interested in metaphysics and all things spiritual," Rebecca said. "He was a member of a secret order called the Rosicrucians. When I was a child, many wise and wonderful people passed through the doors of this house, which, as you know, lies at the foot of one of the mightiest Power Spots in all of Britain."

Rebecca sat down at the kitchen table. I joined her.

"As I told you before, my father was a Royal Air Force pilot. During the Second World War, he was stationed in India where he heard stories about Shamballa, the Great White Brotherhood, and ascension. When the war was over, he returned home and devoted practically all his time to his spiritual and metaphysical studies. He became obsessed with the thought of finding Shamballa, the City of Light, which he believed was the headquarters on Earth of the Ascended Masters who belonged to the Great White Brotherhood. According to my father, Shamballa was located in the higher dimensions above what is now called the Gobi Desert."

"Yes, I remember. Elmar told me a little about the expedition right before he... passed over to the other side."

Rebecca gave me a quick look and then continued. "My father was convinced that an Ascended Master by the name of Djwal Khul—also known as 'The Tibetan'—could show him the way to Shamballa. It was said that from time to time, Djwal Khul took on earthly form and could be found in the area surrounding his ashram in the Himalayas. With this in mind, my father decided to organize an expedition and go to the Himalayas. Finally in 1948, he left with the 16 members of his expedition. All men—it would be more accurate to say—who had in fact been called to join his expedition. Because the members of his expedition found my father in the most mysterious ways. Your grandfather Elmar was a good example. Apparently another Master who went under the name of Stanley Donne sent Elmar to England to join the expedition. But this was something I only learned about later."

As I listened to Rebecca, I started eating a bit more of the breakfast I'd begun before.

"They'd been away for almost a year," continued Rebecca. "In the beginning I received regular letters from my father with news about the progress of the expedition. But then six months went by and no letters came. I knew the expedition was moving into territory no Westerner had ever set foot in before so I didn't worry. And every day I wondered if they'd really found Djwal Khul and Shamballa..."

Rebecca picked up the picture again and looked at it closely as if she was trying to recall something that had happened a long, long time ago. Then she continued, "Then one glorious spring day, there was a knock on the front door of this house. I opened the door and there stood a young man I'd never seen before. He had a strong face, the blond hair of a Scandinavian, bright blue eyes and a very special aura. It was Elmar... and for me... love at first sight... "

Rebecca gently let her hand caress the old photograph. "On that fateful day, Elmar told me the sad news... that he was the only member of the expedition who had survived." Rebecca's voice trembled slightly as she recounted the events of that day. "He told me how they were trapped in a terrible blizzard in a high pass and had died, one by one. In the end, only my father and Elmar were left. Right before my father passed over to the other side, he made Elmar promise that if he survived he would take care of his only daughter."

"And Elmar survived," I said slowly feeling myself getting sucked into Rebecca's tale. "But how? What happened to him?" I wondered if he found Shamballa… this was one tale he never told me.

"The Ascended Master Djwal Khul saved Elmar from frozen death on that high pass."

"Djwal Khul? The Master the expedition was looking for?"

"Yes, exactly. Djwal Khul rescued Elmar and took him to his ashram high up in the mountains. There he taught Elmar many things—about the nature of consciousness, the soul and its evolution—information that was and is vital to humanity if humankind wants to ascend into the higher dimensions. After Elmar was initiated into the secret teachings, Djwal Khul sent him back into the world to assist the Ascended Masters in preparing humanity for the ascension into the 5th dimension. They did this because they knew the end of the 20th century and the beginning of the 21st would be a critical time for humanity."

I nodded, trying to take in all she was saying.

"It may be difficult for you to understand what it was like at that time Starbrow, because nowadays there are so many books and so much information about spiritual development and spirituality. Today there are so many teachers and almost everyone can learn about spirituality if their souls are ready. The so-called New Age movement is just one sign of these developments, one of the many things that happened before you were born. But in Elmar's time—and before Elmar began his mission in 1948—spirituality and metaphysical teachings…especially in the West… were only available to a select few. There were groups scattered here and there—closed secret societies like the Rosicrucians and the Freemasons— but that was about it. As far as ordinary people were concerned, information about consciousness and the evolution of the soul and spiritual development were very difficult, if not impossible, to obtain. At that time, most people just never heard of these things. It wasn't a part of their lives or consciousness at all. So an important part of what Djwal Kuhl wanted Elmar to do was to help make this kind of information available to all of humanity—and to begin the worldwide activation of humanity so that the people who were ready for it could begin to learn about these things and become aware of their true potential."

"Elmar never told me anything about all this—or at least not in the way you're telling me now."

Rebecca actually laughed. "That's not what I heard Starbrow! You grandfather told me many times that he tried to tell you about many of these things but you weren't very interested!"

I smiled faintly. It was true enough. "I guess you're right. I wasn't very interested in these things… back then…but… well… what happened after that… I mean when Elmar came back?"

"Another part of Elmar's mission was to help reactivate the main Power Spots on Earth—the Light Grid."

"The Light Grid? But I thought it was only the Guardians of the Power Spots who could activate the Power Spots with their interdimensional keys?"

"That is true, but Elmar was your predecessor. His task was to pave the way for you, the next generation, and your work, so to speak. In Elmar's time, many of the Power Spots had fallen into decline. They were either forgotten or run down and polluted by negativity. So you see, Elmar's task was to pave the way for your work."

"But first he came here to Glastonbury to see you?"

"Yes, Glastonbury was the first stop on his journey—for two reasons as you can now see. One was to fulfill his promise to my father—and the other was to visit Glastonbury Tor, which is, as you well know, one of the mightiest Power Spots on Earth. And because Glastonbury Tor is the Heart Chakra of the world, it is one of the most important links in the Light Grid."

I nodded, thinking how much Elmar could have told me if only I had listened. "So what happened then… to you and Elmar?"

"Well as I said I fell in love with Elmar the moment I saw him and fortunately for me, he returned my love. So we lived here together for many years. True to my father's wishes, this house continued to be a meeting place for seekers and pilgrims and all those who were interested in the nature of the soul and in spiritual development. Elmar and I often meditated on top of Glastonbury Tor, and Elmar initiated me into many of the secret teachings of Djwal Khul and the Masters. But in the end, it was time for Elmar to move on. His restless soul yearned to wander again and it was his destiny and preordained mission to crisscross the globe, reactivating the Power Spots. So Elmar began his many journeys."

"And you stayed here?"

"Yes. If Elmar was the wanderer, the traveler, I was the fixed point, the home base. My mission was to stay here and build a spiritual center."

"So you and Elmar kept seeing each other?"

"Oh yes Starbrow. Your grandfather and I loved each other—and still do. So of course he always returned to me. We saw each other at regular intervals between his journeys—and he often stayed here for extended periods of time."

I laughed and took another bite of bread. "So that's why Elmar visited just about every country in the whole world. He wasn't just an archaeologist and art dealer as he told most people!" I exclaimed. "How could I have been so dumb... and not see he was on a mission! Now I'm beginning to understand things a whole lot better Rebecca... but what about... Gail? Is Elmar her father?"

Rebecca smiled and shook her head. "No, he's not."

"Really?" I asked in surprise.

"Well Starbrow... destiny sometimes has a strange way with us... anyway, this is what happened. In 1968, exactly 20 years after the first Shamballa expedition, Elmar decided to organize a new expedition to the Himalayas. He wanted to meet Djwal Khul again and find Shamballa."

"Really...he never told me about this...?"

"It was all very mysterious," Rebecca continued. "This new expedition had exactly the same number of members as the first expedition and they left at exactly the same time of year, and..."

"What happened?"

Rebecca's voice became softer. "Many months went by and I heard nothing from Elmar. No news at all. But I wasn't worried because I was used to Elmar being away for long periods of time... sometimes a year could go by and I didn't hear from him. But in the end, I knew something was wrong. Then I got news that the expedition had been trapped in a blizzard—just like the first expedition—and that all the members of the expedition had been killed, buried under a huge avalanche."

I looked at her in surprise.

Rebecca sighed. "Of course I was devastated—completely besides myself with grief. First my beloved father and then Elmar—the love of my life."

Rebecca got up and went over to the window. The morning was slowly becoming brighter—and the gentle sunlight lit up her fine, wise face. I could see why Elmar returned her great love.

"My biggest support during that time—which was probably the most difficult time in my whole life—was David. David had been a friend of the house for many years—he was a true seeker and a true friend to both Elmar and myself. In the end, David and I began a relationship and then one day to my great surprise I was pregnant. Nine months later, I gave birth to Gail."

"So David is Gail's father?"

"Yes."

"But what about..."

Rebecca's face lit up. "Then on another glorious spring morning, a few months after Gail was born, there was another knock at the door. And guess who was standing there, alive and well on my front porch?"

"Elmar?"

"Yes, Elmar. I nearly fainted. I thought I must be seeing things, that the Sight was playing tricks on me. Elmar was so surprised at my reaction that I realized it wasn't a vision and that he was really still alive. Then I fainted—right there on the front porch!"

"So why didn't he send word to you and let you know he hadn't been killed by the avalanche."

"When I came to, Elmar told me why. Apparently, when the expedition reached a certain point on the journey, Elmar had a vision in which he received guidance from Djwal Khul. The Master told Elmar that only he could continue and that the rest of the expedition should return. The group decided to follow the Master's instructions and return—leaving Elmar to continue alone. Since he knew he might be gone for more than a year, he gave the members of the expedition a letter they were supposed to give to me explaining the situation."

"But you never got the letter?"

"No, because on the way down the expedition was trapped in a blizzard and buried under an avalanche."

"And with them, Elmar's letter," I said.

"Yes," said Rebecca. "And as far as anyone knew, Elmar was still a part of the expedition when tragedy struck."

"It must have been a terrible shock."

Rebecca kept looking out the window. "Yes, it was a very…challenging time," she said softly. "In fact, it was the only time I ever doubted Elmar's and my mission."

For a few moments, neither of us said a word.

But my curiosity overcame me.

"So what happened with you and David after Elmar's return?"

"When Elmar returned, David retreated. He knew how much I loved Elmar—he was truly a gentle soul. Thankfully we remained close friends—and he was still, after all, the father of my beloved daughter."

"So you and Elmar were together again?"

"Yes, we were together again and have been until now… when all the things we worked for with such dedication for so many years are finally about to come to fruition."

Rebecca turned away from the window and looked at me. "Planet Earth is about to ascend into the higher dimensions. It is now possible for all of humanity to ascend with Planet Earth. The next generation of Starseeds—including you Starbrow—is awakening and beginning to carry on the work that Elmar and I and many others began."

I looked away from her. "But if all the work that Elmar and you have done for so many years is now finally about to bear fruit, why did Elmar have to die?"

"Elmar is not dead. You should know that by now, Starbrow! He has left his physical body to carry on his work on the other side, in the higher dimensions, in Shamballa, as you well know. And it is now up to you to carry on his work here on this side."

I shook my head. "But what can I do? The Light Grid has been destroyed. As far as I know, I might be the only one left of the 600 volunteers. Even if I could get into contact with the Ashtar Command, what good would it do? The starships have disappeared. STARDAY has been cancelled."

Rebecca sat across from me.

"Starbrow! Look at me!" she said as her clear eyes pierced my soul. "Do not let your grief over the death of your friends overshadow the task that is before you. You are our only hope. If the Ashtar Command cancels STARDAY now, who knows how long it will be before humanity gets a chance like this again?"

"But what can I do?"

"What on earth are you talking about? Haven't you just been on the Ashtar Command and Ascended Masters' crash course in ascension?"

"Yes, but..."

"Have you already forgotten everything you learned about the Force in the Blue Temple? Have you forgotten what Saint Germain taught you about the mightiest spell in the Universe?"

I looked at her in surprise.

"There is no need to look at me like that Starbrow. While I watched over you this night, you were delirious and talked about your adventures. And Elmar told me even more when I saw him here in this house yesterday."

"Yes… you said Elmar was here… what exactly did he say?" I was reluctant to hear her answer because deep down inside I already knew what she was going to say.

"He said the same thing he said to me the last time he was here in his physical body. That was one week ago, right before the Earth changes and your sudden awakening."

"Elmar was here a week ago?"

"Yes. He came to Glastonbury one last time, right before his departure for the higher dimensions."

"What did he say?"

"He said that you had a very important role to play in the great events that are now taking place on Planet Earth, but that you were only just beginning to understand it. He said that you needed all the help you could get."

"But why did he have to leave us right now when I need his help most of all?"

"Do you still not understand, Starbrow? Elmar didn't just leave his body to carry on his work in the higher dimensions, he also left it because he knew that it was probably the only thing he could do that would shake you up enough to get you to accept the invitation to the Ashtar Command's training program."

I bowed my head in shame. I remembered those fateful hours before I made up my mind to accept the Ashtar Command's invitation to be transubstantiated up to the Mothership. What she said was true. If it hadn't been for the shock of Elmar's sudden death and his last words to me, I never would have had the courage to accept the invitation…

"You see, my friend," Rebecca said. "For those who are willing to look a little below the surface, there was always a deeper meaning to Elmar's every action."

For a long while I didn't say anything. I felt as if a heavy weight was bearing down on me. In the distance I could hear the sound of helicopters circling around Glastonbury Tor.

"But what am I going to do Rebecca?" I said at last. "And where am I going to find the strength?"

Rebecca took my hand. "When I spoke to Elmar yesterday—do you know what his last words to you were?"

I lifted my head and looked into Rebecca's clear eyes.

"He said, 'Tell Starbrow to remember everything he has learned—and to fight like a warrior.'"

7

Sisters of Avalon

After our talk, Rebecca led me back to the bedroom where I had slept the night before, changed my bandages, and put some of her special potion on my burns. Although I had burns on my hands, arms and legs, and cuts and bruises almost everywhere, I was healing fast.

Rebecca was amazed. "You are strong, Starbrow," she said as she gently finished putting on the new bandages. "You are healing very fast indeed."

"Before you told me about Elmar's mission, you said you had a plan to get me out of Glastonbury."

"That's right," she replied. "Did you ever hear of Chalice Well?"

"Chalice Well... well not really...but..." I hesitated because somewhere deep inside me a voice whispered *yes*...

"Well," she continued, "at the foot of Glastonbury Tor there is a smaller hill called Chalice Hill. According to legend, the Holy Grail lies buried deep within the hill."

"Really? The Holy Grail that King Arthur and the Knights of the Round Table were searching for?"

"Yes. And there is also a well at the foot of Chalice Hill, called Chalice Well. The waters of the well come from the hills to the north and run through subterranean passages underneath Chalice Hill and Glastonbury and then continue south running past Wearyall Hill. For thousands of years, people have known of the healing power of this water, so pilgrims have come from the far corners of the earth to drink this refreshing, life-giving water. Around the well, there is a truly lovely garden—an oasis of peace—that we call the Chalice Well Garden."

"What's all this got to do with getting me out of here?"

"Well... as I said, there is an ancient underground network of waterways and tunnels running from Glastonbury Tor to Wearyall Hill a few miles from here. Some say these tunnels were built thousands of years ago by the same people who built the gigantic stone circles at Stonehenge, Avebury and Callanish. Chalice Well is partly fed by the water that runs through these tunnels."

"I still don't understand what this has got to do with me."

"Well... I was thinking that if we could somehow get you down into Chalice Well, you could make your way through the underground tunnels that run all the way to Wearyall Hill. That way you would emerge on the other side of the army and police blockades that are holding Glastonbury in an iron grip."

"But didn't you just say that water runs through these tunnels?"

"Yes... but not any more."

"What do you mean?"

"Starbrow, I am a member of an order called 'Sisters of Avalon'," she said. "This order is a kind of modern-day version of the priestesses of Avalon—so we meet at auspicious occasions like the solstice and equinox to pray and meditate at interdimensional gateways such as Glastonbury Tor and Chalice Well. Last night, Sister Ravenheart went to Chalice Well to pray and to her great surprise the well was dry."

"Dry?"

"Yes completely. Not a drop of water."

"Really? How can that be?"

"Glastonbury Tor and Chalice Hill are very intimately connected so apparently the destruction of Glastonbury Tor has blocked the underground stream of water that flows down through the hill. That means the tunnels must now be dry too."

"And you want me to crawl through the tunnels?"

Rebecca nodded.

"How can you be sure the tunnels aren't still filled with water? Has anyone ever been down there?"

"No one's been down there, so we can't be sure, Starbrow," said Rebecca, shaking her head.

I lay back on the bed and gazed at the ceiling, thinking about what she said.

"And you say that there's an opening at the foot of Wearyall Hill? How far is it from the Chalice Well to Wearyall Hill?"

"About 2 to 3 miles."

"2 to 3 miles? And you want me to crawl 2 to 3 miles underground! That's quite a plan. And how are you even going to get me down to the well itself?"

107

"Well here's my plan. As I said, on special days the Sisters of Avalon walk to Chalice Well to pray and meditate. Today we will do exactly the same. We will join together and walk to Chalice Well to pray for peace and healing on Earth. And you will join us, disguised as a priestess of Avalon!"

"A priestess of Avalon..." I couldn't help laughing. "I've heard that one before!"

"I'm sure you'll have no trouble playing the part," said Rebecca giving me a mischievous look.

I laughed again, wondering how much Elmar's wise companion really knew about me!

"So you like my plan?"

"It's the most far-fetched plan I've heard in a long time, but yes, I actually do like it. And besides, do I have any choice?"

"Good." Rebecca rose. "I'll summon the other sisters and begin the preparations immediately. But first I need to know where you plan to go once you get out on the other side."

"Where I plan to go? Good question. You say that you want me to try to contact the Ashtar Command and tell them not to cancel STARDAY..."

"Yes," she replied. "How did you contact them the last time?"

"I was at home in my apartment in Copenhagen. But really Rebecca, I don't think it's got anything to do with the location—it's more about raising your vibrational frequency."

Rebecca was silent for a moment.

"Then maybe you should go to one of the Power Spots in England that haven't been destroyed yet by the army."

I looked out the window—hoping for a hint about what I should do. A strong wind was dancing in the few trees that hadn't been knocked down by the storms and explosions.

A wind from the Western Sea...

Then suddenly I saw in my mind's eye the vision that Rebecca's song had awoken in me last night when she brought me back to life—the vision of those six shining figures standing on the shores of Planet Earth.

Six shining figures with the wind in their hair.

Six shining souls listening to the endless murmur of the sea.

Six friends who had been together... since the beginning...

A deep sense of peace and knowingness washed over me.

"What are you thinking, Starbrow?" Rebecca asked.

With that, the vision of the six disappeared as suddenly as it had appeared. I blinked, wondering about my strange vision. Who were the six shining figures standing on the shores of Planet Earth? This was the second time I'd seen them in the last 24 hours.

"Do you know where you will go?" she asked gently.

"The only thing that comes to mind is..." I said slowly.

"Yes?"

Great pounding surf, tall cliffs, and a windswept coast.

"The only thing that comes to mind..." I said again, "is... the Crystal Cave."

She was looking at me intently.

"You know... off the coast in Cornwall... it's beneath Tintagel Castle," I continued, not knowing exactly what I was going to say. "In my memory, it is a place with a very high vibrational frequency... at least that's how it was when I was there last... but that of course was a very, very long time ago."

There was a moment of silence.

Then Rebecca said, obviously trying to feel her way to Tintagel, "Sounds right to me. And Tintagel is more or less deserted at this time of year—so that's good and it's not that far away. Only a three-hour drive from here."

"All right Rebecca, then it's decided," I said. "It's back to Tintagel for me."

After we agreed that I should head for the Crystal Cave under Tintagel Castle, I decided to take a shower. Since there was no electricity again, I took a candle with me.

I got a shock when I saw myself in the mirror.

I really looked different.

Besides the burns on the left side of my face—my long hair was completely gone!

Starbrow's long golden locks had disappeared! All that was left was a close crop of short brown hair.

I wondered who cut it.

"It was me," said Rebecca, standing in the doorway. "I'm sorry Starbrow, but I had to. Your hair must have caught fire in the explosion, so there wasn't much left anyway. You were such a mess when we found you. Gail helped me clean you up."

I had to laugh. With my ultra-short hair, bandages, burns, and gray pajamas, I looked more like an escaped convict than Starbrow the seer with the long golden locks! The person I was in the days up to the explosion seemed to have disappeared.

"It's probably for the best," I said trying to sound cheerful. "At least no one will recognize me now!"

"It's amazing how fast you are recovering," said Rebecca. "If you continue to heal so fast, it won't be long before your burns will be gone too."

I carefully touched my wounds. It was true—I was healing very fast. Compared to how much pain I was in the night before, I was already so much better.

"Yes, it's true..." I said slowly. "As a matter of fact the DETI agents said something about me and my friends having perfect health and strength."

"You will certainly need it," Rebecca said. "I'm going downstairs to summon the sisters and plan the procession. I've put some clothes for you on the bed."

Rebecca closed the door. I kept on staring at myself in the mirror.

Slowly it began to dawn on me that there was something else, something very important that had changed about me.

I could neither see nor feel the shining star on my brow.

My star was no longer there.

Quite simply, it had disappeared.

That meant the last trace of Starbrow was gone.

Rebecca had warned me that there hadn't been any hot water since the Earth changes began so I took a quick icy shower and then put on the clothes Rebecca had laid out on my bed. A pair of jeans, a t-shirt and a warm sweatshirt. There was also an old raincoat, and a pair of running shoes.

When I went downstairs, I found Rebecca in the living room, busy studying a map.

"I've sent Gail and Lance out to summon the sisters," she said. "Right now I'm trying to plan your route. Go out in the kitchen and fix yourself a sandwich if you're hungry. You can turn on Lance's portable TV—the one that's hooked up to the generator—if you want to watch the news. It's on the kitchen table."

I went out to the kitchen and made myself a sandwich. Even though I'd just eaten a few hours ago, I was still hungry. So I turned on Lance's little TV set and bolted down the sandwich.

"... almost 24 hours ago one could see this fantastic sight in the sky above London's Tower Bridge..." said the BBC newsman as the clear blue sky over London's Tower Bridge was being shown. A few miles above, there was a huge four-sided pyramid of golden light. Underneath, an enormous crowd of people was gathering. Some were singing, some were shouting, some were trying to sit down and form a large circle for meditation. It was obvious that the police and the military were having a hard time keeping the crowds in check.

"... but suddenly at 12:23:19 English time, this and all the other golden pyramids hovering over the other major cities around the world disappeared... as suddenly and as mysteriously as they had appeared..." the newsman continued. While he spoke the picture began to shake slightly—obviously the cameraman was so shocked by the sudden disappearance of the golden pyramid of light he was filming that he couldn't hold still.

The picture then panned to the White House. Huge crowds of protesters with torches were trying to get past a massive contingent of police and military. Another newsman was on camera saying, "Never before have so many conspiracy theories been circulating in Washington as there are now—and throughout the night, hundreds of thousands of Americans have marched past the White House and Capitol Hill protesting against what they call 'the American government's unfounded hostility towards our intergalactic guests'. The protesters included such prominent people as talk show hostess Oprah Winfrey and former Apollo astronaut Edgar Mitchell."

The picture changed again, this time it was an aerial view of the smoking ruins of Glastonbury Tor. A newswoman picked up the story and continued: "Speculation continues as to whether the sudden explosions and destruction of more than a hundred of the world's national shrines and major tourist attractions including Glastonbury Tor in England and the Great Pyramids in Egypt have anything to do with the Ashtar Command's sudden disappearance. Unofficial sources at the State Department are saying there is reason to believe that the Ashtar Command may have been using the strategic, geographical location of these old monuments to control the deeper layers of the Earth's crust and

111

weather systems—causing the present havoc on Earth. In any case, there are grave doubts as to the intentions of the space beings and there continues to be many unanswered questions. At the moment, only one thing is clear. The starships have disappeared—and so has the good weather," concluded the newswoman grimly.

Her report was followed by quick glimpses of the many places around the world that had been hit by earthquakes, volcanic eruptions, hurricanes, and storms during the past few days. "At the same time, the massive clean-up and rescue operations following Wednesday and Thursday's global weather catastrophes continue," continued the studio anchorman. "There are no official figures yet, but government estimates indicate that several hundred thousand people may have been killed—and millions of people have been wounded. Unofficial estimates also say that as many as a 100 million people may have been made homeless by the catastrophes. At the moment, some 75-80% of the world's population is without electricity, many vital communication networks have been damaged, and much of the world's transport systems are inoperative. In addition, the acute lack of food, water and medicine continues to grow. Yesterday the United Nations declared a global state of emergency..."

I turned off the television.

A moment later, Gail and Lance had returned from their expedition. They said the army and the police had searched almost every house in Glastonbury and were now beginning their search all over again, this time with dogs. It wouldn't be long before they came back.

Rebecca returned to the kitchen and talked briefly with Gail. Then she turned to me and said, "Starbrow, we're almost ready. The sisters will be here at two o'clock—in less than an hour. Then we'll begin our procession down to Chalice Well."

Rebecca spread out a map of southern England on the kitchen table. "If everything goes according to plan, you will emerge from the tunnels at the foot of Wearyall Hill... right here," she said, pointing to the spot on the map where the hill was located, a few miles southwest of the Tor. "When you're out, walk in this direction... towards the town of Street and then continue along this road," she said pointing to the road from Street," and follow it through the old forest to the village of Sutton Mallet where one of our contacts will be expecting you."

"How far is it?"

"It's about 10 miles from Street to Sutton Mallet."

"10 miles through an old forest?"

112

"Yes, but if you stay close to the road it should be easy to find your way."

"But won't the road be watched?"

"That of course is a risk. But if you walk far enough from the road so they can't see you, you should be able to get past them."

"And when I get to Sutton Mallet?"

"Go to 19 Hunters Lane, where Mrs. Baker—one of our sisters—lives. The phones are not working, but I've contacted her telepathically and told her that you're coming."

"Telepathically? And what if she doesn't get your message?"

"Just knock on the door and say the secret password, the one we Avalon Sisters use in special emergencies. It's 'Tuatha Dé Danann—May the stars shine on your path'. Then tell her that I sent you and that she must lend you her car."

"Tuatha Dé Danann... May the stars shine on your path... I like that."

"Once you have Mrs. Baker's car, you can drive directly to Tintagel. I've marked the route on the map."

I studied the map—it all looked pretty straightforward. Tintagel wasn't more than 150 miles from Glastonbury.

"Of course there's no telling how the roads are after all the tornadoes and storms," said Rebecca. "So you might have to improvise."

"Is there any way I can get in touch with you?"

"No," said Rebecca. "Only on the inner plane."

It was almost two o'clock. The Sisters of Avalon were beginning to arrive and I could hear many voices from my room upstairs where I was making my final preparations for my journey. Rebecca had given me a handy little backpack stuffed with sandwiches, crackers, fruit, water enough for a couple of days, and an extra set of clothes. Plus a few maps, a compass, a wristwatch, and two hundred pounds. There was also a small silver flask with some extra ointment for my burns. But most important of all was the headlamp, the kind miners wear. How Rebecca got a hold of it I never found out, but I knew that without it I wouldn't be able to see a thing once I was underground.

There was a knock at the door.

"Come in."

It was Gail. She was dressed in a long, white flowing robe that went down to her ankles. It had wide, billowy sleeves and a hood. "We're almost ready now," she said. "Here, put on your priestess robe."

She held up a similar robe before me.

"This belongs to sister Eilan. She's a bit... er... heavier than the rest of us so it should fit you nicely."

I got up and looked at the dress.

"Come on, it won't bite!" laughed Gail. "Here, let me help you."

The robe was big enough to put on over my sweatshirt and jeans and backpack. She was right—it fit me nicely. I pulled the hood down over my head.

"You look like you were born to be a priestess of Avalon!" Gail chuckled.

"If only you knew..." I said, laughing back.

We went down to the living room. About thirty women were gathered in there, all dressed in the same long white robes as Gail and I. They greeted me kindly.

"Welcome, Sister Starbrow!" Rebecca smiled.

She too was dressed in a long white robe and in one hand she held a long, wooden staff with a crescent-shaped handle. "Are you ready to go to Chalice Well and worship the Goddess?"

I nodded.

"It's two o'clock." Rebecca clapped her hands. "Let us go forth—May the Goddess protect us."

The women silently filed out the front door. Rebecca and I were the last ones. Lance stood in the doorway and looked up at me with his big eyes. "Goodbye, Starbrow. I hope you find your star again soon."

I bent down and pressed his little hand. "Goodbye, Lance. Take good care of Rebecca and Gail."

The procession moved down the garden path. I looked up at the old white house where I had been a guest. A crescent-shaped sign hung above the front door; it read: *Avalon Bed & Breakfast—where pilgrims meet.*

When we came to the main road, the women began to walk two by two with Rebecca and me now in the middle of the procession. My face was hidden by the hood and I kept my hands folded like the other priestesses.

There is something very familiar about this, I thought as we walked along. I took a deep breath and continued.

Fallen trees, bushes, smashed benches, and garbage cans were strewn all over the place so we picked our way carefully among the debris. Many

114

of the cars and houses we passed had broken windows and several sheds had completely collapsed. People were busy cleaning up.

We continued down the narrow road that runs past Glastonbury Tor towards Chalice Well Garden. The sidewalk became so narrow that it was difficult for the sisters to walk side by side, but they did their best. Overhead, two military helicopters flew by. There were heavy clouds above, but no rain.

"Stay by my side the whole way," said Rebecca. "If they ask any questions, let me do the talking. They'll probably stop us at the entrance to the Garden. That's where the road leading to Glastonbury Tor begins and it will be heavily guarded."

The procession rounded a corner and the road sloped downwards. Two men who were clearing away the debris looked at us curiously.

"What sacred day are you celebrating now Sisters?" asked one of the men.

"We are on our way to Chalice Well to pray for Avalon's violated earth," replied one of the sisters.

Up ahead I could see the stone wall that surrounded Chalice Hill Garden. Two jeeps were blocking the road next to the Garden that led up towards the Tor—and everywhere I looked, there were soldiers and police officers—and quite a crowd of the local people.

The atmosphere seemed tense. Apparently, the residents of Glastonbury had not taken kindly to having their 'national monument' blown off the face off the earth. As we approached, we could hear the angry voices of the people in the crowd. Some of the soldiers were trying to calm them down and behind them I saw two of the American DETI agents talking on their phones. I recognized one of them—it was Sorvino, the guy who seemed to be Nevis' right hand man. He had a bandage on his head. So Nevis and I were not the only ones who had survived the explosion.

The procession reached the angry crowd, which reverently made way for the priestesses to pass. And so we finally came to the entrance to the Garden. A jeep and a police car were parked in front of the entrance and there were soldiers and two policemen standing there. I pulled the hood further down over my head.

"I'm sorry, but the Garden is closed," said one of the soldiers.

Rebecca left my side and walked up to the soldiers.

"Closed? Whatever do you mean?" she asked.

"The army has closed the Garden for the time being."

"Why?"

"There's an investigation going on. You'll have to come back another day."

Rebecca bowed her head.

So much for that plan, I thought.

The two priestesses in front of me looked as if they were about to turn around and walk back.

Then Rebecca lifted her head and pounded her staff into the ground.

"How dare you deny the Sisters of Avalon entry to the sacred grounds of the Goddess!" she said loudly.

"I'm sorry, ma'm," said the soldier. "But the Garden is closed until further notice."

Again, Rebecca pounded the ground with her staff.

"For thousands of years, the Sisters of Avalon have worshipped the Goddess at Chalice Well, the Well of Life. You cannot deny us entry in this terrible time of trouble."

I knew Rebecca was holding the soldier with her piercing gaze. He looked away and mumbled, "I have my orders..."

People in the angry crowd behind us who'd overheard the conversation started booing and shouting at the soldiers.

One of the local policemen walked over to the soldiers and said. "Is this really absolutely necessary? The people of Glastonbury have suffered enough as it is. You are only making matters worse by denying these innocent Sisters access to their holy shrine."

There was a moment of silence. Then the soldier grumbled and said, "Okay, okay... but we'll have to keep a close watch on them."

"Only women are allowed to participate in our holy rituals!" said Rebecca, hotly.

"Listen, Your Worshipfulness, if we allow you to enter, you'll perform your ritual under our supervision–or not at all."

Rebecca was silent for a moment. Then she took a deep breath and said, "Okay Sisters, follow me!"

Even after many days of heavy storms and the destruction of Glastonbury Tor, it was still evident that Chalice Well Garden was a beautiful place. The Sisters of Avalon walked slowly and reverently through the garden along a pathway that led beneath blooming apple trees and lovely birch trees. In many places, the trees had been knocked down or damaged by the storms, but many still stood.

Two soldiers walked on each side of the procession, watching our every move. I buried myself even deeper in my robe.

In the northern corner of the Garden, between Chalice Hill and Glastonbury Tor, we came upon Chalice Well itself. The thirty women stepped down onto the stones that surround the well as the four soldiers placed themselves in position not far from the procession.

In the middle of the stones, there was a wooden lid with an elaborate iron grate around it covering Chalice Well. The priestesses formed three consecutive circles around the opening while two of the priestesses opened the lid.

The priestesses pushed me to the edge of the well. I could see that the well itself was carved from large blocks of stone and was about fifteen feet deep. Now it was completely dry and empty. I could see the bottom, which was covered with bluish clay, which still looked moist. There was a muddy, blood red substance on the walls of the well and on the bluish-clay bottom.

The Blood Well... said a voice deep inside me.

The priestesses pushed me even closer and I saw that that down inside the well on one side there was a carved chamber, which was large enough for a person to stand in.

The Chamber of Initiation... said the voice inside me again, and for a brief moment I seemed to remember having stood in that chamber once, naked with the icy cold water all the way up to my neck.

I shook off the vision and tried to focus on the present moment. At the back of the carved stone chamber, I thought I could make out a dark opening.

"The Goddess is with you," Rebecca whispered at my side. "There is the entrance to the underground tunnels."

The inner circle of priestesses extended their hands to lower me down into the carved chamber in the side of the well.

"Stop!" yelled one of the soldiers as he pushed his way through the women. "What do you think you are doing?"

"We are sending down one of our sisters to pray to the Goddess to send back the water," Rebecca said.

The soldier gave me a suspicious look.

I bowed my head.

"What are you going to do down there?" he asked me.

I coughed and tried to sound as much like a woman as possible. "Pray for the water to come back and once again fertilize the blessed soil of Avalon..." My voice cracked.

"You have quite a cold, don't you Sister?"

I nodded.

"What's your name?"

"Dana… Sister Dana," I said in a low voice.

You fool! I thought to myself. They'll never buy that!

"Kind sir," said Rebecca, placing herself between me and the solider, "you are interrupting our ceremony!" He kept staring at me suspiciously.

"You didn't mention anything about lowering one of your sisters down into the well!"

"There are a great many things about our rituals you don't know!"

The soldier did not move—but continued to eye me suspiciously.

Then suddenly, with one quick movement, he pulled back my hood.

"What the hell! You're no woman!"

The soldier raised his machine gun and aimed it straight at me.

"What's going on here?" he cried.

The three other soldiers also raised their machine guns.

I'd been discovered.

Our plan had failed.

8

The Blood Well

The soldiers were pointing their machine guns straight at me.

The one closest to me said, "Hands behind your head! Now!"

Slowly, I lifted my hands and placed them behind my head.

I looked over at Rebecca. Our eyes met.

The soldier took a step towards me. The other three soldiers were making their way through the priestesses.

Rebecca raised her hands and clenched her fists as if she was calling upon the protection of the Goddess.

The moment she did that, all thirty priestesses threw themselves between the soldier and me. They almost knocked him over.

"Hey, what are you doing?" he yelled. "Move back or I'll shoot!" He lashed out violently at the women.

By accident, he hit Rebecca on the side of her head and she fell hard onto the stones. Blood trickled from the side of her head.

"Rebecca!" I cried.

"Jump, Starbrow! Now!" she moaned.

The white sea of priestesses threw themselves in front of the soldiers who brutally pushed them aside.

"Now, Starbrow!" Rebecca cried again looking up. "Go!"

I turned and looked down the well at the small stone chamber carved in the side.

At that very moment, the foremost of the soldiers had gotten free from the priestesses and lunged towards me.

I jumped down into the stone chamber, just in time.

I landed on the hard stone floor and threw myself at the dark, narrow opening in the side of the chamber.

"Stop or we'll shoot!" I heard the soldiers yell above me.

Machine gun fire ripped through the well, but I had already pushed myself through the opening.

119

On the other side of the opening was a kind of tunnel leading downwards into darkness. Machine gun fire continued to pound the chamber behind me as I plunged further into the tunnel. The sides of the tunnel were hard and stony and were now shaking. Earth and stone started falling from the ceiling. The machine gun fire was too much for the old well. The tunnel was collapsing!

I hurled myself frantically forward as earth and stone continued to rain down upon me.

Suddenly my hands were gripping at nothing but air.

The tunnel went suddenly downwards.

The stone underneath me was so slippery that I slid directly down for several yards and landed with a thud on the wet stones at the bottom.

Now I was in total darkness.

Above me I heard an ominous rumble, which continued for a few seconds and then stopped.

Then there was complete silence.

I could hear nothing, see nothing.

I fumbled through my backpack and found the headlamp Rebecca had given me. I turned it on.

I was lying in a long tunnel.

The tunnel was about six feet high and six feet wide. Water was dripping from the ceiling.

I got up and pointed the headlamp in the direction of the narrow opening that I'd just come through.

It was no longer there.

The stress of the machine gun fire had obviously been too much for the old well. The opening had completely collapsed and now the ancient entrance to the underground tunnels was sealed—with tons of stone and earth.

No one could get down into Chalice Well anymore.

And no one could get out.

I looked up and down the tunnel.

Unless of course I found another way out.

I directed the light down the dark tunnel. I couldn't see the end of it. Parts of what I could see seemed to be natural, while some of it seemed to be made by human hands. Obviously this was one of the tunnels Rebecca had told me about. I looked back, to the north. I wondered if the water had been blocked forever, or only temporarily? Then I thought of Rebecca and the priestesses above. What would happen to them?

No use thinking about that, I thought. If the heroism of the Sisters was to make any sense, I had to continue now, right away and fulfill my mission.

I took off my priestess robe and fastened the headlamp on my head.

A light on my brow I thought ironically.

Then I started walking down the tunnel as fast as I could.

As I walked I realized that the tunnel was covered almost everywhere with the same red substance I'd seen in the stone chamber of Chalice Well. I bent over and scooped up a bit of the water from one of the puddles and tasted it. The icy cold water tasted like iron. I guessed it was the iron that gave the stones their reddish sheen.

The Blood Well.

I pressed on in the darkness.

The long tunnel continued, sometimes turning to the right, sometimes to the left. But always more or less in the same direction.

About a quarter of an hour later, the tunnel suddenly branched out in five different directions. Two of the branches continued straight ahead. One went sharply to the left. The other two turned to the right, but one of these tunnels was so narrow that you'd have to crawl through it if you went that way.

I took out the compass and the map of Glastonbury. Wearyall Hill lay to the southwest of Chalice Well. According to the compass, I should take one of the two tunnels that turned to the right. I bent down to examine the narrow tunnel. Unlike the other four tunnels, it looked as if it was a natural tunnel, not built by human hands. I remembered that Rebecca said the same people who built Stonehenge had built these tunnels—so why would they make a tunnel you had to crawl through. It didn't make sense to crawl on all fours to Wearyall Hill.

I stood up and started down the other tunnel that led to the right. After a few minutes, I consulted the compass again. This tunnel seemed to be going more or less directly southwest—I seemed to have made the right decision. I walked even faster.

After another fifteen minutes, the tunnel divided itself once again—this time into three. I stopped and studied the three openings. The middle opening continued straight ahead. The opening to the right also seemed to go straight ahead, while the opening to the left wound its way sharply downwards to the left.

I consulted the compass again. Southwest was now to my right and none of these three tunnels seemed to be going in the right direction.

I wondered what to do—and then thought of what Elmar—and my guardian angel Ticha—had told me, once upon a time not so long ago.

Follow your heart, for your heart alone knows the way.

I closed my eyes and focused my attention on my heart. The moment I did this, I felt a faint tingling between my eyebrows. I turned and looked back at the tunnel I'd just come from.

He is very close.

Agent Nevis.

He knows I am down here. And he's thinking about me right now. He knows that I am still alive.

But what can he do? The entrance to the tunnel at Chalice Well was completely blocked. No one could get down here now—unless he tries to blast his way through?

I quickly put my compass in my pocket and started walking down the middle tunnel as fast as I could.

The thought that Nevis was close behind me made me start to run. But it was difficult going because the stones were covered with the reddish slime and were very slippery. The tunnel continued straight ahead for a few minutes and then started to veer to the right.

Good, I thought… now it's going southwest towards Wearyall Hill!

When I turned the corner, the tunnel became higher and wider.

I stopped.

A pale light was glowing from somewhere on the left side of the tunnel.

What could it be?

I slowly walked over to where the light was coming from and stood before an indentation in the wall. The stones really did glow with a pale reddish-white light.

Strange…

I turned off my flashlight. In the darkness, the glow of the stones was even brighter. I slowly ran my hands over the stones wondering what it was. It seemed like the light was coming from behind, inside the rock wall. As if something was buried inside the rock. Something that glowed with this reddish-white light.

A reddish, white… cup.

Yes, there was an old cup buried inside the rock.

As I looked at the cup with wonder, I felt a sudden warmth in my chest, which spread out from my heart and made me tingle all over.

The Holy Grail.

I was overcome with awe and was just about to kneel down before the shining cup when I heard a faint sound coming from the tunnel behind me. It sounded like far-away thunder. I turned around and turned on my flashlight again. I couldn't see anything in the tunnel behind me but darkness. But the rumbling continued.

I wondered if Agent Nevis had blasted his way down into the tunnels.

I looked down at the ground and studied my reflection in the puddles of water around my feet.

The puddles of water around my feet!

Water! I gasped.

With sudden horror, I realized what was happening.

Nevis had not blasted his way through the blocked entrance.

He had done something far worse.

Since he couldn't get down into the tunnels, he had decided to release the blocked up waters and flush me out! In some devilish way, my unrelenting pursuer had managed to blast away whatever was blocking the underground waters.

The mighty waters of Chalice Well were rushing back through the tunnels.

Rushing straight towards me!

The distant rumbling was coming closer.

I took one last look at the Grail and began to run down the tunnel as fast as I could.

As soon as I left the wide, high place in the tunnel where the Grail was buried, the tunnel became narrower again, diminishing back to its previous size. The ominous rumble was growing louder. How far could it be to the opening at Wearyall Hill? Rebecca said two to three miles in all. I must have been in the tunnels for almost an hour now. How far could it be?

I had to be there soon.

I started looking for an opening in the tunnel's ceiling. I slipped on the wet stones and fell forward into a huge puddle of water. In less than half a second, I was back on my feet running down the tunnel.

The rumbling behind me grew in intensity until it sounded like an enormous wave was about to crash right behind me. I looked back.

In the darkness behind me I could faintly see a roaring mass of water rushing towards me at great speed, like a dam whose pent-up waters had finally been released.

The water was not more than a hundred yards away!

The whole tunnel was filling up with water, sweeping away everything on its path.

I charged forward with all the speed that I could muster up.

123

The tunnel began to wind its way upward. I ran over the slippery stones like a madman.

Upwards, upwards!

I could feel the sheer pressure of the water behind me now. Just a few more seconds and the mighty waters would crash into me and smash me into the sharp rocks along the sides of the tunnel.

The tunnel turned even more sharply upwards. I fell and crawled frantically forward and upwards. I couldn't be far from the surface now. If the underground waters were going to emerge through another opening, it had to be here. Somewhere. Somewhere close by.

But how close? How close?

I got up and charged forwards.

But it was too late.

The thunderous sound of crashing waters drowned out all else.

Then the mighty water slammed into me with great force.

I closed my eyes, prepared to pass over to the next world.

The Land at the End of the World

The mighty waters of Chalice Well crashed into me.

I felt myself hurled forward by the icy cold water and smashed with great force into the rocky tunnel walls. Then I was carried onwards by the surging water like a rag doll, thrown upwards towards the ceiling of the tunnel. Everything seemed to be happening in slow motion and I knew in a microsecond I would be dashed to pieces against the ceiling, smashed like a ship against the rocky shore.

The red stones in the tunnel's ceiling shone with a faint reddish glow, with the same reddish glow I'd seen coming from the Holy Grail...

In the next moment I crashed into the tunnel's ceiling.

But instead of smashing into solid stone, I shot upwards through the tunnel's ceiling. Upwards towards the faint light that was coming from above.

I wondered if I was seeing the light from the other side...Maybe I was already dead and this was the other side?

The light came closer and closer—as if it was coming from above me.

Then I realized I was moving towards the light with much less speed. As a matter of fact, I was hardly moving at all.

That's when I realized I was floating.

Floating on top of the icy cold water—surrounded on all sides by old, mossy stones that were covered with the same reddish slime as the stones at Chalice Well.

Then I realized I wasn't dead or floating in another dimension.

No, I was floating on the icy waters of Chalice Well and the old stones that were surrounding me were the stones of another well.

Another well!

The force of the water had been so great that it had literally carried me up through the opening in the ceiling of the tunnel at the very last second!

The light I had seen was the sky above the well.

Suddenly the pressure underneath me became less and I furiously kicked my arms and legs to keep afloat. I spluttered and coughed, my mouth was filled with water. The walls of the well rose around me—there was still about a yard to the top. It wouldn't be easy to get out.

I dug my fingers into the stony sides of the well and slowly pulled myself upward and out of the water. It was a struggle, but finally I managed to haul myself out of the well. I collapsed onto the grass, spitting water and coughing.

In front of me was a hill. On the top of the hill was an old thorn tree.

Yes!

This was Wearyall Hill!

I'd done it!

I'd made it to the other side!

I lay in the grass next to the well for a while, trying to catch my breath. It was strange... right before I'd been thrown up through the ceiling of the tunnel and out into the well, the water had hurled me against the rocky tunnel with such great force that I was sure I'd been hurt. I'd hit the wall with my left side and now, oddly enough, it didn't even hurt. Then I thought well maybe it was so bad I couldn't feel a thing.

I hesitated to look but then thought what the hell.

I lifted up my torn sweatshirt and to my great surprise I couldn't see a thing. Nothing at all—no blood, no gash, no bruises, nothing. And it didn't even hurt. How could it be? It was impossible.

As I searched my left side, I realized that the burns and bruises I'd sustained when Glastonbury Tor exploded were also practically all gone too. It was amazing. It was as if the skin on my arms was completely new... I could barely see where the burns had been. I pulled down my pants. It was the same with my legs.

It was amazing.

I didn't feel any pain anywhere.

I stood up and had to admit that I felt remarkably well despite the terrible beating I'd just been through.

I went over to the well and looked down at the clear, cool water. I leaned over and scooped up a bit of water and put it to my mouth. It was icy cold and tasted very fresh.

What was it Rebecca had said about the waters of Chalice Well?

126

I remembered the reddish-white cup that I had seen shining in the rocky wall of the tunnel right before I realized the waters had been released and were thundering towards me. It was the same reddish-white cup that I'd seen in that fateful moment when the water overwhelmed me.

Overwhelmed and surrounded me… the healing waters of Chalice Well… so that was it…

Someone… or something… did care…!

I looked around. The well was located between a few small trees that stood at the foot of Wearyall Hill. Fortunately for me, there wasn't a soul in sight. I looked up at Wearyall Hill; it too was deserted. In the fading evening light, I could barely make out what was left of Glastonbury Tor some two or three miles to the northeast. Between the Tor and Wearyall Hill was the town of Glastonbury. Helicopters were circling the town and ruined hill. If Nevis had released the waters to flush me out of the tunnels, then he must know that I was now no longer in Glastonbury. He would be hunting me right this very moment.

I looked around.

My backpack was gone. The crashing water had torn it from my back, which meant that all my food, extra clothing, ointment, and most importantly, the maps were gone. I was glad I'd studied Rebecca's maps before I set out.

I went back to the well and scooped up a few more handfuls of the cold water and gulped them down. Then I pulled the hood of my raincoat over my head and started walking westward as fast as I could.

The rain was coming down in bucketsful as I slowly drove down the windswept high street of Tintagel village in Mrs. Baker's old Mazda. After I'd escaped from the underground tunnels, I had spent most of the evening and night walking the 10 miles to Sutton Mallet. When I arrived in Sutton Mallet, Sister Baker had obviously received Rebecca's telepathic message because she welcomed me most kindly, exactly as Rebecca said she would—and promptly gave me her old Mazda. After that it had taken me almost six hours to drive to Tintagel because southern England was more or less immobilized by the violent Earth changes of the past few days. Luckily the road to the Cornish coast had only been seriously hit by tornadoes in one place, just a few miles before Tintagel.

127

And luckily for me, the rescue teams had already cleared away most of the debris and placed makeshift ramps over the worst holes in the roads.

And now finally I was in Tintagel again—back where it all started—1,500 hundred years ago.

Yes it was right here… some 1,500 years ago that Sananda gave the Great White Brotherhood's formula to Merlin and the other volunteers.

It was amazing to think that now I was back.

But the village that had grown up here was now a gloomy ghost town.

Even though it was nine o'clock in the morning, there wasn't a soul in sight. As I drove down the main street, I noticed that most of the Bed & Breakfast places and shops and restaurants on Tintagel's high street had names like 'King Arthur' this or 'Camelot' that. But on this particular morning, it seemed that every single one of them was closed.

When I came to the end of the high street I stopped. I was dead tired having driven non-stop since I left Mrs. Baker's house at three in the morning. I almost couldn't keep my eyes open.

But there was no time to sleep just yet. I had to find the Crystal Cave first. I searched the deserted village for a clue. Branching off to the right of the high street was a narrow road that seemed to run in the direction of the coast. I drove that way and when the road swung to the left, I sighed with relief. Suddenly the whole coastline stretched out before me in all its awesome beauty—the towering cliffs of Cornwall and the great Atlantic Ocean.

I followed the road to the end near the rocky coast and stopped in front of an old spooky-looking place called 'King Arthur's Castle Hotel'. There wasn't a soul in sight here either. So I parked the car, put on my raincoat, and stepped out into the howling wind and rain.

I walked over to the wall that ran alongside the hotel. The view of the coast was spectacular. I immediately recognized Tintagel Head about a half a mile from where I stood. The tall rocky island still looked exactly like I remembered it from my past life as Dana except for one thing—Tintagel Castle was gone. As far as I could see, all that remained of the proud fortress were a few ruins. A long wooden staircase and bridge ran from the landward part of the fortress over to the ruins on the rocky island itself. I remembered how Gaius, Loran, Aran and I had walked across a similar bridge to meet King Arthur and Merlin more than 1,500 years ago.

I climbed up on the stone wall, trying to figure out how to get to the island—and to see if I could see the little cove that was once at the foot of Tintagel Castle. I couldn't see any cove or beach from where I stood, but

I could see a pathway that ran from the other side of the hotel down along the cliffs and all the way around to Tintagel Head.

Just what I'd been hoping to find.

I headed straight for the pathway. Once on the pathway, I discovered that Tintagel Head was further away than it looked. It took me almost 20 minutes of hard going on the winding pathway before I could see Tintagel Head again. This time when it did, I could also see the little cove at the foot of the island. Big waves were crashing in, but there was no beach.

Then I realized why—it was high tide.

The beach would only be visible when it was low tide.

It was all coming back to me. But of course! You could only get to the Crystal Cave at low tide.

I scanned the rocky sides of Tintagel Head trying to remember exactly where the Crystal Cave had been located.

But of course, it was right there! It was just as I remembered. Exactly. I could just barely see the opening in the side of the island right after the waves broke against the rocks and began to recede. That had to be the Crystal Cave!

Now all I could do was wait for low tide.

I continued along the path until I came down to the cove. Directly behind it were two wooden houses. Both were boarded up, closed. Probably some kind of tourist shops during the season. At least nobody was in sight at the moment.

I peered down at the cove. An old stone stairway led down, right into the water. I carefully walked down the slippery steps until I could go no further—the pounding surf was crashing into the steps right where I stood, spraying me with icy cold salt water.

I wondered how long it would be before the tide went down. As far as I could remember, it was late afternoon in my past life when we walked across the beach to the Crystal Cave. I looked at my watch. It was quarter to ten. There was nothing I could do except wait.

I sat down with my back against the stone wall and looked out at the great ocean before me. As far as the eye could see, there was nothing but waves and water and pale gray sky.

This must be the end of the world I thought.

The sound of the pounding waves had a relaxing, almost hypnotic affect on me and it wasn't long before I drifted off into the land of sleep.

The land of sleep is also the land of dreams. And to begin, my dreams were chaotic, a kaleidoscope of images and events, until suddenly it was there again... that very special dream. Or was it a vision? There was something very familiar and comforting about it, something I knew so well. That very special feeling... that very special light.

The light from... the six shining figures... standing on the shores of Planet Earth.

The waves of the great ocean pounded relentlessly onto the shore. The wind howled. The gulls wailed. A deep peace washed over me. It was as if time stood still.

Slowly a light began to grow on the horizon.

The six shining souls spread their arms wide and welcomed the day.

The new day and the new world that awaited them.

The new day they had traveled through time and space and the dimensions to bid welcome to.

The new world they had passed stars, suns and galaxies to experience.

Here, on the windswept shores of Planet Earth...

It was the sound of gulls chattering that woke me. They'd landed all around me, an entire flock, hunting for food. I sat up and they disappeared to all sides. The rain had subsided somewhat and the stairway below me was no longer under water. The sea had retreated and half of the little cove had now become a small rocky beach. I looked at my watch. It was two o'clock in the afternoon. I had slept for more than four hours!

I got up and quickly walked down the steps to the beach and walked over to the large opening in the side of Tintagel Head. There were several large rocks around the opening, obviously the ones I'd seen earlier protruding dangerously from the water when the tide was up.

The sound of my feet crunching on the pebbles echoed through the cave as I walked into it. The cave was about 20 feet high and 30 feet wide. Its walls and ceiling were covered with thousands of seashells. It made me remember the clear, shiny walls of Merlin's Crystal Cave.

Further inside the cave, there were many huge rocks and boulders. I climbed over them until I reached the center of the cave. Daylight was streaming in from the other end of the cave, which now seemed to open to the sky. It had been closed the last time I was in the cave so I went and took a look. From this end of the cave, there was a spectacular view of the

Cornish coastline stretching far to the south. But looking down at the fierce waves pounding the shore beneath the opening, I realized no one could get out of the cave at this end—not at high or low tide. I went back to the center of the cave.

So this was it.

The Crystal Cave.

The place where I was supposed to try to get in contact with the Ashtar Command again.

But how?

I suddenly realized I'd been so focused on getting to the Crystal Cave that I hadn't thought at all about what I was actually going to do once I got here. How was I then going to get in contact with the Ashtar Command? When I first met them, I'd been transubstantiated up to their Mothership from the bedroom of my apartment in Copenhagen.

But I knew it didn't have anything to do with the location… because what was so special about my bedroom?

I began pacing back and forth in the cave.

Think, man, think!

What would wise, old Jacob say? Or do?

He would think it through—logically. He would say…

Where is the Ashtar Command?

In the higher dimensions.

How does one get to the higher dimensions?

I could almost hear Jacob's voice from far away,

Remember everything you've learned, Starbrow! Remember everything you've learned.

How does one get to the higher dimensions?

By raising one's consciousness.

And how does one raise one's consciousness?

By… focusing on the Force.

The Force… ah…

Like a fine breeze, like a distant echo, I remembered the mighty Presence I had experienced when Jacob, Janus and I had focused on the Force in the Gobi Desert… or when we were about to be hit by the tornado.

But the thought of it also made me sad. Back then we'd been three—the three of us together—to do it. We helped and supported each other—with the staff, the sword and the star.

Now I was all alone.

All alone… here at the end of the world.

I do not know how long I sat in the Crystal Cave staring blankly at the walls of the cave. I only know that it was the tingling sensation between my eyebrows that made me look up.

Someone was coming.

Coming down to the Crystal Cave.

I got up.

What was that sound?

The waves were pounding on the rocks, the gulls were crying, the wind was howling.

But there was also something else. Something more.

Carefully I made my way back to the cave opening and looked out. A big wave came crashing in… right in front of me. More than three quarters of the little rocky beach in front of the cave was gone!

The tide was coming in fast.

I had to go back at once or be trapped in the cave by the ocean.

I took one step forward… and froze.

I heard a familiar sound from above.

Helicopters!

Five military choppers were hovering about a hundred yards above the wooden houses back on the shore.

I sprang back into the cave and pressed myself against the wall. The tingling sensation between my eyebrows grew stronger.

He's found me!

My unrelenting pursuer.

I couldn't imagine how, all I knew was that somehow Agent Nevis had found me again.

I ran into the cave and continued all the way to the opening in the other side. I climbed onto the boulders lying in front of the opening and looked up. About fifty yards above me, there was another military helicopter and about a half a mile up the coast, a coast guard ship heading fast towards Tintagel Head.

I was surrounded on all sides.

"Stop! Do not move!" boomed a voice from the chopper above.

I leapt back as machine gun fire crackled and a torrent of deadly bullets tore through the rocks around me. I slipped on the slippery stones and felt a sharp pain in my left arm.

The firing continued and I retreated back into the cave.

"Stay where you are!" said the voice from the helicopter. "You are surrounded!"

I half ran, half stumbled back to the center of the cave. Then I stopped and realized that I had left a trail of blood all the way from the opening to where I was now standing.

I looked at my torn raincoat and saw blood oozing from my left arm—it throbbed painfully. One of the bullets had apparently grazed my arm.

I looked around frantically. I could hear the choppers on both sides of the Crystal Cave and saw the water rushing into the cave as the tide came thundering in. The water was already up to my knees.

If I didn't go back now it would mean certain death.

But if I went back he would catch me.

There was only one way—up!

For each wave that came pounding in, the water rose threateningly and I could already feel the mighty tide pulling me... pulling me back to the ocean. The sound of the helicopters was almost drowned out by the sound of the waves that came thundering into the cave. The throbbing in my left arm grew worse.

I scrambled up onto the highest rock at the center of the cave.

I had to make a decision.

The sea or the Force.

I closed my eyes and focused all my attention on my breathing. On the air flowing in and out... like the great ocean that was flowing in and out.

The Force was like the Ocean.

Omnipresent and Omnipotent.

I remembered how I had sat right here, in the Crystal Cave, and focused on the Force with Jacob and Janus as we repeated the formula after Merlin...

...and Sananda.

The Most Radiant One.

Once upon a time...

In the beginning.

I opened my mouth and said it slowly,

"In the beginning: The Force."

As soon as I'd said those words, I felt new strength welling up inside me.

Immediately.

And I realized it didn't matter if I felt I didn't have the strength to raise my consciousness by myself. The Force would do it for me. Because the Force didn't care one bit what I felt.

133

The Force was All-Powerful.

Unchanging.

Unbreakable.

Invincible.

A huge wave came crashing into the rock I was sitting on, but I did not heed it. Instead I climbed further up the rock and shouted at the top of my lungs:

"IN THE BEGINNING: THE FORCE
HERE AND NOW: THE FORCE
AT THE END OF THE END: THE FORCE
HERE, THERE, EVERYWHERE: THE FORCE
FROM ALPHA TO OMEGA: THE FORCE
IN HEAVEN, UPON EARTH: THE FORCE
IN THE GREATEST, IN THE SMALLEST: THE FORCE
IN FIRE, IN WATER, IN EARTH, IN AIR: THE FORCE
IN ME, IN YOU, IN EVERYONE: THE FORCE
ABOVE ME, BELOW ME, AROUND ME: THE FORCE
IN ME, THROUGH ME, FROM ME: THE FORCE
IN MY THOUGHTS, IN MY WORDS,
IN MY ACTIONS: THE FORCE
THE FORCE IS ALL IN ALL
ALL LIFE, ALL INTELLIGENCE, ALL LOVE
THE FORCE IS THE ONE AND ONLY REALITY
AND SO IT IS!"

As I focused on the Force, the thousands upon thousands of shells on the walls of the cave began to twinkle like stars on a dark night. Every cell and atom of my body began to pulsate and vibrate. I forgot all about the pain in my left arm.

A rubber speedboat appeared in the cave opening. It was filled with armed men.

But I heeded them not. All my attention was on the Force.

I AM THE FORCE.

The men in the rubber boat sped into the cave; Agent Nevis was sitting in front of the boat. He was so close that I could see the burns on the side of his face. Two of his men raised their machine guns.

"Hands behind your head!" shouted one of them.

I AM THE FORCE.

The rocks and the waves and the agents began to fade.

The twinkling lights of the Crystal Cave and my vibrating body melted into one.

The men in the boat reached the rock where I stood.

Nevis jumped out and tried to grab me.

But it was too late.

I was already far, far away.

10

My Past Is No Longer What It Used to Be

The first thing I noticed was the smell of flowers. I opened my eyes and discovered that I was sitting with my back against a cherry tree that was in full bloom. The tree's lovely pinkish flowers were swaying in the gentle breeze. Above me, the sun was shining brightly and the sky was the clearest of blues.

I breathed deeply and took in the sweet scent of the flowers. Yes, there were many cherry trees here, in this part of the Relaxation Forest.

And yes, there could be no doubt about it; I was back in the Relaxation Forest.

I'd never been anywhere else where I felt such a deep feeling of peace and tranquility. The trees, the grass, the flowers and even the birds circling around the treetops above were all surrounded by the same warm golden aura.

I looked down at myself. I was still wearing my tattered jeans, sweatshirt, raincoat, and sneakers, but I felt a lot more whole and at ease than I'd felt in a long time. And my left arm didn't hurt any more.

I stood up.

So I'd actually done it.

I'd actually raised my consciousness enough in the Crystal Cave to be transubstantiated up into the Ashtar Command's Mothership.

But what a close shave it had been. Agent Nevis had been so close...

"Yes, it really was a close shave," said a soft, melodious voice above me.

I looked up. Sitting on one of the branches of the cherry tree was a beautiful woman with long, golden hair. She too was surrounded by that warm golden light.

"Ticha!" I cried in joy.

With effortless ease, my guardian angel jumped off the branch. But instead of falling directly to the ground, she fluttered down slowly like a cherry blossom drifting its way to the ground. She landed in front of me with a big smile on her face.

"Greetings, Starbrow."

"Starbrow?" I said, smiling back and looking down at my torn clothes. "I don't think there's much Starbrow about me at the moment."

"I wouldn't say that," she said with a twinkle in her eye. "There's just a bit more warrior over you than before."

"Warrior! You can say that again! In the last couple of days people have been trying to catch me, blow me up, drown me, shoot me... I tell you those crazy agents have been chasing me across half of England!"

My guardian angel didn't say a word—it seemed all she could do was smile.

"Everything has gone wrong!" I continued woefully even though she kept on smiling. "It's been one disaster after another on Earth..."

Ticha nodded and said slowly. "I know Starbrow. Developments on Earth haven't gone quite according to plan."

"Now that's an understatement if I ever heard one! Do you realize what's happened? Jacob and Janus are dead, the Light Grid has been destroyed, STARDAY has been cancelled... and you say things haven't gone quite according to plan!"

"Now, now Starbrow... don't you go jumping to conclusions," Ticha said to my great surprise. "Things aren't always what they seem to be."

"Now what could you possibly mean by that?"

"Commander Ashtar will explain it all to you in a little while. He's waiting for you in his briefing room."

"Commander Ashtar is waiting for me?"

My guardian angel nodded.

"That's excellent..." I said, a bit surprised that the Commander of the Intergalactic Fleet himself was waiting for me. "I've come to tell Ashtar that he must not cancel STARDAY."

"I know, and you have my full support. But before you talk to him, there is something you should see."

"What do you mean?"

"I mean there is something... something important that you should see before you talk to Ashtar."

"What is it?"

"You will see what it is when you go back to a past life."

"Another regression?"

"Yes."

"Oh no," I said in surprise. "Now?"

137

"Yes now!"

"You must be joking."

"No," she smiled, "I'm not joking at all... "

"But there's no time..."

"Maybe, maybe not." There was that mischievous twinkle in her eye again.

"But..."

"It's important that you see it. Very important." There was something about the way she said this that made me realize I really didn't have any choice.

"But..."

"Trust me, Starbrow. You won't regret it."

"Observe your breathing... just watch the air flowing in and out of your body... all by itself..."

The deep voice of the Keeper of the Cosmic Library echoed through the Pyramid of Time. I felt myself sinking deeper and deeper into a state of deep relaxation. Soon there was only my breathing. Everything else slowly faded out from my awareness... My brief meeting with Ticha, our walk through the Relaxation Forest to the Cosmic Library, meeting the Keeper again... All of it just seemed to fade away and disappear into the nothingness. And now there was only the deep, calm sound of the Keeper's voice and my breath flowing in and out...

"Imagine that you are standing in front of an elevator," I heard the Keeper say. "The doors open and you step into the elevator. Ask your Inner Wisdom, your Higher Self, which floor it is Highest Wisdom for you to visit."

I focused my attention on the many buttons on the elevator's wall panel. So many floors, so many lives...

But I knew at once what floor my Inner Wisdom wanted me to visit.

"5th floor."

I pushed the button and the elevator started to move. I felt myself rising upwards. After a short while the elevator stopped.

"The doors have opened," said the Keeper. "Now look out of the elevator and tell me what you see."

I looked out.

On the other side, there was complete darkness.

"What do you see?" asked the Keeper.

I stepped out of the elevator and looked around.

No, it was not complete darkness after all.

High above me, innumerable stars were shining.

And below me... the landscape was wrapped in mist.

As my eyes grew accustomed to the darkness, the misty landscape began to take form. Woods, fields, rolling hills, a village. And a few miles away... a great hill towered up in the middle of the landscape.

"That is Glastonbury Tor," I said. "I am back in Avalon again."

"Do you see anything interesting?"

As always I felt myself drawn to the great hill. I focused on its grassy sides, the clear lake surrounding it, the stone circle on the hilltop.

A stone circle... and water surrounding the hill...

So I was far back in time again.

As I bent my gaze towards Glastonbury Tor I felt myself first float, then fly towards the hill. Quickly I passed over woods and fields, over the village of Glastonbury and the small church, until I came to the shores of the lake that surrounded the hill.

The swaying reeds were wrapped in the heavy mist. There were only a few leaves left on the trees. A cold wind blew from the east.

A tall figure, wrapped in a long, dark blue robe, was standing on the lakeshore. His hood was pulled back and the wind blew through his white hair and long beard. He was leaning on a massive oak staff.

Merlin.

I hovered a few yards above him, studying my old friend and master. Although his hair was white and his beard was long, he looked younger than I remembered him when I had sat with him in the Crystal Cave as Dana.

Merlin didn't notice me. He was looking straight ahead as if he was trying to penetrate the mist with his clear gaze. I followed his gaze.

Something was coming through the mist.

A white boat.

The boat was slowly but surely making its way across the waters of the lake, heading directly towards the old wizard. Two tall figures—a man and a woman—were standing in the boat. They were both very slender and there was something majestic about them, and they seemed to be surrounded by a golden light. About five yards from the shore, the man stopped the boat.

"Greetings, Merlin," said the man.

139

"Greetings, Rayek." The wizard bowed reverently towards the man. "And greetings to you, Rayel," said Merlin bowing even more deeply to the woman.

"It is well that you could come so swiftly," said Rayel.

"Your visit must be of great importance," said Merlin. "I have felt the urgency of your call for many days now."

"Yes, our visit is of great importance," said Rayel. "The Prophecy of Starwarrior has come to pass."

Merlin looked at the two Star Elves in surprise.

"The Prophecy of Starwarrior? Are you certain?"

"Yes," said Rayek. "What you have sought for, for so long, has finally happened. The two souls were born just a few hours ago, here in Britain."

"The two souls?"

"Yes," said Rayel. "Remember the Prophecy:

> *When the One with the Sight*
> *is reunited with the Warrior from the Stars*
> *the Perfect Being will be born*
>
> *From the Perfect Being*
> *will come the Single Eye*
>
> *From the Single Eye*
> *will come the Perfect World*
>
> *And then the Angels sing"*

"The Single Eye..." said Merlin slowly, reaching far, far back to a time long past.

"That which you prophesied so long ago, Merlin, has now come true," said Rayek. "When these two souls work together in harmony, they will be given access to the Lost Teaching of the Single Eye."

Merlin nodded, still looking as if he was remembering something that had happened a long time ago. "Yes..." he said, almost whispering, "...the Lost Teaching of the Single Eye...The Single Eye that can raise the entire collective consciousness of humanity to great heights."

"Yes," said Rayel. "And never before has our need been so great—as the Goddess well knows!"

"Indeed my friends, God is great!" Merlin cried out, spreading his arms wide and looking up at the sky, which was almost completely shrouded in the mist. "An auspicious occasion I dare say, and an opportunity of extraordinary dimensions."

"Yes my friend," replied Rayek, "but we must indeed take care lest this unexpected opportunity slips out of our hands!"

"What do you mean?"

"We are not the only ones in Britain who know that the two souls have just been born."

"Really? Who else knows?"

"Morgause. She is on her way to them as we speak."

"Morgause!" cried Merlin, clenching his staff. "Does that dark enchantress really believe she can use them in her mad scramble for power? Even she would not dare kill them."

"No," said Rayel, "she will not kill them, but she can prevent them from ever working together."

"You must reach the two babes before Morgause does," said Rayek.

"Yes, I must," said Merlin, "but do you know who they are?"

"Yes, they were born a few hours ago. They are twins."

"Twins!"

"Yes."

"Twins... now that is interesting. Who is their mother?"

"Luned."

"Luned? The priestess who was sent into exile?"

"Yes."

Merlin winced. "I told Viviane not to send her away. It would have been far better for all of us if Luned had stayed in Avalon. Then the twins would have been safe with us now. Do you know where Luned and the babes are?"

"No," said Rayek. "But there is one man who does. The man who got her with child."

"You know who he is?"

"Yes," said Rayel, "his name is Cydwir."

"A Welshman?"

"Yes. But he has been converted into the Christian faith. He is a monk at the church of Glastonbury."

"Ah ha..." said Merlin sighing, "so that was why Luned would not reveal his identity. I must go to him at once."

"Yes," said Rayel. "You must go with all speed... with every moment that passes, our doom draws nearer..."

The Keeper of the Cosmic Library interrupted me.

"Now go forward to the next important event in that life," he said.

My surroundings changed and the next moment I found myself floating above a tiny stone cottage. In fact, it was not much more than a good-sized hut. A chill wind blew over the little cottage, which was nestled between the hills. There were mountains in the distance.

I focused my attention on the little cottage and floated down to the front door. Out of sheer habit, I stuck out my hand to open the door, but since I had no hands or body I simply floated straight through the door.

The cottage had only one room and it was sparsely furnished. There was a bed, a wooden table, and two chairs. A fire was burning low in the fireplace. A young woman was lying on the bed, wrapped in thick blankets.

It was the banished priestess Luned.

In her arms, she held her two tiny newborn babes.

I floated down to her side. She couldn't have been more than twenty years old—with long, blond hair and a beautiful, finely chiseled face. Her eyes were open and she had a blissful smile on her face.

But she was not looking at her newborn babes; rather she was gazing towards another realm, the invisible realm.

She is dying I thought. *Her mission on Earth is ending.*

I bent over her, but she did not see me. The twins moved a little, but they did not cry.

They were a boy and girl—so pure, so innocent. They had just arrived and now she was departing...

"Look at the woman," said the Keeper of the Cosmic Library. "Is she someone that you know in this life?"

I looked into Luned's eyes with their other worldly gaze.

Why yes, there was something very familiar about her.

"Who is she?" the Keeper asked again.

I looked at her more closely.

Who is she? I thought. She seems so familiar…

But of course!

Luned was...

"Rebecca!" I cried. "Luned is Rebecca! Rebecca Randall from Glastonbury!"

Suddenly the priestess sighed and for a brief moment her body shook slightly. Then she lay completely still. It seemed to me as if a gentle breeze rustled through the room. A moment later, a shining figure rose up from Luned's body and began to float upwards.

"Rebecca," I said. "She is leaving her body."

"Yes," the Guardian said. "Her time on Earth during this lifetime is over."

The shining figure was so bright and clear that I almost couldn't look at it. For a moment, she hovered above the twins and then with a swish, she rose up towards the ceiling and disappeared to the other side.

The bright light was gone. The only light left in the room came from the dying embers in the fireplace.

I moved close to the lifeless body on the bed. There was a look of complete peace on Luned's face.

"What about the two twins?" said the Keeper, "do you know either of them in this life?"

I looked at the two newborn babes. They really did look alike—no one could be in doubt that they were twins even though the baby girl was a bit smaller than the boy. She had a shock of golden-reddish hair on her little head—and yes, there was also something very familiar about her too. I looked into her eyes. They were clear and gray-green.

I was not in doubt.

"The girl is me," I said. "She is Dana."

The little girl made small cooing sounds and kicked her little arms and legs. I bent over her.

It was truly amazing. I was witnessing my own birth!

"So that's why Rebecca feels like a mother to me," I muttered. "She really was my mother in a past life, if only for a very short time."

"The individual souls in a soul group have a tendency to incarnate at the same time and in the same place, because they are often working on the same mission," said the Keeper.

"What a nice thought," I said.

"What about your twin brother?" asked the Keeper, "do you know him too?"

"My twin brother? I didn't know Dana had a twin." I wondered why it never came up when I had my past life review of my life as Dana.

Strange, very strange.

I turned towards the little baby boy. Although he looked like Dana, he was bigger and the few tufts of hair he had on his head were darker than Dana's. I looked into his eyes. They were clear and gray-green too, just like my own. I had seen them before as well—but where?

"Do you know him?" It was the Keeper. "Take a good look."

I kept staring at the baby boy's eyes.

"Yes... I know him," I said slowly.

"Who is he?"

143

Although I had no body, I suddenly had the feeling that the point between my eyebrows was beginning to pulsate. The little boy wiggled in his dead mother's arms and began making faint sounds.

Where had I seen those eyes before?

Where had I seen that smile? That face?

The tingling sensation in my forehead grew stronger.

Who was he? Where had I seen those eyes before?

The answer came rushing towards me with the force of a jumbo jet, but I couldn't believe it.

"Who is he?" the Keeper asked again.

"No!" I cried in horror. "No! It can't be true!"

I felt myself being hurled back in the room as if I had just received a savage kick in the gut.

"No! No!" I shouted, covering the eyes I didn't have with the hands I didn't have.

"Who is he?" the Keeper was asking for the third time.

The tiny baby boy and Dana continued to make faint gurgling sounds. I felt sick. I thought I was going to throw up.

What I had just seen could not be true.

"Who is he?" the Keeper asked again.

My twin brother was Gavin.

Gavin! Lord Gavin!

The Lord Gavin who betrayed me and killed me years later at the foot of Glastonbury Tor. The Lord Gavin who killed Jacob and Janus. Again and again. Would it never stop!

Lord Gavin!

Agent Nevis!

My unrelenting pursuer!

I stumbled blindly towards the door in my invisible body. "No! It cannot be true!" I hollered.

"You know in your heart that it is true," said the Keeper calmly.

"But why? Why?? It can't be true…!" I cried though I knew in my heart that it was.

The Keeper was as calm as ever. "It is important that you know your past, before you can move on," was all he would say.

I was so distraught I hardly heard his words. It was pure madness. A terrible blackness was engulfing me. "Why… why! Why are you doing this to me! Why are you doing this to me!" I was terrified, filled with despair. "Ticha, Ticha!" I cried, "Help me, please help me! Get me away from this madman! Ticha!"

"Ticha was the one who has asked me to guide you through this..." said the Keeper, still not budging.

I did not stay to hear more. Instead I threw myself and my invisible body at the door and flew out to the other side. I kept flying for several yards until I bumped into a black horse. I was so surprised that I stopped halfway inside the horse. Then I leapt sideways and out of the horse. Neither the horse nor its rider noticed me. I was just about to continue my wild flight when I realized who the rider was.

Morgause.

I stopped and turned around.

Morgause dismounted and tied the reins around a stake in front of the cottage. She looked like she was somewhere in her early twenties, with red curly hair and large full lips. Although she was dressed for traveling, it was obvious that she was wealthy. There was a kind of vulgar beauty about her. She walked up to the door of the cottage and knocked.

She is coming for the twins.

She is coming for Gavin and me.

When no one answered, Morgause slowly opened the door. For a moment I stared at the cottage and hesitated. Then I turned away.

I just couldn't believe it.

Lord Gavin, Agent Nevis, was my twin brother!

My own brother was my murderer!

"Things are not always quite what they seem to be," the deep voice of the Keeper said inside me.

"But why?" I cried. "Why me? It's just not fair!"

"Even the very Wise cannot see the end of all things."

"Spare me your fucking words of wisdom!"

"It is true nevertheless."

"But why? Why does Ticha want me to know this? What good can it possibly do?"

"The only way to answer that question is to follow the story to its end."

"But I have followed the story to its end!" I shouted. "I know what happens! Gavin kills me! And he kills Loran and Gaius! And then he kills them again in my present lifetime!"

"You have followed *your* story to its end, you mean. But what about Gavin's story?"

"What do you mean?"

"I mean just that—what about Gavin's story."

I could hear the twins crying inside the hut.

The door opened.

Morgause was standing in the doorway with Gavin in her arms.

She had wrapped him in warm blankets, but he was screaming loudly. Inside the cottage, Dana was screaming too.

"To find out how the whole story ends, you have to follow Gavin's story to its end, too" said the Keeper.

"What do you mean by that?"

"Move over to Gavin and enter his body."

"No!" I protested, "You can't be serious!"

"Yes I am," said the Keeper, "You have to enter Gavin's body if you want to follow the story to its end."

"You must be mad!"

The Keeper did not reply.

Morgause opened a saddlebag and took out a backpack. She dumped the contents of the backpack in the saddlebag and then put little Gavin into the backpack with his head sticking out. Then she strapped the backpack on so it hung in front of her, down her chest. Gavin was crying disconsolately.

"Place yourself behind the baby and then enter his body," said the Keeper.

"But how can I enter another body? I know that Gavin is my twin brother, but he's not me. I am Dana!"

"Since the two of you are twins, I can temporarily morph your etheric bodies together so that you are more or less able to experience his life."

"But why? What's the point of all this?"

"Patience, my friend. All will be revealed in due time."

Morgause undid the reins and mounted the horse.

"But what happens to little Dana?"

"You know what happens to Dana. Merlin finds her and brings her to Avalon, where she is raised to be a priestess."

Morgause turned the horse around and started to ride. Both Dana and Gavin were screaming loudly.

"Now…this is your last chance," said the Keeper.

To hell with it I thought. *Things can't get any worse than they already are.*

I focused on Gavin and floated up behind his little back.

Then I stepped into his body.

146

The moment I touched Gavin's body it was as if I became one with it—and not just with his body. It felt as if everything Gavin's soul knew at the moment he had incarnated in this lifetime in Britain flooded my consciousness... Who he really was... where he had came from... why he'd come... who the other souls were he was working with... it all seemed to flood my consciousness at such great speed that I simply could not grasp it.

And the feeling of being one with Gavin continued to grow as Morgause began to gallop away from the cottage with Gavin's tiny body bouncing up and down on her breast.

And yet it was not quite the same as when I went through my past life as Dana. In that past life regression, I was quite literally Dana. I was inside her body, inside her consciousness, I felt what she felt, I thought what she thought, there was nothing else.

But now with Gavin it was different. Although I experienced everything that he experienced, it was in a more detached way. It felt more like watching yourself in a dream... watching from the outside.

The cottage was already far behind and Gavin was still screaming. When Morgause came to the bottom of the next hill, she turned and began riding north.

"Move on to the next important event in that lifetime," said the Keeper.

The windswept hills and the cold starry night disappeared.

And then it was morning.

The waves of the ocean were pounding against high cliffs. Not far from the coast, a medieval battleship was plowing through the great swells.

A tall, proud warrior was standing on the helm of the ship.

I knew that the warrior was Gavin.

Lord Gavin.

But when was it?

"It is 30 years later," said the Keeper.

"30 years?"

"Yes. Move closer to him..."

11

Gavin Speaks

Lord Gavin was standing on the prow of the North Star, watching the magnificent coastline of Cornwall pass by. Summer was drawing to a close and the brilliant rays of the sun cast their beautiful light on the great cliffs that lined the coast. The wind was with them that day and the warship quickly made its way to their destination, Tintagel Castle.

Feeling very content, Gavin surveyed the coastline. Even though Gavin had never been to Cornwall before, there was something about the landscape that made him feel at home.

Which was rather strange considering the fact that he'd never felt very much at home on the island kingdom of Orkney where he grew up and spent the first 25 years of his life. No it was true, he'd never felt really at home on Orkney. Not during the first 12 years of his life when he lived with his parents, Garulf, a poor fisherman and his wife Ellyn. Nor during the next 13 years, when he lived at the court of King Lot of Orkney where he was raised—to the surprise of many—with King Lot and Queen Morgause's unruly sons.

Gavin smiled at the memory. Yes, to be sure it had been quite a surprise when suddenly one day Queen Morgause's footmen knocked on the door of the humble fisherman's hut and announced that they'd come to take Gavin with them to the castle. Ellyn wept and wailed, while Garulf had stood as if stricken to stone. For some reason, 12-year-old Gavin reacted to the summons with strange indifference.

Somewhere deep inside I always knew this would happen.

I did not belong among the fishermen.

Nor did Gavin belong at the court of King Lot of Orkney even though there was really no reason for him to feel that way. The royal couple's five wild sons welcomed him with open arms because to them, he was just another boy they could play and fight with. And as time passed, a strange sort of mother-son love began to grow between Morgause and Gavin. So all in all, it was a good life; Gavin had all the comforts of a young nobleman and the chance to attain wealth and power. It wasn't long before young Gavin showed that he had both a keen mind and great skill as a warrior. He might not have possessed the same savage strength as his five foster brothers, but he was more clever and calculating than they were—and because of this he always beat his five foster brothers in combat. Always.

But despite all this, Gavin did not really feel at home. It was only after another boy was brought to the court to be reared that Gavin felt, for the first time in his life, a kind of kinship with another human being.

The new boy's name was Mordred and he was two years older than Gavin. And just as there had been rumors when Gavin was brought to the court; there were again rumors that Mordred was another one of Morgause's bastard children. One tale that circulated at that time even claimed that Mordred was the result of a fateful night when Morgause had seduced young King Arthur himself.

Gavin and Mordred quickly became best friends and though they never talked about it, Gavin knew that Mordred like himself did not feel very at home in the north either.

Both knew their destinies lay elsewhere.

In the south of the kingdom.

The North Star sped around another bend in the coast and suddenly the entire coastline lay before him like pearls on a beautiful necklace. Indeed, here were the Southern Lands of the kingdom he and Mordred had longed for, glimmering like precious jewels in the sunlight.

But south is enemy country Morgause had always told them.

It was here that the tyrannical King Arthur kept leading Britain into one bloody war after another, urged on by his counselor, the evil wizard Merlin. It was here that King Arthur and Merlin had conceived one disastrous alliance after another as they slowly but surely steered Britain towards death and destruction. All that kept Britain from certain doom was the efforts of King Lot of Orkney and his allies.

Gavin remembered how in their fiery youth, he and Mordred had sworn that one day they would cast the conceited and foolish Arthur from his high throne. And day by day the longing to leave their cold home in the north grew, until finally, when Gavin was 25 and Mordred 27, King Lot permitted them to journey south to King Arthur's realm. King Lot thought that having two loyal knights in the south might prove a wise strategy when the time came to cast Arthur from his throne.

The two knights quickly proved their worth in battle and before the year was out, both Mordred and Gavin held positions of honor and responsibility in Arthur's war-torn country. But their posts were not in the Southern Lands as they had hoped. Mordred was stationed in eastern England where he spent his time fighting the Vikings, the eternal enemies of Britain. And Gavin was stationed at one of the forts along the northern border of the kingdom, where he kept watch on Hadrian's Wall, fighting a constant battle to keep out the wild tribes. For more than four bloody years, Gavin had fought countless battles against the wild Picts and Scots—battles that put all his skill as a warrior to the test. By the time he reached his 30th birthday, Gavin was a hardened veteran with many gruesome battles behind him

During those battle-filled years, Gavin saw nothing of Mordred, and their youthful dream of casting Arthur from the throne slowly began to fade. That was until eight days ago, when a messenger arrived in secret, bringing Gavin a letter from Mordred.

It was the first time Gavin had heard from his foster brother in years. Now Mordred wrote that he had become a Knight of the Round Table and that because of this, he was privy to King Arthur and Merlin's plans. At the moment, Arthur and Merlin were summoning the Knights of the Round Table and other important emissaries to a secret meeting at Tintagel Castle. Based on this knowledge, Mordred and King Lot had devised a cunning and ambitious scheme to put an end to Arthur and Merlin's New Vision and take the throne of Britain. The time to act had come at last.

Four days after the letter from Mordred had arrived, yet another letter came.

This time, it was not from Mordred, but from King Arthur's trusted chamberlain, Sir Cai.

The letter bid Gavin set sail immediately for Tintagel Castle where he was to carry out a very delicate, secret mission for the King.

Although the letter did not explain what the mission was, it was exactly what Mordred had told Gavin to expect.

Obviously something was afoot at Tintagel Castle and the plotters, Mordred and King Lot, were moving their pawns into place. With the end game of their cunning scheme to cast Arthur from his throne fast approaching, it was obvious that Gavin had an important role to play.

Gavin stood on the deck of the North Star, waiting for the important cargo he was supposed to transport to the coast of Somerset to arrive. His ship was moored to the stony pier in the sheltered cove next to Tintagel Head. The sun was rising above Tintagel Castle and it was high tide. This was the only time that ships could sail all the way up to the pier to load or unload goods.

In the distance, Gavin could see King Arthur's chamberlain, Sir Cai, escorting four people and their horses down towards the pier.

According to Sir Cai, whom Gavin had immediately reported to when he arrived in Tintagel late last night, the three and their young servant were on a secret peace mission. Gavin's mission was to sail the four of them up along the northern coast and then put them and their horses ashore on one of Somerset's beaches. No questions were to be asked. After this Gavin was to return to his northerly post on Hadrian's Wall.

Gavin had heard quite another story from his foster brother Mordred, who he met later that same night in the deepest secrecy. More than four years had passed since Gavin had seen Mordred last, and his foster brother had changed greatly. His eyes seemed colder, his speech more bitter, and his hatred of Arthur and Merlin seemed to burn more fiercely than ever before.

Mordred told Gavin that the three emissaries and their young servant were on a mission to Avalon, the priestesses and druids' island in the Summer Country. Their mission was an important part of the wizard Merlin's hitherto most ambitious plan to become the ruler of all Britain. Because of this, it was of the most utmost importance to King Lot and Mordred's plans, that the four never reached Avalon.

That is why the delicate task was given to Gavin.

Only he could be trusted to carry out this deception in complete secrecy.

Gavin's task was to sail the four up along the coast where the North Star would be unexpectedly boarded by one of King Lot's warships. Under the pretense of wanting to speak to Lord Gavin, Lot's soldiers would kill the ten soldiers assigned to Gavin's ship by Sir Cai as well as the ship's seven sailors. After that they would kill Merlin's emissaries and their young servant and then sink the North Star. Gavin would be the ship's only survivor. When he came ashore, he was to send word to Sir Cai that the ship had been attacked by pirates—and that he was the only survivor. In this way, Gavin could retain his cover until he received further instructions from King Lot. The plan could not have been simpler.

Gavin coldly watched Sir Cai and the four emissaries approach the ship.

151

Although it was a warm late summer morning, the four were dressed in long robes; their faces buried in their deep hoods. Two sailors from the North Star led their four horses up the gangplank.

It's a pity those horses will never reach land Gavin thought.

The four emissaries bowed in farewell to Sir Cai and then walked up the gangplank. As they stepped on board the ship, each of them bowed respectfully to Gavin. As they did, he was able to catch a glimpse of their faces.

The first was a big, broad-shouldered man with blond hair. He bowed and smiled confidently at Gavin.

Not much magician in this fellow Gavin thought. He looks more like a warrior to me. I better keep an eye on him.

The next was a man in his late twenties. He had deep, brown eyes. The sunlight was reflected on something that hung about his neck.

A crucifix.

A Christian on his way to Avalon.

This is beginning to get very interesting.

The third envoy, who was shorter than the others, stepped lightly across the gangplank.

A woman.

"Welcome to the North Star." Gavin bowed.

The woman bowed and for a brief moment their eyes met. She was very beautiful, with a fine face and golden-red curly hair. As he looked into the woman's eyes, Gavin suddenly felt a strange tingling sensation between his brows. The tingling sensation spread all the way down through his body.

"Thank you, my Lord," the woman said.

She turned and walked on.

Gavin blinked uncertainly.

The fourth guest, a young lad, stepped on board and bowed, but Gavin took no notice of him. Instead he looked after the woman, dazed.

One of the soldiers chuckled softly at his side. "She's a pretty one, isn't she?"

Gavin nodded mechanically.

Yes, she was certainly a pretty one. No doubt about that.

But Gavin had met many beautiful women in his life without having his whole body tingle...

He shook his head and gave the order to pull up the gangplank.

Tingling or no, she would be dead tomorrow.

12

Treachery

The men on the North Star were fidgeting nervously. A menacing-looking warship was fast approaching Gavin's much smaller ship. It wasn't more than a few minutes ago that the ship had come charging out from a hidden cove where it seemed the ship had been hiding and waiting for them. The warship sported King Lot of Orkney's standard and signaled that it wanted to make contact with the North Star.

Gavin tried to calm his men. At least officially, Arthur and Lot were allies. There was nothing to be nervous about. They probably just wanted information about something.

But still the crew seemed nervous. Did they sense that something was up?

Gavin headed for the cabin at the rear of the ship where his passengers were. He thought it wise to inform the four travelers that King Lot's ship was approaching—and that everything was under control. If he didn't, they might wonder what was going on and become suspicious.

As Gavin approached the cabin, he felt a strange sense of unease. In fact, Gavin had felt uneasy ever since the four travelers boarded the North Star yesterday morning. It was most peculiar.

Above all it was the beautiful woman who made him feel uneasy. Not that he'd seen much of her during the last two days, but when he did, he felt uneasy. He even knew her name—it was Dana. He overheard the young servant calling her one morning as she watched the sunrise.

Dana...

Gavin stopped in front of the cabin door. His heart pounded in his chest and as he raised his hand to knock on the door, it trembled slightly.

Why?

It made no sense at all.

During the last four years, Gavin had killed countless men in circumstances far bloodier than these—without even flinching. He had even taken the lives of many wild Scottish women with his deadly sword. Why should he care about these four travelers? They were Merlin's accomplices, sent out as part of the wizard's dark web of deceit to enslave all of Britain.

Gavin knocked hard on the door.

The young servant opened the door. The three others were standing behind him. Dana had a half open bag in her hand. It looked as if they were packing.

"One of King Lot's warships is approaching," Gavin said. "They have signaled that they wish to board and speak with us."

Dana ran over and opened a hatch.

"How can this be?" she cried.

"There is no reason why they should suspect anything," Gavin said. "You just stay in the cabin, and I'll take care of them."

Gavin quickly closed the door again. Inside the cabin he could hear the big, broad-shouldered fellow loosening his sword from its sheath.

Well, that was that.

I'd best keep a close watch on the warrior.

Lot's ship was now alongside the North Star. There must have been at least a hundred men on board, all of them armed to the teeth. The men on the North Star nervously waited for Lot's men to throw across a gangplank.

Gavin walked up to the prow. Strong hands placed a plank between the two ships. The captain of Lot's ship walked across the gangplank, accompanied by his soldiers. He was old, in his early forties, and scarred from many battles.

Gavin recognized him at once. It was Captain Muldwar, a man he'd seen many times during his younger days at the court of King Lot.

"Captain Muldwar." Gavin bowed. "It's been a long time."

"Yes Lord Gavin, it has." The Captain bowed.

When they saw this friendly exchange, Gavin's men relaxed visibly. It was no secret that Lord Gavin came from Orkney, so when they saw that their captain knew the warship's captain, it made them feel much more at ease.

During this exchange, Muldwar's soldiers had placed themselves along the whole length of the warship—and now his soldiers also boarded the North Star.

"What can I do for you?" Gavin asked at his most accommodating.

Suddenly from the warship, thirty bows were raised and aimed at Gavin and his men. More than fifty of Muldwar's soldiers drew swords from their sheaths.

"Order your men to put down their weapons," said Muldwar.

The ten soldiers that King Arthur had sent with Gavin, looked at him in surprise.

Gavin did not move or react.

The leader of the ten soldiers pulled out his sword.

The next moment, thirty arrows whizzed through the air. The leader and five other men fell onto the deck, riddled with arrows. The other four managed to pull out their swords, but it was too late. Muldwar's men were upon them. For a few seconds, swords clashed and cries were heard on the deck of the North Star. But very soon, Arthur's soldiers and Gavin's seven sailors were cut down, one by one, outnumbered as they were by Lot's men.

The last soldier standing aimed a heavy blow at Captain Muldwar, but before he reached the Captain with his sword, Gavin rammed his sword through the man's belly in one swift stroke.

For a brief moment, the soldier looked at Gavin in surprise—and then fell to the ground, dead.

"Much obliged," said Muldwar.

Gavin and Muldwar turned towards the cabin in the stern of the ship. Now it was time for the four travelers.

Gavin and Muldwar ran down the steps.

One of Muldwar's soldiers kicked open the cabin door.

The cabin was empty.

Gavin paced restlessly back and forth on the deck of Orkney's big warship. The sun was about to set and still there was no news from Captain Muldwar and his men.

After Gavin and Muldwar discovered that the cabin was empty, they realized that the four travelers were fast swimming ashore. The captain and 40 men lowered their boats and rowed swiftly after them. The last Gavin saw of Captain Muldwar and his soldiers was them disappearing into the tall grass on the top of the cliffs.

But that had been more than three hours ago—and still there was no news. It was impossible that the four could escape Muldwar and his vastly superior force.

So why hadn't they returned?

Could the four really have escaped their pursuers?

The thought that they might have managed to escape filled Gavin with a strange mixture of fear and relief. Fear because it meant that his participation in Mordred's deadly scheme might now come to light. And relief because...

The strange tingling between his brows was there again. Gavin put his hand to his forehead and closed his eyes. He was surprised that he could clearly see in his mind's eye the young woman Dana walking calmly between old trees... trees that swayed without a wind. Her three companions were walking behind her.

"The Star Elves have driven off our pursuit," she said. "At last we can take a rest."

The vision faded and the strange tingling in Gavin's forehead receded.

Gavin opened his eyes and looked towards the coast—he could see nothing.

He knew with a sudden certainty that Captain Muldwar and his men would not return.

Gavin turned and began giving orders to the remainder of Lot's soldiers. Boats were lowered into the water. It was time to row men and horses ashore.

In less than half an hour, Gavin and twenty of Lot's riders were thundering through the Summer Country, headed for the great hill that towered high to the southeast.

Now it was up to Gavin to make sure the four never reached Avalon.

Much later that same night, Gavin dreamt that he was walking inside a great stone circle. Although he'd never seen the place in waking life, Gavin knew that the stone circle was the legendary Stonehenge, told of in many tales.

The great stones were wrapped in a heavy mist. A cold wind blew through the circle.

Gavin could see a robed figure standing between two great stones on the other side of the circle.

The figure began to walk slowly towards him.

"Gavin," the figure said.

There was something familiar about the voice, as if it was a voice that he had known and loved before, but not heard for countless ages.

The figure stopped right in front of him. Gavin could not see the face, which was covered by the deep hood.

"Gavin," the figure said. "Beware of this rash and wanton deed that you are about to commit."

An icy cold enveloped Gavin's heart. He wanted to open his mouth to speak, but he was unable to move. He stood as if rooted to the ground.

"Gavin..." said the voice again, "beware of this rash and wanton deed..."

The figure drew back its hood.

The light was so bright that Gavin could not see the face clearly.

"Gavin, beware..."

Suddenly the figure began to fade.

A moment later, one of Lot's soldiers was shaking Gavin.

"Wake up my Lord, Bretach has found footprints."

Still lost in the mist and stones, Gavin looked at the soldier and tried to focus on what he was saying.

"Footprints?"

"Yes my Lord, footprints of the four we seek. It looks as if they're headed for Glastonbury, just as my Lordship predicted."

Still dazed, Gavin looked at his surroundings. It was dark in the camp that he and Lot's men had made on the outskirts of the Whispering Forest. Most of the twenty riders that Gavin had brought with him on the hunt for the four travelers were still wrapped in their blankets sound asleep. Not far from them the trees were swaying, but there was no wind.

"Do you want to see the tracks, my Lord?"

Gavin did not answer. Instead he put his hand to his head, trying to fathom his strange dream. Who was the shining figure in the dream? What rash and wanton deed was he about to commit? Was it ending the lives of the four sorcerers?

"My Lord, do you wish to see the tracks?" the soldier asked again.

Gavin sat up. The first signs of dawn were appearing on the eastern horizon. Soon it would be morning. Why ponder the meaning of a dream at all? Gavin knew he had no time for strange premonitions or dreams. It might delay him and weaken his resolve. Now was not the time for questions, now was the time for action.

157

He drew his sword from its sheath and looked at it as it glinted coldly in the pale moonlight.

"Shall I wake the men, my Lord?"

"Yes. The four are on their way to Glastonbury," said Gavin. "There will be no stopping until we have sent them to their graves."

Gavin resolutely put his sword back in its sheath.

The riders were waiting for Gavin's signal. For several minutes, they had been hiding in the bushes on top of a rocky plateau, watching the four travelers below.

Gavin sat silently in his saddle with a faraway look in his eyes. Down below on another flat shelf of rock not far away the four travelers were surveying the landscape. There were woodlands all around.

Gavin, who was keeping perfectly still, watched as the knight and the monk started to go down from the ledge. The woman, Dana, remained standing on the flat shelf of rock, gazing at the great hill that rose up on the horizon, about five miles away. Gavin knew it must be Avalon, the sacred island of the priestesses and druids. The young servant walked up to Dana and said something.

Dana turned around.

"There's something I must tell you," Gavin heard her say as she began to follow the knight and the monk, who were already halfway down from the rocky ledge. At that very moment, Gavin stirred as if he had been awakened from a dream. He raised his hand.

"Now!" he cried.

Ten of his twenty riders lifted their bows.

"Loran! Gaius!" Dana was calling to the others as she began her descent. "Wait for us! There's something I must tell..."

Ten arrows whizzed through the air. One of them landed deep in the monk's right arm. He tumbled forward, crying out in sudden pain.

"Get down!" cried his companion, the knight.

The four rushed frantically forward, tumbling down the slope.

The ten riders let loose another deadly burst of arrows at the travelers. One pierced Dana's cloak, but she kept tumbling downwards towards the bottom. When the travelers reached the bottom, they began to run desperately towards the trees.

Gavin and his riders drew their swords and began the descent from the ledge where they had been watching. When they reached the bottom, the four had just made it to the forest.

"There's no way they can escape us now, my Lord," cried one of his men as the riders charged after them in hot pursuit.

Inside the forest, the four had run up a tree-clad hill close by. Gavin and his men dismounted and led their horses through the trees up the hill. After a few minutes they arrived at the top, looking in all directions for their prey.

"There they are!" cried one of the riders, motioning to the right.

Gavin caught a glimpse of someone running between the trees at the foot of the hill.

"After them!"

The riders hurried down the right side of the hill where they mounted their horses and then charged after the four. Suddenly they came upon a fast-rushing stream. They waded through on horseback and halted on the other side.

"Where are..." began one of the riders, but he never finished the sentence.

Someone came flying down from the branches overhead and landed on the horse right behind the rider. Then with a stroke as quick as lightning, he cut the soldier's throat. The horses neighed fiercely as Gavin and his men reached for their swords.

It was the broad-shouldered knight, Loran.

Loran hurled his dagger into another rider's belly. The rider fell forward in the saddle, dead. Gavin lashed out at the knight, but he ducked adeptly.

"Gaius!" cried the knight.

The monk came flying down from the branches above and landed on top of another rider. The horse reared on its hind legs, knocking the rider out of the saddle. The monk grabbed the reins.

"Ride, Gaius, ride!" cried Loran, as he sprang out of reach of several swords.

The monk went off at a gallop.

"Bows!" cried Gavin.

Four of the riders drew their bows.

The powerful knight knocked two more riders out of the saddle, jumped onto one of the horses, and headed full speed towards the archers.

But Gavin blocked his way. With a deft blow, he almost managed to knock the knight off the horse. Blood gushed from the knight's side and he stumbled backwards.

Gavin's men let loose their arrows. Two struck the monk in the back. He fell off the horse and landed on the ground with a loud thud.

"No!" bellowed Loran ferociously.

With a furious cry he threw himself at Gavin. The two men tumbled to the ground. Gavin tried to get up, but the knight was faster. He kicked Gavin hard in the stomach. Gavin tumbled backwards and landed on the ground.

Then something very odd happened. As time stood still, Gavin watched the knight make a strange movement. He seemed to be drawing his sword and ramming it into Gavin's side.

Gavin moved to ward off the blow and prepared himself to feel the bite of cold steel in his side.

But to Gavin's great surprise, he felt nothing.

Gavin and the knight looked at the knight's hands in surprise.

His hands were clenched as if they were holding a great sword, but there was nothing there.

Loran was holding nothing but thin air!

Loran cursed and made another odd movement, this time as if he was putting an invisible sword back into its scabbard.

Gavin and his men looked on in amazement.

Had the knight lost his mind?

Loran took advantage of his pursuers' surprise and delivered a cruel blow to the side of Gavin's head.

For a brief moment, everything went black for Gavin.

This time the knight grabbed a real sword, one from a fallen rider, but it was too late. The other riders had surrounded him. One of them stabbed Loran savagely in the back. He let out a great cry and fell to his knees on the grass. Gavin grabbed his sword, but before he had time to strike, one of the other riders rammed his sword through the knight's belly.

Loran was dead before his body hit the ground.

One of the riders turned over the monk. He too was no longer in this world.

Gavin rose to his feet. "Where are the other two?" he cried.

The riders looked around warily. There was no sign of the woman or her young servant.

"They are on their way to Avalon!" cried Gavin. "After them! They must not reach the island!"

*Darkness had fallen across the land and the mist lay heavy over wood
and hill, when Gavin, with only 18 riders left, reached the stretch of open
land between the forest and the island of Avalon. Gavin had divided his
men into smaller groups who were now galloping across the fields. They
were no more than a mile and a half from the lake that surrounded the
island.*

*All of a sudden, Gavin brought his horse to a halt. He motioned for the
four men behind him to stop as well. Was that the sound of a horse
neighing in fear he'd heard to his left? Gavin turned and tried to pierce
the darkness and the mist with his gaze.*

Yes. She is there.

*Gavin turned his horse and charged to the left. The riders rode a couple
of hundred yards, until they saw a dark shape lying in the grass.*

It was one of their own men.

He was dead, a dagger deep in his chest.

The riders drew their swords and advanced cautiously.

*A few yards ahead they came upon another dead rider. He had a deep
gash in his head. Not far from the rider was his horse—also dead—killed
by a massive blow to the neck.*

*Slowly the riders advanced through the mist with great care until they
came upon another figure lying in the grass.*

This time it was the young woman.

She did not move.

The five riders surrounded Dana.

*Gavin motioned to two of the riders. They dismounted and pointed their
spears at her.*

"She's still alive, my Lord," said one of the riders.

The riders lifted her to her feet.

*Gavin got off his horse and walked over to Dana. He could see the
brunt of a spear point protruding from her right thigh. Her clothes were
soaked in blood, but she didn't seem to notice her wound. In fact, she
seemed very calm.*

Gavin held the point of his sword to Dana's chest.

*Their eyes met and again Gavin felt the strange tingling sensation, not
just between his brows, but also in his heart. He had to hold the hilt of his
sword tightly to keep it from shaking.*

Dana did not seem to have any fear of Gavin.

161

She smiled at him as if she knew something he did not know, something very sweet and peaceful.

"Where's Aran?" asked Gavin threateningly as he tried to master the strange feelings that were welling up in him.

Dana did not answer.

Instead she kept looking deep into Gavin's eyes.

In that instant, Gavin realized he didn't have the faintest idea who this woman was. Who was she really, this mysterious, beautiful woman that he had traveled so far to kill?

The strange feeling inside Gavin became so intense that he knew if he allowed it to continue a minute longer he would not be able to carry out the deed he had come to do.

Using all the force of his will, he looked away from Dana. "After the lad," he cried to his men. "She is just trying to win him time."

Four of Gavin's riders galloped off into the mist.

Then Gavin turned and with a quick stroke drove his sword into Dana's chest.

She gasped and went limp in the arms of the two riders who were holding her. They released her lifeless body and she fell to the ground. Gavin pulled his sword from her body and put it in his sheath. Then he walked over to his horse without looking back.

13

The One With the Sight

For hours, Gavin and his men searched for the young servant, but to no avail. Young Aran had escaped—and was by now either in Avalon on the other side of the mist-covered lake or somewhere else, far, far away. In all probability, Aran's escape meant that Gavin's treachery would be discovered—unless of course, Lot and Mordred cast King Arthur from his throne very soon. Whatever the case, there was nothing Gavin could do but return to the island kingdom of Orkney in the north with Lot's men.

Under cover of night they buried the bodies of the three travelers and the four of their own men who had been killed during the frantic chase. After they had hidden all traces of their deeds, they began their journey back to the coast and Lot's warship. After riding for a few hours through the woods, sleep was about to overcome them so they camped beneath a cluster of old oak trees. They built a fire and shared food and wine, and then one by one the men fell asleep.

Except one. Gavin.

Instead, he sat staring into the fire, drinking on occasion from the wine pouch at his side. After he killed Dana, instead of disappearing, the strange uneasiness in him had grown even stronger.

Gavin gulped down another swig of wine. What was wrong with him? Why did he feel so strange? Was it because Dana was a woman? Or was it because she was a priestess of Avalon? The white robes and the exquisitely crafted silver belt and dagger she wore underneath her cloak left little doubt as to her identity. She was one of the Goddess worshippers, the first people of Britain. Gavin had heard many rumors about the priestesses and druids of Avalon, some good, some bad. Maybe the woman had bewitched him or placed a curse on him.

In his mind's eye Gavin again saw Dana's beautiful, peaceful face. Dana... who looked at him so sweetly the moment before he had pierced

163

*her heart with his sword... as if she had known something about Gavin,
some deep secret that he did not know...*

Gavin shook his head and took another mouthful of wine. Then he threw
some more branches on the fire. All the men were sleeping soundly, some
around the fire, others under the old oak trees. Grey-white mist danced
around the trunks of the trees.

Grey-white mist... like the mysterious mists of Avalon, like the
mysterious visions that now filled his mind...

Gavin shook his head again. Then he looked up through the ancient
branches of the oak trees. There was an opening in the mist—and through
the opening, he could see many stars. Among them there was one lone
golden star, which shone far more brightly than any of the others.

"Well met on this dark night," said a deep voice.

Gavin sprang to his feet with a start.

On the edge of the camp, shrouded in mist, stood a tall figure.

Gavin blinked. Was the figure real or just another one of the strange
and horrible visions that were tormenting him on this endless night?

Gavin cleared his throat. "Who goes there?" he cried into the dark.

"Just a weary traveler in the night."

The figure was walking towards Gavin. The mist parted and in the light
from the campfire, Gavin saw it was an old man. His hair was white and
he had a long beard. He was wrapped in a dark blue cloak and he leaned
against a massive oak staff with symbols and runes carved into it.

Out of habit, Gavin reached for his sword.

The old man held up his right hand with open palm and said, "There is
no cause for alarm, my friend. All I seek is a little warmth and company
before I continue my journey."

Gavin took his hand off his sword.

No. There's been enough killing for one day.

Now the man stood almost before him. Their eyes met. The light of the
fire reflected in the old man's eyes and made them look like black coals
that hid a sleeping fire. Gavin sensed that the man was very old, far older
than he seemed to be.

"You are welcome to sit by the fire," said Gavin.

The old man smiled and bowed. Then he sat down by the fire, not far
from Gavin, warming his hands in front of the fire. The rest of Gavin's
men snored on; none of them having noticed their unexpected guest. But
then again, they had all drunk deeply of the wine. All of them, including
Gavin...

164

The old man made himself comfortable by the fire. "Even if it is late summer, it is still good to warm oneself by the fire," he said. "Now all one needs is a bit of wine to quench a traveler's thirst."

Gavin handed the wine pouch to the old man.

He accepted it gratefully. "You are truly kindness itself," he smiled as he drank deeply. "Ah!" he said, wiping his mouth. "Warm both inside and out!" He handed the wine pouch back to Gavin.

Gavin took the wine and turned his gaze back at the fire.

The old man looked at the men sleeping scattered around the campsite for a while. Then he turned towards Gavin and said, "Judging by your tired men and beasts, you have been riding hard and far today."

Gavin did not answer. He kept staring into the fire.

"All sleep the sleep of the very weary," continued the old man, trying to start a conversation. "Except you."

Gavin was still silent.

The old man was silent for a while as he poked at the flames with a stick.

The minutes tickled by slowly and as Gavin stared into the fire, it seemed to him that the dancing flames became white-robed priestesses with deep, penetrating eyes...

"I can see that something lies heavy on your shoulders, my friend." It was the old man speaking again.

The old man's voice startled Gavin and the dancing visions vanished. For a moment Gavin had almost forgotten the old man, lost as he was in his visions.

Gavin looked at the old man for a moment and then turned back towards the flames.

The old man was watching him kindly.

"Why not unburden yourself to an old man?" he said. "It will ease your heart... and then you will be able to sleep peacefully, I am sure."

Gavin drank again deeply from the wine pouch and felt the warm drink relaxing his mind and body.

Not really knowing why—whether it was because he had drunk too much or because of the old man's deep, soothing voice—Gavin heard himself say in a low voice, "A deed was done by me this day of which I am not proud."

The old man smiled. "I suppose most of us can say the same at some point in our lives. But few indeed have the humility or the wisdom to admit it. But you, I can see, are a man who is both wise and kind-hearted."

"Kind-hearted?"

"Yes. How else can you explain the fact that you are the only one who is unable to sleep this night... when all of you took part in the deeds you speak of?"

Gavin looked at the old man. There was something very reassuring about his manner. What harm could it do to tell him what was on his mind? He would probably never return to this place again or see the old man again. This place, this accursed place... Somerset, the Summer Country, with Avalon, its beating heart...

"Yes, we all took part in the deeds of this day," said Gavin, again marveling to hear himself speak so openly.

"Yes?" the old man said kindly.

"Yes," said Gavin again. Then he took a deep breath and looked up again through the opening in the mist above as if to steady himself. The large golden star was still shinning brightly. "But I it seems am the only one who is tormented by strange visions this night."

"Strange visions?" The old man looked at Gavin in surprise. "You speak like a wizard!"

"Like a wizard..." Gavin looked down and shook his head. "No, I'm no wizard. More likely I'm just bewitched."

"Bewitched? Whatever do you mean?"

Gavin did not answer. In his mind's eye he saw Dana. Beautiful, peaceful Dana...

"Who has bewitched you?" the old man asked again. "A woman?"

For the first time, Gavin looked directly at the old man.

"Aha!" smiled the old man. "I can see I am near the mark. So we're talking of an enchantment of the more pleasant kind!"

"No." said Gavin shaking his head. "It's not what you think."

"Then what is it?"

Gavin took another swig. "It is foolish, absolute foolishness..."

"And yet it torments you and keeps you from sleeping."

Gavin looked at the old man again. His eyes were deep and black, deep and black like burning coals... Deep and black like Dana's eyes... Dana...

"How terrible can this secret of yours be?" said the old man. There was something almost hypnotic about his voice. Gavin suddenly felt very tired. But he knew that he would not be able to sleep unless...

"It is foolish, absolute foolishness through and through..." he mumbled.

Silence hung over the camp. Gavin looked up between the branches of the oak trees at the large golden star high above, shining as it did... forever and ever...

166

"I don't know how it happened..." Gavin wondered to hear himself speaking like this to a complete stranger. "I don't know how... but suddenly it was as if... as if a door inside me opened."

The old man looked at Gavin with new interest. "A door inside you?"

He waited for Gavin to continue, but Gavin fell silent again as if voicing his thoughts was too painful.

"What did you see on the other side of the door?" the old man asked slowly.

"Strange things, strange visions," replied Gavin almost whispering. "They keep haunting me, even now."

Again the camp was silent. All that could be heard was the sound of the fire cracking softly and the giant oaks swaying above them. The old man was quiet for a long time as if he was pondering Gavin's words.

After a time, he said, "If it can be of any comfort to you, my friend, you are not the only one who has been visited by such visions."

Gavin looked at him. "What would you know about that?"

"A great deal," he answered. "And I know that it can be a frightening experience for one who is untrained... to suddenly experience the Sight."

"The Sight?"

"Yes. It is obvious that the strange visions you speak of are the first stirrings of the Sight in you."

Gavin did not reply.

The old man continued kindly, "The Sight must be strong in you, my friend, if you can experience the other realms like this without any form of training."

"The other realms?"

The old man nodded and made a slight circular movement with his wrinkled hand over the flames. For a moment it seemed to Gavin that he again saw dancing figures in the flames. Dancing, white-robed priestesses...

"Yes," said the old man. "With the Sight you can see into the other realms. Just like the priestesses and druids on the holy isle of Avalon do."

"Avalon?" Gavin looked up in surprise when the old man spoke the name of the fabled island. Dana had been a priestess on Avalon. Dana... Avalon. Gavin felt the strong tingling sensation again, this time surging up his spine to the point between his brows.

The old man moved closer to Gavin and studied his face and his eyes. "Yes, my friend," he said. "It is obvious that the Sight is very strong in you."

Gavin looked away from him and stared into the fire.

The old man kept looking at him intensely. "Tell me, who are you, a man with the Sight, among such fell warriors?"

Gavin did not reply. The pulsating sensation between his brows continued.

The silence around the campfire was so thick it could be cut with a knife. When Gavin didn't answer, the old man tried another line of questioning. "At least tell me where your home is. Are you from the Summer Country?"

Gavin took a sip from the wine pouch. "The Summer Country? No, no."

"Where are you from then?"

Gavin wiped his mouth. "I come from Orkney."

"Orkney? That is indeed far from here."

Gavin smiled to himself. Suddenly it seemed to him that he saw the great bare cliffs of Orkney, where he had played as a child, dancing in the flames.

"And what may I ask, brings you to the Summer Country?" asked the old man.

Gavin was silent for a while as the memories of his childhood danced in the flames.

"I was sent here," said Gavin, handing the wine pouch to the old man.

"Sent here? By whom? By your parents?"

Gavin shrugged. "In a manner of speaking."

The old man drank deeply once again. "Who are your parents?" he said, wiping his mouth.

Again, Gavin smiled to himself. In his mind's eye, he could see himself as a boy, running wild along the cliffs while Ellyn and Garulf admonished him to be careful. That was until that fateful day when...

Yes.

That is a good question.

Who were my parents?

"My parents were fishermen."

"Fishermen?" The old man handed him back the wine pouch. "You look like a nobleman."

"Garulf and Ellyn were my parents for the first 12 years of my life only."

"Really... for the first 12 years only? That is strange... why was that? What happened to them? Did they die?"

"No, they didn't die," shrugged Gavin thinking it could do no harm to tell this old man about his origins.

"Then why were they only your parents for the first 12 years of your life?"

"When I was 12 years old King Lot and Queen Morgause's men came and took me to their castle," he said, matter-of-factly.

"Really?" said the old man, obviously startled by the revelation. "Did you say Queen Morgause?"

"Yes," said Gavin. "Morgause, wife of King Lot. Do you know of her?"

For a moment the old man looked intensely at Gavin. Then he turned his gaze to the flames. "Yes, I know her all too well..."

Now it was Gavin's turn to be curious. How could this old man know Queen Morgause of Orkney?

But he had no time to ask because the old man continued, "Why did Lot and Morgause's soldiers take you to their castle?"

"Because I was to be raised there."

"Really? But why?"

In his mind's eye, Gavin now saw himself and the royal couple's rowdy sons romping playfully in one of their many contests....

Yes, that's another thing I've wondered about all my life.

Why did they bring me to the castle to raise me?

Why did my whole life change like that in the twinkling of an eye?

What is the answer to the riddle of that fateful day?

Gavin shook his head and sighed. "I don't know."

"You don't know?"

"No I really don't."

Both Gavin and the old man were silent. There was a change in the air as the stars began to fade and the dawn of a new day was fast approaching.

But Gavin heeded not the change of air, nor the flames, which sprang to new life as the old man added more branches to the fire. To Gavin, his surroundings seemed to fade and became more and more distant.

More and more distant.

Until there was nothing but...

... a song.

Fair words to a fair, gentle melody... Fair words calling... calling Gavin from far, far away...

Who will solve the riddle?
Who will tell the tale?
Who will ride on after us?
After we set sail?

169

Who will know the magic sign?
Who will find the gate?
Who will wake up to their fate,
Before it is too late?

I knew you when the mystery was still untold
I knew you in your younger days, before you grew old
I knew you in your sunny days, the days of wine and mirth
I knew you in the summertime, way before your birth

The old man's voice and words... and the melody... all of it seemed to lull Gavin, whose head moved closer and closer to the flames... as if by leaning closer to the flames he would be able to hear each word of the song more clearly and see the images, which now unfolded before his eyes even more clearly...

Who will solve the riddle?
Who will tell the tale?
Who will ride on after us?
After we set sail?

Who will know the magic sign?
Who will find the gate?
Who will wake up to their fate,
Before it is too late?

I knew you when the world was young and meadows still were fair
I knew you when you hid the secret in your golden hair
I knew you in your younger days, the days of silver song
I knew you, yes I knew you, before the days grew long

Gavin was now so close to the flames... so close to the images, at once strange and familiar that seemed to dance and unfold in the flames...

Who will solve the riddle?
Who will tell the tale?
Who will ride on after us?
After we set sail?

Who will know the magic sign?
Who will find the gate?
Who will wake up to their fate,
Before it is too late?

The old man stopped singing. Gavin kept on staring at the flames as if enchanted. He didn't seem to see or hear the old man moving closer to him. Gavin paid him no heed until the old man said, "What do you see in the flames, my friend?"

When Gavin didn't reply, the old man repeated his question. "What do you see in the flames?"

Gavin opened his mouth slowly. "I see... I see... strange visions..." He thought his voice also sounded distant, as if it came from far away.

"What do you see?"

"I see... I see... mountains..."

"Mountains?"

"Yes..."

"What more do you see?"

Gavin squinted. It was difficult to see anything but the mountains...

"What do you see besides the mountains?" the old man asked again, this time more firmly, as if giving a direct command..

"I see..." said Gavin opening his mouth again slowly, "I see... hills..."

"Hills?"

"Yes... and a little cottage... it's more like a stone hut... It is night... It is cold..."

"Yes? What else?"

Again Gavin was silent.

"What more do you see?" the old man was persistent. "What do you see inside the stone hut?"

Gavin frowned, his head moved closer to the flames, closer to the stone hut...

"Inside the hut..." he whispered, "there lies a woman."

"A woman?"

"Yes... a beautiful woman... with long, blond hair..." At the sight of the woman Gavin felt a sudden warmth in his chest.

"What more?" the old man asked. Suddenly his voice was very close, very eager. "What more do you see?"

"I see... two babes... two newborn babes... lying in the woman's arms..."

"Two newborn babies?"

"Yes..." Gavin smiled. "They must be twins..."

"Twins! Holy Mother Goddess!"

The old man leapt to his feet.

His sudden outburst made Gavin snap out of the trance. The vision was gone.

"Twins!" cried the old man again, almost prancing now.

Gavin felt a pair of strong hands on his shoulders. The old man was standing right behind him. His hands were trembling.

"Twins!" the old man laughed. "Ha ha! But of course, of course! What a fool I have been!"

Gavin freed himself from the old man's surprisingly strong grip and got up. He turned towards the old man.

"What are you talking about?"

"Twins!" the old man laughed again. "But of course! That is why the Sight is so strong in you! That is why Queen Morgause adopted you when you were 12 years old!"

"What are you talking about?"

Again the old man placed his hands on Gavin's shoulders in excitement.

"My dear friend, for more than 30 years I have been looking for you all over Britain!"

Gavin again removed the old man's hands.

"I have no idea what you are talking about!"

"My dear friend, this is nothing less than a miracle! And to think that you and I should meet like this! And tonight of all nights! It cannot be a coincidence! Indeed the Goddess is great!"

Gavin shook his head.

The old man must be crazy.

I should have never let him into our camp.

When the old man saw Gavin shaking his head in disgust, he raised his hand in protest and said, "My friend, I know that this may be hard for you to understand, but you must trust the Sight and what it tells you. The reason why Morgause took you to her castle was because Garulf and Ellyn were not your real parents!"

"You don't need to be a magician to figure that one out," said Gavin in irritation. The old man's words made him remember how people had whispered about his true origin all those many years. It was no secret that many believed Gavin to be yet another of Morgause's bastard children. Perhaps she had conveniently placed him with the poor fisher couple for a few years to avoid the wrath of her husband.

The old man shook his head as if reading Gavin's thoughts. "Morgause is not your real mother either, my friend!"

Gavin clutched the hilt of his sword.

Again the old man raised his hand. "The woman that you saw in the flames a moment ago was your real mother! Her name was Luned and she was a priestess of Avalon!"

Gavin let go of his sword.

"A priestess of Avalon?"

"Yes! She had the Sight, just like you do!"

The old man made a circular movement with his one hand and then, before Gavin had a chance to react, he pressed two fingers directly on the point between Gavin's brows. The moment the old man's fingers touched his forehead there was a great flash of light in his head. It only lasted a split second, but for Gavin, it seemed to last a very long time because in that flash of light, he saw the first years of his life from his conception and birth to his abduction and his childhood in Orkney. It was as if the first years of his life, which had always been hidden by a veil, were now revealed to him by the old man's touch.

"You see, my friend," the old man said in a kindly voice. "Your mother was Luned, priestess of Avalon—and you were one of the two babes you saw lying in Luned's arms before."

As the powerful visions faded, Gavin reeled backwards.

"I apologize for the intense activation of the Sight, my friend," said the old man, "but it was necessary that you see."

Gavin groaned and held his head.

"But even without the Sight," continued the old man, "I know what you saw is true because I myself was there. You see I came to the cottage where Luned lay but a few hours after Morgause had ridden off with you!"

Gavin continued to hold his head as if he was in great pain. Somehow, even though the visions had gone, Gavin knew, with a deep inner knowingness that what the old man had shown him was the true...

"Rode off with me?" Gavin stammered.

"Yes," he said. "You see my friend, it was vitally important for Morgause to separate you from your twin sister immediately because she knew that the two of you are the two souls spoken of in the Prophecy of Starwarrior!"

"The prophecy...? What prophecy?"

"What prophecy!" The old man clapped his hands together in delight. *"The Prophecy of Starwarrior!"* he laughed. Then he began pacing back and forth in front of the fire, speaking half to himself and half to Gavin.

"The Prophecy of Starwarrior... I remember it as clear as yesterday...

> *When the One with the Sight*
> *is reunited with the Warrior from the Stars*
> *the Perfect Being will be born*
> *From the Perfect Being*
> *will come the Single Eye*
>
> *From the Single Eye*
> *will come the Perfect World*
>
> *And then the Angels sing"*

Gavin looked at the old man in wonder, not understanding a word of what he was saying.

The old man stopped and walked solemnly over to Gavin. He pounded the ground twice with his staff. *"You see my friend, you are one of the two souls spoken of in the Prophecy of Starwarrior!"*

Gavin shook his head.

He must be mad... he must be mad...

The old man continued excitedly. *"According to the Prophecy, two great souls—the One with the Sight and the Warrior from the Stars—would one day be born here in Britain. And the prophecy tells that when these two great souls work together in harmony, they will open the door to the Lost Teaching of the Single Eye."*

Gavin turned away from the old man and stared at the world around him. Everything was as before. All his men were still sleeping—none of them had even noticed the approach of the old man and his sudden outburst of wild enthusiasm and excitement.

Maybe this is only a dream.

"... according to the oldest legends in Britain, the Lost Teaching of the Single Eye can drastically raise the collective consciousness of all humankind," continued the old man solemnly, *"and thus create peace and harmony in Britain. And God knows my dearest of friends that we need peace and harmony now more than ever before. It is indeed a blessing from the Great Mother that I found you tonight of all nights!"*

174

The old man placed his hand on Gavin's shoulder. "You must understand my friend, you are one of the two great souls spoken of in the Prophecy. Your real parents are Luned and Cydwir. And your twin sister is Dana, a priestess of Avalon!"

Gavin leapt back in terror and grabbed the hilt of his sword.

"Dana?" he cried.

"Yes," the old man nodded. "Dana, priestess of Avalon. The Sight is very strong in her too, just as it is in you. She is your twin sister!"

"My twin sister?"

"Yes."

The strange tingling between Gavin's brows grew stronger, stronger than it had ever been before. He looked frantically back and forth from the smoldering flames to the old man's deep, coal black eyes. But no matter where he looked, he saw the same thing—the same vision. The same vision of an icy cold stone cottage and a beautiful young woman drawing her last breath... as the red-haired baby was taken from her side...

Dana, with the beautiful red hair...

Dana, with the deep, penetrating eyes...

Dana, his beloved twin sister...

"You see," the old man smiled. "The Sight is as strong in you as it is in your twin sister Dana."

"My twin sister..."

"Yes. Do you know her?" asked the old man in sudden wonder.

Gavin let out a huge groan and buried his head in his hands—desperate to shut out the visions. But it was useless. With eyes open or closed, all he could see was himself driving his sword through Dana's heart. Driving his sword... driving his sword... right into...

Dana, with that beautiful, peaceful expression on her face... with that expression of infinite sweetness...

Dana, his twin sister...

Gavin was shaking uncontrollably.

The old man did not seem to notice. Instead, he put his hand on Gavin's shoulder and said. "It is no coincidence that I met you here tonight, my friend, of that I am now sure! As fate would have it, I am on my way to Avalon to meet your twin sister this very day. You must come with me."

Gavin raised his trembling hands. So tightly had he been gripping his sword, that one of his hands was completely covered in blood. He must have gripped the blade instead of the hilt in his panic. Now blood gushed from his hand.

Or was it Dana's blood?

Blood from Dana's heart, from when his sword had mortally wounded her...

My own sister's blood.

My own blood.

So exalted was the old man, that he did not notice Gavin's bloody hand or his violent trembling, instead he patted him on the back and continued, "It will be a wonderful reunion when we come to Avalon... a wonderful reunion, my friend."

Gavin took the blade of his sword in the other hand and squeezed it so blood now gushed from the other hand as well.

Blood, all is blood. Dana's blood. My own blood.

"No..." cried Gavin, "no!".

"But why not, my friend?" cried the old man in surprise. "It is your divine destiny—yours and Dana's. The two of you have been born to do great things. And when you work together in harmony, you will open the door to the Lost Teaching of the Single Eye. The Single Eye that can raise the collective consciousness of all humanity and bring peace and harmony to Britain and all the world!"

Gavin kept clenching the blade tightly.

"No..." cried Gavin again.

"But my friend, why not? I know with the Sight you can see that what I say is true..."

"No..." Gavin let out a great cry that echoed through the forest.

So great was his cry that Gavin's sleepy men arose and leapt to their feet in surprise, grabbing their weapons. Not knowing what was happening, they ran towards Merlin and surrounded him.

But it was too late.

Gavin had already fled with a great cry... deep into the dark forest...

"That is enough for now..." said the Keeper of the Cosmic Library. "You have seen enough of Gavin's story. Now return to this room."

The moment the Keeper spoke these words, I felt myself being pulled out of Gavin's body and his consciousness. Gavin and the dark forest began to fade.

"Return to the room," said the Keeper again. "Return to the chair you are sitting in."

Gavin and his story faded into the distance. The last thing I saw in my mind's eye was Gavin running through the dark woods with a sword covered in blood in his bloody hands...

"Slowly open your eyes," said the Keeper.

The vision was gone and I was again aware of my breathing, the beat of my heart, and my body in the alpha chair in the Pyramid of Time.

Slowly I opened my eyes.

The Keeper of the Cosmic Library was standing in front of me; Ticha was at his side, emitting a faint golden glow.

I didn't move or say anything. I just kept staring straight ahead, right past the Keeper and Ticha, at the golden stones that were part of the walls of the pyramid.

The minutes ticked by. My two guides remained motionless before me—not moving or speaking.

I paid them no heed. Instead, I got up and walked right past them out of the Cosmic Library without looking back.

I was sitting with my back to one of the great trees in the Relaxation Forest, watching a lively brook make its way through the forest. The clear water swirled and danced over the shimmering stones as it made its merry way through the lush forest. I remembered how Jacob and Janus and I had passed by this stream many days ago, the first time we were led to the Cosmic Library, to view our past life in England.

Our past life in England...

And now I realized, that life was not, after all, exactly what I had thought it was.

Nor was Lord Gavin, Agent Nevis, after all, exactly what I had thought he was either. Nothing it seemed in my past was exactly what I thought it was.

And what about the present, my present? What about all the things that had happened in the last couple of days? What about now?

I sat there wondering just how many other things I might have misjudged during the last days and weeks...

What else had I misunderstood...?

I got up and walked along the brook, following the stream as it turned to the left. Above the treetops, the sky had that incredible blueness that only the sky in the Relaxation Forest can have. And like everything else in the forest, the sight of the sky filled me with a deep sense of peace.

But I did not stop to enjoy the blueness of the sky. Instead I continued walking while in my mind, I went through the events of the last hours and days again and again. From great heights I had fallen far during the last terrible days. What was really going on—in the past and right now? And how would the things I'd just seen in the Cosmic Library influence what I was going to do now?

After a while, I sat down again with my back to another tree and watched the babbling brook.

There was no doubt in my mind as to what Jacob and Janus—and even Elmar and Rebecca—would want me to do. But they were all gone, in some other dimension now, and I was here alone. All alone at the end of the world.

My thoughts thundered back and forth—and the hours passed. I knew if I'd been on Earth, the sun would soon be setting.

But here it didn't.

Instead a golden figure appeared at my side.

"We might be in the higher dimensions," said Ticha, "but that doesn't mean that time isn't still moving swiftly down on Earth. Have you decided what you're going to do?"

I nodded. "I want to talk to Ashtar."

14

The Big View

Commander Ashtar's private briefing room looked remarkably like the great hall where the 600 volunteers met Ashtar, Sananda, and the other Star People just a few short days ago. Even though to me it felt like several lifetimes ago. Ashtar's briefing room, like the great hall, had a very harmonious shape and smooth, silvery etheric walls. The only furniture in the room was a long, ellipse-shaped table that seemed to grow right out of the floor. Around the table were 12 pea-pod-shaped armchairs like the ones I'd seen in the great hall of the Mothership and in the Cosmic Library. On one side of the room, there was a huge window with a magnificent view of the starry heavens. Close by floated my home, blue-white Planet Earth.

But I had no time for the breathtaking view; all my attention was focused on Ashtar.

The Commander of the Intergalactic Fleet sat at the end of the long table, his body surrounded by a strong white light. I stood at the other end of the long table, my eyes fixed on him.

"The Ashtar Command must not cancel STARDAY," I said as firmly as I could.

"We have not cancelled STARDAY," I heard Ashtar's voice saying inside me.

"But why then are your starships gone?"

"They are not gone."

"What do you mean?"

"The starships are still hovering above all Earth's major cities and capitals."

"I don't understand. According to the news..."

"But even though the starships are still in place above all the Earth's cities, it doesn't necessarily mean that the human beings on Earth can see them."

I looked at the Commander questioningly. "What do you mean?"

"Because of the destruction of Earth's mightiest Power Spots and the resulting deactivation of the Light Grid, the level of humanity's consciousness and its vibrational frequency has fallen drastically. That is why human beings can no longer see the starships. The vibrational frequency on Earth has quite simply fallen so low that human beings can no longer see the starships because they are operating on a much higher vibrational frequency."

"So the starships are still floating above all the Earth's cities—it is just we people who can't see them?"

"Precisely."

"And that's because our consciousness has fallen so drastically that we are unable to perceive the starships because they are on a higher frequency?"

"Precisely."

"So what will happen on STARDAY—on Friday?"

"There won't be a STARDAY."

"But didn't you just say that you haven't cancelled STARDAY?"

"We haven't. The starships are still there. And they will remain there until Friday. But because the collective consciousness of humanity is so low, the inhabitants of Earth won't be able to see the starships or experience STARDAY. So in fact, it is humanity itself who has cancelled STARDAY."

"But it's not everyone on Earth who is afraid or feeling hostile towards you," I objected. "There are millions of people who are welcoming you, millions of people who now have new hope thanks to the New Vision and the promise of STARDAY."

"I know, my friend. But there is nothing I can do about that. All this is a matter of Universal Law. As long as the collective consciousness of humanity is as low as it is, humans will not be able to experience STARDAY."

"But so many good things have also happened since we anchored the New Vision and you announced STARDAY. You have no idea how many great global group meditations there have been—with millions of people working together to lift the collective consciousness. More and more people on Earth are truly waking up and remembering who they are. My grandfather's lifelong companion, Rebecca Randall, who has worked with ascension almost all her life, says that a great consciousness revolution is really taking place on Earth right now."

Ashtar rose from his chair and walked over to the huge window. Three large golden pyramids were on their way to the Mothership from Planet Earth.

"I know that there have been many wonderful developments," the Commander said, "and I am truly glad to see them. But I still cannot change the Natural Laws of the Universe. As long as humanity's collective consciousness is as low as it is, human beings will not be able to experience the starships or STARDAY."

"But then what will the starships do on STARDAY—on Friday?"

"They will return to the Intergalactic Fleet and await the day when the collective consciousness of humanity is again high enough for human beings to experience a STARDAY."

"And when will that be?"

"I cannot say. It depends on humanity and what it does. Remember what you have learned—the Intergalactic Fleet may not interfere with the evolution of souls. We are here to guide and inspire, not to do the work for humanity."

"So you're just going to abandon the sinking ship at the very last moment?" I said indignantly. "And fly off to safety in the higher dimensions, while humanity perishes in the collective panic and chaos caused by all the Earth changes!"

Ashtar turned towards me, "Things are not always quite the way they look."

"Maybe not," I continued hotly, pointing at the Earth, "but it sure looks like the end of the world down there! Hundreds of thousands of people are dying, nothing is working, whole cities have been eradicated, millions of people are homeless..."

"You are only taking a very short view of things, my young friend."

"But Commander, if only you could see what's going on..."

"I can," replied Ashtar calmly. "It's you who cannot. As I said, you are only looking at the short-term perspective. If you could see the big view—the long-term perspective—you would see there is a higher purpose to what may appear to be total chaos."

"What higher purpose can there be to so much destruction?"

"The end of the old world is necessary to make way for the beginning of the new world," the Commander answered. "The end of the old age is necessary before a new age can begin. In the larger perspective, all souls live forever. The only things that are really being destroyed at this time are all the old limiting structures and fear-based thought patterns that are keeping humanity in bondage. All this apparent destruction is making way for the new to be born."

I turned to the window. The three pyramids were now close to the Mothership and were preparing to land on a landing site off to my left. In the distance, I could see more starships leaving the Earth's atmosphere.

"How long will it be before humanity's collective consciousness is again high enough to release a STARDAY?" I asked.

"In Earth time? Probably several centuries."

"Several centuries?"

Ashtar nodded.

"Several centuries? But didn't you just say that the end of the old world was making way for the beginning of the new?"

"Yes, and so it is. But this transition is not usually something that happens overnight. Mother Earth is ascending into the higher dimensions and She will continue to do so. Human beings will also gradually ascend into the higher dimensions, first the most spiritually aware, then the next level of beings, until all of humanity eventually does the same."

"And this ascension will take several centuries?"

"Yes probably."

"But is there time enough for this, if Mother Earth is about to ascend into the higher dimensions right now?"

"Probably not."

"Probably not? What do you mean?" I looked sharply at the Commander, trying to decipher his cool. "What will happen then? Will there be another axis shift as Mother Earth tries to ascend?"

"Probably."

"Oh my God…When?"

"No one knows. It might be in two years time it might be in twenty. It all depends on the collective consciousness of humanity."

I turned away from the window and began pacing back and forth in the room.

"I can't believe this! After all that we've been through, establishing the Light Grid, anchoring the New Vision in humanity's collective consciousness—and now we're right back where we started!"

"I think you are taking it all far too seriously, my friend. Remember that the soul is immortal and that the limiting beliefs that are causing the majority of humans so much pain have no substance at all in reality. It's all just an evil dream that most humans are dreaming at the moment. Sooner or later, all beings are destined to awaken and remember their true nature."

182

"Sooner or later! In several centuries you mean! Unless we're totally wiped out by an axis shift!"

Ashtar came back from the window and sat down at the end of the table. "I am sorry, my friend, but that is the way the Universe works. The level of consciousness is always equal, identical and interchangeable with the vibrational frequency. And it is one's vibrational frequency that determines one's experiences, be it on a personal or a planetary level."

"But what if humanity lifts its collective consciousness by Friday?"

"Then humans on Earth will again be able to see the starships and the ships will land on STARDAY just as originally planned. And with STARDAY on Earth, Mother Earth will quickly and effortlessly continue her ascension into the 5th dimension together with all humankind."

"And there will no longer be any risk of an axis shift?"

"No."

"Then that's it," I said, "that's what I must do. I must lift the collective consciousness before Friday so that we can have STARDAY on Earth."

"That is a noble thought, my friend," said Ashtar with a smile. "And I do not doubt that you mean it with all your heart. But to lift the entire collective consciousness of humanity single-handedly to quantum level 5 in just four days, I am afraid that is beyond your power."

"Why?"

"You are forgetting everything you learned about the nature of consciousness. In order to lift the collective consciousness to quantum level 5, you need a critical mass of enlightened human beings on Earth. That means 1% of the Earth's entire population must raise its consciousness drastically. And as you know, this translates into 60 million human beings."

"We did it before with the New Vision, why can't we do it again now?"

"Because when you did it before, the New Vision was amplified and increased 600 times by the volunteers and then another 100,000 times by using the Light Grid. But the greater part of the 600 volunteers are no longer on the Earth Plane and the Light Grid has been destroyed."

"But there's got to be another way to create a critical mass!"

"If there is another way, it is not known to me."

"I can't believe you don't know any other way!" I said hotly. "You're the Commander of the Intergalactic Fleet, you visit galaxies and dimensions as easily as people on Earth drive their car from one city to another—and yet you are telling me you've never heard of any other way—not in any other galaxy—of raising the collective consciousness of a planet! I don't believe it!"

Ashtar raised his eyebrows, somewhat surprised at my sudden outburst.

"There's got to be another way, Ashtar! There's got to be!"

Our eyes met. Ashtar's gaze was as powerful and as intense as ever, but I didn't flinch.

The Commander rotated slightly in his chair and surveyed the shining starry sky outside the window once again.

"You won't find this officially registered anywhere, but if you really want to know I have actually heard rumors that three souls, known as the Three E Masters, once lifted the entire collective consciousness in the Umtarion-system in just a few hours—without the use of either a positive New Vision or a planetary light grid."

"The Three E Masters?"

"Yes."

"In the Umtarion-system? Where is that?"

"In a galaxy far from the Milky Way Galaxy," Ashtar replied. "Hundreds of thousands of years ago, the Umtarion-system was a 3rd and 4th dimensional planetary Test Zone where the level of development resembled Planet Earth's in many ways. The collective consciousness of the souls there was catastrophically low. Because of this low collective consciousness, a devastating disaster threatened to completely destroy the planet and wipe out all life on it in just a few days. But according to the rumors, the Three E Masters managed—in just a few hours—to create a critical mass of enlightened souls, thus lifting the collective consciousness high enough to avert the catastrophe."

"In just a few hours? How did they do it?"

The Commander pressed the tips of his fingers together and looked at me thoughtfully.

"According to one of my closest advisors, they used a method described in the Lost Teaching of the Single Eye."

"The Lost Teaching of the Single Eye? What is that?"

"No one knows for sure and there are quite a few theories about the matter. Some say the teaching allows you to skip several steps in the evolution of both personal and planetary consciousness—in other words the teaching triggers a kind of 'hyper-enlightenment' one could say."

Hyper-enlightenment? The Lost Teaching of the Single Eye? Where had I heard this before...

"Other theories maintain it 'kick starts' the evolution of consciousness—again some type of 'hyper-enlightenment'," continued Ashtar. "One colleague even says it can be dangerous—not so much to the collective consciousness—but to the souls who experience this hyper-

184

enlightenment because the leap from their current level of consciousness to the Single Eye can be so intense and drastic..."

"Ashtar! That's it!" I cried, jumping forward.

"That's what?"

"The Lost Teaching of the Single Eye!"

"What about it?"

"I can access the Lost Teaching of the Single Eye!"

"I'm sorry, my friend, but after the Three E Masters lifted the collective consciousness in the Umtarion-system they vanished without a trace and no one has ever seen or heard anything about them or their Teaching since."

"But I have!"

The Commander looked at me in surprise. "What are you talking about?"

"I've heard about the Lost Teaching of the Single Eye!"

"What do you mean?"

"The Prophecy of Starwarrior!"

"Starwarrior? What is that?"

Barely able to contain myself, I blurted it all out. "1,500 years ago, in my past life in Britain—when we, the volunteers, were given our mission to anchor the New Vision in the collective consciousness—the wizard Merlin made a prophecy. And according to this prophecy—the Prophecy of Starwarrior—two souls would one day be born in Britain at the same time... and if these two souls learned to work together in harmony, they would be able to access the Lost Teaching of the Single Eye!"

"Did Merlin really say that?" Ashtar looked even more surprised. "He never told me that."

"Well it's the truth and now I understand why Ticha—my guardian angel—wanted me to see my past life again! Oh thank you, Ticha!" I cried and began dancing around the room.

Ashtar looked at me as if I'd completely lost it.

I walked back over to the Commander again and continued eagerly. "You must understand Ashtar—one of these two souls was me! The other soul was my twin brother Gavin..."

I stopped up short.

In my excitement I'd momentarily forgotten all I'd learned about Gavin's tragic story.

"And?" said Ashtar. "During that life, did you access the Lost Teaching of the Single Eye?"

"No."

"Why not?"

"Because…" I looked away and said slowly as it began to dawn on me what I was actually going to say, "my twin brother killed me."

"Your own twin brother killed you?"

"Yes."

"Why?"

"Well... that's a long story." I looked intensely at the Commander. "But Ashtar I know who my twin brother is in this lifetime. He's the head of the CIA agents who destroyed the Light Grid. If only I could find him and make him understand… if only the two of us could work together in harmony… then we could access the Lost Teaching of the Single Eye and lift the collective consciousness enough for STARDAY to take place and not to be cancelled!"

"Just hold it right there," said Ashtar. "Didn't you just tell me that your twin brother killed you in your past life?"

"Yes."

"But if your twin brother killed you in a past life and in this life has already destroyed the Light Grid, what on Earth makes you think that you can get him to change his mind by telling him this?"

I didn't answer.

"You have to admit that it sounds a bit farfetched."

I walked back to the window well aware that Ashtar was studying me from the other end of the room. Neither of us spoke.

The minutes ticked by. Then Ashtar got up and walked over to my side and said, "The real reason I asked you to come to this meeting was to tell you that your mission on Earth is now over."

"What's that supposed to mean?"

"As I said before, it will most likely take many years—perhaps even centuries—until the collective consciousness of humanity is once again high enough to release a STARDAY. But you are not required to stay on the Earth-plane until this happens. You have done your duty and now you can stay here in the Mothership until the starships return in four days. After that, the Fleet's personnel will be reorganized. Some will remain in orbit around Earth, while others will be stationed elsewhere, and yet others will go home. The same goes for you. You have many choices. You may stay here for a while or return to your home planet if you wish. Or travel through the galaxies and dimensions, if you so desire."

I didn't say anything.

Ashtar put his hand on my shoulder.

186

"Your mission on Earth is now over. You have done everything you could and more."

I didn't respond. I just kept staring out of the window. More starships were returning to the Mothership from Earth.

They're coming back already I thought.

Returning from their mission.

Their mission, which is now over.

Just like mine.

Then I thought about Jacob, Janus, Elmar, Rebecca, all my brave companions and dearest friends, who lifetime after lifetime had given everything they had to spread peace and enlightenment on Earth.

They'd given everything to bring us to this very day.

This very day... and Ashtar was telling me I could quit and go home.

I clenched my fists.

"No," I said.

"What do you mean… no?"

"I mean no! I'm going back to Earth, Ashtar. If there's just the slightest chance that I can lift the collective consciousness enough for STARDAY to happen, I must go back and try."

"But Starbrow, the chances that you will succeed are virtually nil."

"I don't care. I'm going back, I have to."

There was a long pause.

Then Ashtar said, "I must tell you Starbrow that if you go back, this time you will be on your own. The Ashtar Command and the Ascended Masters will not be able to help you because we are not allowed to interfere. Your guardian angel is not allowed to interfere. If you are captured by the army or the CIA, you will probably end up spending the rest of your days in a high-security prison with no chance of escape—or you might even be executed."

"It doesn't matter, " I said. "All my friends are dead anyway."

"I am not sure you understand my young friend. It won't be like before. There will be no special dispensation this time. Even if we would like to, we will not be able to help you. You will literally be completely on your own."

"I don't care. I'm going back."

"My friend, this decision I think is..."

"I'm going back, Ashtar. You can't change my mind."

The Commander of the Intergalactic Fleet looked at me with his kind, grave eyes.

Then he looked at the Earth floating in space and turned back to the room, making a circular movement with his hand.

"Monka," he said into thin air. "How much does humanity's collective consciousness and vibrational frequency need to be lifted in order for STARDAY not to be cancelled?"

A voice replied inside my head though I couldn't see Monka anywhere, "At present the collective consciousness is fluctuating between quantum level 4.0 and 4.1, Commander."

"So you're saying almost an entire dimensional frequency?"

"Almost, yes."

"And how long is it precisely until STARDAY?"

"Exactly 4 days, 7 hours and 43 minutes in Earth Time."

"Thank you, Monka."

Again Ashtar made a circular movement with his hand. Then he turned back to me. "There you have it. Most of humanity is now fluctuating somewhere between quantum level 4.0 and 4.1. In order to reach quantum level 5 and release a STARDAY, we need a critical mass of enlightened human beings. In other words, 60 million people must wake up from the collective dream in 4 days."

"I'm going back, Ashtar."

Again there was silence in the briefing room.

Then Ashtar said, "What do you intend to do when you get back to Earth?"

"Find my former twin brother and tell him the truth. And use the Force. Isn't that what you've been telling us to do all along?"

A faint smile spread across Ashtar's lips.

"Yes, that is what we have been telling you to do," he said.

"I'm going back."

Ashtar kept on smiling. Then he turned towards Earth, floating peacefully on the horizon.

"I have supervised many planetary dimensional shifts in my time as a Commander. And I have to admit that none of them have been quite so problematic as Test Zone Earth. And rarely I must say, have I witnessed such courage and determination as yours. No matter how your adventure ends Starbrow, the Ashtar Command will not forget you."

I said nothing. Instead I just stared at that beautiful, mysterious blue-white planet I had called my home for so many lifetimes.

"Although I cannot help you once you have returned to Earth, I can do one last thing for you," said Ashtar. "I can transubstantiate you to any location on Earth you wish."

"Good," I said. "I want to be transubstantiated back to the exact same spot I came from."

"Back to the Crystal Cave? But the army will capture you immediately?"

"That's exactly what I want. No sense in wasting any more time."

Ashtar laughed. "You are not just stubborn, Starbrow, you're quite the daredevil too! But the Wise often say that desperate circumstances sometimes require desperate acts."

"There's no time to waste," I said taking a deep breath. "So let's do it."

The Commander of the Intergalactic Fleet raised his hand. Our eyes met briefly.

"The Force is with you."

"The Force is with you, Ashtar."

The Commander made a quick circular movement with his hand. Instantly I felt a tingling at the top of my head. It spread down throughout my body until my whole body was vibrating and pulsating.

Ashtar and the briefing room shimmered and turned to light. For a moment, I floated in a place outside of time and space.

The next moment I was under water.

A powerful wave slammed me into one of the rocky walls of the Crystal Cave. I felt a stab of pain in my left side as the icy waters of the Atlantic filled my nose and mouth. I struggled fiercely to reach the surface and came up just in time to be slammed into the cliff wall by a new wave. The power of the wave almost knocked me out, but I remained conscious. In the lull before the next wave, I caught a glimpse of the pale gray light coming from one of the openings into the Crystal Cave. I gasped for air and struggled to keep afloat. The Crystal Cave was almost completely under water now.

Another new wave was coming. I took a deep breath and dove underneath the wave and let the powerful tide take me. It pulled me towards the opening of the cave.

As the wave subsided, I surfaced again and swam with all my might towards the cave opening. Every time a wave came, I dove under and swam on until I finally reached the opening. I dove under again and let myself be pulled out into the open sea.

I gasped for air when I surfaced and was tossed about by the fierce waves in the cove by Tintagel Head. Now the rocky beach was completely gone and a cold wind was howling in from the west. Grey rain clouds were above. With my last strength, I headed towards the broken stone stairway in the side of the cliff that led down to the cove. I struggled

189

against the current and kept swimming towards the stone stairway. Several times, I was afraid the powerful waves would pound me to death on the great rocks that now protruded from the turbulent sea, but I kept my aim on the stairway.

With my last strength, I reached the stairway and pulled myself out of the water, collapsing on the cold stones and gasping for air. My body was numb with cold. I knew I had to move or die.

Then I realized that I was not alone on the cliffs.

About a mile away, two military helicopters were hovering in the air, their searchlights moving across the windswept cliffs, probably looking for me. Two more choppers were circling above the ruins of Tintagel Castle. On the island, men with dogs were searching the rocky slopes. About a mile from the coast, two coast guard ships were searching the choppy water with powerful searchlights.

Right above the cove, about 50 yards away from me, behind the two boarded up wooden houses, there were two military helicopters and some police cars. I recognized DETI Agents Sorvino and Jackson standing by one of the choppers, studying a map. Agents and soldiers were milling around. I guessed there were at least 30 of them—agents in civilian clothes, soldiers and police officers—the lot. Over by the other chopper, I recognized the hefty DETI Agent Hama working with a team of British agents pulling equipment out of the helicopter.

In the middle of all this stood Agent Nevis, talking on his phone. A long black bag was slung across his shoulder.

So far, no one noticed me.

I got up and walked up the stairs. The wind beat against me. I was completely soaked and freezing. My left arm throbbed where the wave had slammed me into the cliff wall. I reached the top of the stairs and made straight for Nevis who was standing with his back to me, talking on the phone.

I kept on walking.

Nevis finished his conversation and put his phone in his pocket. He was still standing with his back to me.

I wasn't more than ten yards away from him when the agents, soldiers and police officers all seemed to discover me at the same time.

"Stop!" cried one of the British agents.

"Major, watch out, he's right behind you!"

From every direction, guns and machine guns were whipped out. Agents and soldiers started running towards me. It was as if everyone realized at the very same moment that the man they were moving heaven and earth to find had actually walked right into their camp.

"Stop!"

"Don't move, stay right where you are!"

I took no notice of what they said but kept walking straight towards Nevis. I didn't take my eyes off him.

An agent and a British soldier were right in front of me.

"Stop!" cried the agent.

But I just kept walking towards Nevis.

The soldier moved as if he was about to slam his machine gun into my side, but my fierce determination seemed to paralyze him. I kept walking towards Nevis.

"Major! Watch out!"

Nevis turned around.

His face was blank. Obviously he had no idea what was going on.

"Greetings, Ben!" I said. "I have something important to tell..."

"Stop him!" cried Sorvino, looking around for men to answer his call.

My intent was so pure and my determination so strong that it seemed to clear the path before me, despite the fact that there were soldiers and agents everywhere.

Nevis didn't move. It was hard to tell whether he was surprised to see me or if he was merely waiting to see what I would do.

"I have something important to tell you, Ben..."

Suddenly I felt a sharp blow on the side of my head. For a moment everything went black and my legs gave way underneath me. It was Sorvino's pistol butt... I tasted my own blood.

I was on my knees in the grass.

"I have something important... to tell you... Ben..." I gasped.

Hands grabbed me from all sides and pressed my face to the ground. My hands were wrenched unto my back and I was handcuffed.

"No! I must... talk to Agent Nevis..."

"You're going to have plenty of time to do that where you're going, mister," snarled Sorvino. "Search him!"

I tried to get up, but they kept me pinned to the ground as they searched me. The side of my head throbbed painfully.

"So where have you been the last couple of hours?" Hama mumbled. "Trying to swim across the Atlantic Ocean?"

I tried to turn my head so I could see Nevis. He was standing right over me, looking down at me. He had cuts and burns on the side of his face just like Sorvino, Jackson and Hama had.

"He's clean Major," said Sorvino. "He's not carrying. Are we going back to headquarters?"

Nevis nodded. "Yes. Radio the other units and tell them we have him. Put him in helicopter 1. Contact General Hecht in Newquay and tell him we're on our way."

The agents pulled me to my feet and began dragging me towards one of the helicopters. I tried to turn towards Nevis.

"You must listen to what I have to say, Ben," I said.

"Don't worry, my friend," he said. "Soon you will tell me everything your heart desires. Before this day is over, I will know everything there possibly is to know about you and your adventures."

Nevis turned and yelled to his men. "Get him out of those wet clothes and into a thermo suit immediately. I don't want him dying on us now!"

The orders were carried out on the spot and then, dressed in a thermo suit, I was bundled off to the chopper, surrounded by agents on all sides.

In less than two minutes, the whole fleet of choppers had lifted off and was flying in close formation along the rocky coastline of Cornwall. Then the group turned as if with one movement and began flying south at great speed. I tried to turn my head and look back. The Crystal Cave and the ruins of Tintagel Castle already lay far behind us in the gathering dusk. I wondered how long it would be until I saw the green hills of England again.

PART TWO

12 STONES

1

Prisoner No. C22

I was all alone, in the deepest dungeon of the CIA.

All alone in Cell C22 in Cellblock C at the bottommost level of CIA headquarters in Langley, Virginia.

I was lying on a bed, a hard wooden plank, the only piece of furniture in the tiny cell, staring at the ceiling. There were no windows or openings of any kind in the cell.

A dim light from the ceiling lit up the room. There was a small camera in the corner.

So I'm not all that alone.

Since I had been transubstantiated back to Agent Nevis and DETI, the American agents hadn't let me out of their sight for as much as a nano-second. Agents Sorvino, Jackson, Hama, as well as a small army of British MI6 agents, soldiers and police, had surrounded me constantly, watching my every move, all the way from the ruins of Tintagel Castle to Northolt Royal Air Force Base outside of London. At the base, I was moved with great haste to the DETI agents' own Special Task Force Carrier plane, which flew us all the way to the United States, more precisely to Andrews Air Force Base outside Washington DC. From there a short, heavily guarded chopper ride took me directly to CIA headquarters in Langley, where an impressive contingency of agents led me through several retinal scans, meter-thick metal doors, voice identifications and laser fences, only to lock me up here, in Cell no. C22.

Surprisingly enough, the only person who had not monitored my every move was Nevis—the one person I wanted to talk to. After the agents took me into custody at Tintagel, Nevis spent most of his time talking on the phone giving orders. And I almost didn't see him at all on the Special Task Force Carrier. If I hadn't known better, I could almost have believed he was trying to avoid me. But he'd promised me back in Tintagel that I'd get to tell him everything… *everything*… before the day was over.

If that was true, what was he waiting for?

I looked up at the silent camera in the corner. Was he sitting somewhere in some high-tech observation room studying me?

I closed my eyes. There was no sense thinking about it. As long as I couldn't talk to Nevis face to face, my only job was to think about something else, something completely different...

... to think about the Force.

With all the determination of a warrior.

So I did. I focused all my attention on the Force.

Stronger than electricity.

More powerful than nuclear energy.

Mightier than the sun.

My invisible but omnipresent ally.

Ever since the DETI agents' Special Task Force Carrier left England, I had used all my time focusing on, meditating on, and thinking about the Force.

The most powerful ally in the Universe.

With my eyes closed, I meditated on my breath throughout the flight until I began to feel the Presence, the Power, the Deep Peace, that was my true nature, that was everyone's true nature. Even when my eyes were open, I kept my mind focused on the Infinite, Eternal and Immortal Presence that was the Source of All Life and the Intelligence behind All the Universes and All the Dimensions.

Minute by minute, hour by hour, no matter what passed before me... be it straight-faced soldiers, intense-looking agents, storm-ridden landscapes, flooded roads and highways, landscapes darkened by the lack of electricity... whatever it was... I kept my focus on the Force... thinking about It and meditating on It.

Wrapped in thermal blankets, wearing a thermal suit after my icy swim in the Atlantic, my head throbbing where Sorvino hit me with the butt of his gun, guarded and pushed around by silent agents, I made myself shut out all physical and mental distractions. I kept telling myself I was a warrior now—a warrior of spirit—and that my only task was to focus on the Force.

Only once during the whole trip to America did I lose my focus on the Force. It happened when we were nearly halfway across the Atlantic. I had fallen into an uneasy sleep, but even in sleep, I was grimly determined to keep my focus on the Force. Then suddenly, that mysterious vision of the six shining figures standing on the shores of Planet Earth welled up from the depths of my being. The vision touched me so deeply that for a brief space of time it transported me into another realm... but the dream quickly past and the six shining figures on the windswept shore were gone... and I was once again surrounded by watchful agents. I sighed and directed my attention to the Force again.

At times it felt as if I was fighting a desperate battle to preserve the last shreds of my sanity, but I kept on, kept reminding myself to maintain the attitude of a warrior and so again and again I turned my attention back to the Force, back to my true nature, back to everyone's true nature.

Until there was nothing else in my mind.

Until...

I heard the electronic click of the cell door.

I sat up on the hard bed.

Two agents and four guards were standing in the doorway, motioning for me to follow them.

The agents silently led the way and the four guards walked behind me, down the long narrow hallways. After I had passed through a retinal scan, my escort took me to what looked like an interrogation room.

The room was lit by a long neon light on the ceiling. On one side of the room, there was a long dark glass wall. In the middle of the room, there was a table and chairs. One of the chairs was covered with leather padding and there were straps with buckles hanging from the armrests.

Next to the chair was a man in a white uniform who looked like a doctor. He was filling a syringe and tapping on it with his nail. Next to him was a metal trolley crammed with vials and syringes.

The man signaled to the guards to put me in the padded chair. They sat me down and began tightening the straps around my chest, waist, wrists, arms and legs.

"Hey!" I protested. "What do you think you're doing?"

Nobody paid any attention to me.

"Get your hands off me! I've come to talk with Ben Nevis!"

The guards finished buckling me up so it was impossible for me to move.

"You'll get a chance to talk to Agent Nevis in a moment," said one of the agents and then they left the room.

I turned and looked at the long dark glass wall because I had the feeling that someone on the other side was watching me.

Was it Ben Nevis? Why wouldn't he talk to me?

The man in the white uniform pulled up a chair and sat down next to his trolley, apparently finished with whatever he was doing.

I was just about to close my eyes and focus on the Force, when two men entered the room. One of them was Agent Nevis. The other was a heavy-set man who was gray and balding. Like Nevis, he too was dressed in civilian clothes.

Nevis closed the door behind them. The two men seated themselves on the other side of the table. I looked at Nevis. He looked tired.

The older man fixed his gaze on me and smiled. "So this is the man my best Agent and special units have been chasing halfway around the world?"

I didn't answer but just kept looking at Ben Nevis.

"This is my boss, General Peter Elson, Director of DETI," said Nevis without emotion. "He is going to ask you a few questions about your collaboration with the Ashtar Command."

"It's you I want to talk to Ben," I said. "It's you. And it's of the utmost importance that you hear what I have to say."

"Well, then go ahead and tell Agent Nevis what you have to say," the General said good-naturedly.

"What I have to say is for his ears only."

General Elson looked questioningly at Ben Nevis. Nevis shrugged. The General turned towards me again, this time looking more serious.

"Okay, let me be frank. We all know that the Ashtar Command has used the so-called Power Spots to manipulate the deeper layers of the Earth's crust and our weather systems. And we all know that you and the other groups of volunteers have collaborated with them."

"You don't know what you're talking about," I said. "The Intergalactic Fleet is here to help humanity ascend into the higher dimensions, just like Ashtar says."

"If they're here to help humanity, then they sure have a peculiar way of doing it," said the General. "Their manipulation of the Earth's crust and weather systems has cost hundreds of thousands of people their lives, made millions homeless, and eradicated entire cities!"

"You don't understand," I said again. "If it wasn't for the Ashtar Command, all life on Earth would be eradicated by now. It is because of them that there's still hope for a future for humanity on Earth." Then I turned to Nevis and said, "And that's why I have come back, Ben. You must listen to what I have to say. It is of utmost importance for the future of humanity."

General Elson leaned back in his chair for a moment. Then he signaled the man in the white uniform to come over.

"Give him the truth serum," said the General.

200

"How long has it been since he ate?" asked the man.

"At least eight hours," said Nevis.

"Good. That means the serum will take effect right away."

The man pulled up my right sleeve.

"Truth serum!" I laughed. "For crying out loud, I've been telling you the truth the whole time!"

The man picked up the syringe he'd prepared and searched my arm for a good vein.

"Come on!" I laughed. "Give it to me! Give me two! Let the truth be told!"

I felt the needle slide into my arm.

2

The Hour of Truth

Everything looked blurry. Agent Nevis and General Elson looked blurry. When they opened their mouths to speak they looked blurry and when they talked, it sounded blurry. And there was a long delay before I heard what they said—and then there was this strange echo after their words. My body felt heavy in an odd sort of way.

"Okay. Let's start from the beginning," I heard General Elson say. He sounded friendly enough. "Tell me... how did a nice young fellow like you... from a nice, little country like Denmark... make contact with nothing less than the Intergalactic Fleet?"

"Now... that's really... a good question, man... a good question." I didn't really have control over my jaw muscles and my voice sounded strange and far away. Kind of like I was drunk or something... very drunk.

"From the beginning, please," said General Elson.

"From... the beginning?"

"Yes, from the beginning. How did it all begin?"

"In the beginning... Well in the beginning I came... from the stars. That's right, just like the Ashtar Command... Way up there, far out in space, man. Together with Jacob and Janus and Elmar and... and you, Ben!" I tried to turn my head towards Ben Nevis because I wanted to look him deep in the eyes, but somehow my body wouldn't do what I wanted it to.

"You came from the stars too, Ben... Gavin... just like me. And you know what... once we were twins... yeah twins... born in England, a long time ago, and our mother was a priestess... and her name was Luned... now... she's.... Rebecca... Rebecca Randall... now isn't that far out... or what?" My voice sounded more and more strange and disconnected... I was having a hard time hanging in there... like a teenager who was drunk for the first time.

"Merlin... " I continued, "you know, Merlin the famous wizard... the one with the Sight... well... he prophesied that when the two of us work together in harmony... we would be able to access something...something called... the Lost Teaching of the Single Eye... which is supposed to be very remarkable... very remarkable..."

"The Lost Teaching of the Single Eye?" said General Elson.

"Yup, the Lost Teaching of the Single Eye... And according to what I've heard, well man, it can drastically... and I mean drastically and... dramatically... raise the entire collective consciousness of humanity."

"Raise the collective consciousness? Now what does that mean?" said the General turning to Nevis. "Didn't Commander Ashtar say something like that a few days ago on TV?" Nevis nodded yes.

"Yes... that is exactly... exactly what he said," The words were heavy on my lips, "... Lift the collective consciousness... that's what it's all about, man... peace, man... peace and enlightenment for everyone... that was our mission... Jacob and Janus and Elmar and Rebecca and me... and you Gavin, Ben... the two of us were supposed to do it... but the whole thing got messed up, man... messed up..."

"Let's forget Agent Nevis for a moment young man and return to my first question," the General said firmly. "How did you and your two friends get in touch with the Ashtar Command?"

"It was Ticha... she arranged it all... she's the one who deserves all the credit... she's the one... she's the one who made me watch the transmission from Ashtar..."

"Ticha?"

"Yeah... Ticha ... she's my guardian angel..."

"Your guardian angel?"

"Yeah," I said, nodding slowly. "Yup Ticha's the one. She's my guardian angel... Of course she doesn't have wings... at least none I can see... but she sure can fly!" The thought of Ticha levitating in my bedroom made me laugh.

General Elson obviously didn't think it was funny.

"Is this what he told you in England?"

Nevis sighed and nodded. "Yes, it's the same story... almost word for word."

"All right," said the General. "So this Ticha, your guardian angel, contacted you and got you to see the transmission from Ashtar. How did she actually do that?"

"She did it by turning on the … television… man… it was easy… zap zap and there it was… on Channel 75… the Ashtar Command's very own TV channel…"

Nevis nodded again. "That corresponds with the findings of the SETI astronomers."

"All right," said the General turning back to me. "And what did Ashtar say to you when you saw him on TV?"

I tried to move a bit but the straps were too tight. I sighed. It was a drag being tied up like this, but what could I do?

"They invited me… or should I say he invited me… " I continued, "to take part in their very own top-notch intergalactic training program."

"Their intergalactic training program?"

"Yeah… where you learn all about the Force…"

"The Force? What Force?"

"Not what Force… but *the Force*… the one great almighty super-duper-mega-giga Force…"

The two men turned to each other again. "Well, at least it corresponds with the transmission the SETI astronomers picked up," said the General. He looked at me again.

"Okay. So you were invited to take part in the Ashtar Command's intergalactic training program. Then what happened?"

"Then what happened…? I sort of chuckled. "Well can't you figure it out?" For some reason I thought the two of them were incredibly dense. "…I mean it's obvious… I thought I'd lost it man, completely lost it… until Elmar died and told me to follow my heart…"

I looked down at my hands. The thought of my grandfather made me feel like crying. Maybe I was crying. I wasn't sure.

"Elmar?"

"His grandfather, sir," said Nevis. "He died of a heart attack the day after the transmission."

"Elmar is not dead!" I said vehemently and looked up again. I wanted to wipe my eyes, but couldn't move my arms. "He's not dead… he's alive and well… in the Ascended Masters' headquarters in Shamballa…"

"Shamballa?"

"Yes… Shamballa… the City of Light… in the higher dimensions…"

"Wait a second," the General said. "Let's go back to the Ashtar Command and their training program. After your grandfather died, you agreed to join their training program?"

"Yes, yes… I said yes…"

"And what happened next?"

"Well... I was transubstantiated... up into the Mothership..."

"Tran-sub-what?"

"Tran... sub... stantiated..."

"What's that?"

"Beats me man... First you're in one place and then suddenly you're in another place... a totally different place..."

"You mean some kind of teleportation?"

"Yeah ... well you know like in Star Trek man... or just like we did when we were kids playing Dungeons & Dragons..."

"OK so then you were teleported... may I ask from where?"

"From my apartment in Copenhagen... to the Relaxation Forest..."

"The Relaxation Forest? I thought you were teleported up to the Mothership?"

"Well I was. The Relaxation Forest is in the Mothership... the Mothership... is fucking huge man... mile after mile..."

"And it's orbiting Earth...?"

"Yeah man."

"So how come our radar can't pick it up?"

I just didn't have the strength to explain. They were so dense and I was so tired. So I just nodded or rather flapped my head up and down.

General Elson was silent for a while. Then he continued, "So you got transported up to this forest...?"

"Yes... it was the most beautiful forest you've ever seen man... it's a forest of light... it's all light up in the Mothership... the forest, the city, the starships, all of it..."

"Well tell me about the city," he seemed at a loss as to how to continue.

"It's all so... incredibly beautiful," I said, feeling very moved by the thought. "... Everything looks like it's made of light..."

"What do the inhabitants look like? Do they look like humans? Ashtar does."

"Yes. It's funny, isn't it...? The Star People all look like humans... Even though some are tall and some are short and some have bluish or golden skin and some have big almond-shaped eyes... but they all look like humans... the most beautiful humans."

"Interesting. Tell me about their technology, about their starships."

"Their technology... is way beyond me..."

"Did you see weapons of any kind?"

"Weapons!" I laughed. "You discount agents still don't get it, do you... They don't have any weapons... none at all... the Ashtar Command is completely peaceful..."

General Elson got up and started pacing back and forth in front of the table.

"OK... so what happened after you were... transubstantiated... up into this forest of light?"

"I met Jacob and Janus up there... I mean Telperion and Moncler... my two best buddies... who are dead now... dead because you killed them, Ben! Dead again, like you killed them in England!"

I tried to look straight at Ben Nevis, but it was hard for me to focus.

"Let's forget Agent Nevis for a moment," the General said again, "and continue with your training program..."

"Forget about Agent Nevis... that's easier said than done man... when he's my own twin brother, my own twin... who killed me... and you just want me to forget him?"

I tried to focus on Ben again but I just couldn't do it. And it was impossible to move... everything was so frustrating.

"My own twin brother... who killed me! How could you do it...? Even if you didn't know I was your twin... you still had the Sight... you knew something was wrong... you knew it... it was bad Ben, real b·d."

General Elson banged his hand on the table as if he was trying to get my attention. "Let's talk about the training program," he said very slowly. "Did it have anything to do with the Earth's Power Spots?"

"You knew something was wrong, Ben..." I went on. "You did."

General Elson turned towards the man in the white uniform. "How much did you give him?"

"The standard dosage," he replied. "You can see from his movements that the drug has taken affect."

"You knew something was wrong..." I said again, "... and when Merlin told you the truth... you knew what you'd done!"

Ben Nevis said nothing.

"Give him another shot," said the General.

"Another shot? But his nervous system..."

"Just do it, George. The world is about to go under and we haven't got much time. Give him another shot."

"When you'd heard what you'd done Gavin, you went mad..." I cried. "Mad... and you ran into the forest with your insides screaming... all alone with your shame..."

I vaguely sensed a new needle in my arm.

"But you came back, Ben... you came back... just like I did ... back to this lifetime... back for another shot at it..."

206

"Look, I am going to ask you just one more time young man" General Elson said, trying to sound friendly but he didn't fool me. I knew he was pissed. "Did your training program have anything to do with the Earth's Power Spots?"

"The Power... Spots...?" I was feeling the effect of the new injection. "The Power... Spots... have all been blown to pieces... blown to pieces... by you, by Gavin... mad...screaming... maniac..."

Suddenly I was tired, so very very tired, but the General wasn't about to give up. "How did the Ashtar Command use the Power Spots to control the deeper layers of the Earth's crust and weather systems?"

"Oh come on, man... " I was having a hard time talking, "...you still don't get it... do you..."

"Get what?"

"You should get it man... you CIA agents are supposed to be so damn smart.... and tough... and champions.... champions of the Good and of justice... and then guess what! The Ashtar Command turns up on the scene, bringing the people on Earth the greatest opportunity in the entire history of mankind... and you just don't get it..." I groaned.

"What opportunity?"

"STARDAY dummy! What do you think I'm talking about? I mean, come on man... didn't you guys hear a word of what Ashtar said... STARDAY... we're talking about a mega-giga-super-duper-day... a new era of peace and enlightenment on Earth... hunky dory good times for everybody... no more Earth changes... no more axis shifts... and then you wannabe X-Files agents get so freakin' paranoid that you blow up all the Power Spots and ruin the whole thing... you just don't understand what you're missing... what all of humanity is missing..."

"What are we missing?"

"Ascension man... good times... like ascending into... the higher dimensions..."

"What has that got do with the Power Spots?"

"Forget about the Power Spots... all the Power Spots... have been blown to bits anyway..."

"So the Ashtar Command can no longer use the Power Spots?"

I flapped my head from side to side. "No, no... nothing can raise the collective consciousness now... nothing... except... except the Single... Eye..."

I felt so drunk and weird and completely out of control that I almost didn't know what I was saying.

"So what is the Ashtar Command going to do next?" the General asked. "They seem to have left Earth, but maybe it's only temporary? Maybe they're just waiting... biding their time until the right moment..."

"No man... they're leaving... they're out of here, man... they've had enough of us... and it's all your fault, Gavin... you blew up the Power Spots... you killed Jacob... you killed Janus... now it's going to take several hundred years before they come back..."

I bowed my head, all the fight gone out of me.

"So it's going to take several hundred years before the Ashtar Command comes back?" General Elson's voice also sounded as if it was coming from far away.

"I don't know... they might never come back... I don't know..."

"Agent Nevis tells me that you were up on the Ashtar Command's Mothership again, after the destruction of the Power Spots?"

"Yes, yes... in the Relaxation Forest... not that it was very relaxing this time! Because my guardian angel made me watch myself... get killed by my own twin brother... the madman...Mad Gavin... and he's sitting right there!"

"Now he's telling us that story again! I wonder why he keeps going back to that story..." The General sounded truly confused. "What's this Gavin got to do with anything?" He turned to the man in white. "How much did you give him?"

"Two full doses," the man said. "It's the absolute maximum. So he must be telling the truth."

"Yes unless of course all this space mumbo jumbo has completely blown his fuses," the General mumbled and closed his notebook.

"But it's not too late, Ben!" I cried trying to muster up energy from somewhere... I looked at Nevis as well as I could. "It's not too late Ben... I have come back... if you and I work together in harmony... we can access ... the Lost Teaching... of the Single Eye..."

The General leaned across the table. "Where are the Ashtar Command's spaceships now?"

"It's not too late, Ben... it's not too late... with the Single Eye we can raise the collective consciousness... like the Three E Masters did... which means that STARDAY won't be cancelled..."

The General raised his voice. "I am asking you a question young man: Where are the Ashtar Command's spaceships right now?"

I turned towards him, very slowly. "The starships are where they've always been... we just can't see them..."

"And where might that be?"

"In the higher dimensions..."

"In the higher dimensions...?" The General said slowly, raising his eyebrows and looking at the dark glass wall again. "I wonder what the National Security Council will make of that?"

Nevis said nothing.

"The National... Security Council..." I said, trying to face the glass wall and finding it too difficult. "The National Se..cur..ity..." Talking was getting more and more difficult. "...should get its act together... and should... drop its insane paranoia trip!"

Then I heard General Elson say way off in the distance, "If they don't think this young man is totally crazy, the National Security Council will have to seriously reevaluate its entire strategy... seriously reevaluate."

"Crazy... that's what they all say... they all say that I'm crazy... even the Ashtar Command says I'm crazy... crazy to go back to Earth... back to my own murderer... back to the end of the world..."

"I doubt if we'll get much more out of him at present." The General got up.

I laughed. "Even Ashtar says I don't have a chance... humanity doesn't have a chance... it's all fucked up... fucked up at quantum level 4 point 0... 4 point 0..."

"I'll notify the Director at once," said the General and opened the door. "Then they'll have to analyze our data. You can keep questioning him if you want, Ben. I'll be in my office if you find out any more."

General Elson left the room.

"Yup, bye bye... But you, Ben!" I said and turned towards Nevis. "You have the Sight! You know I'm telling the truth... you know...you have the Sight like me... we're twins..."

Nevis just sat in his chair and didn't move.

"Can't you do anything but stare at me?"

He didn't answer me, but just kept staring at me.

"I know you have the Sight Ben... I know it. Why the hell don't you use it?" I started to sob. I just couldn't bear it anymore.

Nevis got up and walked over to the door.

"Hey, Ben, man! Where... are you going... we have to work together in harmony you and I... or it will all be over..." The tears were streaming down my cheeks.

Nevis opened the door. "Take him back to his cell," he said to the guards.

The guards half dragged, half carried what was left of me back to my cell and threw me, none too gently, on the bed. And there I lay as the effects of the truth serum slowly began to wear off. I don't know how long I wandered, dozed and slept in that strange state, but after a while my surroundings began to seem less blurry. And I noticed that I was able to move a little more normally and think a little more clearly. Maybe not that clearly, but at least I was back in my body again... suffering from a killer hangover.

I knew I had to do something to get the poison out of my system as quickly as possible, so I got up and tried to walk back and forth in the cell as fast as I could, hoping it would help get my circulation going.

It was difficult going. After about ten minutes I sat down again, exhausted. I was just about to lie down when the door to my cell opened.

It was Ben Nevis—and he was alone.

He walked into the cell and locked the door behind him. He was carrying a long black bag on his right shoulder. The same bag he'd had over his shoulder in Tintagel—the same bag he'd carried with him the whole way to the United States.

Nevis put the long bag over in the corner and looked at it for a moment. I thought it probably contained another one of DETI's high-tech 'alien detectors'.

But Nevis didn't open the bag. Instead he turned and looked at me as if he didn't quite know how to begin.

Finally he said, "How are you feeling?"

"Terrible," I said, "Like I've got a hangover from hell."

He pulled out a small flask and handed it to me.

"Here. Drink this."

"What is it?"

"An antidote to the truth serum. Drink it. You'll feel better immediately."

I took the bottle, opened it and smelled it. The clear liquid had no smell at all.

"Drink it all."

I put the bottle to my mouth and thought what the hell—if Nevis wants to get rid of me, this is as good a way to go as any. The liquid tasted cool and refreshing so I drank it all.

But Nevis meant what he said. I felt better right away, as if a heavy cloud had been lifted. My mind started to clear.

Nevis nodded towards the camera on the ceiling.

"I turned off the camera," he said, "so no one can monitor what we say. Now you can speak freely." Then he added, "... Now we can speak freely."

"But I already spoke freely. I've been telling the truth all along…"

"I know," said Ben.

I looked at him in surprise.

"I know you told the truth in there," he continued, "or at least what you think is the truth…"

"So what do you think?"

Nevis didn't answer. Instead he walked over and picked up the long black bag.

"Let me ask you something first," he said.

"What?"

He put the bag down in front of me.

"I want you to tell me if you can see what's inside this bag."

"You what?"

"I want you to look inside my bag and tell me if you can see what I've got in it."

I looked down at the bag as he unzipped it.

A shining, almost blinding white light streamed out from the bag.

I blinked.

Nevis grabbed the white light and pulled it out of the bag.

Then he held the light up in front of me.

It was a sword.

A long, shining, silvery sword!

And the light blazed forth from sword edge to sword hilt just like it once did from Moncler's staff, Telperion's sword, and from the star on my brow. The light from the sword was reflected in his gray-green eyes.

"Can you see what I'm holding in my hand?" he asked again.

I nodded.

"Yes. It's a sword."

He seemed surprised by my answer. "Can you really see the sword?"

"Sure I can."

His hands were trembling and there were tiny beads of sweat on his forehead. He looked intensely at the sword and moved closer to me. I could feel the power of the weapon radiating towards me.

"Can you see what is written on the hilt?" he asked.

211

I looked at the shining hilt. There was a large star engraved in the center of the hilt.

"Can you see what's written on the hilt?" he asked again.

I leaned forward. There were glowing symbols engraved around the star.

"I see shining symbols, " I said, "they look like runes."

"What does it say?"

I squinted, trying to read the fiery letters. At first I couldn't decipher them but slowly they became clearer and then I could read what it said.

"Yes, I can read them."

"What does it say?"

Slowly I spelled the inscription out loud:

"S-T-A-R-W-A-R-R-I-O-R."

3

The Invisible Sword

Ben Nevis sat down on the bed next to me and laid the shining sword across our knees.

Then he laughed softly to himself. "You can see the sword too… so that means we've both lost it!"

I touched the bright sword and caressed it slowly. It felt at once cool and warm, strong and beautiful. I grasped the hilt and held it up in front of me.

"The sword of Starwarrior..." I said, gazing at it in fascination. "Just like in the Prophecy."

"The Prophecy?"

"Yeah, the Prophecy of Starwarrior."

Then the words came back to me, the very same words Merlin had chanted in a distant past, on the misty shores of Avalon:

> *"When the One with the Sight*
> *is reunited with the Warrior from the Stars*
> *the Perfect Being will be born*
>
> *From the Perfect Being*
> *will come the Single Eye*
>
> *From the Single Eye*
> *will come the Perfect World*
>
> *And then the Angels sing"*

I felt the power of the sword rippling through my hands and arms out into my whole body.

"The sword is powerful indeed," I said. "Where did you find it?"

213

"I didn't find it," Ben said. "It found me."

"Found you? What do you mean?"

Ben looked up at the camera as if to make sure no one was listening.

"It all started after the explosion at Glastonbury Tor set off that huge, unexpected chain reaction."

"Oh yeah…what happened?"

"Well, first the explosion knocked me out—just like it knocked you out. When I woke up hours later, I was lying in a hospital bed in pretty bad shape… burned and battered…I was just about to call someone for some painkillers when I realized that I wasn't alone in the bed…"

"Weren't alone?"

"No. There was this long, shiny thing lying by my right arm."

"And it was the sword?"

"Yeah, it was the sword."

Ben took the sword from me and held it up in front of him. The light from the ceiling made the long weapon glint like the stars and moons on a clear night. He stared at the weapon, obviously fascinated by it.

"So what did you do?"

Ben smiled ever so slightly.

"At first I thought I was dreaming—or hallucinating. You know, you wake up after an explosion and there's a bright sword in your bed. It was too much. I figured I was suffering from shock. When the nurse came in she confirmed my suspicion because she didn't ask me what this bright sword was doing in my bed. So after that, I was pretty sure I must be hallucinating or something."

I smiled. "I understand. Most people are unable to see interdimensional weapons, unless they have the Sight."

"Interdimensional weapons?"

"Yeah. I'll explain later. Go on."

"Well", said Ben chuckling, "interdimensional weapons or no, when the next nurse came in, I decided to ask her why there was a sword in my bed. She immediately rushed out and got the doctor. He couldn't see any sword either, so he gave me a tranquilizer and told me to get some rest. He mumbled something about people going into shock after traumatic experiences.

"When I woke up a couple of hours later, the sword was still there. This time I discovered I could actually touch it. I picked it up and found it was very light. Not only that, it fit my hand perfectly… almost as if it had been made for me…"

Ben's eyes shone as he talked about the sword.

214

"What happened next?"

"Well all my next visitors—the doctors, nurses, some of my agents, some members of our English liaison team—couldn't see the sword either. So I didn't mention it to anyone, I just figured it was my own private little hallucination. My agents told me that every one of the 144 Power Spots had been completely demolished by violent chain reactions of explosions just like the ones at Glastonbury Tor and that all the starships had disappeared at exactly the same time. Which certainly indicated that we were right that the Ashtar Command was using the Power Spots to control the deeper layers of the Earth's crust and weather systems."

I was just about to object to the conclusions he'd drawn from the explosions, but I decided to wait and hear him out.

"I was also told that almost all the agents in the 144 special units had been killed by the explosions and that so had the 451 volunteers. That is except you. And you still hadn't been found. But that didn't surprise me."

"What do you mean?"

"I already knew that the explosion hadn't killed you."

"How did you know that?"

Nevis looked at me for a moment as if he was trying to remind himself how I looked. Then he looked at the shining sword again.

"I don't know why but all of a sudden I could see you. I don't have the faintest idea why this happened; I just know it did. So when our English liaison team told me they still hadn't found you, it didn't surprise me. I even knew you were still in Glastonbury—hiding. In fact, while I was lying in the hospital, I had a glimpse of you lying in a bed just like me, wrapped in bandages, just like me. I even saw the white bed you were lying in and the view from your window—the burnt out remains of Glastonbury Tor."

I looked at him in surprise. "So that was how you knew that I was at..." I stopped short because I realized that it might not be a good idea to mention Rebecca Randall's name.

Ben smiled as if he'd read my thoughts.

"Yes, that was how I knew that you were in one of the houses in the area around Rebecca Randall's house."

I didn't say anything.

"At that time I didn't know exactly which house it was," he went on, "but I knew the house was near the foot of Glastonbury Tor so I immediately gave orders to search all the houses around the hill. As soon as I could walk, I resumed command of the operation."

"And what about the sword?"

"The sword was still there. I could touch it, handle it, feel it—but no one else could. So I put it in this bag and kept it secret while I searched for you."

Ben got up and started pacing back and forth in the cell, frequently looking down at the sword in his hand.

"When I came to Rebecca Randall's house I was sure that you were there. And even though we searched the house and never found you, I was still sure you were there."

Ben looked at me intensely but I said nothing. I remembered how close he'd been to finding me at Rebecca's house and how I'd felt this strange connection with him even though it was only later—up in the Mothership—that I learned that Ben and I had been twins in a past life. And that Rebecca Randall had been our mother...

"So the hunt for you continued," Ben continued. "We searched every house, shed, and garden in Glastonbury. And all the while, the sword was with me and all the while I was the only one who could see it. During the hunt, I discovered something else that was odd about the sword."

Again I noticed how his eyes shone when he talked about the sword.

"Every time I got near Glastonbury Tor—or what was left of it—the sword would shine more brightly as if the hill was a magnet that was drawing the sword to it. And there was more. I started having these weird experiences, or at least I thought they were weird since nothing like this ever happened to me before."

"Like what?"

"I'm not sure what to call what I experienced. You could say it was… a kind of remembrance or dejá vu. Or maybe it was just more strange visions."

"What did you see?"

"The past."

"The past?"

"Yes. As I walked around Glastonbury, I had this odd feeling that I'd been there before… had seen the place before. Which of course is nonsense since I've never been to Glastonbury before."

"I know what you mean," I said, smiling, "I've had that feeling, too."

"But it was more than just a feeling," said Ben. "In certain places, I suddenly saw... how can I explain it?" Ben stopped as if he was looking for the right words.

"Inner visions?"

"Yes, exactly. Inner visions. I saw myself dressed as a medieval knight, wearing armor and a sword. And…."

"And what?"

Ben was silent for a moment as if he was trying to find the right words again.

"The funny thing was that even then… I was hunting someone."

"Hunting?"

"Yes."

"Hunting who?"

"You."

I felt a cold shiver run down my back.

Our eyes met for a moment and then Ben again started pacing back and forth in the cell again.

"So what did you do about these inner visions?" I asked.

"Nothing. I kept telling myself they were just the delusions of a man who was wounded and exhausted—and I kept on searching for you. And finally that afternoon we had news of you. You'd escaped down into Chalice Well and unfortunately one of the soldiers who spotted you had blown up the entrance to the well and completely blocked it. And we couldn't get a word out of Rebecca Randall and her fellow sisters."

"I hope you didn't do anything to the sisters," I exclaimed hotly, "they've got nothing to do with…"

"You needn't worry," said Ben. "I barked at them very softly."

"So where are they now?"

"Oh they're probably in custody somewhere, being questioned by the British MI6. But I seriously doubt they'll get a word out of Rebecca Randall, she's one tough cookie."

And she was your mother I thought and then the melody line ran through my head… *when will you wake up to your fate, before it is too late…?*

Ben continued, "My English liaison team thought you must be dead down there, buried under tons of rock and earth. But I knew you were still alive because I had another vision—this time of you walking through dark tunnels with a miner's headlamp attached to your forehead. I asked one of the local Glastonbury constables who told me that yes, as a matter of fact, there were legends and stories of underground tunnels underneath Glastonbury Tor and the surrounding hills."

"So then you decided to drown me alive!" I said dryly.

"Is that what you think?" Ben looked surprised. "Releasing the waters wasn't my idea. We tried to blast the rocks away that were blocking the entrance to the tunnels. But for some reason, the only thing that happened was that we released the underground waters."

"You can say that again!" I said. "I was only a few seconds from drowning. It's a miracle that I got out of there alive."

"But nevertheless you did because a few minutes later I had another vision, this time of you standing at the foot of a great hill—a hill with a thorn tree on top. When I asked, the English constables told me that there was a hill with a thorn tree southwest of Glastonbury Tor called Wearyall Hill"

"So the hunt continued."

Ben nodded.

"How did you know that I was in Tintagel?"

"I didn't know for sure but I kept seeing you—first walking through a dark forest, then driving an old car on a highway. Finally I saw you heading towards the entrance of a large cave in the side of a rocky island. On the top of the island, there were ruins of an ancient castle."

"And then you knew that I was in Tintagel?"

Ben laughed. "You have no idea how many rocky islands with old castle ruins there are in England! But I had pictures of all the rocky islands sent to me immediately… and as you can imagine, at that point the British agents started to think I was something of a super sleuth since I seemed to have this uncanny knack for constantly being able to predict your whereabouts!"

Now it was my turn to laugh. "Yeah, the Agent with the Sight!"

"As soon as I saw the picture of Tintagel Castle," Ben continued, "I knew you were there. So we headed straight to Tintagel and arrived there late in the afternoon. Funny, but as soon as we arrived, I had that strange feeling again that I'd been there before, that I'd stood exactly where I was standing before… on that rocky coast. Anyway, once we realized you really were in the cave beneath Tintagel Head, we were sure we had you. There was absolutely no way you could escape—but still you did—right before our eyes. It was too much. You just disappeared into thin air."

"When I disappeared, could you see where I'd gone?"

Ben shook his head. "No. As a matter of fact that was the first time since I woke up in the hospital that I didn't have any idea where in the world you were."

I laughed. "That's probably because I was no longer in this world. I was in the higher dimensions, just like I told you, in the Ashtar Command's Mothership."

Ben nodded. "So you say. And yet, one and a half hours later you suddenly reappeared out of thin air and gave yourself up freely."

He fixed his gaze on me. "Why did you come back? If you really were up in their spaceship, why did you come back? Did they send you back?"

"No," I said. "That's what I have been trying to tell you. I chose to come back."

"But why?"

"If you'd just let me tell you the whole story—right from the beginning—maybe you'll understand why. And maybe you'll understand all the things that have happened to you in the last few days a little better."

Ben stopped in his tracks and put down the sword.

"OK, you win," he sighed. "Tell me the whole story—tell me everything—and start from the beginning… the very beginning…you understand."

"Okay," I said. "From the very beginning… as your boss General Elson would say..."

Then I told Ben everything that had happened during the past two weeks, starting with my very first meeting with Ticha on Ocean Drive, the transmission from Ashtar, and my experiences with Jacob and Janus in the Relaxation Forest. Then I told him about the Cosmic Library and our past lives in England. I explained the concept of the Shadow Earth to him and told him about the threat of an axis shift that would wipe out all life on Planet Earth. Then I briefly sketched our adventures in the higher dimensions and told him what we learned about the Force on the road to Shamballa.

When I told him about the star on my brow and about Jacob's staff and Janus' sword, Ben didn't say a word but stared at his sword in amazement.

Then I explained to him how the 600 volunteers had been sent back to Earth to activate their Power Spots and the Light Grid so we could anchor a positive New Vision in the collective consciousness—and how we meditated in the tower on top of Glastonbury Tor for 24 hours—a meditation that culminated in the radiant vision that had spread all over the Earth. Then I recounted how Jacob, Janus and I had woken up the next morning and walked down from Glastonbury Tor to met Ben and his agents, who took us into captivity, none too gently, as he well knew.

I even told Ben about the vision I had when they arrested us—that he had been Lord Gavin, the man who betrayed and murdered us in our past life in England.

"How strange," said Ben in surprise, "you mean to say you could really see that I was Lord Gavin, come back from the past to haunt you again?"

"Yes," I said, "it was spooky."

Ben shook his head. "You know you said something like this after we gave you the truth serum."

"I'm sure I did," I said, nodding, "since it's the truth."

"But how can you know for sure that I am Lord Gavin?"

"Aren't you starting to get it man?" I replied impatiently, "I have the Sight, just like you do! "

"The Sight?"

"Yeah, I can see things, just like you can. I know things, just like you know things. Remember back in England how you knew where I was all the time…."

Ben nodded slowly. "OK, I am starting to get it. But tell me more about this thing you call the 'Sight'."

"Well obviously, the Sight is the ability to see. The priestesses and druids of Avalon said the Sight was the ability to see into the past and the future and into different worlds and different dimensions. And it seems we both have it!"

Ben was quiet for a while, then he sighed and said, "All right, go on; tell me the rest of it."

So I continued from the explosion at Glastonbury Tor where I was knocked out just like he was—and how Rebecca Randall's grandson found me. I told him about Rebecca and how she helped me. I told him about my escape, my trip to Tintagel and about how I finally managed, at the very last second, to raise my consciousness high enough to be transubstantiated up into the Mothership just before he caught me in the Crystal Cave.

"And now it really gets interesting" I said slowly, "because this was when I learned about the Prophecy of Starwarrior." Then I went on to tell about Merlin's Prophecy of the two souls—and of my great shock when I discovered that Gavin and Dana were the two twins that were spoken of in the Prophecy.

"You and I were twins?"

"Yes."

"So that means we're supposedly the two souls spoken of in the Prophecy?"

"Yes it does. I take it the One with the Sight—Starbrow—is me. And the Warrior from the Stars—Starwarrior—is you."

"Tell me again what the prophecy says about us."

I repeated the prophecy again.

"When the One with the Sight
is reunited with the Warrior from the Stars
the Perfect Being will be born

From the Perfect Being
will come the Single Eye

From the Single Eye
will come the Perfect World

And then the Angels sing"

"I guess it means what it says Ben... that when the two of us are reunited, when the two of us work together in harmony, the Perfect Man will be born, and we will be able to access the Lost Teaching of the Single Eye."

"Which is what?"

"Well, according to Merlin and Commander Ashtar, the Single Eye bestows the ability to drastically lift the collective consciousness."

Ben nodded slowly, as if he was really trying to understand what I was talking about.

I continued my tale and explained to Ben in detail how the Keeper of the Cosmic Library morphed my consciousness to Gavin's so I could see his life—Ben's past life—through his own eyes. I told him how Morgause separated us right after we were born and about Gavin's childhood and friendship with Mordred, about their plot to destroy King Arthur and Merlin—and finally how Gavin, without knowing it, had killed his own twin sister Dana, who was me.

"Did Gavin really kill Dana?" asked Ben, shaking his head.

"Yes. He drove his sword through her heart..."

When I said these words, Ben suddenly dropped his sword on the floor—with a loud, crashing sound.

I looked at Ben in surprise; his hands were shaking.

"Gavin stabbed Dana... in the heart?" Ben asked slowly.

"Yes," I said, wondering at his reaction. "But as I said, Gavin didn't know Dana was his twin sister at the time."

Ben was quiet for a moment. I sensed he was really upset, but he pulled himself together and picked up the sword.

"OK," he said, clearing his throat, "go on."

So I continued and told Ben how Gavin met the wizard Merlin that terrible night and how Gavin, when he learned the truth, had run in horror into the dark forest—overcome by madness.

I waited a few minutes to let Ben digest all this and then went on to tell him what I did after the past life regression. I described my meeting with Ashtar and how I learned there might be a small chance of lifting the collective consciousness enough so that STARDAY would not be cancelled—that is if Ben and I could work together and access the Lost Teaching of the Single Eye. Then I explained that if we succeeded and STARDAY actually happened, the threat of new Earth changes and an axis shift would be gone forever.

"So now you can understand why I decided to come back, Ben. When Ashtar saw I wouldn't change my mind, he had me transubstantiated back to the Crystal Cave, where I gave myself up."

When I finished, the cell grew quiet—very quiet.

Ben got up and started pacing back and forth again in the cell.

Finally he stopped.

"If you'd told me this story a week ago I would have said that you were stark raving mad and that all those Dungeons & Dragon games you played as a kid had gone to your head. I'd probably even say so right this minute if it weren't for the fact that I'm standing here in your cell with a sword in my hand that shines in the dark! A sword that no one else can see but you and me! It's madness, madness... unless of course we've both gone stark raving mad. Which I must say is also a very likely explanation."

I laughed softly. "If it can be of any comfort to you Ben, I know exactly how you feel. Think about how it was for me, this young guy walking around Copenhagen bored out of my mind. And then one day—boom—I find this beautiful woman who glows in the dark and tells me she's my guardian angel floating in the middle of my bedroom! I mean man... if you had told me two weeks ago just a fraction of what has happened to me during the last couple of days, I would have thought I'd completely lost it! And yet today I cannot deny any of it. It's all true. It all happened to me, just like I've told you. It's all just as real as the shining sword in your hand."

More silence.

"But I still don't understand why you decided to come back to Earth," said Ben after a while. "Ashtar made you a wonderful offer when he said that you could end your mission on Earth and go on an..." Ben was smiling now, "... intergalactic holiday or whatever you call it. Why didn't

222

you accept his offer… especially when you knew that humanity's chances of survival are just about nil?"

"Oh come on Ben, how could I just walk away and leave Earth with a clear conscience if I knew that there was just the tiniest chance that STARDAY would not be cancelled if I came back and found you?"

"But I killed you and your friends in a past life! If you really believe in that reincarnation stuff and the story you just told me, how can you ever forgive me?"

I thought for a moment and then replied, "Well Ben, for one, you didn't know what you were doing. You'd forgotten who you really are, just like I for most of my current life had forgotten I'm Starbrow.'"

Ben looked at me and said hotly, "But even if you forgot your true identity, you still didn't kill your own twin sister!"

I shook my head. "That's true… but if you think I returned to Earth because of you, Ben, you've got it all wrong. I returned for one reason and one reason alone and that's to raise the collective consciousness enough so that STARDAY isn't cancelled. And unfortunately—or maybe fortunately—you're the only chance I've got of doing it. For some mysterious reason, our destinies are entwined. I can only achieve my goal by working with you!"

Again Ben started pacing back and forth in the cell.

"But why you and me? It doesn't make sense. How come the collective consciousness can only be raised if the two of us work together?"

"I have no idea, Ben. No idea… All I know is that according to the Prophecy of Merlin for some reason, the two of us, if we work together in harmony, will have access to the Lost Teaching of the Single Eye."

"And what is the Lost Teaching of the Single Eye?"

"I haven't got a clue. All I know is that according to Ashtar, the Three E Masters once drastically raised the collective consciousness in an entire star system by using the Single Eye."

"And who are the Three E Masters?"

"Again I don't know. I'm just telling you what Ashtar told me."

"Okay, okay," mumbled Ben. "And what will happen if the two of us, according to this prophecy, work together in harmony and access this teaching?"

"Well as I said, both Merlin and Ashtar say the Teaching of the Single Eye is able to raise the entire collective consciousness of a planet drastically. So that means if the collective consciousness here on Earth is raised drastically before Friday, then STARDAY won't be cancelled."

"And then what happens?"

"Well, then the starships of the Intergalactic Fleet will land as planned and a new era of enlightenment and peace will begin on Earth, exactly like Ashtar said in his transmission. And there will no longer be any danger of Mother Earth making a total axis shift."

"And all this might happen if you and I work together in harmony? Don't you think it's all a bit far out."

"Well Ashtar didn't seem to believe it, but it's the only hope we've got."

Ben stared at me for a while and then he began walking back and forth again, waving his sword in the air.

"How do you know the Ashtar Command hasn't lied to you and isn't really out to invade Earth and exterminate all of humanity? How do you know that it's all not just one big intergalactic scam?"

"I can't tell you how I know Ben, I just know. And besides, both you and I know that with their super technology, the Ashtar Command could easily take over the Earth right now if they really wanted to. But they aren't doing that because that's not what they're up to. Really Ben, if you'd just start listening to your heart, you'd realize you know all this already."

Ben sighed and shook his head.

"Well Ben, I've told you everything I know…so it's up to you now… you've got to decide whether to help me or not."

"Whether to help you or not! Are you out of your mind? Do you realize what you're asking me to do? I mean everything you've just told me is so far out… it makes no sense whatsoever! How do I know that all this is not just something you've cooked up… something you've dreamed up in your fantasy Dungeons & Dragons world?"

I stared at him coldly and said, "Ben, you are the Warrior from the Stars!"

"Forget it!"

"You are Starwarrior!"

"No!"

"Sooner or later, you're going to have to face your true destiny."

Ben turned away from me and gazed intensely at the sword. It shone fiercely from sword tip to sword hilt, as if it wanted to confirm the truth of my words.

"You know in your heart what I am telling you is true."

"You don't realize what you're asking me to do!"

"Yes I do!"

"I'm a CIA agent, not some New Age group meditation leader!"

"And what about the sword? The fact that your interdimensional weapon suddenly shows up must be a sign that you're ready for ascension, ready to remember your True Self and carry out your true mission."

"Which is?"

"To create peace and harmony on Earth. Is there any other mission? Isn't that what you have been working for all your life as a CIA agent?"

Ben didn't answer.

"Right before my grandfather Elmar died, he said to me that *once in every person's lifetime, the soul is called to ascend into the higher dimensions, but that only very few heed that call.* This is your call, Ben. Now is your time."

He still didn't say anything.

After a while he turned and looked at me.

"So tell me, my fine friend… just how do you see the two of us working together in harmony?"

"Well for one, you could start by getting me out of here."

Ben laughed out loud.

"I must say! You really do have a great deal of faith in my abilities! You're the most wanted man on the entire planet and we're in one of the most heavily guarded buildings in the world. Even if I believed your story and wanted to help you get out, it would be completely impossible."

I didn't answer; I just kept looking at him.

Ben shook his head and turned away from me. Then he picked up the long black bag and put the sword back in it. Slowly, very slowly, he zipped up the bag so the light from the sword no longer lit up the cell.

Then he walked over to the door and opened it. He looked at me one last time and walked out of the room, closing the door softly behind him.

I heard the lock click into place.

I was alone in the cell once again.

I just sat there for a while, staring at the door. Then I lay down on the bed with my hands under my head.

So that was it.

Now I'd done what I came to do.

Now I'd done all I could do.

I'd told Ben Nevis my story.

Our story.

The story of our past and of our possible future.

Why had he walked out like that? Without saying a word? I wondered what he was thinking.

225

And guessed I would never know.

All I knew was that I was all alone again in the deepest dungeon of the CIA.

I guessed Ashtar was right… I'd probably acted foolishly…incredibly foolishly. And now I'd have to pay for my foolishness and spend the rest of my days rotting away in some prison cell while humanity slowly built a new civilization on the smoldering ruins of the old world.

The rest of my days.

Well it didn't really matter.

I'd done what I knew in my heart was right.

The rest... was up to the Force.

I closed my eyes.

And for the first time in many days, I slept deeply and peacefully.

I woke up and opened my eyes, feeling a change.

Something was different.

Then I realized that the light on the ceiling was out. It was pitch dark in the cell and I couldn't see a thing. I wondered if the light had gone out by itself or if someone had turned it off.

I got up and fumbled my way to the door. I tried to open it, but it was still locked.

I was trapped in the darkness.

I made my way back to the bed and sat down again and focused my attention on the Force.

I AM THE FORCE.

I AM...

Suddenly I heard a sound coming from the direction of the door.

Then the door opened and light came streaming into the cell. The light was coming from a flashlight.

The figure holding the flashlight was Ben Nevis.

"Hurry up!" he said. "We only have a few minutes before they turn on the back-up generators and the lights go on again."

I got up and rushed to the door. Ben had already disappeared out of sight.

I looked down the long dark hall. It was quiet and empty. Ben was already far down the corridor. The light from his flashlight cast long shadows on the walls. Over his shoulder, he had the black bag with Starwarrior's sword.

"Come on," he signaled to me. "And hurry up!"

I rushed after him as fast as I could. When we came to the end of the long corridor, which didn't seem to go anywhere, Ben stopped in front of a door on the left side of the corridor. He took out a key and opened it.

The door led to a new corridor of cells. There were cell doors on both sides. Cellblock B was written on one of the walls. Here too, it was completely dark and deserted.

I wondered where he was taking me.

Ben stopped in front of one of the doors.

"Where are we going?" I asked.

"I'm getting you out of here. Isn't that what you want?"

Ben took out another flashlight and handed it to me. I turned it on.

"So what are we doing here?"

"Before we say goodbye to my old workplace for good, we have two allies I think we should take with us."

I looked at him questioningly.

"Two allies? What are you talking about?"

Ben had another key in his hand.

I looked around warily. There wasn't a sound anywhere; nothing could be seen nor heard in the long corridor.

"Do we really have time for this?"

Ben smiled. "I don't suppose you'd want to continue your intergalactic adventures without your two friends?"

"My two friends?"

Ben inserted the key in the door in front of him.

"The Wizard and the Elf King."

I stood as if turned to stone.

"Your two friends Jacob and Janus aren't dead. They survived the explosion, just like you and I did. And they're right here... locked up in this wing of Cellblock B."

4

Escape From DETI

I stared at Ben and stammered.

"Are you saying that...?"

"Yes. Apparently your two friends are made of the same tough fiber as you."

"But...?"

"DETI thought it would be a whole lot easier to get you to talk if you didn't know the other two were still alive."

"And Jacob and Janus are here?" My world rocked.

Ben turned the key and opened the door.

"Come and see for yourself," he said, walking down the corridor towards a cell door a little further down the hall.

He opened the door to a cell. I pointed my flashlight into the small, dark cell. It looked exactly like the one I had been in. The room was completely empty except for the bed in the corner.

A young man with short red hair was lying on the bed. He was dressed in the exact same gray shirt and pants that I had on. His right arm was hanging in a sling. He had cuts and bruises on his face and neck.

But there was no doubt who it was.

"Jacob!" I cried, running into the cell.

"Who's there?"

Jacob sat up, blinded by the sudden light from my flashlight.

"Jacob! It's me!"

"Starbrow? But...?"

"Jacob!"

"Starbrow!"

Jacob leapt to his feet and we gave each other a huge bear hug.

"This is further out than far out!" I laughed. "I thought you were dead!"

"I thought you were dead, too!"

"I can't believe it!"

"But how on Earth..." began Jacob.

We suddenly heard a loud crashing noise coming from outside in the corridor. It sounded as if someone had slammed a door open with great force.

"Take that you scum-sucking DETI bastard!" we heard a voice shouting from further down the corridor.

Then we heard another thud. As if someone had thrown a heavy object at the wall.

When I realized what was happening I ran out into the corridor shouting, "Janus... Telperion... No! Janus, wait!"

Ben's flashlight was rolling down the corridor.

Two figures were lying in a heap in front of an open cell door—the one pounding the other mercilessly. There was a big crack in the wall right next to where they were fighting as if someone had smashed it with a battering ram.

"How does that feel, huh! You bastard!"

"No Janus! Wait!" I ran down the corridor.

"This one is for England! This one is for the Light Grid! This one is for Moncler! This one is for Starbrow!"

In vain Ben struggled to free himself from Janus' iron grip. But such was Telperion's strength and ferociousness that even Ben's lightning-fast reflexes were no help.

"Janus!" I cried, "It's not what you think it is! Stop, STOP!!!"

Janus was on top of Ben and was just about to throttle him with his powerful elven hands. Blood trickled from Ben's nose as he tried to free himself from Janus' iron grip.

"Janus! Stop! He's here to help us!"

I tried to push Janus away, but he didn't even notice me.

There was only one thing to do. I shouted in his ear at the top of my lungs, "It's me! Starbrow!"

Janus turned to stone and looked up in amazement.

"Starbrow?" he said, not letting go of Ben's neck.

"Yes! It's me, Janus!"

"But how..."

"Let him go..."

Janus gasped, his mouth wide open. Then he saw Jacob standing next to me. "Moncler?"

Jacob smiled sweetly. "Greetings, Telperion!"

"Moncler! Starbrow! You're alive! But how... what's going on?"

"Let him go Janus. It's Ben Nevis who's freed us!" I said. "He wants to help us."

"Help us?"

"Yes!"

Janus looked down at the bleeding man whose neck he was still clutching. Slowly he let him go.

Ben gasped and stuttered, holding his neck…"We've only... got….a few minutes... until they return…"

I put my hand on Janus' shoulder. "Listen Telperion, we've got to hurry. All hell is going to break loose in a few minutes."

"But…" Janus was having a hard time taking it all in, "but… this scumbag killed us in a past life and destroyed the Light Grid…"

"Janus, it's not the way you think it is. Ben has decided to help us now."

"Help us?"

"I don't have time to explain now. You're just going to have to trust me unless you want to spend the rest of your life down here!"

Janus looked at Ben with loathing. Then he pushed him away in disgust and got up.

"Starbrow!" he laughed. "You're alive!"

"You bet I am!" I cried.

We embraced each other heartily.

"And you Moncler!" Janus laughed.

"Yes! We're all bloody alive!" Jacob laughed and joined the joyous embrace.

"This is just too far out! But how did it happen?"

"If the three of you don't get a move on quicker than quick, this is going to be the world's shortest reunion." In a moment Ben was on his feet again. He'd picked up his flashlight and was now wiping the blood off his face with his shirtsleeve.

"Is he really going to help us?" asked Janus again. "Him? The bastard of all bastards?"

"Yes," I said. "But there's no time for explanations now. Just do what he says. It's our only chance of getting out of here alive."

Ben had already walked past us and was now at the end of the corridor. He opened the door with his key. I followed him as fast as I could. I felt Jacob and Janus hesitate behind me for a second—and then come pounding down the hall after me.

We were back in the corridor where my cell was. Ben opened the door at the end with a passkey and walked through a big room and over to a big metal door. Everything was dark and deserted here too.

"What's happened to the lights?" I asked.

"Since we lost power after the earthquakes, CIA headquarters has been running on power from our own power plant on the Potomac," said Ben, "But the flooding yesterday knocked that out too, so headquarters has only been running on back-up generators. We don't have enough back-up to supply the whole compound, so only the most important areas, like your cell block, have electricity."

"And you turned off the back-up generator for this building?" Jacob asked.

"Exactly. But it won't take long for them to realize what's wrong and hook up another generator."

"Where is everyone?"

"Right now I figure most of the guards are stuck in the surveillance room waiting for the electricity to go on so they can get out. You see the doors are electronic, so they can't get out—at least not for the moment. And everything else is out too for the moment, including the cameras, the lasers, the sound sensors and the retinal scanners."

Ben inserted his passkey into the metal door. He turned the key and pushed.

It didn't budge.

"Damn!"

"What?" I said.

Ben turned the key again and this time pushed with all his strength. The door still didn't move.

"What's wrong?" asked Jacob.

"The door won't open."

"Isn't there another way out?" I asked.

"Only by passing through the retinal scan. And in order to do that, we need electricity."

"Nice plan," said Janus.

"Can't we force our way through the door?" I asked.

"No, that would take a tank. This door is made out of four layers of metal."

"Can we generate enough electricity ourselves by connecting the system to your flashlight battery, just for a couple of seconds?" asked Jacob.

"Exactly what I'm thinking," said Ben. "It might work for a couple of seconds, which is all we need."

He handed his flashlight to Jacob. "Here."

Ben took out a knife and cut the sides of the panel. Then he pulled it from the wall, without severing the wires.

"Starbrow, you know I'm a firm believer in miracles, but honestly, can we really trust him?" Janus whispered as Ben and Jacob worked feverishly on the wires. "Yes, we can," I whispered back. "If we get out of here alive, I promise I'll explain everything."

"There you go!" cried Jacob.

The buttons on the panel lit up. Ben pressed several of them and a machine shot out of the wall on the right side of the door. Ben placed his head on the glass screen. It was a retinal scanner.

"Coolness!" said Janus. "Like in Mission Impossible!"

The metal door whizzed open. Darkness awaited us on the other side of the door too.

"Quick, " said Ben, motioning us through the door.

We stepped through the door as fast as we could and it closed behind us.

"I thought the retinal scan only gave clearance to one person," said Jacob.

"So it does."

"But what if they find out that four people just passed through?"

"That's why I've brought this—just in case." Ben opened his jacket. He had a machine gun strapped to his side. He took it out and released the safety catch.

"Let's move," cried Ben urgently.

Ben led us through another large room and down a long corridor. At the end of the corridor there were some desks with computers and TV monitors. But like everywhere else, it was totally dark. All the screens were blank—and there wasn't a soul in sight. As we passed the desks, I suddenly had the impulse to look behind them. Two security guards were laying there, eyes closed and motionless.

I looked for Ben, but he was already at the end of the corridor. He didn't seem to have noticed the guards at all.

Ben led us through another door and out into another corridor.

Suddenly he stopped.

We could hear voices coming from one of the corridors to the left.

Ben turned off his flashlight and motioned for us to be quiet. I turned off my flashlight. Ben peered slowly around the corner. We could hear the sound of voices and footsteps.

Our guide stood like stone for a few seconds then motioned for us to follow him. He quickly led us past the corridor to our left. After a few seconds, he turned on his flashlight again. We were standing in front of two large swinging doors.

Ben pushed the doors open and we stepped into a spacious kitchen. Someone was lying behind one of the doors. An agent, dressed in civilian clothing. His eyes were closed and he did not move, just like the two security guards we passed before.

"Is he dead?" whispered Janus.

"Non-operational," said Ben as he continued through the kitchen.

"Non-operational? What's that supposed to mean?"

Ben did not answer. Instead he led us through the kitchen into an empty canteen.

Ben stopped in front of the canteen exit and peered out carefully.

"Shit!" he hissed.

"What is it?" I asked.

Ben signaled for us to take a look. On the other side of the door, there was a wide hallway leading to one of the building's exits. There was a metal detector in front of the exit. Next to the metal detector, there were six armed guards. They had machine guns. The only light they had was coming from their flashlights.

"Talk about bad luck," whispered Ben. "They've posted six guards at this exit. Usually there's only two."

"What about the other exits?" I asked.

"This one is the least guarded because it's only used by kitchen staff. We'd have no chance of getting out through any of the other exits. If we're going to get out, it's got to be through this one."

"So what are you going to do?" asked Janus.

"You're forgetting I'm still their superior officer. Now you three are going to walk down the corridor in front of me with your hands behind your heads. I'll walk behind you with the machine gun. I am transferring you to another cell block for security reasons. Now move."

I turned off my flashlight and put it in my pocket. Ben swung the door open. I stepped out onto the corridor with my hands behind my head. Janus was right besides me. Jacob followed us, one hand on his head, the other hanging in its sling. Ben walked behind us, machine gun in hand.

"Who's there?" called out one of the guards.

They beamed their flashlights in our direction.

"It's Major Nevis," said Ben. "I am transferring three prisoners to cell block G for security reasons."

"Is everything okay, sir?"

"So far yes," answered Ben. "There must be some problem with the back-up generators."

233

We were halfway down the corridor now. The guards were eyeing us suspiciously.

"We've had no word about a relocation of the high priority prisoners, sir."

"Of course you haven't, the electricity's..."

Suddenly the whole corridor was bathed in light.

The metal detector lit up and the cameras along the corridor began to move in our direction.

The power was back on.

One of the guards grabbed a walkie-talkie and started speaking into it very rapidly.

"Just what we need!" whispered Janus. "Now what?"

I looked at Ben. He motioned us to keep moving.

We were at the exit. Two of the guards were blocking the door—two on our left, two on our right.

"Sorry sir, but we have no notification coming through of any relocation of prisoners. It's probably because of the blackout but we'll have to wait until we get clearance, sir."

Out of the corner of my eye I could see that Ben was starting to sweat.

What would he do now?

Suddenly a high-pitched siren tore through the building. It was the alarm. They'd discovered our escape!

The guard in front of us raised his machine gun. "What's going on here?"

"Let me through," said Ben. "I am relocating the prisoners. We have a serious crisis situation in cellblocks B and C."

"Why are you bleeding, sir?"

I looked at Ben. Janus had really given him a bashing and now the blood was beginning to trickle from his nose again.

Janus and I looked at each other.

Ben didn't move.

Janus turned to the man in front and said, "Your shoes are untied."

The guard's eyes flickered with uncertainty for a fraction of a second.

Without a moment's hesitation, Janus slammed the guard's machine gun up into his face and pushed him into the guard standing behind him.

"Watch out, they're making a run for it!" cried Ben.

The four other guards turned towards me. At that very moment, Ben threw himself to the right, slamming his machine gun into the back of one guard's head. Then he punched the other guard so hard he fell down. The two soldiers on my left were watching Ben in confusion.

That was all the time Janus needed. He threw himself at them and they all landed on the floor with a loud crashing sound.

One of the other guards had managed to get up again and was now lashing out at me. He hit me hard in the stomach and I buckled over. Again, he lashed out at me, but before his second blow hit home, Ben threw himself at him and pushed him up against the wall. A moment later, he was lying unconscious on the floor.

When I looked up again all six guards were 'non-operational' as Ben would say.

Ben gave Janus a hand and helped him to his feet.

"Your shoes are untied!" Janus laughed, dusting himself off. "That must be the oldest trick in the book! I can't believe he actually fell for it!"

Jacob looked disapprovingly at Janus. I knew he didn't approve of what just happened and was about to say something but there was no time. Behind us was the sound of footsteps coming up fast.

"Let's get out of here!" cried Janus.

We charged through the metal detector, which also began to beep, and out through the door. A little further off to our left was the entrance to the main building, which was now swarming with guards. In front of us was a large parking lot. We ran towards the parked cars. Behind us alarms were howling everywhere.

"Freeze!" someone yelled to our right.

Two guards came running towards us, aiming their guns right at us. Several more came running from another building a little further away.

Ben raised his machine gun and fired. Bullets ripped through the concrete right in front of the guards. They ran for cover behind a car.

"This way!" Ben shouted.

Ben ran through the parked cars with the three of us on his heels. We'd only gone a few paces when a heavy-set guard jumped out from between two cars to our left.

"Freeze! Don't move!" he shouted, pointing his gun towards us and holding it with both hands.

But Ben was faster. With a lightning quick move, he knocked the gun out of the guard's hand with the edge of his hand. Then he punched the man in the side of his head. The guard collapsed without a sound.

"Hurry! This way!" cried Ben and ran on among the parked cars.

Ben stopped in front of a dark blue Jeep Cherokee. He yanked the back door open, told us to get in and cover ourselves with the blankets. We did what he said as he ran around to the driver's seat. Two seconds later the jeep was moving fast.

After about 10 seconds the jeep stopped again.

"I'm sorry Major Nevis but the alarm's gone off and no one is allowed to leave the area," said a voice.

"I have special clearance," said Ben.

"What clearance?"

We heard a machine gun being cocked.

"This clearance. Now open the gate."

The tires screeched and the jeep accelerated. We heard something crash in front of the car, then the sound of machine gun fire from the guards at the gate behind us. The back window was shattered and pieces of glass came raining in over us. It was a good thing we were covered by blankets.

The jeep made a sharp, screeching turn and we were thrown to one side of the back compartment. Ben drove faster, zigzagging through who knew what. Car horns were honking on all sides as tires screeched and cars slammed on their brakes.

After a few more minutes, we again heard the sound of gunfire from behind us. The jeep was swaying from side to side.

"Give me a hand up here!" cried Ben.

We pulled off the blankets. Both the front and back windows of the jeep were totally pulverized. Cool night air pounded against our faces as we sat up. Ben was driving extremely fast, swerving back and forth from one side of the road to the other.

Right behind us, two big black Cadillacs were gaining on us. In both cars, agents were leaning out the windows aiming machine guns at us.

"Use this!" Ben threw us a machine gun.

We looked at each other in surprise.

A new onslaught of bullets came towards us from the foremost Cadillac. We threw ourselves down in the back.

"Hey, what the hell are you doing?" yelled Ben. "Use the machine gun!"

The nearest Cadillac was now right next to our jeep and all of a sudden it swerved and slammed into us. We were thrown to the right side of the car as we heard tires screeching in front of us. The jeep swerved, narrowly missing a van that was coming straight at us. A new torrent of bullets rained over us from the other Cadillac, which was also gaining on us.

"What the hell are you doing?" shouted Ben again. "For Christ's sake shoot!"

"We don't believe in violence!" cried Jacob as the car swerved.

The front Cadillac slammed into us again.

236

"Great!" cried Ben heartily as he drove for dear life, "You guys want me to help you escape from the entire US army so you can save the world. And now you tell me that you won't use violence! Couldn't you have told me that before?"

The jeep skidded past another oncoming car as a new torrent of machine gun fire lashed at us.

Janus grabbed the machine gun and aimed it at the Cadillac behind us.

"What are you doing, Janus?" cried Jacob incredulously.

"The Force is with them," yelled Janus and shot at the front tires of the Cadillac. The car swerved dangerously toward the side of the road as the driver struggled to maintain control, but it was too late.

The Cadillac crashed into the ditch.

"Groovy," laughed Janus. "I always wanted to be James Bond for a day!"

"But," cried Jacob again only to be interrupted by Ben who shouted, "Watch our side!"

We ducked down just in time as another volley of gunfire pulverized the windows to our left. The other Cadillac was so close now that it rammed into our side. Ben started firing at the car's tires with one hand while continuing to drive with the other at breakneck speed.

"Hold on!" he shouted as he slammed on the brakes.

We were hurled forward as the jeep skidded and slowed down.

As the Cadillac roared past us, Ben fired at its back tires. They exploded and the car began to skid.

Ben slammed down the accelerator again and raced after the Cadillac, which was now swerving back and forth. He slammed the jeep into the side of the car. That was too much for the Cadillac—it skidded out of control and ran off the road, crashing into the trees along the roadside.

Two seconds later, Ben was driving again at full speed, weaving in and out of cars on both sides of the road.

5

Journey to the Mountains

"We've got to get rid of this car quick," muttered Ben, mostly to himself. We were crossing a pretty big river.

Jacob and I looked at each other, but said nothing.

"That's the Potomac River," said Ben dryly, "we're headed south now." There were no lights on the bridge and very few cars, which Ben quickly passed. The cool night air beat against our faces through the jeep's broken windows.

"South?" I asked. "What's your plan?"

"First of all, we've got to get ourselves another car," said Ben. "In a few minutes, the choppers will be over us."

Ben took the first exit, turned off the main road, turned left again, and presto, we were in the middle of suburbia. We were on a street with lots of houses and nice gardens, but many were badly damaged by the recent storms and Earth changes. It was dark everywhere. In a few of the houses, candles were burning in the windows.

Ben scanned the cars parked along the street. He stopped next to a silver-gray BMW in front of a house that was completely dark. It looked as if there was nobody home.

"Take the wheel and turn the jeep around," Ben said to me.

Ben jumped out of the car. We climbed out of the back and I got in the front and turned the jeep around.

Ben took out his gun and fired a few shots at the BMW's door. The car alarm went off. Ben tore the door open and silenced it with one precise blow.

"Well I'll be...!" said Janus, watching Ben work. "Talk about a complete turn-around... How on Earth did you manage this, Starbrow?"

"Well, it's a pretty long story " I replied, grinning, "All I can tell you right now is that some pretty mind-boggling stuff has happened to him in the last couple of days."

"Such as?"

"I promise I'll tell you the whole story as soon as we get out of here. All you need to know right now is that Ben's and my destiny are entwined in the strangest way—and that this is going to affect the whole destiny of humanity too. Without Ben, there's no way we can lift the collective consciousness by Friday."

"Lift the collective consciousness by Friday?" said Jacob. "What in the world are you talking about Starbrow?"

At that very moment, Ben drove the BMW over to the jeep. He jumped out, came over to the jeep, and opened the floor lining of the back compartment where we'd been lying. Underneath was a small arsenal of guns, machine guns, knives, rifles, explosives, and even something that looked like a bazooka...

Ben tossed a machine gun at each of us. Then he slung several machine guns and a big bag with weapons, knives and explosives over his shoulder.

I stared at the cold killer weapon in my hands.

"We can't... use these," I said.

"You don't know our pursuers," said Ben as he opened the trunk of the BMW. "Without weapons we haven't got a chance."

"We're not supposed to use violence on our mission," I said.

Ben threw the weapons down into the BMW's trunk. Then he looked at the three of us. "How are you going to manage without weapons?"

"We have other weapons besides violence," I said.

"Like what?"

I threw the machine gun Ben had just given me into the trunk. "I'll explain it to you later," I said. "For now, let's just get out of here."

Jacob threw his weapon into the trunk too, but Janus just stood there, looking reluctantly at his weapon. Jacob snatched the machine gun out of his hands and threw it into the trunk too, saying, "Come on Telperion, get a grip! Have you already forgotten the lesson we learned on the West Bank? That violence only leads to more violence."

Ben just looked at us and shook his head. Then he slammed the trunk of the BMW shut, got into the jeep, and drove it back to the parkway that ran alongside the river. He drove off the road and headed straight towards the river. When he was close enough, he slowed down, jumped out of the jeep, and watched it plunge into the water.

Then he ran back to us and jumped into the driver's seat of the BMW while the rest of us piled in after him. He jumpstarted our new car in a

239

flash and we were on our way, tearing down the parkway that ran alongside the river.

"Not a minute too late," said Jacob, pointing back downriver towards the bridge. Several choppers were flying up the river.

Ben nodded. "Once they realize I'm the man behind your escape, they'll expect me to change cars. So we'll have to get ourselves another vehicle again very soon."

Again Ben drove fast, but not quite as fast as he did before. "We don't want to attract undue attention right now," he said.

A few minutes later, Ben took another left and then headed down another road—but all the time it seemed he was keeping more or less parallel to the river. We couldn't see the choppers anymore.

"Where are you taking us?" I asked.

"The CIA knows everything about my secret hideaways. They know all about my friends and contacts. It's standard procedure. So I'll have to take you somewhere that they don't know that I know."

"And where might that be?"

Ben didn't answer but just kept passing cars. I looked at the clock on the dashboard. It was almost three o'clock in the morning in Washington DC. Which meant that it was eight in the morning in England.

"I don't know why," said Ben suddenly, "but in my mind's eye I keep seeing a vision of my Uncle Ernest's cabin up at 12 Stone Mountain. I haven't been there in 15 years."

"In your mind's eye?" said Janus.

"Yes. Your friend Starbrow here calls it the Sight."

Jacob and Janus stared at Ben in amazement.

"Why do you think you're seeing this in your mind's eye?" I said.

"I don't know, but I guess it's because I have a strong hunch that we should go there."

Janus shook his head in disbelief. "The Sight? A strong hunch? What have you done to him, Master Starbrow?"

I chuckled, "I told you some pretty mind-boggling stuff has happened to Ben!"

Jacob interrupted. "Where's 12 Stone Mountain?"

"It's about a three and a half hour drive west from here—in the Appalachian Mountains, where this river—the Potomac—actually begins. It's pretty wild and uninhabited up there. In fact, my Uncle Ernest's cabin is one of the few dwellings in the area."

"What about your Uncle Ernest? Won't he be there?"

"No, he's only up there on holidays and in the summer."

Ben drove through a small town. When he came to an all-night supermarket, he drove straight into the parking lot and pulled up beside a nice Land Rover.

"If we're going up into the mountains, we'd better get ourselves a vehicle that's a bit more suitable."

"Now this has truly got to be the Mother of All Excellent Surprises," said Janus from the backseat in his most kick-ass of voices. "Just when I thought the two of you were both dead and gone—and far away in some other dimension—I find myself sitting with the both of you in a stolen Land Rover, driven by none other than the man who almost did us in— Special Agent Ben Nevis himself. And if that wasn't enough, this very same Special Agent Nevis now claims to have the Sight and has fallen prey to having 'strong hunches' and such. All I can say Starbrow is a lot sure must have happened since we saw each other last!"

I turned around in my seat (I was sitting in the front) and looked at my two friends in the back seat and laughed. It was four in the morning and still dark outside, but it was the best laugh I'd had in a month of Mondays.

"You're absolutely right," I said, still laughing, "but before I tell you my story, let me hear yours. What happened to you guys after the explosion at Glastonbury Tor?"

"Well, my story's not that exciting," said Janus. "After the explosion, I woke up in a bed in an airplane guarded by two DETI agents and this nurse. We were up in the air and I can tell you I felt pretty lousy, all covered in bandages and with lots of burns. They told me it was Sunday evening, so apparently I'd been unconscious for more than two days. After a while Ben here comes into the cabin and tells me that Glastonbury Tor has been blown off the face of the Earth and that you two have been killed by the explosion. You can see why he isn't—or at least wasn't— exactly my favorite person. He also told me that all the Power Spots had been destroyed and that the starships had vanished. Well anyway after all that cheerful news I have to admit I kind of lost hope of us ever doing any good around here."

I looked at Ben in surprise. "You mean to tell me Jacob and Janus were on the same plane as me when we flew to the US?"

Ben nodded. "We thought it would be easier to get at least one of you to talk, if you didn't know the other two were alive."

"Nice gesture," I snorted and turned back to Janus. "What happened after that?"

"Even though I'd been unconscious for more than two days, I recovered with amazing speed, at least according to the nurse. But my golden elvish locks and long, pointy elven ears were gone—and so were my golden chain mail armor and my two-handed sword. All the things that made me Telperion were gone!"

"Yeah I know," I said. "The same thing has happened to me. The star on my brow and all the things that made me Starbrow also disappeared."

"Same here as you can see." Said Jacob, waving with his right arm even though it was in a sling. "Moncler's magic staff, my wizard's cloak and spell book, all of it vanished right after the explosion."

We stared at each other and realized that this was the first chance we really had to take a good look at each other. And it was true; we were really changed. Now all three of us had ultra-short hair and we were all dressed in these dingy gray CIA prison uniforms. When you added the remains of all our cuts, burns and bruises to the picture, we really did look like a bunch of convicts or prisoners of war.

As if reading our minds, Ben broke in and said, "Yeah, we've got to get you into some other clothes so you don't look like three escaped convicts. Let's hope Uncle Ernest has some extra clothes up in his cabin."

We laughed and Janus continued his story. "After I got over the first shock and was considering some wild escape, the plane landed at some military base and I realized we'd arrived in Washington. They transported me under very tight security to CIA's headquarters and locked me up in that tiny cell. After a while Agent Nevis here and some General named Elson interrogated me."

"Did they give you the truth serum too?"

"Yeah. Two whole doses. But as you know since we have absolutely nothing to hide I told them everything that I knew about the Ashtar Command and about our adventures. I couldn't figure out if they were going to use the information for anything or if they just thought that I had completely lost it. Anyway, after the interrogation they took me back to my cell where you guys found me."

"My story is pretty much the same as Janus'," said Jacob. "I too woke up Sunday night in a bed in an airplane all battered and bruised and with a broken arm. Two DETI agents and a nurse also guarded me all the time. Then after a while Agent Nevis showed up and told me exactly the same story he told Janus. That Avalon and the Power Spots had been destroyed—that the explosion had killed you both—and that the starships had disappeared. According to him, STARDAY was cancelled. Not very uplifting news to say the least, but I tried to keep my spirits high. After Nevis left the cabin I tried to focus on the Force, but for some reason I kept falling asleep all the time and every time I dreamt about my past life as Gaius the monk in England."

"Me too!" exclaimed Janus as if he'd totally forgotten.

Jacob turned towards him.

"The same thing happened to me," said Janus, nodding in agreement. "Both on the airplane and even in the cell, I kept dreaming about my past life as Sir Loran."

"You both kept dreaming about your past lives?" I looked at Ben. "Interesting, indeed. What did you dream?"

"My dreams covered pretty much the same story as the one that we saw in our past life regression when we were up in the Mothership," said Jacob, "except this time there seemed to be more focus on Lord Gavin."

"Yeah," said Janus, "There was definitely more focus in my dreams on you too Ben."

"This is getting more and more interesting," I said. "So what did you learn about Lord Gavin that you didn't know before?"

"It's hard to tell," said Jacob, "but it felt as if there was something important I should know, but I never really found out what it was."

"Yeah I kept waking up with the same feeling," said Janus. "But what about you, Starbrow? How in the name of wonder did you manage to convince this bugger to finally come to his senses?"

"Well it's a long story… but let me start at the beginning… when I woke up surrounded by flames and burned bodies after the explosion at Glastonbury Tor…"

Jacob and Janus were all ears as I told my tale. When I told them about meeting Elmar's life-long partner Rebecca Randall and her plan for me to get in contact with the Ashtar Command, they were very surprised.

"Really?" exclaimed Jacob. "Rebecca and Elmar wanted you to contact the Ashtar Command and tell them not to cancel STARDAY? I wonder why? Especially since it was obvious that the Ashtar Command withdrew because humanity was so hostile towards them."

"That was exactly my first reaction when she said it. But Rebecca was adamant and told me it was important to remember that not everyone on Earth was hostile to our intergalactic guests—far from it. And she also reminded me that the New Vision and the whole idea of STARDAY had initiated massive changes in the consciousness of humanity…"

Then I told Jacob and Janus about the global group meditations and about how millions of people were beginning to wake up and remember their true nature—and that all this was happening right now, as we spoke.

"But there was more that I didn't know about," I continued. "There was also Elmar and Rebecca's mission."

"Their mission?" said Janus.

"Yes," I said. "Rebecca told me that the events that we are witnessing today are really the culmination of their mission, which involved many decades of hard work and sacrifice. Then she explained that it was their mission to help make humanity ready for ascension into the higher dimensions. From that perspective, she said it was obvious that STARDAY represented a unique opportunity for humanity to take a quantum leap forward in its evolution, an opportunity that we had to do everything in our power to take advantage of."

Jacob and Janus were quiet for a while, digesting Rebecca's story. Ben said nothing.

"Okay," said Jacob, finally breaking the silence, "so I take it you accepted Rebecca's appeal and decided to contact the Ashtar Command and speak on behalf of humanity."

I nodded in consent.

"So what happened next?"

I continued my tale and told my friends about my desperate escape from Glastonbury and flight through England and about how I was transubstantiated up into the Mothership from the Crystal Cave just a fraction of a second before Ben captured me…

When he heard this, Janus let out a gleeful hoot and gave me an affectionate slap on the back. "I've got to hand it to you Starbrow, you're definitely improving!"

"But you're not going to guess what happened next! I woke up in the Relaxation Forest and met Ticha!"

"You were in the Relaxation Forest without us!" cried Janus. "It's not fair! It's just not fair. While the rest of us were going through hell, you were chilling out in the Relaxation Forest with your guardian angel!"

"Truth to tell it wasn't all that relaxing!" I laughed at Janus' consternation. "I was intent on talking with Ashtar right away, but Ticha had other plans. Plans that just happened to turn my view of the world completely upside down."

Jacob laughed at the thought of our guardian angels, "Yeah, they do seem to have a knack for turning everything upside down!"

"Yeah, tell me about it. Anyway guys, this time the change in my world view was drastic to put it mildly… beyond my wildest dreams!"

Then I told them how Ticha had insisted that I do another regression to our past life in England—the same past life the three of us had seen together. Then I told my friends about the Prophecy of Starwarrior, about the Lost Teaching of the Single Eye, and about how I discovered that Gavin and Dana were twins.

Jacob and Janus stared at me in disbelief.

"You and Gavin were twins!" cried Janus. "Oh man, that's the most far out thing I've heard in a long time! You're saying you found out that your own twin brother was your murderer!"

"Yeah, that's exactly what I'm saying."

"Oh God…" Janus held his head and groaned.

"I must admit I was pretty shocked too… in fact I tried to run out of the Cosmic Library… but Ticha wouldn't let me!"

Janus shook his head. "Talk about far out! Gavin was Dana's twin brother!"

My two friends kept looking back and forth from Ben to me. "At least that explains why the two of you look so much alike," muttered Janus under his breath.

I looked over at Ben. Throughout this whole conversation, he hadn't said a word. He just kept on driving. There was no telling what was going on in his mind.

"Funny," said Jacob slowly, "but now that I think about it, I realize that the first time we met Ben I was so occupied with the news about STARDAY and with everything that was going on that I didn't allow myself to really notice the resemblance. But when I woke up on the airplane and Ben came in to talk to me, I remember how struck I was by how much he looked like you Starbrow. It was totally weird."

"Yeah, it's true," said Janus, letting it all sink in. "The same facial features, the same color eyes, same color hair… and well… there's something else as well, something that's hard to define."

"And now it turns out that you and Ben were twins back then in England," chuckled Jacob. "That really does take the cake!"

"Yeah," said Janus, grinning too, "Quite a little surprise your guardian angel had up her sleeve Starbrow! But why do you think she wanted you to see this?"

"That's what I thought too," I said. "The Keeper of the Cosmic Library said the only way for me to answer that question was to go through that past life and see it from Gavin's point of view."

"Ugh!" cried Jacob, "But is that possible?"

"Well apparently it is," I replied, "because I did it. I don't know quite how the old Keeper managed it. But I remember him saying it had something to do with the fact that we are twin souls so he could temporarily morph our bodies together, which made it possible for me to see Gavin's life from his point of view."

"Ugh! Talk about a disgusting thought!" cried Janus.

"Yeah, you can say that again," I said, looking sideways at Ben. "Nor can I say it was a particularly pleasant experience." Again I looked over at Ben, but his face said nothing.

Then I told them how the story unfolded once I was morphed to Gavin's body... about how Gavin and Dana were separated from each other at birth—and about Gavin's strange and lonely childhood and life, about his friendship with Mordred, how they plotted against Arthur and Merlin, and how finally, in the end, he unwittingly killed his own twin sister.

My two friends listened in silence.

Then I told them how Gavin met Merlin that fateful night—and learned the truth about himself and his twin sister... and about how, in the end, his hands covered with blood and his heart crying with shame, he had run into the dark forest overcome by madness.

"Gavin covered with blood..." whistled Janus. "Talk about bad karma!"

"Yeah," said Jacob, "That is some story! Who would ever have guessed that Dana and Gavin were twins? And Gavin kills Dana without realizing who she is! Once again we see that reality sure does beat fiction!"

I looked over at stone face again, but still he said nothing. He seemed completely absorbed in the dark highway before us.

Then I told them about my meeting with Ashtar in his private briefing room.

"So Ashtar actually told you that STARDAY hasn't been cancelled?" said Jacob in surprise.

"Well, technically speaking, it hasn't been cancelled," I replied. "If humanity's collective consciousness is raised an entire dimensional frequency, from quantum level 4 where it is now, to quantum level 5, STARDAY will not be cancelled and the starships will land as planned."

"And what will it take for that to happen?" asked Janus.

"A critical mass of enlightened human beings. At least 60 million enlightened beings or 1% of the Earth's population before Friday."

"At least 60 million enlightened beings... in just three days?" said Jacob.

I nodded.

"So what will it take to achieve that?" asked Janus. "The New Vision again?"

I shook my head. "No that won't work. According to Ashtar, the Light Grid was completely destroyed and most of the 600 volunteers are no longer on the Earth plane. So that possibility is completely out of the question."

"What did he suggest instead?"

"As a matter of fact, Ashtar didn't suggest anything. He said that it would probably be several hundred years before humanity's collective consciousness would again be high enough to release a STARDAY."

"Several hundred years? That sounds depressing. What will happen to the Intergalactic Fleet in the meantime?"

"It will withdraw and continue to monitor the evolution of humanity. But there will be no STARDAY."

"What about Mother Earth?" asked Jacob. "Will She make an axis shift in 2-3 years as Ashtar predicted right before we volunteers were sent back to Earth?"

"Ashtar said it was highly probable. But he couldn't tell whether the axis shift would come in two years or 20. That depends on the collective consciousness of humanity."

Jacob and Janus were silent for a while as they digested this new information. Ben drove off the highway and headed up towards the hills. We were really out in the country now, surrounded on all sides by woods and fields.

"So after that cheerful piece of news Ashtar sent you back to Earth?" said Jacob.

"No. I myself chose to come back."

"Why?"

"I kept asking Ashtar if there wasn't any other way to raise the collective consciousness. Finally he told me that he had heard rumors about three souls—called the Three E Masters—who once raised the entire collective consciousness of some faraway star system by using the Single Eye."

"The Single Eye? What's that?" asked Janus.

247

"I don't know and neither did Ashtar. Nobody seems to know. But that made me remember Merlin's Prophecy of Starwarrior."

Again I slowly recited the Prophecy for Jacob and Janus:

> *"When the One with the Sight*
> *is reunited with the Warrior from the Stars*
> *the Perfect Being will be born*
>
> *From the Perfect Being*
> *will come the Single Eye*
>
> *From the Single Eye*
> *will come the Perfect World*
>
> *And then the Angels sing"*

"So what's that supposed to mean?" asked Janus.

"According to Merlin, Dana and Gavin were the two souls spoken of in the Prophecy. The One with the Sight and the Warrior from the Stars— they were Gavin and Dana or Ben and me if you prefer. Anyway, according to the Prophecy, if we work together in harmony for some reason, we will be able to access the Lost Teaching of the Single Eye— whatever that is. But as far as I can understand, it's the Teaching the Three E Masters used to raise the collective consciousness in that faraway star system."

"There's just one small problem, isn't there?" said Janus. "Gavin killed you in our past life! And Ben nearly did in this life. Doesn't sound all that harmonious to me."

I said nothing.

"So despite this cheerful assessment," chuckled Jacob, "you decided to return to Earth anyway because you had this crazy idea that if you could work in harmony with Ben this time around, the two of you would be able to access the Lost Teaching of the Single Eye—and raise the entire collective consciousness by Friday so STARDAY doesn't get cancelled."

I nodded.

Jacob grinned out loud. "Got to hand it to you Starbrow, that's quite a gamble... but then again you were always something of a dreamer!"

"Something of a dreamer!" cried Janus. "Now that's the understatement of the year if I ever heard one! First of all, the guy you're supposed to work together with to achieve all this also happens to be your very own

248

murderer from a rather eventful past life… and also happens to be in this very life one of the main reasons why STARDAY is going to be cancelled to begin with!" Janus was really getting worked up. "And not only that, as far as I can see you haven't got the least bit of evidence that this so-called Prophecy from your past life is real and valid in this lifetime! And to make matters worse, you don't even know if these so called three E Masters actually exist or if they're in hibernation in some star system a billion light years from here…"

"There, there, Janus," said Jacob, trying to calm him down a bit. "At least old Starbrow was right about one thing. Ben seems to have decided to start working with him… for reasons that are quite beyond me…"

"Yeah, that's true," laughed Janus turning to me again. "Tell us oh Wise One, how on Earth you managed this small miracle?"

"Well I'm getting to it… I'm getting to it… just give me a chance brothers!"

Then I continued my tale. I told them how Ashtar had transubstantiated me back to the Crystal Cave, where Ben and his team took me into custody and brought me back to America for interrogation just like them. When I came to the part of the story when Ben came to my cell, Ben motioned for me to open the long black bag, which was wedged in between the front seats.

"Ben stepped into my cell and asked me if I could see—this!" I said, opening Ben's bag. The blinding light of the sword filled the car. I seized Starwarrior's shining sword and held it up before my two friends.

"Holy smoke!" cried Jacob.

"Cool sword man, cool sword!" muttered Janus.

For a moment Ben turned around and looked at my two friends in surprise. Then he looked back at the road. "So now the four of us have completely lost it!" he mumbled.

"Can you guys read what it says on the sword hilt?" I asked.

Jacob leaned forward and examined the sword, letting his hand glide slowly across the glowing symbols and runes that were engraved around the star on the hilt.

"Starwarrior," he said slowly.

"Who is Starwarrior?" asked Janus.

"Ben," I said. "Starwarrior is Ben's cosmic name, just like Starbrow is my cosmic name. This sword is Starwarrior's interdimensional key."

"She's a real beaut, she is," said Janus caressing the smooth steel admiringly. "How'd you get a hold of her, Ben?"

"I didn't," he answered. "The sword found me. When I woke up after the explosion at Glastonbury Tor, the sword was lying on the bed next to me. But I was the only who could see it. You guys are the first people I've met who can see the sword."

Jacob and Janus didn't say a word as Ben recounted his experiences with Starwarrior's sword and how he discovered he had the Sight and then hunted me over half of England.

Finally Janus couldn't help but laugh. "Starwarrior! No one in their wildest dreams could have imagined this—that the Warrior from the Stars, Starbrow's other half, was none other than Lord Gavin, Agent Nevis. This is further out than far out!"

"But Starbrow," interrupted Jacob, "you're saying that all this about Starwarrior's sword was something you first found out about when Ben stepped into your cell?"

"Yes, and even after we talked in the cell, I wasn't sure what Ben would do. But at least at that point I knew there was nothing more I could do. I kind of felt at peace after that… like it was really all up to the Force after that."

No one said anything for a while.

"There's another thing I wonder about," said Jacob after a while. "If all three of us survived the destruction of our Power Spot, maybe some of the other 600 volunteers also survived."

"We captured groups of volunteers at 126 of the 144 Power Spots," said Ben.

"126..." I said. "And 139 groups returned from the Worm Hole."

"Which must mean that 126 of the 139 groups made it to their Power Spot in time," said Jacob.

"So how many volunteers is that in all?" asked Janus.

"The 126 groups consisted of a total of 451 volunteers, including you three," said Ben. "426 of the 451 were killed by the explosion at the Power Spots—and so were thousands of agents and soldiers. You were among the lucky ones."

"426 of the 451 volunteers who made it to the Power Spots were killed?" I said. "Does that mean that besides us, 22 other volunteers are still alive?"

"DETI doesn't know for sure. You're forgetting that the whole world is in complete chaos. And in many places the explosions at the Power Spots were so powerful that the rescue workers are still digging people out. The 22 missing may be alive somewhere—but they may just as well be buried under tons of rock and earth. Your guess is as good as mine."

"That means as far as Starbrow's wild plan to raise the entire collective consciousness is concerned, we can't count on anybody but the three of us," muttered Janus.

. I didn't say anything.

Janus continued, "What about the Ashtar Command and the Ascended Masters? Can't they give us a hand?"

"No," I said, shaking my head. "Ashtar made it very clear that they're not allowed to interfere. It's up to humanity."

"And how much time do we have?"

"Like I said… until the moment when STARDAY should commence on Friday the 10th of April at 00:00:00 Greenwich Mean Time."

Janus looked at the clock on the dashboard. "And it's now 4:32 in the morning here in the US on this fine Monday morning which I believe must be the 6th of April.

"Which means it's 09:32 GMT," calculated Jacob, "so that leaves us three days and 14 hours to raise the entire collective consciousness."

"Well, that's a whole lot better than the last time," grinned Janus, "when we had less than 48 hours!"

"Yeah," said Jacob, "but last time, the power of the New Vision was magnified 60,000,000 times thanks to the concerted efforts of the 600 volunteers using the 144 Power Spots. Now we've got nothing."

"That's very encouraging, Master Wizard," said Janus. "So what do you suggest?"

"Don't ask me, ask Master Starbrow. He's the man with the plan."

It was almost eight in the morning when Ben finally turned onto the dirt road that led up to 12 Stone Mountain and Uncle Ernest's cabin. The sun was up and from time to time it sent its bright rays down through the gray rain clouds that hung over the mountain tops. The Appalachians were an impressive mountain range, which Ben told us ran all the way from Canada in the north to Georgia in the south. Our destination, 12 Stone Mountain, was only one of the many mighty mountains that made up this long chain.

I stretched and yawned. We had been driving for hours now and had only stopped twice. Once to "borrow" some gas from a truck parked by the wayside and once to move a tree that was blocking the road.

"Let's hope Uncle Ernest has left some supplies in the cabin," said Ben. "I think we could all use a nice hot cup of coffee."

"Hear, hear!" said Janus. "And some chow!"

The Land Rover reached the top of another ridge. More hills and mountains came into view and we could see how, mile after mile, we kept getting closer to the majestic peaks towering in the distance. Here and there, we caught a glimpse of a lake or a stream glinting in the sunlight. It was wild country.

After a while Ben pointed to a cabin in the distance. "That's my uncle's cabin over there at the foot of 12 Stone Mountain." We hadn't seen another house or any other sign of civilization for quite a long time.

"Pretty cool place to have a little hideaway," said Janus.

"Until I joined the army when I was 20 I used to spend all my summers up here," said Ben.

"So you know the place well?" I said.

"Like the back of my hand. In the summertime I used to trek up in the mountains for weeks in a row."

It wasn't long before Ben was pulling up in the front of a nice wooden house with a big front porch. We all got out of the car and inhaled the fresh, clean air. Then we climbed the steps up to the porch. Ben peeked in the front windows. "No one's here." Then he walked over the front door and kicked it open with one deftly aimed kick.

"Welcome to Uncle Ernest's Cabin!"

We walked in and found ourselves in the main room—a nice big room with a stone fireplace and open kitchen. An impressive stuffed moose head hung over the fireplace. There were a couple of worn sofas and armchairs in front of the fireplace. Jacob, Janus and I all plunged simultaneously into the sofas and yawned. Ben went over to the kitchen and started rummaging through the cabinets.

"There you go!" he said and held up a bag of coffee. "Looks like my uncle was here recently. Lucky for us there's some canned food here too. It's going to be baked beans and sausages for breakfast boys!"

While Ben was fixing us breakfast, we pulled off our prison uniforms and got into some extra clothes Ben had found for us upstairs. It felt good to be out of those uniforms and into something more normal—some old lumberjack shirts and jeans.

Fifteen minutes later, the four of us were busy munching away at the baked beans and sausages Ben found—and washing it down with strong coffee.

"Ah!" sighed Janus speaking for all of us, "now that sure feels a whole lot better." A collective sigh of contentment passed through the room.

"You're well on your way to paying back some of that bad karma, Ben!" continued Janus as he sat back in the sofa.

"Speaking of karma," said Jacob, downing another swig of coffee. "What about your grand plan, Master Starbrow? If we're going to raise the whole collective consciousness of Planet Earth by Friday, I don't believe we have time to slip into the 'holiday in the mountains' mode right now… do we?"

"That's right," Janus chimed in, yawning. "You two had better start working together in harmony right now so we can access this here famous Lost Teaching of the Single Eye."

"You're right." I stopped eating and looked at Ben.

He didn't say anything.

"Well, what are you two waiting for?" said Janus.

I cleared my throat, "You see, the thing is..."

"You haven't got a clue as to what to do," said Jacob bluntly.

"Yeah, that's… more or less it!"

"Wait a moment!" cried Janus. "I thought you said that the two of you were going to work together in harmony?"

"Well yes they are," said Jacob, "but what does that actually mean… you know in practice?"

Ben and I said nothing.

"I can't believe you two!" cried Janus. "You've dragged us all the way out here into the middle of frigging nowhere to save the world and now it turns out you don't have a clue as to what we're supposed to do!"

I still didn't say anything.

"But what was it the Prophecy said about you two?" asked Jacob.

"It said that when we work together in harmony we would be able to access the Lost Teaching of the Single Eye," I repeated.

"When you two work together in harmony..." Jacob, ever the thinker, said thoughtfully. "In one way at least, one could say that that's exactly what the two of you have been doing the last couple of hours."

"OK Master Wizard," said Janus, "if that's true then where is the Lost Teaching?"

"Just give them a moment," said Jacob, still looking very thoughtful.

Janus threw up his hands in disgust. "Well while the two of you are harmonizing yourselves, the least I can do is take a little nap." Janus sunk down in the sofa and put his feet up on the coffee table.

Ben's eyes met mine—and I could see he didn't have the faintest idea what we were supposed to do either.

I turned to my buddies.

"Listen guys, instead of taking a nap I strongly suggest that we begin to meditate on the Force again. Ever since Glastonbury, we've really lost it..."

Suddenly a car started honking loudly out front.

We all froze.

Ben motioned for us to be quiet. He snatched his machine gun and rushed over to one of the windows.

"Damn!" he hissed under his breath.

"Who's there?" I whispered.

"Uncle Ernest—and two of his friends. Talk about bad timing!"

We could hear footsteps and the sound of voices approaching the cabin.

"Can't you just tell them to leave us alone because we're on a top secret mission to save the world?" said Janus.

"I guess I'll have to. Stay where you are and don't say a word."

Ben put his machine gun back on the table and covered it with his jacket. Then he walked over to the door.

He grabbed the doorknob and flung the door open.

"Uncle Ernest, I..."

"Why Benjamin, my boy!" cried an enthusiastic voice from the porch.

"Uncle, I'm afraid that..."

"What a pleasant surprise!"

A burly, half bald man with a jolly red face practically pushed Ben back into the cabin as he embraced him in a huge bear hug.

"I can't believe how much you've grown my boy! Come have a look— my dear boy Benjamin is back!"

Before Ben could say another word, Uncle Ernest's two friends were also inside the cabin hugging Ben heartily.

"Delighted to see you again, old chap!" said the other man, a distinguished-looking elderly gentleman with an English accent, who was wearing a worn but immaculate tweed jacket. He looked like he'd just stepped out of an old Sherlock Holmes movie.

"Hi Emmet," said Ben, looking more than perturbed.

"Why Benjamin," cried Ernest's other friend, a little slender old lady with round wire glasses and smooth silvery hair gathered in a neat little bun, "This is indeed a lovely surprise Benjamin my boy!"

"Hi Emma," said Ben, actually hugging the little old lady.

Ernest clapped his hands together in delight, "And I can see you've brought some friends along too Ben! Now isn't that splendid. Absolutely splendid! I think this calls for my finest whisky. We simply must celebrate Benjamin my boy!"

"But Uncle Ernest!" cried Ben, clearing his throat. "I'm sorry, but my friends and I just don't have time to celebrate right now. Haven't you been listening to the news Uncle Ernest? The whole world is about to go under!"

"Nonsense, my boy," said Ernest as he slapped Ben heartily on the back. "There's never a better time to celebrate than the present moment!"

6

Uncle Ernest and His Friends

Before we knew what hit us, Uncle Ernest and his two friends had invaded the cabin and were busy introducing themselves to Jacob, Janus and me. For some reason, Ben seemed to be completely unable to deal with the situation.

"I must say it's an honor," said Emmet, shaking my hand warmly.

"I can't tell you how delighted I am to meet dear Benjamin's friends," followed Emma, shaking my hand just as warmly as Emmet. "And my... what a startling resemblance there is between you and Ben!" she said with a twinkle in her eye.

Ben tried in vain to get his jolly uncle to understand the seriousness of the situation.

"Uncle, you're not listening to me! I am being serious, quite serious. The situation really *is* serious! *Very serious Uncle Ernest*!"

"Oh come, come, my boy. Nothing is really worth losing your peace of mind over! You know that!"

"It's got nothing to do with me losing my peace of mind..." said Ben. He was starting to sound really irritated.

"You should listen to your Uncle Ernest," said Emma soothingly to Ben while she was eagerly shaking Jacob and Janus' hands. "It's never a good idea to lose your peace of mind... no matter what is going on."

"It's got nothing whatsoever to do with that!" said Ben. "Nothing whatsoever. Now uncle, you must listen..."

"Even though it's still quite early in the day, I think we could all do with a nice shot of my finest whisky," said Ernest as he pulled a bottle from one of the cabinets.

Jacob, Janus and I were looking at each other in complete surprise. What was going on here?

256

"I said we don't have time for that now..." said Ben again, trying to cut through the incomprehensible whirlwind that seemed to have taken him over.

"Nonsense my boy! Nonsense!"

Ernest passed a couple of glasses to Emma and Emmet who then passed them on to us. Before we knew it, Ernest was pouring whisky into our glasses and the seven of us were standing in a circle, whisky glasses in our hands.

"Cheers, my boy!" said Ernest, raising his glass to Ben and the rest of us.

"Cheers!" cried Emma and Emmet in unison.

"Uncle, you are being very kind. But we just don't have time for..."

"Nonsense," said Emma. "Nothing can be that much of a hurry now can it?"

"Yes it can," I said, trying to come to Ben's assistance. "As a matter of fact time is of the essence."

"I'm quite sure the four of you will have plenty of time to do absolutely everything that has to be done," said Emmet calmly.

"Well, I'm not that sure," I said. "Not at all…"

"And what then? What if you don't have time to do whatever it is that is so important?" said Ernest laughing and taking a good swig of his whisky.

"Then it will be all over," I said," … all over."

When they heard that Ernest, Emmet and Emma simply roared with laughter.

"I must say," said Emma, the tears running down her cheeks, "it's been absolutely ages since I've heard anything that funny! The young man actually said… 'Then it will all be over!' As if anything is ever over…"

"How very right you are my dear," said Ernest, drying his eyes, "nothing is ever really over. And even if one doesn't have time to do whatever it is that must be done this time around, you can be sure you'll have plenty of time to do it the next time around!"

"But you don't get it..." I cried.

"No, I'm happy to say we don't!" said Emmet, still laughing heartily.

Ernest and Emma joined him in laughing heartily at what I'd just said.

"Man, these three are really beginning to annoy me!" muttered Janus under his breath.

"Now, now, now," said Emma kindly. "Nothing is really worth getting annoyed over either!"

And with that, they all burst out laughing again.

Janus turned red and clenched his fists, looking like he was just about to explode.

"I see the four of you were having breakfast," said Ernest motioning over to the kitchen table. "Mind if I join you? And what about you, Emma and Emmet? Will you join me for some baked beans and sausage!"

"Sounds good to me," said Emmet and Emma in unison again.

"This is a nightmare," moaned Janus. "… a complete nightmare!"

"Don't you know that bad dreams can be hazardous to your health, young man?" said Emmet. "That's why the wise always advise us to dream good dreams!"

Janus looked as if he was just about to strangle Emmet. "Help me for Christ's sake Ben! Can't you do something about these lunatics? We've got more important things to do than babysit for a bunch of raving idiots."

But Ben had no time. Uncle Ernest had already cornered him in the kitchen as he was pouring some baked beans into a saucepan. "So what brought you to these parts, Benjamin?" Ernest was asking him.

"That's exactly what I'm trying to tell you. We're on a top secret mission."

"Why that sounds very exciting," said Emma sweetly as she took a dainty sip of her whisky.

"What's going on my lad?" asked Emmet.

"Well," said Ben, sounding now for the first time like he was going to take charge of things again, "the CIA has really made a mess of things."

"Oh, it can't be that bad," said Emma.

"Yes, as a matter of fact it really is very bad," I said.

"You know what I always say to myself when I meet someone who seems to be acting foolishly?" said Emma. "I always say that all I can do to help is pray that they will become wiser. And in the meantime, if they suffer, it means that kindly Mother Nature is teaching them a valuable lesson, a lesson they need to learn..."

"Yes, yes, of course that's true in some cases," I said. "But we're talking about a catastrophe of gigantic proportions here."

"Oh it can't be that bad," said Emma again in her sweet little voice.

"You have no idea how bad," I said.

"You must know my dear boy, it's not a good idea to focus on how badly things could turn out," Emma continued sweetly, "because what you focus upon grows. Haven't you heard that?"

"Yes, yes, of course..."

258

"Well that's good. And so you must also know that you can only focus on one thing at a time," she went on. "So I better understand that you're feeling so stressed young man... trying to think about two different things at the same time..."

"But I'm not stressed!" I objected. "And I'm not thinking about two different things at the same time..."

"Well you sound stressed to me."

"I'm not..." I cried and then said, "Okay forget it... so I am stressed. But the fact is the whole thing depends on the four of us..."

"Sounds to me as if this young man feels he's carrying the weight of the world on his shoulders!" laughed Ernest.

"I guess we can thank our lucky stars that he's not," laughed Emmet. "Because fortunately for all of us, things don't work like that."

Then the three of them burst out laughing again.

I looked at Jacob for help. He was the only one who hadn't said a word since Uncle Ernest and his friends arrived.

"Let me tell you a little story, my boy," said Emmet patting me on the shoulder. "In the old days, when we used to go to Europe on one of the great ocean liners, we never worried about getting there safely. And do you know why? Because we had confidence in the Captain. We knew that the Cunard or the French Line wouldn't put one of their valuable ships in incompetent hands. So if we woke up in the middle of the night and the weather was rough and stormy, we didn't run up to the bridge to tell the Captain to be careful or to ask him if he was sure he was on course. No, my boy, we stayed in our cabins and slept soundly because we knew the Captain was on the bridge. And the same goes for Life in general. The Captain *is* on the bridge."

"What on Earth has a story about old ocean liners got to do with anything!" fumed Janus.

"If you ask me, I think it was an excellent story, Emmet," said Emma smiling and pressing Emmet's hand warmly.

"Okay," said Ben trying to explain. "This is the situation. The whole world is in chaos."

"Well, " said Emma, "sometimes one needs a bit of chaos to shake up the old order. And after that, when the dust settles, everything usually looks a whole lot better."

"Yes, yes," said Ben. "But in this case we're talking about hundreds of thousands of people who have just died, hundreds of millions of people that are homeless..."

"I tried being homeless once," interrupted Ernest, "and it was actually quite interesting. As far as I remember, I learnt several valuable lessons from the experience too."

"Yes, of course. But the whole world is in a state of emergency and many people have lost everything..."

"I've always said you can't lose what really belongs to you," said Emma.

"For Christ's sake, will you let the man finish!" cried Janus. He was really having a hard time controlling himself.

"It's kind of difficult to explain," said Ben, "because it's got something to do with the different levels of consciousness. But the fact is that unless the four of us raise the entire collective consciousness of humanity before Friday, the future of humanity looks very bleak."

"It can't be that bad," said Emma for the third time.

"You sound as if you're worried that the whole universe is going to blow up!" said Ernest as he poured the hot beans and sausages on to the three empty plates on the kitchen counter and handed them to Emma and Emmet.

"You three are just too much!" cried Janus, pounding his fist on the table. "And what would the three of you do if the whole universe was about to blow up? Just keep on drinking whisky and eating baked beans?"

"What I would do if the whole universe blew up?" said Emmet softly as he stuffed a portion of baked beans into his mouth. "Well young man, I would just let it blow up. And when the dust settled, the Captain would still be on the bridge, and I would still be alive somewhere, ready to carry on."

"This is just too much!" said Janus, fuming. "You three are the most idiotic bunch of annoying..."

"Janus, wait a minute," said Jacob softly.

Janus, Ben and I looked at Jacob. It was the first time our friend had said anything since Uncle Ernest and his friends arrived.

"Well what?" said Janus, still fuming. "What?"

"Maybe you should just… just ... listen to what the three of them are saying."

"What do you mean?"

"I mean exactly that… just think about what these three have actually been saying."

Janus looked at Ernest, Emmet and Emma.

Suddenly the three of them were completely silent.

They'd also stopped eating and drinking and were now sitting very quietly, looking at each other with the most mischievous look in their eyes, as if they'd just told us the joke of the century and were waiting for us to get it.

"Jacob, what on earth are you talking about, man?"

"I'm talking about what the three of them have actually been saying."

"A lot of irritating nonsense!" said Janus. "That's what"!

"Then you haven't really been listening to what they have been saying," said Jacob.

"OK man. Just tell us what you're getting at Jacob, will you please?" I said feeling rather annoyed myself. "We don't have time for any more fun and games."

"Well," said Jacob. "Didn't you say that the Prophecy of Starwarrior said that when you and Ben worked together in harmony, you would be able to access the Lost Teaching of the Single Eye?"

"Yes."

"And suppose we presume that during the last couple of hours, the two of you have been working together in perfect harmony."

"Yeah... so?"

"So then you should now have access to the Lost Teaching of the Single Eye. The same teaching that the Three E Masters used to raise the collective consciousness of an entire star system."

"And...?"

I still didn't get where Jacob was going with all this.

"Well...what's the first letter of Ernest's name?

"E," I said.

"And what is the first letter of his two friends' names...?"

"E," I said again.

"Exactly," said Jacob quietly.

I was still completely blank.

"Ernest... and Emmet... and Emma," I said again.

"Yes," said Jacob again.

And then like an explosion, it dawned on me.... "The three Es."

"Exactly."

"Jacob, are you saying..."

I stared in amazement at those three very unusual characters who were now sitting silently at the table, looking down at their baked beans. Then I noticed that their lips were trembling as if they were about to roar with laughter again and I realized that they could hardly contain themselves a second longer...

"You mean to tell me that the three of them are..." I heard myself saying.

Jacob nodded.

"... The Three E Masters!"

7

The Law Never Forgets

In a split second, Ernest, Emmet and Emma were rolling with laughter again and clapping their hands as the tears rolled down their cheeks.

"Are you really the Three E Masters?" I asked again in amazement.

My question set the three of them laughing again.

"Well, what do you think?" asked Emmet.

"Well, you're not exactly... the way I thought you'd be."

"Didn't anyone ever tell you that you shouldn't judge a book by its cover?" said Emma, drying her eyes again.

"Yeah, sure. But I kind of thought that you would be more like the other Ascended Masters we've met. With big shiny auras and not..."

"And not what?" Emmet asked.

Again the three of them were rolling with laughter.

"Oh God," said Emmet, drying his tears. "It's a frigging miracle that the four of you ever found us!"

Janus looked suspiciously at the three of them.

"But why all the secrecy? Why didn't you just tell us right away that you were the Three E Masters?"

"But we did," said Ernest. "You were just so occupied with saving the world you didn't seem to notice!"

The four of us stared at them in total bewilderment. Chubby Ernest with his ruddy face and bald head, proper Emmet in his old-fashioned tweed jacket, and tiny Emma with her round glasses and neat little bun. No, they certainly didn't look like the other Masters we'd met on our way!

"That means your Uncle Ernest was one of the Three E Masters all along and you never knew it Ben..." said Jacob slowly.

Ben shook his head, utterly confused.

"Well, we had to keep an eye on the boy somehow," said Ernest as he patted Ben on the shoulder. "In case he woke up one day and remembered who he was."

"But why didn't you just tell him right away?" I asked.

"All in good time," said Emmet. "But in any case, you're forgetting the Prophecy of Starwarrior. It's not until you and Ben work together in harmony that the two of you are able to discover us, even though we've been here all along."

"But I still don't understand why you didn't just tell us right away who you are?" said Janus.

"But we did," said Ernest. "You were so busy saving the whole world that you didn't pay attention."

"Well is there anything wrong with that?" I asked.

"You can say what you like about these boys," said Emma, "but one thing is for sure… they certainly don't lack optimism."

"True," chuckled Emmet. "Only it's a pity they have so little spiritual understanding!"

Emmet's remark once again set the three of them rolling with laughter.

"Okay, so we overlooked the fact that you're the Three E Masters," I said. "But it can't be all that bad."

"Oh yes it can!" said Ernest, laughing even more.

"Couldn't you be just a bit more constructive instead of laughing at us all the time?" said Janus. He was still really pissed.

"Yes, yes, quite right," said Emmet as another tear rolled down his cheek. "It's just that it's been such a long time since I've met such pathetic ascension candidates as the four of you!"

Peals of laughter filled the cabin.

I looked at Jacob and Janus, and then at Ben. I still had difficulty believing that these three dusty old characters really were the Three E Masters who had supposedly raised the collective consciousness of an entire star system.

"All right," said Ernest to Emmet and Emma. "I guess we'd better be a little more supportive, don't you think."

"Yes," said Emma with a smile.

"Well boys, what can we do for you?" asked Emmet, straightening his tie.

"Ehm…" I said, "You can teach us about the Single Eye… for starters…"

"Why do you want to learn about the Single Eye?" Emma asked.

"So we can raise the collective consciousness of humanity to quantum level 5 by Friday so that STARDAY won't be cancelled."

"He's really quite the optimist, isn't he?" said Emmet.

"According to Commander Ashtar, the three of you lifted the collective consciousness of an entire star system with the Single Eye," I said.

Ernest nodded. "It's true."

"That was in the Umtarion-system," said Emma. "The souls that hung out in that system back then were really sweet."

"We've been looking for you because we want you to share the Lost Teaching with us so we can raise the collective consciousness here on Earth," I said.

Ernest, Emmet and Emma didn't reply, instead they just smiled blissfully and looked expectantly at Ben. Ernest went over to his nephew and patted him proudly on the shoulder as Jacob, Janus and I looked on.

But Ben didn't respond, rather he wrenched himself out of Ernest's fatherly grip and ran over to the window. The rest of us followed him with our eyes.

"Damn!" cried Ben when he got to the window. Suddenly he had that wild look on his face and we realized that a sound like distant thunder was approaching the cabin.

"What is it?" Janus cried.

"They've found us!"

"Who's found us?" asked Ernest.

"My former employer—the CIA!"

We all ran over to the windows. Above the trees that stretched out in all directions we could see eight military helicopters soaring straight toward the cabin at breakneck speed. Looking down the winding road that led up to the cabin, we could just make out the police cars and jeeps that were roaring up the hill towards us.

"How did they find us so fast?" cried Jacob.

"I don't know," cried Ben. "No one should know about this cabin! Unless they tracked us somehow."

Jacob, Janus and I were looking out the windows in horror. The helicopters and police cars were closing in on us very quickly. It wouldn't be long before they'd have us surrounded!

Ben was calculating fast. "That must be the local sheriff and his men," said Ben, pointing at the cars heading our way. "And by the look of those choppers, General Elson's got assistance from the Special Forces. We've got to get out of here right away!"

Ben ran over to the table and grabbed his machine gun and his backpack.

"But what about the Lost Teaching..." I cried.

"If we don't get the hell out of here right now, it's game over boys!" shouted Ben. "And this time you won't have me or any shining swords to set you free! Now move!"

Ben was already at the back of the cabin where he broke a window with the butt of his machine gun. "There's no time to think!" he yelled. "Just run! Head for the hills!"

I looked over at Ernest, Emmet and Emma. They seemed totally unaffected by the situation.

"If you don't get a move on it right away you can forget all about raising the collective consciousness!" cried Ben, already outside the cabin. "Now move, MOVE!"

The sound of the choppers was almost upon us.

Jacob, Janus and I gave each other a quick look—and then hopped out the window and took off like greased lightning after Ben.

In a few seconds, we were far from the cabin. We were already surrounded by great trees on all sides, running as fast as we could. We headed straight into the forest that stretched before us in endless miles up the mountain.

Ben was already quite a ways ahead of us, leaping over fallen trees and weaving his way in and out of the undergrowth. After a few minutes, Ben stopped by a babbling brook and waited for us to catch up with him. When we reached him, we turned and looked back. It was impossible to see the cabin anymore butt we could hear the roar of the choppers.

"Sounds like they are landing as close to the cabin as they can," said Ben.

"What about your uncle and his friends?" I asked.

"It's not them they're after—it's us. In 30 seconds, they'll realize we're not in the cabin and they'll be after us again!"

Ben turned and leapt across the stream—and began to run again through the trees as fast as he could. We followed. After a few minutes, he changed course and began running to the right up another hill, across some big rocks in another stream, then crisscross over several moss-covered rocky precipices. He seemed certain of his wild zigzag course as he led us higher and higher up into the mountains.

A couple of minutes later we heard the choppers take off and whiz out in different directions. Ben stopped to listen.

"That's good, "he said as we tried to catch our breath, "they've split up."

"Where are we going?" said Janus as he wiped the sweat from his forehead.

"Upwards." Ben pointed to the mountaintops that towered high above us.

"And after that?"

Ben didn't answer. He was already on his way again. Upwards and ever upwards he led us without a stop in a wild zigzag course through the forest.

Suddenly we heard the sound of choppers approaching.

"Over there! Quick... into the bushes!"

Ben pointed to some bushes at the foot of the rocky precipice where we stood.

The sound of choppers was almost upon us. We jumped down from the rock face and landed hard in the bushes. Then we crawled deeper into the dense leaves and branches, huddling together under the bushes.

The choppers were right above us now.

The power of their propellers made the bushes above us shake. A couple of the trees not far from us that had almost been knocked over by the storms of the preceding days broke in two and came crashing down. One large pine tree cracked and came thundering down alarmingly close to us.

Two helicopters hovered right above us. They were so close that through the leaves, I caught a glimpse of soldiers in army-green uniforms scanning the terrain from both sides of the chopper.

Suddenly it turned and zoomed on, further up the mountainside.

"Special forces," said Ben as we crawled out from under the bushes.

"How good are they?" asked Janus.

"The best of the best. I'm pretty sure their next move will be to place a couple of units on the ground."

"What do we do?"

"Move on!"

The choppers could no longer be heard and we were back on our feet again. This time Ben led us in a more direct route straight towards the top of the mountain. The higher we climbed, the less dense were the trees, so at times Ben had to stop and survey the terrain for the least exposed route towards the top. The going kept getting more and more steep and in several places, we had to half run, half crawl over the mountain's steep rocky sides.

Suddenly Ben slowed down. We had come to a series of huge moss-covered boulders that protruded from the side of the mountain like the crooked green teeth of a giant. Ben got down on his hands and knees and started to crawl in between two of the boulders. We got down and

267

followed him, gasping for breath. When we were halfway through, Ben suddenly disappeared from sight.

"Where did he go?" asked Janus.

"Down here," we heard Ben's voice echoing back to us from a little further ahead.

We followed the voice and found out why we couldn't see Ben. The rocky passageway split in two and Ben had taken the left turn. We crawled after him and found ourselves underneath a natural roof with a big black hole in it.

"I'm in here," Ben cried.

I crawled through the dark opening after Ben; Janus and Jacob were right behind me.

For a few seconds everything was dark.

Then suddenly I could see Ben. He'd turned on his flashlight and was standing right in front of me.

We discovered we were inside a deep cavern, approximately six feet high and thirty feet long. Ben walked over to the end of the cavern, looked around and sat down. We followed him and sat down next to him, happy to be able to get a chance to rest after our breakneck flight up the mountainside.

"I am going to allow us a short break," said Ben. "We can rest for a few minutes—until they send the bloodhounds after us."

"The bloodhounds?"

"I'm sure the Special Forces will make use of the sheriff's bloodhounds. The only question is how long it will take them to get the dogs up here."

"And then the hunt continues," I said. "And all the while we're getting further and further away from the Three E Masters and the Lost Teaching of the Single Eye."

"Yeah," said Janus, shaking his head, "the Three E Masters who just happened to be Ben's uncle and friends. I still can't believe it!"

"It's as much news to me as it is to you," said Ben. He walked over to the cave's entrance and sat down.

"And you mean to say that all the time you've known them they never said a word about who they really are or about the Single Eye?" I asked.

"Nope." Ben replied, shaking his head. He took off his backpack and began rummaging in it.

"Oh come on, Ben, you can't be serious that you don't know more about them," I said. "You said yourself you used to spend all your summers up here when you were a kid."

Ben took a compass and knife out of his backpack. "That's right."

268

"Then you must have spent a lot of time with them."

"Yeah I did. In fact they raised me. You see both my parents were killed in a car accident when I was four years old. Ernest adopted me and took me up to the mountains where I lived on a farm with him and Emmet and Emma. We used to spend all our summers here at the cabin."

"Adopted you? So Ernest is not your real uncle?"

"No, no." Ben continued searching his backpack. "I'm not related to any of them. 'Uncle' was just something Ernest used to call himself."

"The Three E Masters adopted you? This is getting to be more and more weird."

"I told you I had no idea they were the Three E Masters!"

"Speaking of the Three E Masters," said Janus. "Maybe we should just ask them what the Lost Teaching is, instead of trying to dig it out of Ben—who doesn't seem to remember anything anyway."

"Great idea Janus," laughed Jacob as he wiped his sweaty face on his shirtsleeve. "But somehow I don't think going back to the cabin would be such a good idea right now."

"But there's got to be some way we can get in touch with them again," I said.

"I don't suppose you happen to have their cell phone number so we can just call them up, Ben?" asked Janus sarcastically.

"Nope. And even if I did, it would be much too risky to call them now. The CIA will definitely hold them under strict surveillance."

Our conversation was interrupted by the sound of a chopper again. It sounded as if one was approaching to our right. We stopped talking and didn't move. Ben grabbed his machine gun.

The chopper sped over us. A minute later, the sound of the chopper was fading into the distance. We relaxed and breathed a little easier again.

"But we have to do something—and fast," I continued. "We've only got three days until STARDAY and every second counts. We've got to get hold of the Three E Masters somehow or other."

"Let's just analyze the situation for a moment," said Jacob. "The Three E Masters know we've fled up into the mountains. And obviously they know we want to get in touch with them so we can learn about the Teaching of the Single Eye—without being captured by the CIA. So don't you think they'd try to meet us somewhere? Somewhere you used to go to when you were a child, Ben? Some secret place that only the four of you know—that would be safe now that the CIA's after us?"

"12 Stone Falls," said Ben.

"12 Stone Falls? What's that?" I asked.

"Ever since we started up the mountain I've been seeing 12 Stone Falls in my mind."

"What's 12 Stone Falls?" asked Janus.

"It's a waterfall further up the mountain situated in a little dell. When I was a kid Ernest and his friends used to take me up to the waterfall to teach me..."

"Go on, to teach you what?" I said.

Ben avoided my gaze and looked out of the cave.

"I... I can't remember."

"You can't remember!" snorted Janus. "When you were a kid you were raised by none less than three Masters who raised the collective consciousness in an entire star system—and you can't remember! Come on Ben, I don't believe it. How come you can't remember? Did you fall and hit your head or something... or are you just suffering a severe case of memory loss?"

Ben shook his head.

"What happened, Ben?" I asked.

"I don't want to talk about it."

Jacob, Janus and I looked at each other in surprise. I turned to Ben again.

"Ben, you've got to tell us what happened. Our mission might depend on it."

Still no answer; Ben just kept staring out of the cave.

"Ben, you've got to tell us what happened."

Ben was silent for several seconds. Then he said quietly,

"My wife was killed."

"Killed?"

"Yes, killed."

I looked over at my two friends again.

"How was she killed?"

"We were so young. I was only 20 and she was 19. We'd just gotten married and were celebrating our honeymoon in New York City. On our way back to the hotel late one evening, three crazy junkies cornered us and pushed us down a dark alley. One of them had a knife. He grabbed my wife and I tried to free her. In the commotion, he got desperate and he stabbed her—right in the chest. One of the others hit me from behind so I passed out. When I came to, I found myself in a hospital bed. The doctor told me my wife was dead. The junkie had stabbed her right in the heart and she died immediately. And with her, the life she bore also died."

"The life she bore?" said Jacob. "You mean she was pregnant?"

"Four months pregnant."

I looked at Ben, utterly amazed. He just kept staring out of the cave.

"A knife in the heart?" I said.

"Yes."

Ben said no more. The rest of us were silent for a while.

"A knife in the heart..." I said in a low voice. "So now I better understand why you dropped your sword back in the cell when I told you about your past life. About how when you were Gavin, you stabbed Dana in the chest and killed her."

Ben still said nothing.

Jacob and Janus shot me a look.

"Gavin stabbed Dana in the heart and killed her..." said Jacob slowly. "And 1,500 years later, Ben's wife is stabbed in the heart and dies…"

A great stillness descended on the cave. All that could be heard was the mountain wind in the trees and bushes outside.

"I'm truly sorry, Ben," I said. "No matter what you did in the past, you surely didn't deserve..."

"If what you boys are telling me is really true, it's not a question about deserving," said Ben.

"Ben is right," said Jacob. "It's the Law of Cause and Effect. Karma. As you sow, so shall you reap."

"Yeah, but still, we're talking about 1500 years later!" cried Janus. "Talk about waiting a long time before settling an account."

"The Law never forgets," said Jacob.

Ben smiled faintly.

"So what happened after that?" asked Janus.

"After I lost my wife and baby, I just couldn't go back to the mountains and my old life... the memories were too painful. So I joined the army."

"What about Ernest and Emmet and Emma? Didn't you tell them what happened?"

"Yeah, I wrote them a letter."

"But didn't you talk to them—or call them or something?" asked Jacob.

"No. And I haven't had any contact with them for the last 15 years."

None of us said anything for a while.

Janus was the first to break the silence. "At least this explains your relationship to Ernest and his friends a little better."

"Which brings us back to the Three E Masters," I said. "Time is running out and we have to find them. And according to Ben's intuition, 12 Stone Falls is the most likely place to find them. How far is it to the waterfall, Ben?"

Our guide stood up and put on his backpack.

"Usually I'd say half a day's march. But today I say a quarter of a day's march because I know the mountains like the back of my hand—and we're in one hell of a hurry."

8

The Stanza of the Ancients

For four hours, Ben led us on—through narrow mountain passes and along the windswept sides of the mountain—ever higher and higher. During the first two hours, we had to run for cover more than once, hiding under the nearest bush or rock as our pursuers came thundering up the mountainside in their choppers. But after that, we didn't see or hear any more choppers, nor did we meet any agents or soldiers on the ground.

Still Ben kept moving ahead at a relentless pace, finally leading us through a tree-covered valley to our destination. It was about 1 o'clock in the afternoon on Monday when we finally arrived at 12 Stone Falls—a mighty waterfall that roared for about fifty yards straight down the steep mountainside at the other end of the valley. For a moment as we entered the valley, the gray clouds parted and the waterfall shimmered like a rainbow-colored curtain in the afternoon sun. Otherwise all was quiet in this wild and beautiful place, and there was no sign of the Three E Masters.

Ben led us quickly up along the right side of the waterfall—half running, half climbing—towards a narrow ledge that was about 30 yards above our heads. As we got closer to the ledge, which seemed to wind its way along the side of the mountain, we could see that it passed right through the roaring waterfall.

After several minutes of climbing we finally came to the ledge. It was little more than a foot wide; barely enough for someone to walk on it, but Ben didn't hesitate. He was already moving along the ledge with his back to the cliff wall, heading straight towards the waterfall. There was nothing for it but to follow him. As we approached the roaring waterfall, spray covered us like a cool rain. But even then Ben didn't stop, instead it looked like he just walked straight into the waterfall—and disappeared from sight.

I followed, wondering what was going on. But then I understood. Looking up I realized that a few yards above our heads a huge rock formation jutted out from the side of the mountain making the water arch slightly outward before it fell down the side of the mountain into the valley. And there where the water arched, there was an opening or gap behind the waterfall. Ben was standing in that gap now with his flashlight in hand, waving to me to follow him.

I followed and stepped behind the waterfall and into the gap—without even getting wet.

The gap opened into a cave behind the waterfall, which was surprisingly large. It must have been about five to six yards to the roof of the cave and about thirty yards to the other end, and maybe twelve to fifteen yards from wall to wall. The cave's rocky floor slanted slightly downwards— and in the middle of the cave there was a large pool of water—created I guessed by water from the falls, which must have gradually dripped down into the cave.

"Nice little hideaway," whistled Janus as he and Jacob entered the cave behind me.

"But no E Masters," observed Jacob.

He was right. There was no one in the cave.

"Well maybe they haven't arrived yet," said Janus. "After all, the three of them look way beyond retirement age."

"Way beyond retirement age!" cried Jacob. "If they could lift the collective consciousness of an entire star system, I'm sure they'd be able to whisk themselves up to this little cave in no time if they really wanted to."

"Well then where are they if they're so bloody quick?" said Janus as he started walking down towards the pool of water.

Ben was already standing by the water.

The four of us placed ourselves around the pool of water and Ben turned off his flashlight. Daylight seeped in through the hidden openings on both sides of the waterfall and dimly lit up the cave.

"So here we are—at the famous 12 Stone Falls," said Janus. "And there's still no sign of the Terrific Trio. So what do we do now?"

No one answered. Instead we stood perfectly still and listened to the roaring waterfall as the sound from it reverberated inside the cave. The rays of the sun made the falling water dance with rainbow colors… red, orange, yellow, green…

I looked in Ben's direction—and realized that he hadn't heard a single word of what we had been saying. He was just standing there by the water's edge, staring at the pool with this faraway look in his eyes. Then I realized his lips were moving as if he was talking to some invisible presence.

"What are you saying, Starwarrior?" I said to Ben.

"Oh," he said softly as if I'd startled him. "Now I remember what it was Ernest, Emmet and Emma taught me when I was a child and they brought me up here…"

We all looked at him. He was still staring at the pool. There was a faint smile on his lips as if he was remembering something pleasant.

"Well, what did they teach you Ben?" I asked.

He shook his head. "It's nothing really. Just an old rhyme."

"A rhyme?"

Ben nodded. "Well actually Ernest and the others called it "The Stanza of the Ancients" and they said it was very important that I never forgot it."

"Why was it important?" asked Jacob.

"I don't know. They said that even if I forgot everything else, it was very important that I never forget the stanza."

"Well, if it's so important, can you remember it?" asked Janus.

"Yes," said Ben, still with that faraway look in his eyes.

"Well, let's hear it then!" said Janus.

For a moment Ben didn't say anything. Then, without taking his eyes off the pool, he slowly chanted:

"12 stones
brought here from the Ancient lands

12 stones
put here by the Masters' hands

12 stones
underneath the Sea of Glass

12 stones
revealing what will come to pass"

The moment Ben uttered these words, the moving waters of the pool became completely still.

Like a Sea of Glass.

Like magic.

275

And underneath this Sea of Glass, we could suddenly clearly see the bottom of the pool.

A bottom... of rainbow colors. Because there, on the bottom of the pool, there was a row of glimmering stones—each about the size of a human hand. And each glowing stone had a different color—one was pearly white, one was ruby red, one was emerald green, one was cobalt blue. And I realized that in all there were ... 12 stones!

We stared in fascination at the 12 shining stones on the bottom of the pool. They were incredibly beautiful, but it was impossible to see if they were natural or man-made.

"12 stones... revealing what will come to pass," said Janus. "What does that mean?"

We turned towards Ben again but he didn't look back at us, he just kept staring at the 12 shining stones.

"You know what guys!" exclaimed Jacob suddenly sounding very excited. "I think you two, Starbrow and Starwarrior, should say the stanza together and see what happens."

Ben and I both looked at Jacob. "What are you thinking Jacob?" I asked.

"Didn't you say that the Prophecy of Starwarrior says that when the two of you work together in harmony you will be given access to the Lost Teaching of the Single Eye?"

"Yes..."

"Well then try saying "The Stanza of the Ancients" together and see what happens. If the Three E Masters told Ben it was so important maybe it's because the stanza will release the Teaching."

"Hmm," I said. "That's an interesting thought. Okay," I said, looking at Ben. "Let's give it a try."

I walked over and stood next to Ben and looked down at the 12 shining stones. They seemed even more beautiful than they were just a moment ago.

Then we said in one voice:

"12 stones
brought here from the Ancient lands

12 stones
put here by the Masters' hands

12 stones
underneath the Sea of Glass

12 stones
revealing what will come to pass"

With each word we spoke, the 12 stones seemed to become brighter and brighter. And not only that—the still waters of the pool became even more still and started to shimmer—truly like a Sea of Glass. A Sea of Glass that was slowly expanding... Or was it just my imagination?

No, I realized it wasn't!

The Sea of Glass was really getting larger and larger!

Slowly but surely spreading out in all directions!

The four of us stepped back in amazement. Truly Jacob had been right, there was something about "The Stanza of the Ancients", something strange and wonderful and powerful that transformed the water of the pool into a shimmering sea of translucent glass that was spreading out in all directions. It was even underneath our feet! It was everywhere... under us, in front of us, behind us and spreading out in all directions. And as the Sea of Glass grew, the cave, the waterfall, the mountain, and the valley outside all completely disappeared.

We all stared in amazement. It was magic. In just a few seconds, everything around us had disappeared.

And now, all that remained was the vast, immense shimmering Sea of Glass we were standing on that spread out in all directions, as far as the eye could see and on into infinity.

We blinked, staring wide-eyed at the vastness of infinity that was enfolding around us in all directions.

It was awesome.

So awesome that we were stunned... speechless.

And indeed no word was uttered as we stood there drinking in the mystery The Stanza of the Ancients had released.

It was utterly fantastic, unlike any place or space I'd ever seen before.

As I tried to take it all in I realized that I'd never experienced such a sense of vastness... of clear, empty open space before. And yet it was not an openness or an emptiness that was empty in the normal sense of the word. No, on the contrary, it was an emptiness and an openness that was vibrantly alive, crystal clear, profoundly rich, intelligent and aware. I couldn't explain it to myself but I just knew that there was something about the vastness of this space we were experiencing that was more

277

alive, more vibrant, more aware, more intelligent than anything I'd ever experienced before.

And so we stood there as if turned to stone.

As we stood there in silent amazement, the thought dawned on me, just out of the blue, out of the great empty openness that we were standing in and upon, that for a brief moment of no time we were actually experiencing the Vast Mind of God Him-Herself...

"Look," whispered Janus in the most awestruck of voices, looking down at the Sea of Glass right underneath our feet.

Jacob, Ben and I followed his lead and looked down. Underneath our feet, the Sea of Glass was solid and deep like clear ice or solid crystal yet at the same time, completely pure and transparent... like a diamond.

And then we saw what Janus meant. Underneath our feet lay the 12 glimmering stones. But how they had grown! When we first saw them, they looked about the size of a human hand, now each stone was man-size! Honey yellow, kingly amethyst, apple green...

"12 stones brought here from the Ancient lands..." said Jacob dreamily.

"12 stones put here by the Masters' hands..." whispered Janus.

"12 stones underneath the Sea of Glass..." I followed slowly.

"12 stones revealing what will come to pass," said Ben at last.

The moment we uttered the words of The Stanza of the Ancients, I heard something behind us. Something that sounded like a gentle breeze, blowing our way. And then I felt it, felt a gentle breeze caress me. First it seemed to caress my face, then it moved on and caressed the rest of my body until I felt myself completely enveloped by this gentle breeze. And it was so fine, so very fine... fresh, and somehow kind and gentle. And as it caressed me, it made me feel as if all my cares and worries had simply left me... that they somehow just slipped away... leaving me pure and empty. And I knew my three friends were feeling the same.

Feeling that fine healing wind.

"What brings you to the 12 stones?" said a clear voice from behind us. And we knew that the fine healing wind came from the voice. Because the voice was just like the fine healing wind... so fine, so clear, so gentle and yet firm that I felt the voice and the fine healing wind were one.

Slowly, ever so slowly, we turned in the direction of the voice.

As we turned, a gentle, golden light fell on our faces, which also seemed to come from the voice. A voice and a wind and a light of infinite gentleness and kindness.

278

All seated on…

A great white throne.

A great white throne that looked as if it had grown or been carved directly out of the Sea of Glass.

And on this great white throne sat a woman.

And she was tall and slender, clothed in a long gown that seemed to blend together with the bright golden-white light that was emanating from her. Everything was so bright that it was hard to tell if she was clothed in a golden-white gown or in golden-white light… perhaps they were the same.

But the most striking thing about the woman was her face.

Her features were fine and delicate, beautiful beyond words and her dark hair fell gracefully like waves that were tumbling down to her shoulders.

On her lips was the faintest of smiles, a smile of such perfect contentment and peace that the moment I looked at her I felt as if every single care I ever had in my whole life was lifted from my shoulders and my mind. Just one look at that smile of perfect contentment made them disappear…

And then there were her eyes.

Looking into her eyes I felt the same way I first felt when I gazed at the great infinite Sea of Glass that was surrounding us. It was as if I was looking into the Vast and Infinite Mind of God Her-Himself.

And o! my heart leapt!

And o! I thought to myself!

I would give anything to glimpse for just a moment the glorious and exalted thoughts that led to the look in the eyes of this radiant woman!

"Greetings o! travelers from a far land," said the woman, her eyes, her face, her whole being, smiling at us like a radiant sun that was casting its blessed rays on some gray and misty land. And then came the sound of her voice—brilliant and clear—like the 12 shining stones underneath our feet, sparkling like endless rainbows with never-ending beautiful colors caressing us from on high. "What brings you to the 12 stones?" she said, repeating her first words to us.

So stunned were we by the sight of this glorious woman that none of us dared utter a word. Instead the four of us kneeled as if on cue before her. Even Ben seemed moved beyond words.

"Arise, dear friends!" said the woman. "There is no need to kneel before me. Here there is neither high nor low. Or have you forgotten everything that we taught you, Starwarrior?"

279

There was such friendliness in the woman's voice, such kindness, that we all dared look up again.

Ben was now staring at the woman looking utterly confused.

"Emma?" he said, his normally very firm voice quaking slightly.

"Yes my dear boy, it is I, "said the woman, smiling. "Surely you have not forgotten your Aunt Emma?"

"Aunt... Emma? Is it really you?" said Ben slowly, looking completely bewildered.

We were all staring at the radiant woman before us in amazement. But there was no doubt about it. Although she looked very different now, somehow she also looked very much the same. And we knew in our heart of hearts that the queenly woman before us was in truth Emma, Uncle Ernest's old friend with the round glasses and neat little bun. Only now, so much more radiant and beautiful, it was no wonder that none of us recognized her at first!

"But...?" stammered Ben, still having difficulty meeting her clear gaze.

"Have you forgotten, my dear Starwarrior?" she said. "Such is the effect of looking at the 12 stones. Such is the effect of giving your attention to the radiant Light of Truth."

"Is this..." stammered Moncler, gesturing at the Sea of Glass underneath and all around us. "Is this place... the Truth..." he muttered, unable to complete the sentence.

"Ah, Moncler!" said Emma. "The Wise Wizard should know better than to think that anything the eye can behold can possibly be the Truth. Because Truth is unchanging, whereas anything and everything the eye can behold is impermanent, forever changing."

Moncler lowered his gaze and said nothing.

"So, travelers from a far land," she said again. "In Absolute Truth there is no time, but in the dream of Planet Earth that you are presently dreaming, time is passing swiftly. So let me ask you again: Why have you come here? What brings you to the 12 stones?"

None of us answered. We just stood there, spellbound, drinking in the purity, the holiness, of this glorious woman and the glorious vastness surrounding and emanating from her.

Finally, I mustered up the courage to speak.

"Your Holiness..." I said slowly.

"All is Holy, Holy, Holy," said Emma. "I no more than you. So only utter that word if by me you mean you."

Emma looked at me, transfixing me with her gaze. Here eyes were deeper than deep, like the vast and infinite Sea of Glass around us. And just for a moment I had the strange and wonderful feeling that her eyes, her whole being, and the entire vast Sea of Glass all around me, were really just a mirror that was being held up before my eyes. And in that mirror all the glorious holiness I was seeing was nothing but the reflection of my own glorious holiness.

Emma nodded. "You see indeed, Starbrow. All is Holy, Holy, Holy beyond words."

I smiled back at her, feeling more confident. "Dearest Emma," I said. "We have come to ask you to give us the Lost Teaching of the Single Eye."

"The Lost Teaching of the Single Eye?" said Emma with a glint in her eyes. "Lost? Or merely forgotten?"

I didn't know what to say.

She smiled again. "So why my dear friends are you seeking the Lost Teaching of the Single Eye?"

"So we can raise our consciousness and the entire collective consciousness of humanity," I said, "so we can have STARDAY on Planet Earth."

"And why, O Master Starbrow, do you want to have STARDAY on Planet Earth?"

"Because… it will prevent an axis shift… and because STARDAY will give all human beings a greater opportunity to learn about higher consciousness and their own true inner potential."

"And, why, O Sinless One, do you want to give all human beings a greater opportunity to learn about higher consciousness and their own true inner potential?"

"Because…" I said slowly, "learning about your own true potential and nature is… Peace and Harmony and Love and Joy and Unlimited Freedom."

Emma smiled. "And why, Most Precious Child, do you want all human beings to experience Peace and Harmony and Love and Joy and Unlimited Freedom?"

"Because… because…" I stopped, searching for words.

"Yes?" said Emma, watching me carefully. "Tell me, you who seek the Secret of Secrets, why do you want all human beings to experience Peace and Harmony and Love and Joy and Unlimited Freedom?"

"I… I… I just do…" I stammered, "because… Peace and Harmony and Love and Joy and Freedom is… Good."

"Aaahhh…" said Emma, smiling radiantly and sighing with great contentment, "The Good!"

When Emma said the word "the Good" it was as if the entire Sea of Glass and the 12 stones beneath our feet and the great throne and even Emma herself all began to glow even more brightly. As if the very word "the Good" made everything around us sing with joy.

Again Emma bent her penetrating gaze upon me. "So you want all human beings to experience the Good?"

"Yes, yes…" I said slowly. "I guess that's why. I don't think I can really explain why… I just…"

"You don't have to explain why, O Holy One," said Emma. "With the Lost Teaching of the Single Eye you will see why. And all will be clear."

Emma turned her gaze away from me and looked straight at Ben. "What about you, O Warrior from the Stars? Why do you seek the Lost Teaching of the Single Eye?"

Ben didn't answer. He just stared at Emma and our fantastic surroundings with a look of awe and disbelief on his face. There could be little doubt that this was no ordinary experience for him!

"Well, my Dear One," said Emma. "Now that you have come all this way, don't you want to see what is around the next corner?"

After a long silence, Ben finally said, " Well… yes, yes…I do."

"So why are you seeking the Lost Teaching of the Single Eye?"

Ben was quiet for a moment and then he whispered slowly, "I don't really know… It's all so fantastic… but still… I just I have this feeling that if I could find the Teaching I might get an answer…"

"… an answer to what?"

"To… the whole thing," said Ben thoughtfully. "You know… to the purpose of my life, to the purpose… of the whole thing… of everything..."

"Why do you want to know the purpose of your life and of everything?"

"Because… If I do then maybe it will make sense, I mean then maybe there'll be a meaning behind all of it."

"Why do you want it all to make sense, why do you want there to be a meaning to it all?"

Now it was Ben's turn to smile. "Because it's nice when things make sense, when there's a meaning to it all."

"Why is it nice?"

"Because then it's like life is not so chaotic or meaningless. It means that there's a higher purpose to life, that there's some kind of intelligence or wisdom or meaning behind it all."

"And why, O Wise One, do you want this Intelligence, Wisdom, Meaning?"

Ben shrugged. "Well, doesn't everyone want Intelligence, Wisdom and Meaning?"

Emma nodded. "Yes, everyone most certainly does want Intelligence, Wisdom and Meaning. But why?"

Ben was silent for a moment. Then he said, "Because... Intelligence, Wisdom and Meaning is nice... because when things make sense... it's Good."

"Aaahhh!" Emma sighed and smiled again. "The Good!"

And once again when Emma said the word "Good", it was as if the Sea of Glass, the throne and her very being again glowed even more brightly. As if her whole being resonated like a musical instrument to these words... as if the word "Good" itself was her keynote.

"So what you are saying is that Master Starwarrior is seeking the Lost Teaching of the Single Eye for the exact same reason that Master Starbrow is seeking it...because you are seeking the Good?"

Ben nodded slowly. "I guess so, though I don't know why, I..."

"Patience," said Emma. "With the Lost Teaching of the Single Eye all will be revealed."

Then she turned towards Jacob. "And what about you, dear Moncler, student of Wisdom and Intelligence Unbounded? Why are you seeking the Lost Teaching of the Single Eye?"

"Well," Jacob said with a smile. "I guess it's basically for the exact same reason as Starbrow and Starwarrior. Because I believe that with the Teaching I will be able to experience more Peace, Harmony, Joy, Love, Intelligence, Wisdom—in other words, the Good."

Emma's eyes sparkled as if she was very satisfied with his answer. "And when, O Radiant One, would you like to experience this Good, this Peace, Harmony, Joy, Love, Intelligence and Wisdom?"

"When?"

"Yes. When?"

Jacob was silent for a moment. Then he said, "Well, to be honest..."

"There is nothing but Honesty here, my friend," said Emma. "And even if you are dishonest, that too will be seen in the Light of Honesty."

"Well, to be honest," nodded Jacob, "I wouldn't mind experiencing the Good I am seeking right now!"

"Yes," smiled Emma, "if we are honest with ourselves, we all want the Good right now. Not tomorrow, not in a million years. But now."

Then she continued, "And for how long do you want to experience the Good that you are seeking?"

Again Jacob was silent for a moment. Then he smiled and said, "Well of course I want to experience the Good all the time—that is forever!"

Emma smiled back at him. "Yes, you are truly honest. We all want to experience the Good that we are seeking now and forever. We all want it to be Permanent. Unchanging."

Emma then turned her gaze to Janus. "So, Telperion, my Brave Brother, why are you seeking the Lost Teaching of the Single Eye?"

Telperion and Emma's eyes met. My brave friend looked more thoughtful than I had seen him in a long time.

"Well," he said. "I guess I could come up with all kinds of reasons. But if I ask myself why I want what I want, the answer is ultimately the same as Moncler and Starbrow and Starwarrior's. Because I am seeking the Good."

"Very good, O Holy One. You are seeking the Good. And where do you want this Good to be, this Good that you are seeking?"

"Where?"

"Yes, where?"

Janus scratched his head for a moment. "Well, I guess I want it to be… here!" he said laughing.

Emma laughed too. "Don't be shy, dear One! The Lost Teaching is without limits. So only the one whose aspirations are without limits can step onto its Limitless Pathway."

She continued, "So you want the Good that you are seeking to be here. And for whom or for what do you want this experience of the Good?"

Again Janus was quiet for a moment. Then his face lit up in a smile. "Of course, I see it now! I want everyone and everything to experience the Good. That's what this whole mission is about!"

"Exactly, dear friend," said Emma. "We all want the Good we are seeking to be here, there and everywhere. Everywhere Present. For everything and everyone. Infinite. And Limitless."

With that Emma stood up and clapped her hands. The sound of her clapping was very loud—yet not loud in the way that we normally perceive loudness. It wasn't unpleasant at all, but rather loud and powerful in a pleasant way. And when she clapped her hands you felt that she was somehow doing it to shake you out of your normal way of seeing things and draw you closer to her way of seeing things.

"So, dear friends," she said. "By answering my questions you have in fact already taken the first step into the Lost Teaching of the Single Eye. Because the first step in the Lost Teaching of the Single Eye is to understand that everyone is seeking the Good."

Emma took a step closer towards us, as if she wanted to bring us even closer to the sweet secrets that she knew. "Everyone is seeking the Good," she said again. "This is Man's Eternal Quest. Everyone without exception—every living, breathing sentient being—is seeking the exact same things—Freedom, Health, Strength, Energy, Support, Abundance, Security, Love, Peace, Intelligence, Wisdom. In short: The Good. And not only is everyone seeking the Good. If we are really honest with ourselves, we want the Good that we are seeking to be now and forever. To be Permanent and Unchanging. Because no one is really satisfied with a Love that is temporary, a Joy that is fleeting, a Peace that is unreliable. No, we want the Good and we want it Now and Forever. And if we are really honest with ourselves we not only want the Good—Peace, Life, Freedom, Love—for ourselves but for everyone and everything else. For the whole human family and all living beings. We want the Good to be Here, There and Everywhere. Omnipresent, Omnipotent, Omniscient."

As I listened to Emma speak about the Good I had an almost uncanny experience… something happened that never happened to me before. I realized that the words she was speaking were not simply words.

The Good.

Omnipresent.

Omnipotent.

Omniscient.

The words she was speaking were signposts.

Openings.

Gateways.

To higher levels of consciousness.

Gateways leading me straight to the actual thing itself. Alive, breathing, present, here and now. Like the fine healing wind that came from Emma and her throne, caressing my whole being with its infinite kindness.

Because Emma truly understood.

And the words she was speaking truly understood.

The longing and desire that was burning in my heart of hearts.

Emma truly understood what was driving me onwards and upwards with every breath I took.

My heart's desire.

The thing that motivated my every decision, my every thought, my every word, my every action.

It was my search for the Good.

And as Emma continued to speak about and describe the Good that everyone is seeking... constantly... ceaselessly... It was as if her words began to dance before me in the forms of images, pictures, visions... of every man, woman and child on Earth... and I saw every man, woman and child on Earth as dear, sweet Emma saw them... always searching, always looking, for the Good... always believing that... *There is Good for me and I ought to have it*... The saint and the sinner say alike... *There is Good for me and I ought to have it*... the prince and the pauper say alike... *There is Good for me and I ought to have it*... You and I say alike... *There is Good for me and I ought to have it*... The birds and the stones say alike... *There is Good for me and I ought to have it*... Man's Eternal Quest... always looking, always seeking, for the Good...

"Truly," said Emma, "Everyone is seeking the Good. When you understand this, your heart and mind will chime in unison with all living beings. You will know that even those whom you at present find loathsome and uncouth are also seeking the Good... the exact same Good that you are seeking."

At my side I suddenly heard Janus clear his throat, as if he was unsure about whether to speak or not.

Emma looked at him. "Speak, O Brave One! Here everything must be held up and measured in the Light of Truth."

Jacob and Ben and I also looked at Janus. He looked a bit uncomfortable.

"Well," he said to Emma. "I can see that everyone is seeking the Good but what I really want to know is: How do we experience the Good that we seek? As far as I can see that's the big question."

Jacob nodded his head in agreement. "Yes," he said, "that's what I've been wondering too."

Emma's eyes glinted but she did not answer Janus' question.

286

Instead a strong, clear voice behind us said, "The answer to your question, Brave Knights of the Good, is the Lost Teaching of the Single Eye."

9

The Good

We turned around slowly and as we did so a great golden light fell upon us. The light came from the voice. And the light and the voice came from...

A tall man.

Like Emma he was seated on a great white throne, which seemed to have simply grown out of the immense Sea of Glass all around us. And like Emma a great light shone from him, enveloping his entire being in a warm, golden-white light.

Very kingly he looked, noble, steadfast and strong. And as I looked at him it seemed to me that a red cross was shining right where his heart was... a red cross that reminded me of the red crosses medieval knights often wore upon their breasts.

"Greetings, my Brave Knights of the Good!" said the man. His voice was kind and glad, yet also strong and firm. It was the kind of voice that filled you with awe and a sense of respect.

None of us said anything. We just looked at the man before us. His face was handsome and strong, his eyes were deep and clear, and the smile on his face was as kind and generous as the summer sun. There was something about the look in his eyes, the smile on his face, the firmness of his voice that made you want to be... well, just like him. That made you want to be good and just and honorable and chivalrous and gentlemanly and fair and honest and trustworthy... just like him, just like a noble knight of old. Looking at him I was reminded of all the good and honorable heroes that I had ever heard of. Of King Arthur, Merlin, Aragorn, Gandalf, Luke Skywalker, Obi-Wan-Kenobi... Here was a man you could trust with all your heart and all your might—and with your very life. He was like the sun that shines without reserve or hesitation on all beings—without any distinction. And when the bright radiance of his being shone upon you, you felt as if all the petty, mean, vain, proud, selfish, unjust, dishonest and cowardly thoughts and actions you had ever thought or done in your life just dissolved like dewdrops in the bright morning sun.

And o! my heart leapt!

And o! I thought to myself!

I would give anything to know the noble and exalted thoughts that were the cause of the radiance of this sun that was shining on me!

"And greetings, Ben!" said the man, smiling broadly to our friend.

"Greetings... Emmet," said Ben, once again taken aback by the stunning transformation of his uncle's old friend. And no wonder! It was certainly a far cry from the elderly English chap in the dusty old tweed jacket we'd met in Uncle Ernest's cabin to this glorious being standing in front of us. And yet there could be no doubt that they were one and the same.

"So..." said Emmet, "to business, my Sincere Seekers of the Holy Grail. You want to know how to experience the Good that you seek— how to experience Permanent, Unchanging Freedom, Peace, Health and Harmony."

"Eh yes, Sir Emmet sir..." I said haltingly, still feeling somewhat stunned by this great being sitting before me.

Emmet was quiet for a moment, his clear eyes studying each of us in turn. Then he said, "Know Most Noble Ones that in order to answer that question, we first have to answer another question. Namely the most thrilling and interesting question of all. The question that has been asked by all sincere seekers since the beginning of time. And that question is: What is Truth? What is the Nature of Reality?"

Jacob nodded eagerly, the Wizard in him warming decidedly at the prospect of even more teachings on his favorite subject. For a moment, he fumbled instinctively after his spell book but immediately realized it was in vain, because since the destruction of Glastonbury Tor, all the symbols of our True Selves had disappeared.

"Once you understand the Truth, the True Nature of Reality, you will also be able to experience the Permanent Good that you are seeking," continued Emmet. "Because the answer to these two questions—'How do I experience the Good that I seek' and 'What is Truth'—are and must be inextricably linked to one and other. Once you have the answer to the one, you have the answer to the other."

"So what is the Truth?" said Jacob, trying not to sound too eager.

"This great question," replied Emmet, "has been asked by all the Awakened Ones on your planet such as Jesus, Moses, Buddha,

Krishna, Padmasambhava, Gandhi, Mary Baker Eddy, Patanjali, Mother Mary and many more—since the dawn of human history. And all have inevitably reached the same conclusions, even though they have been cloaked in different words, stories, teachings and symbols that correspond to the time and place of their sojourn on Earth."

"And what are these conclusions, Sir Emmet?" asked Jacob.

"The first conclusion that the Awakened Ones have reached about the Nature of Reality is this: God is All and God is Good."

The moment Emmet said the word "Good" the same thing happened that happened when Emma said the word "Good". The Sea of Glass, the great white throne, and Emmet's entire being glowed even more brightly, as if the mere mention of the word "Good" made all things more vibrant, radiant and alive.

"So what do I mean by the word 'God' and by the word 'Good'?" said Emmet. "By the word God I mean that which never changes. That which was never born and will never die. That which is Eternal, Immortal and Unchanging. The Absolute. That which has no beginning and no end. That which is you, me, everyone and everything. That which is Infinite, Undivided and One. That which is Free, Independent and Untouched by passing events, thoughts, emotions, and actions. That which is closer than breathing..."

"... nearer than hands and feet," said Jacob, echoing what the Ascended Masters Kuthumi and Serapis Bey had taught us in the Blue Temple. "I get it now."

"Me too," I said. "You are talking about the Force."

"Yeah," said Janus. "The Force."

"The Force..." said Emmet slowly, as if he was tasting a word he'd long forgotten. "Yes, I remember the word now. But just bear in mind that the Force is merely one word—and might I add a very inadequate word as are all names and descriptions of that which is Nameless and Indescribable—of the One Unchanging Reality behind all changing forms. Throughout human history the Absolute, the Force as you call it, has been called many different things by different Awakened Ones in different cultures in different times and places. It has been called God, the Goddess, Spirit, Tao, Nirvana, the Buddha, the Christ, Allah, Jehovah, the Self, Brahman and many, many other names. But the words we use to describe the One Unchanging Reality matter not. Did not your great poet Shakespeare say: *'What's in a name? That which we call a rose... By any other word would smell as sweet.'* And so we can also say the same about the very inadequate names that we use to describe God or the Force. No matter what name we use to describe God or the Force, He-She-It still smells just as sweet!"

We all laughed.

"Yeah, that's a good point," grinned Janus.

Emmet continued, "One of the important things to understand is that God or the Force is not something that is separate from you or outside of you. It is your very nature. It is you! Because your True Self—that which is behind, beyond and independent of your present name, form, physical body and passing sensations, thoughts and emotions, as well as your past and present story—is One with God, the Spirit."

Jacob nodded. "Closer than breathing, nearer than hands and feet."

"Exactly," said Emmet. "Or as the Masters often say *The Highest God and the Inmost God are One*."

Suddenly without warning, just as Emma had done before him, Emmet stood up and clapped his hands together. The sound of the clap grew and grew, and became louder and louder, until it was like the sound of a thousand thunderclaps. And yet it was not so loud as to be unpleasant. Again I had the distinct feeling that Emmet was doing this to give our minds and our consciousnesses a mighty jolt to completely shake up our normal perception of things.

And shake it up he certainly did.

Because suddenly I saw!

Suddenly I saw, as I knew Emma and Emmet also saw, the True Nature of Reality!

Suddenly I saw the One Unchanging Absolute Reality behind all the changing relative forms. And I saw, just as Emmet said, that this One Presence, Power, Life, Spirit, Consciousness, God, Force… was and is not separate from me.

It was and is me.

Closer than breathing, nearer than hands and feet.

So close that all of my life I had completely overlooked it.

So close… like my own face… that I couldn't see it.

And so for a brief moment I saw the One Spirit face to face. The One Spirit that turned back upon itself and became aware of itself—in and through me. And so I also understood why there were so many different names for the One Unchanging Reality.

Because in fact all words are futile.

No words can possibly describe…

That which I AM.

That which every human being is.

291

God.

The Force.

Now. Birthless. Deathless. Eternal. Immortal. Unchanging.

Here. There. Everywhere. Beginningless. Endless. Everywhere Present. The One.

Free. Independent. Unlimited. Uncaused.

Pure Presence, Power, Being.

Perfect, Whole, Complete.

Perfect, Unlimited Life, Strength, Energy.

Perfect, Unlimited Love, Oneness.

Perfect, Unlimited Intelligence, Wisdom.

Perfect, Unlimited Peace, Harmony, Bliss, Joy.

Perfect, Unlimited, Unchanging...

Good!

And then I saw and understood... and the joy of my understanding was like the radiant splendor of a thousand suns all blazing into the sky at once... like a thousand lovers all running into the arms of their beloved at once...

Because now I knew.

Now I knew why everyone is seeking the Good.

Because we are the Good that we seek!

10

The Radiance of Mind

Jacob, Janus and I were laughing so hard that tears came to our eyes. Laughing like we had never laughed before. Laughing like the Three E Masters laughed when they'd laughed so uproariously at the four of us down in Uncle Ernest's cabin. Laughing with a sense of wonder, delight, relief, abandon all mixed with a feeling that it was all so absurdly obvious that up until now we had completely overlooked it. Even Ben was chuckling to himself.

"Ha ha!" I laughed. "Everyone is seeking the Good! And the Nature of Reality *is* the Good!"

"Oh man!" cried Jacob. "But of course! That's it! So absurdly simple that we completely overlooked it!"

"Man oh man!" grinned Janus. "The Good that everyone is seeking is what we are! And not only that—the Good we are seeking is the Nature of Reality! They are one and the same!"

"You said it!" I cried. "The Good that everyone is seeking and God, the Force, our own True Self, are equal, identical and interchangeable!"

Jacob, Janus and I enthusiastically gave each other high fives. Ben did not join in, but he was grinning too so he must have realized something quite good.

"Very good, my Dear Children of the Good," said the voice of Emma behind us.

We turned to face the other E Master. Once again I was struck by the deep sense of peace and contentment that Emma's entire being radiated.

"Indeed," said Emma, "everyone is seeking the Good. Everyone is seeking Life, Health, Freedom, Love, Joy, Peace, Strength."

"And the Nature of Reality," said Emmet from the other side, "the Nature of God, the One Unchanging Spirit, Force, Presence, which is everyone's True Self—is the Good—is Perfect, Unlimited Life, Love, Peace, Joy."

We looked back and forth from the one radiant master to the other on either side of us and bathed in their bright glow of pure Goodness.

"And that of course," said Emma, "is why everyone is seeking the Good. Because everyone is seeking their own True Self. Day and night. This search—Man's Eternal Quest—pushes and pulls and drives us on. And we will never surrender, we will never give up, until we experience the Good, which is actually our own True Self, God, the Good."

Janus laughed heartily. "This is really radical!" he said. "So it must really mean that that which we are seeking, is that which we are seeking with!"

"Exceptional Telperion! Exceptional!" said Emmet. "I couldn't have said it better myself!"

We all burst out laughing again. There was something about this realization that was so clarifying, so uplifting, so liberating, that it just made you feel like singing and dancing and laughing all at the same time. Realizing that the Good that everyone is seeking is really the Nature of Reality made me feel as if some terrible, dark cloud had been removed from the sun or as if someone had removed a dark veil from before my eyes. Suddenly the bright sunlight of a beautiful day was streaming in.

"You know what guys," I said. "This really changes everything a whole lot because before, although we understood that the Force is All, we basically believed that the Nature of the Force was, well, neutral. You know just a neutral energy or substance or force that could be directed for good or evil by our thoughts. But we were wrong! The Nature of the Force, of you, me and everyone else, is the Good, is pure natural Goodness!"

"You're right, Starbrow," said Jacob. "And that really makes a big difference... and makes everything a whole lot easier. Because it means we don't have to create the Good that we seek because the Good is here now. It already exists as the True Nature of everyone and everything."

"But if everything you're saying is true," said Janus, "there's still one thing I don't understand. If the Nature of Reality is that the Force is All and the Force is Good then what is the cause of—pardon my French—all the shit?"

Jacob and I looked at him.

"The shit?" I said.

"Yeah, you know," said Janus, "If God, the Force, is All, and God, the Force, is Good—then what is the cause of all the bad things that happen to people?"

"The bad things?" I said, still not quite understanding what my friend was getting at.

"Yeah," he continued, "you know like sickness and death and unhappiness and war and all the other unpleasant stuff we human beings experience?"

Neither Jacob nor I answered. We were both silent as we pondered Janus' new question.

"He's got a point," said Jacob after a while. "A very good point. If God is All and God is Good, then why do we human beings seem to experience a lack of the Good in our lives? Why do we suffer?"

"Yeah," I said slowly. "That's actually a very good question, Janus."

We all looked at Emmet and Emma. The two E Masters were studying us calmly, as if they had been waiting for us to ask this very question.

But it was neither Emmet nor Emma who answered our question. Instead a voice behind us said:

"I am glad you asked that question, my dear lads! Because no understanding of the True Nature of Reality and of the way to experience the Good is complete without an answer to that question."

The four of us turned in the direction of the voice. There, between Emma and Emmet and their thrones, was another great white throne. And on that throne sat another majestic being of light.

The being of light was a man—and like Emma and Emmet, the man radiated a strong golden-white light. The light that came from him was very pleasant and I thought I could detect a sweet aroma coming from the man, like the scent of roses or some other wonderful flower.

The man on the throne was rather large, almost chubby, with a face as kind as summer and cheeks as red as fresh apples or ripe strawberries. He had a long beard that was as white as snow. He looked very jolly and when you looked at him, you somehow just wished that he would laugh because for some reason you knew that there would be nothing better in the world than to hear him laugh. There was also something very grandfatherly about him. Like the kind, jolly, understanding, wise grandfather you either have or always wished you had. Sort of like Santa Claus, and Gandalf the Wizard, and Merlin, and every wise, kind being you have ever known or heard of all rolled into one.

"Well hello, Ben my lad," said the man in a deep, booming voice.

"Hello Uncle Ernest," replied Ben immediately, unable to suppress a smile at the amazing transformation of his adopted uncle. And truly he looked very different. When we last saw Ernest in the cabin, his face was ruddy and his head bald, and he was dressed in an old lumberjacket.

"And hello to you three young gentlemen," said Ernest. "I am mighty happy to see that you are following in the footsteps of the great seekers, seers, saints and philosophers—on Man's Eternal Quest." The big man sighed. "Ah! There is no greater joy than to drink of the Cup of Knowledge, to quench your thirst for the Divine Knowledge!"

With that Ernest laughed heartily. And truly when he laughed, one felt there was nothing better in the whole wide world than to hear him laugh because his laugh was so all encompassing, merry, and gay. It was positively contagious as it echoed down and around the vast Sea of Glass. So contagious that it wasn't long before all of us—Jacob, Janus, Ben, myself, Emmet, Emma and Ernest were all laughing merrily.

And o! my heart leapt!

And o! I thought to myself!

I would give anything to know the happy and wonderful thoughts that could make someone laugh like that!

After we had all laughed for a while, Ernest motioned for us to come closer, like a grandfather beckoning his grandchildren to gather round for the exciting tale he was about to tell. We all stepped forward, each one of us bathing in the bright rays of his merry presence.

"So, my merry lads," said Ernest, "Now to your question. If God is All and God is Good, why do we human beings seem to experience a lack of the Good in our lives? Why do we experience sickness, unhappiness, suffering, disharmony, and limitation of all sorts? Or you could turn the question around and ask 'If the Force is All and the Force is Good—how then can we human beings experience the Good?'"

Ernest rubbed his hands together as if he was about to tell us something especially delicious or exciting. "In order to answer that question," he said, "we first have to consider another aspect of the Nature of Reality. As you have seen, the Nature of Reality is that God, the Force, is All and God, the Force, is Good. And as you have also seen this One Unchanging Force or Spirit is really none other than your

296

very own self. Although usually you are not aware of this fact, lost as you are in your own thoughts and projections. And that is where—as Janus here so poetically put it—all the shit begins."

"Lost in our own thoughts and projections?" said Jacob. "I don't quite follow you."

"God, the One Force or Spirit, is not just Life, Intelligence and Love," said Ernest. "First and foremost God, the One Force or Spirit is Pure, Unlimited Consciousness or Mind."

"Yes," said Jacob slowly. "That's exactly what the other Masters told us as well."

"Good," continued Ernest. "So your own True Unchanging Self, the One Force, is Pure Consciousness or Mind. And what does Consciousness or Mind do?"

"Do?" said Janus.

"Yes," said Ernest. "What do you as mind do more or less all the time, whether you are aware of it or not, and whether you want to or not?"

"Well let me see," said Janus, "…my mind thinks."

"Exactly," said Ernest. "The Nature of Consciousness or Mind is to think. Just as the nature of the sun is to emit rays of light or the nature of the ocean is to have waves so, in the same way, the Nature of Mind or Consciousness is to have thoughts. They are phenomena that just arise."

Ernest stopped for a moment as if to give each one of us time to assimilate his words. I looked over at Ben. He still looked pretty dazed and amazed at the whole thing, but I could also see that he was listening intently to his uncle's every word.

"So, my dear lads," continued Ernest. "The Force is Consciousness or Mind. Your Mind, remember. And the Nature of Mind is to think, to have thoughts. And as you already know, thought is cause, outer experience is effect."

We all nodded.

"This means that in reality every thought is a thing," said Ernest, "and every thing is a thought. The whole world that we experience is nothing but a thought in our minds."

Ernest directed his clear gaze at each one of us in turn. "Are you with me so far, lads?" he asked.

"Yes," I said. "I think so."

Ernest laughed. "Well, my boy, think twice before you think!"

297

Then he stood up and clapped his hands together loudly. The sound and force unleashed by his vigorous clap was like the sound of a billion waves crashing over you, immense and powerful, and yet the sound was neither unpleasant nor frightening. Once again I felt I'd just received a powerful knock on the door of my consciousness, opening wide my doors of perception.

The next moment a great silence fell.

All was silence and silence was all.

No sound.

Nor anything to see.

The vast Sea of Glass, the Three E Masters, my three friends, had all disappeared.

So had my physical body.

I could sense nothing, feel nothing and… think nothing.

Even the thought or memory of what had been before had disappeared.

It was like that split second of no time when you wake up in the morning and have no idea who you are or what you are—you just know you are. A moment of pure being—without thought or form or a world. But unlike those brief morning moments, this moment of no time, no space, no thought and no form, just continued.

No thought, no form, no space and no time.

Just Pure Being.

Pure Presence.

Pure Existence.

I AM.

God.

The Force.

Peace beyond words, Love beyond words, Bliss beyond words…

I don't know how long I dwelt in that state of Pure Being, Presence, Existence, behind and beyond all thoughts or things. I only know that suddenly I became aware that not only was I Pure Being, Pure Presence, Pure Existence…

But I was also conscious and aware that I was Pure Being.

I was Pure Being Itself being conscious and aware of Itself, of Pure Being Itself.

I was Conscious.

I AM Consciousness!

I AM Mind!

Vast and spacious and infinite like a Sea of Glass…

I AM Consciousness.

I AM Mind.

And in that Vast Consciousness, that Vast Mind, which is me, something suddenly began to stir... like bubbles... ripples... waves... on the surface of the vast Sea of Glass...

The natural radiance of Mind.

And what was that ripple? That radiance?

It was thought!

More and more thought bubbles and thought ripples and thought waves began to emerge and dance upon the surface of my mind... like infinite ripples appearing and disappearing on the surface of a great ocean... like countless rays emitted by the sun...

So thoughts were the natural radiance of my mind!

Now I saw it.

Now I understood in a sudden flash...that thus does the whole world come into being.

Thoughts arising, world arising!

It was suddenly clear.

Because thoughts are things.

And things are thoughts.

One and the same.

Time and space, higher and lower dimensions, sight and sound, universes and galaxies, stars and planets, mountains and oceans, trees and flowers, birds and fishes, human bodies... I now saw that all things and experiences were thoughts in my mind... the whole world of so-called phenomenal experience was but a thought in my mind... appearing and disappearing like waves on a great ocean...

And with that realization I was back in Starbrow's body, back on the Sea of Glass, standing with my three friends before the Three E Masters.

"Wow!" said Janus. "That was intense."

"Amazing!" said Jacob, looking down at his physical body as if he was not quite sure that he was really back in his physical body.

Ernest smiled. "Well done, lads."

I looked down at my so-called physical body. Suddenly it no longer seemed so solid.

"You know," I said. "Although Saint Germain and the other Ascended Masters told us before that our thoughts create our reality, I don't think I ever quite understood it as I do now."

"What do you mean?" said Jacob.

"I think before I really believed in mind over matter," I said. "Before I believed our thoughts had the power to control and shape the outside world. But now I see that *mind is matter*. And *matter is mind*. They are one and the same."

"Or to put it even more correctly," said Ernest. "There is no matter at all. What you call matter is really thought."

We were all silent for a while, each of us trying to grasp the import of this new understanding of the Nature of Mind.

After a while Jacob said, "I see now. Thought is cause and outer experience is effect. Which means that everything is thought. Which must also be the answer to Janus' original question. Because here we have the cause of all our experiences—both the good and the bad."

Janus and I looked at Jacob. I was just about to say something, when Ben to my surprise said, "You mean when your focus and your thoughts are positive, you have correspondingly positive experiences? And when your focus and your thoughts are negative, you have correspondingly negative experiences?"

I looked at Ben. This was the first time he'd really commented on our explorations into the Nature of Reality at all. He still looked pretty dazed and amazed, but obviously his mind was functioning quite well!

"Yes, Ben," said Jacob, "I think that must be pretty much it... the answer to Janus' question about where all the so-called 'shit' comes from." He looked up at Ernest.

"There is nothing wrong with thinking," said Ernest. "As you have just seen, it is the natural activity of Mind, just as waves are the natural activity of the ocean. But suffering and unhappiness arises when our focus and our thoughts are out of harmony with the True Nature of Reality, which is that God is All and God is Good. When our thoughts are out of harmony with the Truth, when we believe ourselves to be separate from God, the Good, when we limit ourselves and others and identify with our thoughts, emotions, and temporary physical bodies, we create suffering and disharmony for ourselves and for others. And that..."

"... is where all the trouble begins," I said. "Yeah, I see it now."

Again no one said a word for while as each of us in our own way contemplated the ramifications of this Great Truth.

After a while Janus had another question, "But here's the million-dollar question, Ernest. How does all this hang together? On the one hand, you say the Force is All and the Force is Good. And on the other hand, you say that our thoughts have the power to create suffering and

300

disharmony. I don't get it. How does this work? Does it mean that our thoughts have the power to change that which is Good to begin with… into something bad?"

We all turned towards Ernest.

But instead of answering Janus' question, the Master made a circular motion with his hand. The next moment four pairs of sunglasses were lying in the palm of his hand. They were strangely shaped and looked like nothing I had ever seen before.

"Cool shades," said Janus.

Ernest handed each one of us a pair of sunglasses. "Put them on," he said.

We all put the sunglasses on.

I jumped back in amazement.

The moment I placed the sunglasses on, everything around me looked very different. Not only did everything look much darker, as you would normally expect from a pair of sunglasses, but everything also seemed strangely… distorted.

11

The Veil

Looking through the strange sunglasses Ernest had given us, everything around us now seemed ugly, twisted and distorted. The Sea of Glass, which before had looked so radiant and beautiful, now looked dark and dull—and positively uninviting. The glass now looked like scorched earth and everywhere around us there were holes and fissures in the ground. The place looked desolate with blackened bomb craters everywhere; it could have been a scene from the hellish land of Mordor in the Lord of the Rings.

"Hey, what the…" exclaimed Janus.

And not only was everything completely changed—the sounds we heard were different too. There was the ominous roll of thunder somewhere in the distance—and a rotten smell in the air like the terrible stench of burnt bodies. The sick, stale air felt hot and dry in my throat.

"Ugh!" I said.

Then I turned back to look at the Three E Masters and when I saw them through the sunglasses I jumped again. Where before there had been three beautiful and majestic beings of light, there now stood three wizened and decrepit beings. They looked extremely old and frail and their bodies were crooked and bent. All three of them stooped almost to the ground. Ernest. Emmet and Emma looked even older than they did back in Ernest's cabin, and not only that, they looked much frailer and uglier.

"What's going on?" I said.

"Can your thoughts change that which is Good into something bad?" said a dull voice. It was Ernest speaking. Even his voice sounded different. "Can putting on a pair of sunglasses darken the whole world? It may seem like it. But does it? Can a cloud harm the sun? Can a wave disturb the ocean? Can a dream or nightmare hurt the dreamer? It may

302

seem like. But does it? Of course not! It's only when the dreamer is caught up in the dream that it seems so terrifyingly real. But once the dreamer wakes up, he or she realizes the dream was just a dream... completely unreal and without the slightest power to harm him or her. It is the same with our experiences of this thing we call Life. Consciously or unconsciously, everything we experience—be it positive or negative—is but a projection of our own mind."

"Well, if that's the case then I'd rather experience Life without this particular pair of shades, thank you very much!" exclaimed Janus hotly.

"Then take them off," smiled Ernest. "As in all of life, you are free to do as you please."

He didn't have to say more. We took off the strange shades immediately and the moment they were gone, the world around us was back to its original beautiful self. The Sea of Glass, the Three E Masters, all our surroundings, once again shone forth in all their radiant beauty. And the light was again spectacular.

Ernest made another circular moment with his hand and the four pairs of sunglasses disappeared.

"I think I understand now," said Janus thoughtfully. "Our negative, limiting thoughts don't change the natural Goodness of Life—because the natural Goodness of Life is permanent and unchanging. But our negative and limiting thoughts seem to put a veil over our experience of life."

"Yes," said Jacob. "And when we look at the world through this veil, what we see is what we call disharmony, trouble, sickness, accident, death—all the bad stuff."

"But once we stop thinking wrongly or negatively about Life," said Ernest, "in other words, the moment we remove the distortion created by our negative thoughts, we see everything the way it truly is. As God, the Good sees."

We were all silent for a while, pondering on what we had just experienced.

After a while Janus broke the silence. "You know what, friends, this must mean that we didn't quite understand the mechanism behind the Power of Thought and the Power of the Word after all."

"What do you mean?" I said.

"Well, up until now, we believed we were supposed to direct our thoughts and words to create the Good we wanted to experience, isn't that right? We thought that we were supposed to create the Peace, Harmony, and Goodness we wanted by thinking correctly," said Janus.

"Yes, that's true," I replied. "But I don't see what you're driving at."

"What he's saying is that according to what we've just learned, we don't in fact need to use our minds to create the Good," said Jacob, "because the Good already exists. All we have to do is focus our attention on the Good which already exists, which is already there."

"Yeah," said Janus. "The Good has always been there and always will be. It's just us who didn't see this, which means that the Good was, is and always will be here, there and everywhere—all the time."

"Do you realize what this means?" I said slowly. "I mean this really makes everything a whole lot easier."

"You said it," said Janus taking a deep breath. "This means we don't have to create the Good by the force of our will as we thought before. All we have to do is focus our attention on it because the Good already exists. The Perfect You already exists. The Perfect World already exists."

"Yes…" said Jacob, also letting this crucial realization sink in.

"It's just…" I stopped and stared at my two friends. "Do you remember the Prophecy of Starwarrior?" I said. "*From the Single Eye will come the Perfect World…*"

My friends looked at me in surprise.

"You're on to something, Starbrow," said Jacob. "*From the Single Eye will come the Perfect World…* The Perfect World, which has been here all along. Finally things are starting to make sense!"

"But what about the Single Eye?" asked Janus. "What's that?"

The three of us turned towards the Three E Masters.

"Just as you, as Mind, can focus on and believe in limitation, negativity and separation from God, the Good," said Ernest, "so you, as Mind, can also turn your attention and identification towards the True Nature of Reality, which is God, the Good."

He then turned towards Emma.

"This activity of Mind," Emma said, "of mentally turning your attention towards God, the Good, is called many different things in different cultures and among different spiritual seekers on Planet Earth. Some call this turning of your attention towards God, the Good, meditation, others call it prayer, some call it mindfulness, still others call it spiritual mind treatment—and there are still other names. But where we come from, we call it *the Single Eye*!"

304

12

The Single Eye

"The Single Eye, of course, does not refer to anything physical," said Emmet. "The Single Eye refers to that quality of one-pointed attention in which all your attention is directed at and on the Truth, the One Force or Spirit, which is altogether Good."

"When your Eye is Single," continued Emmet, "when you focus your attention on God, the Good, the outer world of experience then reflects back this focus to you. The outer world then reflects back more and more experiences of Harmony, Peace, Health and Happiness. The Harmony, Peace, Health and Happiness that is the True Nature of All Things."

"Because your focus determines your experience," said Jacob. "Yeah, I see it now. And it's not because your thoughts are creating this Peace and Harmony, but because by focusing on the True Nature of Reality, you quite simply experience more of it."

"Exactly," said Emmet. "This is what Jesus and Moses and Buddha and all the other Awakened Ones on Planet Earth did when they performed their so-called miracles. In reality they did not *do* anything at all. All they did was shift their attention or focus to the True Nature of Reality, to God, the Good. And because their realization of the True Nature of Reality was so strong, immediately their outer surroundings fell in line and reflected this focus back to them. To those standing nearby, it seemed that miracles occurred. Immediately the blind could see, the deaf could hear, the lame could walk, the sick were healed, water became wine, and even the dead were restored to life. To those witnessing these manifestations of the absolute supremacy of the Divine Mind, it seemed like miracles because they did not understand the magic of attention that you have just learned about. Those who did understand this great law realized that these so-called miracles or acts were in fact just the fulfillment of the law—in other words, the tangible evidence that the True Nature of Reality is Good."

We all sighed at the precision of his explanation and the Sea of Glass twinkled even more brightly.

After a few moments, Ernest continued, "All four of you have already had glimpses of the so-called miracle-working power of focusing your attention on the Force, the Good. You experienced it, for instance, when the three of you focused on the Force as Peace on the West Bank in Israel. You also experienced it when you focused on the Force in the Gobi Desert and when you focused on the Force when that the tornado was about to ram into your car and crush you back in England. And you, dear Ben my boy," said Ernest as he turned towards Ben. "You too have also had glimpses of the miracle-working power of focusing on the Good when you were a child and we took you up here. Although at present you remember very little, it will all come back to you in due time, I promise."

We looked at Ben, but he didn't say anything.

Jacob turned to the Masters. "I think I'm beginning to understand the Lost Teaching of the Single Eye now. So is this how you succeeded in raising the collective consciousness in that far-away star system of yours? By getting a critical mass of the planet's population to focus on the Good?"

Emma smiled. "Yes, that was part of how we did it."

Emmet joined in, "We also gave everyone who was ready to raise their consciousness a formula to help them focus their attention on and meditate on the Good."

"A formula?" I said. "That sounds familiar!"

The Three E Masters laughed.

"Well, Master Starbrow, you might find this formula even more familiar than you expect!" grinned Emmet.

"Well, let's hear it then!" said Janus.

The Three E Masters looked at each other for a moment. Then they walked over to their thrones and sat down—fixing their eyes upon us with their penetrating gaze.

A great silence descended upon the Sea of Glass.

A great silence and a sense of expectancy. The whole place was tingling with it. Waiting as we were, for the magic words that would help the Good look back on Itself and thus experience Itself more fully.

The Holy Grail.

The Pearl of Great Price.

306

The Single Eye.

As we waited expectantly for the Three E Masters to tell us the formula, I had a feeling that the formula they were about to share with us was very old, older than the Earth itself, older than the Universe itself, as old as the Eternal, Beginningless God, the Good Itself.

And o! my heart leapt!

And o! I thought to myself!

I would give anything to hear those magic words! The magic words that would enable me to begin to experience the Good that I am seeking, the Good that is the True Nature of Reality.

And then as if with one voice Ernest, Emmet and Emma began, and these were the words that they spoke:

"IN THE BEGINNING: THE GOOD
HERE AND NOW: THE GOOD
AT THE END OF THE END: THE GOOD
HERE, THERE, EVERYWHERE: THE GOOD
FROM ALPHA TO OMEGA: THE GOOD
IN HEAVEN, UPON EARTH: THE GOOD
IN THE GREATEST, IN THE SMALLEST: THE GOOD
IN FIRE, IN WATER, IN EARTH, IN AIR: THE GOOD
IN ME, IN YOU, IN EVERYONE: THE GOOD
ABOVE ME, BELOW ME, AROUND ME: THE GOOD
IN ME, THROUGH ME, FROM ME: THE GOOD
IN MY THOUGHTS, IN MY WORDS,
IN MY ACTIONS: THE GOOD
THE GOOD IS ALL IN ALL
ALL LIFE, ALL INTELLIGENCE, ALL LOVE
THE GOOD IS THE ONE AND ONLY REALITY
AND SO IT IS!"

Every time the Masters uttered the word *Good*, their entire beings, and their thrones, and the vast Sea of Glass seemed to vibrate in joyous response to the word. And every time they said the word *Good*, my realization that God is All and God is Good became even greater and more powerful. It was as if I knew, and completely and totally understood and felt that God, the Good, is who I really am! Is who everyone and everything really is! And that there was nothing but the Good.

All is the Good.

307

I AM the Good

The Good looking at the Good.

The Good thinking about the Good.

The Good enjoying the Good.

Perfect, Unlimited Life, Intelligence and Love.

Here, Now and Forever.

And so it is!

The last words of the formula echoed from E Master to E Master, from mighty throne to mighty throne, across the great Sea of Glass and straight back to us again.

I sighed with contentment. I felt so uplifted by the words of the formula that it took me a little while to realize that I had heard a formula very much like it some 1,500 years ago...

And then, at the very same moment, Jacob, Janus and I all burst into laughter.

"Oh man!" I cried. "Those E Masters sure have a sense of humor!"

"You said it," grinned Janus. "It's the same formula Sananda gave us 1,500 years ago in the Crystal Cave. You'd think you Masters were working together or something!"

"Yeah the same old formula," I said, "but with one small change!"

"Actually quite a big change!" said Jacob, still laughing. "Because now we know that not only is the Force the One and Only Reality—the Force is also Perfect, Unchanging Good!"

Janus took a deep breath. "And boy does it feel Good to focus on the Good! So is this what the three of you had a critical mass of the population on your star system focus on? This formula?"

"Yes," said Ernest. "Meditating on the formula was part of how we raised the collective consciousness in the Umtarion-system, but that was not all."

"Well, what else did you do?" asked Janus.

The Masters looked at us in silence for a few moments.

Then Emmet said, "You see, dear friends, there is more to having the Single Eye than just meditating on the Truth, on God, the Good. That is the first and most important step. But in practice, it is of equal importance that you put this Truth into action."

"Into action?" I said. "What do you mean?"

"In order for you to fulfill the Prophecy of Starwarrior," said Emmet, "you not only have to focus on God, the Good. In practice, it is also of crucial importance that..."

I didn't hear the rest of the sentence because at that very moment, Emmet's clear voice was drowned out by a loud sound coming from behind us. The sound was very different from anything I'd heard so far in or on or around the Sea of Glass. It sounded like wild animals snarling or angry voices shouting, or a mixture of both.

Surprised, we all turned around.

The moment we turned around, to our even greater surprise, the vast Sea of Glass began to vibrate and disappear.

"Hey, what's going on?" cried Janus.

Turning to the Three E Masters, I cried, "What's happening?"

But when I looked in their direction, they were gone.

Disappeared.

Just like the Sea of Glass—into thin air!

And we were back in the cave behind 12 Stone Falls. Ben, Jacob, Janus and I, facing the pool in the center of the cave.

We looked around in confusion, not understanding what was going on. The afternoon sun was still streaming into the cave from the sides of the waterfall. Everything was exactly the same as it had been the moment before Ben started reciting The Stanza of the Ancients.

Everything was exactly the same except for one thing—the ominous sound of dogs barking outside the cave.

The water in the pool was now agitated and choppy, making it impossible to see the bottom of the pool.

I looked over at Ben. Gone was the dazed and amazed look on his face, back was the stern face of Agent Nevis.

He ran to the entrance of the cave and looked out.

"Who's coming?" I cried.

"The sheriff and his bloodhounds," cried Ben as he surveyed the valley below us. "Backed by quite a bunch of special forces—a lethal cocktail to put it mildly. We've got to get out of here right this minute!"

I turned to Jacob and Janus who were still staring at the choppy water of the pool and looking quite dazed.

"Did you hear what he said?" I cried. "Move your butts now!"

Jacob and Janus snapped to attention and the three of us ran to the entrance to the cave and after Ben who'd left through the opening on the left side of the waterfall. We followed even though Ben was already out of sight. Once outside, it took a moment for our eyes to adjust to the daylight even though the sky was overcast.

We followed Ben's lead. The ledge on this side of the waterfall was just as narrow as it had been on the other side, on our way up to the falls. But

309

there was nothing for it but to move as fast as we could. We followed the ledge as it wound its way upwards along the steep side of the mountain. More than 30 yards below us we could see the little valley—but no dogs or men. But even if we couldn't see them, we could hear the sound of barking dogs.

"Move it!" cried Ben, who was a good way ahead of us on the ledge. Special Agent Ben Nevis was back, fast, alert and ready for anything. But what about all the things we'd just experienced in the cave? What about the Sea of Glass and the Three E Masters and the Lost Teaching of the Single Eye? And what about the last, very important thing the Three E Masters were about to tell us when we were so rudely interrupted? Weren't they going to tell us about how to use the Single Eye in practice? Weren't they going to tell us how to put it into action?

But there was no time to think about it now. Now all we had to do was escape. We ran after Ben as fast as we could.

The higher we got, the narrower the ledge became. Ben stopped a few times to kick off rocks that dangerously blocked our passage. A couple of times the boulders on the ledge were so big we had to climb over them. The drop from the ledge kept increasing. I figured it must have been at least 70 yards to the bottom.

"That's some bungy-jump!" panted Janus behind me as we carefully made our way along the ledge. "I suppose the next thing you'll be wanting us to do is rock climbing, Ben..."

"Quiet!" Ben motioned for us to stop.

The sound of barking dogs was no longer beneath us.

Now it was behind us.

"I think the bloodhounds are onto our scent!" said Ben. "We've got to move faster, before they bring up the choppers!"

We moved along the ledge as fast as we dared. About five minutes later, the ledge finally came to an end and we stepped onto a wide rocky plateau. We all breathed a sigh of relief.

Ben stopped and surveyed the landscape. We threw ourselves on the ground and tried to catch our breath. Although it was cold up here, we were all sweating hard. The sound of barking dogs was getting nearer. Suddenly I thought I could hear the sound of men shouting too.

"So what do we do now?" asked Janus, wiping the sweat from his brow.

"About two miles from here, on the other side of the plateau, there's a canyon," said Ben. "The Sight tells me we should go there. If we can get to the other side of the canyon, it will be difficult for the bloodhounds to track us."

"Then let's get a move on it!" I cried and leapt to my feet.

Ben and I plunged forward. Janus and Jacob followed, breathing hard.

"The Sight tells me! Let's get a move on it!" cried Janus behind me, still trying to catch his breath. "What's going on here?"

"If I didn't know better, I'd say Ben's getting more and more like Starbrow—and Starbrow's getting more and more like Ben," panted Jacob back. "But there's no time to speculate about that now! Just run for your life brother!"

13

Cliffhanger

Ben led us at a swift pace across the great plateau, between pine trees and huge boulders. When we reached the other side, the terrain started to slant downwards again. Before us new mountains and valleys came into view. There were pine trees everywhere—and the sound of running water.

After we'd run for about another ten minutes, the trees came to an abrupt end and Ben signaled for us to stop.

In front of us was a gaping hole—the canyon he'd been talking about.

It was about 30 yards from the mountain where we stood to the mountain on the other side of the canyon. We walked carefully to the edge and looked down. It must have been about 50 yards to the bottom of the canyon where a river pounded its way over rocks and boulders.

We stared down at the raging water, but not even the sound of the water surging down below could drown out the sound of the barking dogs that were getting closer and closer.

Ben ran off to the right with Jacob close behind him. Janus and I followed.

As we ran along we discovered why Ben had led us to this treacherous canyon. The long wooden bridge that spanned the canyon came into view. It was a primitive bridge—made of wooden planks held together by rope—and it sagged in the middle as it swayed back and forth in the wind.

"Whooa dudes!" cried Janus. "Welcome to Cliffhanger!"

Ben stopped in front of the bridge and waited for Janus and me to catch up. The bridge was attached to each side of the canyon by rope wound around spikes that had been hammered into the ground. We stood for a moment and regarded the bridge. It looked positively ancient. Down below in the canyon, there stood a single, lone pine tree on a little island in the middle of the river. It was a huge tree, standing like a silent sentry, solitary, guarding the river as it surged around it.

"Once we get across, we'll cut the bridge down," said Ben. "Then the dogs won't be able to track us any more."

"You think the bridge is safe?" asked Jacob skeptically.

"I hope so, but we better go across one at a time just in case," said Ben. "We don't want the bridge collapsing under the weight of the four of us."

"Very comforting thought!" laughed Janus. "You think the bridge is safe enough for even one person to cross?"

"It was last time I tried."

"Wasn't that about 15 years ago?"

"Yup."

Ben grabbed the ropes with both hands and stepped out onto the bridge and began walking across as fast as he could. The bridge sagged heavily as he made his way over. A minute or two later he was on the other side, motioning for the next one of us to follow.

Jacob took a deep breath and stepped gingerly onto the bridge. He clutched the ropes tightly and looked straight ahead. It was no secret that Jacob was afraid of heights...

He started to walk.

When he was about a third of the way over, the two wooden planks he just put his left foot on broke in half. Jacob slid through the hole, grabbing desperately after the ropes. He succeeded and ended up dangling in thin air.

"Whooaaa!" cried Jacob, desperately holding on to the ropes.

Janus and I held our breath.

Jacob just hung there, clutching at the ropes with all his strength, his legs swinging wildly in the air. We could hear him gasping for breath.

The ropes creaked ominously.

Janus put his foot on the bridge and started out towards Jacob, but Ben hollered from the other side, "Stay where you are Janus! The bridge can't bear the weight of more than one person at a time."

Janus stepped back reluctantly.

"You're going to have to pull yourself back up onto the bridge, Jacob!" shouted Ben.

Jacob tensed his muscles and tried lifting himself up.

"The Force is with you, Moncler!" I shouted.

Jacob managed to lift himself up halfway and was trying to swing one of his legs up onto the bridge when a sudden gust of wind shook the whole bridge and made him fall back.

Janus and I looked at each other.

"This is not good," said Janus, "not good at all. Jacob is scared out of his wits!"

I shook my head and looked at Ben who was shouting with the fearless focus of a military commander for Jacob to lift himself up again. It was the same Ben, who less than an hour ago had stood with us surrounded by the Sea of Glass, listening to the Three E Masters tell us about the Good…

The thought made a light go off in my head and I cried out to Jacob. "Moncler! Remember what we just learned from the Three E Masters!"

Jacob was trying to raise himself up once again but another powerful gust of wind was making it impossible for him.

"The Force is All and the Force is Good!" I shouted at the top of my lungs.

At first I thought Jacob couldn't hear me, so I shouted it again—but then we heard his voice slowly repeating my words, "The Force… is All… and the Force… is Good…"

"Above you, below you, around you—the Good!" I cried.

"Above me…" said Jacob, the muscles in his arms bulging as he tried to raise himself. "Below me… around me…" he said, lifting both his legs with a sudden newfound confidence. "The Good…"

Jacob managed to swing both his legs up on the bridge again.

"That's it, Moncler!" yelled Janus. " You did it! The Force is with you!"

"The Good is with you!" I shouted with all my might.

"Don't put your weight on any one plank for too long!" yelled Ben from the other side. "Hold on to the ropes and fly like the wind."

Jacob nodded, took a deep breath, and rushed forward as lightly and quickly as he could.

I looked back. The sound of the bloodhounds was getting closer every minute. They must have reached the plateau by now.

A minute later, Jacob was on the other side. He turned and gave Janus and me the thumbs up as Ben signaled for the next one of us to cross.

Janus stepped confidently out onto the bridge. He'd never been afraid of anything—not bungy jumping from the Harbor Bridge in Copenhagen or any other kind of physical challenge.

When he came to the hole that Jacob had nearly fallen through, he hopped over it lightly.

"Be careful! Don't hop…" cried Ben.

SNAP!

Janus' elegant little hop was more than the old bridge could handle. It split in two, right where Janus landed.

"Janus!" I cried.

As the bridge snapped, Janus struggled frantically to hold onto the rope as the force of gravity pulled him down towards the canyon below. He was holding on to the side of the bridge, which snapped back towards the side of the mountain where I was standing. The other 20 or so yards snapped back towards the other side of the canyon where Ben and Jacob were standing.

Janus crashed into the side of the mountain with a loud thud.

"Janus!" I cried, looking down at my friend who was hanging there, holding on to the last shreds of the bridge with his one hand. Far below him the planks from the old bridge were already smashed to pieces on the sharp rocks at the bottom of the canyon.

The old ropes creaked alarmingly.

"Starbrow!"

"Telperion! Hold on! I'm coming!"

Janus tried to grab hold of the rope with his other hand… but couldn't reach it.

"Hold on! I'm going to haul you up!" I cried and dug my feet into the hard ground. I started pulling on the ropes with all my strength—huffing and puffing like a maniac. I'd almost managed to pull him up to the top when I heard a shout from below, "No! No Starbrow! The rope's going to snap!" I stopped pulling and looked over the edge. Sure enough, the rope Janus was holding onto was slowly unraveling. My friend was literally hanging on by a very thin thread.

I hung onto the rope, lay down flat, and stretched my arm out and over the edge. There was about a yard from my outstretched hand to Janus.

"Take my hand!" I cried.

With his free hand, Janus tried to reach my hand but there was still about a half a yard between our hands.

Suddenly the canyon around us echoed with the sound of machine gun fire.

I looked up. Ben was firing at someone behind us. I could hear the sound of men and dogs running in the woods behind us!

"Come on, Telperion, take my hand!" I shouted.

Janus tightened every muscle in his body, managed to raise himself up a few more centimeters. I leant out even further over the edge, straining every fiber of my body to the bursting point.

Behind me I heard the sound of soldiers running for cover, trying to escape Ben's machine gun fire.

But there was still almost half a yard between our hands.

I closed my eyes and tried to remember what the Three E Masters had told us about the Nature of Reality.

The Force is All and the Force is Good. Perfect Life. Perfect Intelligence. Perfect Love...

Suddenly I felt something grasp my hand tightly.

I opened my eyes.

Janus had managed to grab my hand!

"Starbrow!" he cried. "What did you do?"

"Telperion!" I cried. "Hold on, I've got you! The Good is with us!"

We clutched each other's hand tightly. Half a second later the last shred of the bridge rope unraveled and fell into the depths.

The full weight of Janus' powerful body in my one hand made me slide further forward and out over the edge.

"Whooaa!" cried Janus.

I dug my feet further into the ground and desperately tried to grab onto something with my other hand. I found a stump of an old tree and held onto it for dear life. I tightened every muscle in my body and tried to pull myself backwards.

It worked.

I stopped sliding forwards and was stable.

"Starbrow!"

"I've got you! I won't let you go."

The only problem was that I had to use both my feet and one hand to keep us from sliding over the edge and falling down into the canyon. That left only one arm for Janus and there was no way in hell I could heave him up with one arm.

For a moment Ben's machine gun fire stopped. I looked up and could see Ben and Jacob having a heated discussion on the other side of the canyon. Behind me I could hear the soldiers and dogs closing in on us again.

"This is one hell of time for them to have a discussion about non-violence!" groaned Janus underneath me.

"Hold on, Telperion!" I said, trying to pull him up. I knew I couldn't hold on to him much longer, he was just too heavy.

"Starbrow! Don't let go!"

I didn't know what to do. In desperation I did the only thing I could think of. I closed my eyes and thought about the One Force, the Good, which is the One and Only Reality. The Force... The Good... in me, in Janus, in everyone. All Life, All Intelligence, All Love and... All Strength.

316

The moment I thought about the Good as being Strength, something strange happened. I felt as if a cool fire had been aroused within me. And with that cool fire, a strength and fierce determination began to grow in my heart.

The strength and determination of a warrior.

I opened my eyes and tensed my muscles. Then, fiercely determined, I began to pull Janus up. To my great surprise it was easy. Suddenly my powerful friend seemed as light as a small child. It was easy as pie!

With one final movement, I pulled Janus all the way up. Or should I say in one effortless movement, the Omnipotent Force not only pulled Janus up from the side of the mountain, but also placed him securely on the hard ground right next to me.

My friend stared at me in amazement.

"Whoa, Starbrow! The Force is definitely with you, man!"

I let go of Janus' hand and looked at my hands. My whole body was shaking—or should I say pulsating—with this amazing Strength and Power.

A new burst of machine gun fire from Ben quickly snapped us out of our euphoria. Apparently, Jacob hadn't succeeded in convincing Ben not to shoot at our pursuers. Janus and I looked back and could hear dogs snarling and soldiers closing in fast.

We jumped to our feet and looked over at Ben who was motioning for us to run along the mountainside, in the opposite direction of the soldiers.

"This is getting a little too intense!" cried Janus. "Let's get out of here!"

We started to run in the other direction, but had run only a few yards when we realized that soldiers were also approaching from that side too.

We were surrounded—there were soldiers everywhere—on all sides now.

The only way out was the deep canyon below.

I looked over at Ben and Jacob. I could see from Ben's face that he knew there was nothing more he could do for us.

Janus and I were trapped.

Ben fired another round at the soldiers behind us but this time the soldiers returned his fire. Ben and Jacob leapt for cover.

Suddenly everything went very quiet as we stood looking down at the canyon with its one lone pine tree standing in the middle of the raging river.

"How far down do you think it is to that pine tree?" I said.

"Oh about 30 yards or so," said Janus. "Why?"

317

The soldiers and the bloodhounds were now charging through the trees. In a few moments, they would be upon us.

I turned and walked back a few paces. I felt the fierce determination of the warrior swell up in me again.

"After all the trouble you had hauling me up from the canyon now you want us to jump back into it?" said Janus laughing when he realized what I intended to do.

I walked back about 10 yards and then turned back towards the canyon again.

"You should have accepted Ashtar's offer to stay in the Mothership, Starbrow," said Janus following me. "Just think about it. Early retirement, endless interdimensional holidays."

I focused on the Good and began to run forward.

"Don't worry brother," I cried as I ran, "if this leap of faith doesn't work, I'll be in the higher dimensions in no time!"

Then I jumped into the canyon.

14

In Fire, in Water, in Earth, in Air

As I soared through the air, heading straight for the pine tree, time stood still.

Those few seconds felt like eternity.

The wind beat against me as I zoomed through the air but I didn't care. My whole focus was on the Good.

The Good that is All and in All.

Omnipresent, Omnipotent, Omniscient.

And as I focused on the Good, I suddenly had this strange feeling—the feeling that a Greater Mind was taking over my mind. And in that eternity of no time, I was all of a sudden able to see everything with the eyes of the Greater Mind. The pine tree I was heading for, the sheer mountainside, the roaring water below… every physical form suddenly seemed to contain a radiant light, an invisible fire that was barely covered by a very thin, transparent veil…

The Good is the One and Only Reality.

I was right above the pine tree now, flapping my arms and aiming for the center of the tree, trying to position myself so I would land feet first.

The Good is All in All. All Life, All Intelligence, All Love. The Good is Defense and Protection.

The moment I thought of the Good as being Defense and Protection, it was as if time slowed down even more.

Much much more.

Much much slower.

Like very slow motion.

It was almost as if I was floating, suddenly weightless in the air. As if a giant invisible hand had placed itself underneath me and was gently holding me up.

An invisible hand?

Holding me up?

319

It can't be true, I thought. *I must be dreaming...*

The moment that thought arose in me, time and gravity returned with a vengeance.

The wind pounded against me and I plummeted straight towards the center of the pine tree at breakneck speed. I could see I was going to crash into the tree with the side of my body. In less than a second...

No, no! Don't think about it!

CRASH!

I hit the tree with a tremendous force. The topmost branches of the tree snapped like matchsticks.

A searing pain shot through my left side. I kept falling at great speed.

CRASH! CRASH! CRASH!

Branch after branch after branch snapped as I fell towards the bottom of the canyon. Each branch I hit felt like a whip lashing across my body.

CRASH! CRASH!

But at least the branches were slowing me down, breaking my fall.

Then with one final, violent crash that knocked all the air out of me, I landed on my back on the soft turf around the pine tree.

I saw stars and blinking lights.

Had I died and passed over into the next dimension?

I looked up.

Was it my guardian angel who was now racing towards me from up above?

Or was it...

"YIPPIEKAYAAAAAIIIIIIII!"

Bruce Willis' trademark Die Hard war cry echoed in the canyon as Janus threw himself from the mountainside with one great bellowing roar.

The blinking lights before my eyes disappeared and I could now clearly see Janus come flying straight down towards me.

I sat up and blinked.

That crazy brother of mine was coming at me head first as if he'd just dived off a diving board!

When he was about halfway to the tree, Janus apparently came to his senses because he tried to turn in mid-air so he'd land feet first.

Unfortunately, a strong gust of wind pushed him slightly off course so it now looked as if he'd land on the other side of the tree, dangerously close to the rapids!

I struggled to stand up but it was difficult because my whole body was racked with pain. My left arm felt like it was on fire.

CRASH! CRASH!

Janus hit the other side of the tree.

Branch after branch cracked as he shot towards the ground like a cannonball. When he was halfway down the huge tree, he hit a very thick branch which amazingly enough did not break on impact but rather swung and catapulted him away from the tree.

Janus landed with a big splash in the roaring river.

"Janus!"

I got up and ran across the rocks and tried to grab my friend before the powerful current took him.

My left arm and hand were covered with blood.

With my right hand I managed to grab a hold of Janus' leg.

But the wet rocks were too slippery.

Instead of holding Janus back, I was pulled into the roaring river.

A moment later I was under water, icy cold mountain water in my mouth. The current took me and I felt myself being pulled downwards.

I struggled up to the surface again and saw Janus struggling to keep afloat a few yards ahead of me.

"Starbrow!" he spluttered.

"Telpe..."

Again the incredibly strong current pulled me under as the river rushed ever downwards.

When I came up sputtering I found myself almost next to Janus.

Right before us was the sound of thunder.

"Watch out, Starbrow!" yelled Janus.

Up ahead we saw the river abruptly disappear.

A waterfall!

And judging by the sound of it, it was no small waterfall.

"WHOOOOAAAAAAAAAAA!!!" yelled Janus and I in unison as we tumbled over the edge in another free fall as gallons and gallons of mountain water covered us. The great waterfall thundered down into a small lake below.

As we tumbled down I could see several large, sharp rocks sticking up from the water, right were Janus and I were falling.

We were headed straight for them!

I tried to open my mouth, but there was too much water. Water everywhere... so instead I thought fiercely...

Everyone is seeking the Good! And the Good that everyone is seeking is Defense and Protection! And the Good is the Nature of Reality!

Therefore the Nature of Reality is Defense and Protection!

The Good is Defense and Protection!

Immediately I saw that radiant glow again. It was everywhere. In the turbulent water, in the sharp rocks below us, in my body!

The Good is Defense and Protection! I thought again adamantly, fiercely. *The Good is Defense and Protection!*

Suddenly I felt something push me from behind—gently yet firmly. The gentle push altered my course! Now I could see that instead of landing on the sharp rocks below, I would land in the water right between the rocks.

The Good is Defense and Protection...

Splaaaash!

I cannonballed into the lake, right between two of the rocks. The force of the waterfall pushed me down deep towards the bottom of the lake.

There was water everywhere—and a roar like thunder. Rocks. Water. Body. Air. Blood. Water...

The Good is...

"Hey Starbrow! You can't give up now!"

Air... Water... Earth...

Solid ground beneath me.

Beneath my body.

I opened my eyes.

I was lying on a flat piece of stone about a yard from the edge of the lake and about 50 yards from the waterfall. Janus was lying on the rock next to me, breathing hard.

"In me, in you, in everyone—the Good..." I moaned.

"You can bet your ass you're Good!" chuckled Janus spitting water in all directions. "Do you have any idea what kind of super stunt the two of us just did?"

"Where are we?"

"We made it Starbrow! We're on land! We're on land!"

"We... made it..."

"You better believe it! In fire, in water, in earth, in air—the Good!"

"The Good... we're on land..." I mumbled.

"Yeah!" laughed Janus. "We're on bloody friggin' land!"

Despite the fact that every bone in my body ached and I was having a hard time catching my breath, I burst out laughing too. I just couldn't help it.

"But how did we get here?" I asked as I started to catch my breath.

"You tell me," sputtered Janus, "...how we survived hitting that pine tree and cannonballing over that waterfall? I don't get it. We should be dead, bro."

We slowly sat up and looked at each other.

"Any broken limbs?" asked Janus.

I looked down at myself. My clothes were torn to shreds, especially on the left side of my body where I'd first collided with the tree—and blood was slowly oozing from the deep gash on my upper left arm.

"That looks pretty nasty," said Janus as he ripped off one of his shirtsleeves. "We've got to stop the bleeding."

He bound up my arm tightly first above the six-inch wound—and then around the wound itself as tightly as he could. So tight that the rest of my arm felt strangely numb.

"And what about you, oh noble Elven King?" I asked when he'd finished bandaging me up. "Are you okay?"

My strong friend got up and looked at himself. His right pants leg and shirtsleeve had been ripped off and he had several nasty bruises across his shoulder. But apart from that he looked pretty OK.

"No broken limbs here," he said. "So I have to admit the Three E Masters' formula is pretty effective! But apparently not effective enough to prevent you from getting that nasty wound on your upper arm."

"It happened because I had a moment of doubt," I said.

"You too?"

"Yes." I said, looking up at him. "When I jumped into the canyon I focused all my attention on the Good. The moment I focused on the Good it felt as if time stopped and gravity disappeared. But then I couldn't believe what was happening—and this nasty gash is the result of my doubting the Good."

"If it's any comfort to you," said Janus nodding in agreement, "the same thing happened to me. I also focused my attention on the Good. Then about halfway down, I realized that landing head first in that pine tree was probably not such a great idea. So I tried to turn myself around in mid-air, but the wind was too strong. Still I kept focusing on the Good—and then suddenly it was as if time stood still and gravity disappeared, just like you say. And then it was like something began to turn me 180 degrees in the air..."

"Something?"

"Yeah," he shrugged. "I don't know what it was... but it was almost like a giant invisible hand or something..."

I nodded. "Exactly my experience. The Invisible Hand of the Good!"

"I thought I was hallucinating or something!" laughed Janus. "And the minute I had that thought, time and gravity came back with a vengeance—and a gust of wind threw me off course so I landed in the river. But I was lucky I guess. My doubting the Good didn't get me in as much trouble as you."

I struggled to get up. Apart from the deep gash in my upper arm, I had lots of smaller cuts and bruises, mostly on my left side. But nothing felt broken.

"It was almost the same when we went over the falls and were heading straight for those sharp rocks," I said. "Again I was focusing on the Good when I felt something pushing me from behind. Thanks to that push, I miraculously missed the rocks."

"Same with me," laughed Janus. "And the next minute the two of us are lying safe and sound on dry land! The Teaching of the Three E Masters is too cool!"

We laughed and slapped our palms together. Unfortunately this gesture of triumph sent a wave of dizzying pain up my arm.

"Sorry dude," said Janus when he saw me pull back in pain. "No more funky moves until we get that arm of yours fixed."

"Okay bro, but where do you think we are?"

We looked around and discovered that the river continued downwards from the other side of the lake. Then we looked back towards the waterfall, only to discover Ben scrambling down the mountainside with Jacob close behind him.

Janus and I walked over to meet them at the bottom.

"Well I never!" smiled Ben as we approached. "Have you two boys ever considered joining the CIA!"

"The Force is truly with you!" said Jacob with a big grin. "That was the most amazing stunt I've ever seen! And no one seems to have any broken bones!"

"Starbrow's got himself a nasty gash on his left arm," said Janus, "but apart from that we're okay."

"You boys were literally hanging up there by a thread," said Ben as he looked at the bloody bandage wrapped around my arm.

"Do you think the soldiers will try to follow us?" I asked.

"Jump off a mountain like the two of you? I don't think so," said Ben. "They're CIA agents—not suicide bombers!"

"We can thank the Teaching of the Three E Masters for being alive," I said. "By focusing on the Good we literally passed through fire, water, earth and air."

"You're kidding," said Ben incredulously. "You mean to tell me the two of you performed all those super stunts by thinking about what the Three E Masters said to us in the cave?"

"Yes, that's exactly what I mean," I said. "If it hadn't been for our focus on the Good, I don't dare think what would have happened to us."

"Shredded to pieces by the tree or smashed to a pulp on the rocks is what would have happened to us!" grinned Janus.

Ben shook his head in disbelief.

"Look guys," said Jacob, "before we start celebrating, let's just think for a minute about where we are because I doubt if those soldiers have given up the chase."

"You're right Jacob," said Ben. "They'll just call in the choppers and then they'll be over on the other side in no time."

"And then the hunt will go on," I said. "And even with the Teaching of the Three E Masters, we can't go on jumping off mountainsides forever. What about our mission?"

"Yeah, what about our mission?" said Jacob. "The further we get from civilization, the less chance we have of lifting the entire collective consciousness by Friday."

"You've got a point there," said Janus gloomily.

"OK," said Ben, "But first we have to get ourselves somewhere safer— so I can take a look at Starbrow's arm. But we do have one advantage. I know this valley and they don't. There's a place not far from here where I think we'll be safe for a while. Follow me."

15

In the Dark

It was raining by the time we reached Ben Nevis' hideaway an hour later. It was an old deserted mine shaft at the other end of the valley. Old rusty railway tracks led to a dark opening in the side of a high rock wall. A pile of rotting wooden beams was stacked on one side of the entrance.

As we approached the mine, everyone walked towards the entrance except me. I didn't have the strength. In fact I was so weak I could barely stand. My left arm and shoulder felt strangely numb.

My head felt light and I began to sway.

"Hey, Starbrow!"

Janus ran back and grabbed me just before I fell to the ground.

"Friends!" he called to Jacob and Ben. "We've got to do something about Starbrow!" Jacob and Ben came running back.

"Starbrow, you fool," said Janus obviously worried. "Why didn't you say something?"

Ben carefully unwrapped the bloody bandage on my upper left arm. The long, deep gash didn't look good.

"Ow!" said Janus sympathetically. "That must hurt."

"You've lost quite a lot of blood," said Ben frowning. "We've got to sew this up immediately."

I smiled faintly. "I don't suppose there's a hospital around here?"

"No," said Ben. "So we'll just have to do the best we can."

He pulled off his backpack and rummaged through it.

"The best we can?" said Jacob, now it was his turn to frown.

Ben pulled out a small first aid kit and took out a needle and thread.

"You must be kidding!" said Jacob.

"We have no way of anesthetizing his arm," said Ben. "But the alternative is bleeding to death."

Ben seemed to know what he was doing. He disinfected the needle with a lighter, while he barked out orders to Jacob and Janus. Then he carefully cleaned the wound with the water they'd fetched.

"Okay," said Ben sitting down next to me. "Now I want you to bite down on this piece of leather and think about something else."

"This is radical," said Janus as he turned his head away. " Reminds me of that scene in First Blood where Sylvester Stallone sews up his own arm while he's out in the wilderness. In the end he..."

"Spare me the movies please! I have AAAAAARRRRGGGHHH!!!" I said screaming with pain as the needle tore through my flesh.

"Hold him, so he doesn't move," said Ben.

Jacob and Janus sat down on each side of me and held me down. Unfortunately, my arm no longer felt quite so numb and lifeless!

"Okay, Starbrow," said Janus firmly. "Now think about something else."

AAAARRRGGGHHH! I screamed.

The pain was unbearable. I kicked but Jacob and Janus held me in an iron grip.

"This isn't good," said Jacob to Ben. "The man is about to faint!"

"Might be for the best," said Janus consolingly.

AAAAARRRGGGHHH! More pain ripped my body as Ben kept sticking the needle into my flesh.

"Fuck," said Jacob. "What the hell are we doing? If the two of you could survive that incredible kamikaze jump into the canyon by focusing on the Good, we must be able to use that focus in this situation too."

"You've got a point," said Janus. "Did you hear that, Starbrow?" he almost shouted in my ear. "Focus on the Good like you did when you jumped into the canyon."

AAAARRRGGGHHH! Ben continued sewing up the wound.

"Starbrow," said Jacob. "Remember that by focusing on the Good, which is the True Nature of Reality, one experiences it. One experiences harmony where there seems to be disharmony. Life where there seems to be a lack of Life..."

ARRGHH! I screamed again.

"Okay, Starbrow," said Jacob. "Now do it. Tell me what you learned about the True Nature of Reality from the Ascended Masters and from the Three E Masters. And tell me now!"

I took a deep breath and tried to focus.

"First, the Force..." I whispered, feeling very faint and in pain. "The Force is All..."

"That's right, Starbrow," said Jacob encouragingly. "The Force is All in All. All Life, All Intelligence, All Love. YOU ARE THE FORCE!"

"Yes..." I said trying to remember the exaltation I'd felt up in the higher dimensions when I realized for the very first time that I was the One Omnipresent and Omnipotent Force. "I AM THE FORCE!" I said weakly.

The pain in my arm was unbearable. ARRGHH! I had no idea how far Ben was with his sewing operation, but it was no use thinking about it. The best thing I could do was think about the Force.

"YOU ARE THE FORCE, Starbrow!" said Janus in a loud voice.

"And let us remember what we have learned about the Nature of the Force," said Jacob.

"Tell me about the Nature of the Force, Starbrow," said Janus.

Making an enormous effort, I replied, "The Nature of the Force is.... Good...The Good..."

The moment I thought about the Good, the true nature of everything, something strange began to happen. I felt like I did when we were in the cave behind 12 Stone Falls standing on that amazing Sea of Glass. It was as if suddenly there was a wind, a fine healing wind that began to caress my face, softly and kindly. And I sighed as the wind caressed me...my face, my body, my arms. Because it was such a fine healing wind... so fine, so soft... that it began to soothe away the pain... all the pain, all the fear, all the tiredness... soothe it—and send it far far away, back into the nothingness from whence it came. For in reality there was nothing but Life. Health. Strength. Energy. THE GOOD.

Somewhere on the edge of my consciousness I still felt a faint pricking sensation in my arm. Was Ben still sewing up my inflamed arm? No I said to myself, don't think about it...

"That's good, Starbrow," said Jacob in a soft, soothing voice. "Just keep focusing on the Good. Remember what the Three E Masters told us about the Nature of Reality. The One Force or Presence is you, me, and everyone and everything."

"I AM the Force," I said dreamily.

"Exactly," said Jacob. "You are the Force. And the One Force is Perfect, Whole and Complete. Untouchable and Invincible."

"Yes," said Janus. "That means that you are Perfect, Whole and Complete."

"Starbrow is Perfect, Whole and Complete," said Jacob firmly.

"Perfect, Whole and Complete," said Janus.

"Perfect, Whole and Complete..." I repeated softly as the fine healing wind within and around me grew in power. The feeling was now so powerful and so blissful that I'd almost forgotten all about my body and my arm.

There was nothing but the fine healing wind.

I was the fine healing wind.

The Good.

"*I am the Good*," I said.

"*You are the Good*," said Jacob and Janus slowly and in unison.

"It has always been so..." said Jacob.

"It is so now..." said Janus.

"It will always be so," all three of us said.

A deep peace descended over me. A deep peace and a powerful sense of well being. Because I knew with absolute certainty that this was the True Nature of Reality. *The Good.*

I do not know whether I drifted away and dozed for seconds or hours experiencing the Good in this blissful state, all I know is that it was Janus' voice that brought me back. He was crying, "Holy Testicle Tuesday...Halle-fuckin-lujah!"

Then I heard Jacob say, "It's a miracle... a bloody miracle!"

I opened my eyes... the Single Eye of the Force in me opened Its eyes...

Ben was standing next to me with the needle and thread in his hands, staring at my arm as if he'd just seen a ghost. "What... what did you do?" he said completely dumbfounded.

"Ha ha!" Jacob and Janus triumphantly slapped their hands together.

"What did we do?" I repeated still in a daze.

I looked down at my arm.

No, you moron! The other arm! I was so completely gone in my focus on the Good that I couldn't remember which arm had the ugly gash!

I looked at my other arm.

Strange. No sign of a gash on that arm either... no stitching, no blood, no nothing.

I looked back at my left arm. No sign of anything there either.

Perhaps it was all just a dream?

Ben was still staring at my left arm, his mouth wide open.

"What did you do?" he said again.

"Ha ha!" Jacob and Janus were still laughing and dancing around us like two maniacs. *"The Good is All in All! The Good is All in All!"*

Still baffled, Ben put his hand on my left arm.

My left arm was all together Perfect, Whole and Complete.

It had always been so.

It would always be so.

And now we saw it.

With the Single Eye of the Force.

That was when I burst out laughing too and leapt to my feet suddenly feeling completely well and strong. All dizziness and weakness were gone. I raised my left arm and Janus and I slapped our palms together with all our might. This time there was no pain, only an incredible feeling of wellness, aliveness, and strength.

"Way to go, Starbro'!" laughed Jacob when I slapped my palm to his too.

Ben was still watching the three of us with this comical, confused look on his face.

"But how? How did you do it?"

I raised my arms and began posing like a bodybuilder.

"I feel as strong as an ox!" I cried. And it was true. I felt stronger, healthier and more energetic than I'd ever felt before. It was amazing.

Janus felt the bulging muscles in my arms. "Hmm!!" he said as he compared my muscles to his. "Check out these biceps! I do believe all this focusing on the Good actually made your muscles bigger too!"

We burst out laughing again.

"I swear," said Ben, "the wound closed itself up right before my eyes!" He was feeling my left arm. "Every trace of blood and stitching disappeared just like that. It looks like absolutely nothing ever happened to your arm! This is way beyond me!"

Ben kept staring at my arm and shaking his head. "First the two of you survive the most insane suicide jump I've ever seen in my life and then you heal Starbrow's arm in the twinkling of an eye. I wonder what the next miracle's going to be?"

"Remember what the Three E Masters told us, Ben," said Jacob. "In truth, these aren't really miracles. All we did was focus on the True Nature of Reality, which is the Good—Perfect Life, Intelligence and Love. And then when we did, this is what we experienced."

Ben shook his head. "This is way beyond me!"

Once my arm was healed, we started walking down the mine. It was a good thing Ben had a flashlight because it was very dark inside. We made

330

steady progress as Ben led us in between rotten beams, barrels, and other abandoned miner's gear that lay scattered all over the place. Water dripped from the ceiling and several times the passage split into several directions, but Ben always seemed to know where he was going. He said he was leading us through the mine to another entrance on the other side of the mountain—which was about an hour's walk from where we were.

As we walked, we talked about everything that happened since we entered the cave at 12 Stone Falls and learned about the Lost Teaching of the Single Eye. A teaching of obviously unbelievable power since it miraculously saved Janus and me when we jumped into the canyon and now it had completely healed my badly damaged left arm.

As we walked, Ben was silent most of the time. Whether it was because he was pondering the Lost Teaching of the Single Eye or because he was beginning to remember some of his forgotten childhood, was hard to tell.

Finally he said, "So you're saying you focused on the Good when you jumped into the canyon?"

"Yes," said Janus. "And we did it again when we went over the waterfall and were about to crash into the rocks. And again when we almost drowned in the lake."

"We also did it when you were sewing up my arm and I was in such pain."

Ben stopped for another look at my arm. It was completely healed, whole and perfect. Then he turned and continued on through the old, decaying mine.

After a few more minutes, he said. "So if I understand things correctly… doing what you guys did—focusing on the Good which the Teaching says is the One and Only Reality—is what we are going to have to do to raise the collective consciousness so that STARDAY can be released? Is that right? Is that what you're saying?"

"Yes, that's what we're saying," said Jacob. "According to the Prophecy of Starwarrior, the Perfect World will come from the Single Eye."

We came to a place in the mine where so many rotten beams had collapsed that for several minutes we had to crawl through, over and around them. Once we got to the other side, Ben said: "But how does its work, I mean practically? Are we just going to sit and focus on the Good until the whole collective consciousness is raised or what?"

I thought about the Three E Masters' last words… what they were saying when we were interrupted by the approaching soldiers and bloodhounds.

"In order for you to fulfill the Prophecy of Starwarrior you not only have to focus on God, the Good. In practice, it is also of crucial importance that..."

In practice it was also of crucial importance... to do what?

We were interrupted so suddenly and had taken flight so quickly that we'd never had time to think about their last words...

"No, not just us," said Jacob. "In order to raise the collective consciousness, we need a critical mass of human beings who focus on the Good."

"A critical mass?" said Ben. "You mean like Ashtar said in the Mothership... the Hundredth Monkey Syndrome I think you called it?"

"Yeah that's right," said Jacob. "In order to raise the collective consciousness, one percent of Earth's population—that is 60 million human beings—must raise their consciousness drastically at the same time."

"I have just one question, Jacob," I said. "It seems to me that to have the Single Eye and focus on the Good is a lot more powerful than the New Vision. And if that's the case, maybe it means we need less than one percent of the Earth's population to create a critical mass? What if we only need 0.1%—that would be only six million people? Or what if it's only 0.01%—that would be only 600,000 people?"

"Good question," said Jacob nodding. "I was thinking the same thing because you're right. It does seem like the Single Eye is a lot more powerful than the New Vision. But how should I know exactly how many people we need to have the Single Eye and focus on the Good to create a critical mass by Friday? What did Ashtar say? Didn't he mention anything about it when you talked to him up in the Mothership?"

"No," I replied. "He just said that by using the Lost Teaching of the Single Eye, the Three E Masters raised the collective consciousness of an entire star system. He didn't say anything about what percentage of the population they actually got to focus on the Good."

"Hmm," said Jacob thoughtfully. "I suppose the Laws of Consciousness must be the same everywhere in the Universe."

Janus laughed softly. "As far as I can see, whether we need 60 million or 600,000 is really a rather moot point at the moment considering the fact there's only the four of us—and right now we're wandering around in some deserted mineshaft in the middle of nowhere with half the US army on our tail! I mean how the hell are we going to escape and get back to civilization for one—not to mention just getting the four of us to have the Single Eye all the time?"

No one replied. We just kept walking, each deep in thought.

We'd been so focused on finding out what the Lost Teaching of the Single Eye was and on escaping from our pursuers that we'd completely forgotten this very important question. How on earth were we going to get one percent of the Earth's population—60 million people—to raise their consciousness drastically and focus on the Good by Friday?

That was when Ben's flashlight went dead. We stood there for a while in the darkness wondering what to do when suddenly a bright light lit up the blackness.

It was Ben's sword. He'd taken it out of his bag.

When he held up Starwarrior's sword, it lit up the darkness before us. Ben started walking down the tunnel again. The rest of us followed, hoping against hope that Starwarrior and his bright sword would lead us to the light on the other side of the darkness.

PART THREE

THE GATHERING OF
THE BROTHERHOOD

1

The Interdimensional Radio

Finally we saw light at the end of the tunnel. It filtered in softly from the entrance on the other side of the mountain and when we emerged, the sun was setting on a wild mountain landscape with valleys and tall peaks in the distance. And then, in the light of the setting sun, we sat down for a council of war.

"Right now the time is 17:44," I said looking at my watch. "Which is 22:44 Greenwich Mean Time. And today is Monday the 6th of April. Which means that we have..."

"... 3 days, 1 hour and 15 minutes to STARDAY," said Jacob.

"That is, if there's going to be a STARDAY at all," interrupted Janus. He didn't sound very optimistic.

I went on: "According to Ashtar, Merlin and the Three E Masters, the Lost Teaching of the Single Eye is able to lift the collective consciousness of a planet to quantum level 5, which should be enough to allow STARDAY to take place here on Planet Earth."

Jacob nodded in approval at my summary of the situation.

"Now that we have the Lost Teaching of the Single Eye," I continued, "the big question is how many people do we need with the Single Eye to lift the collective consciousness here on Planet Earth? Do we need a critical mass of one percent or 60 million people like we did with the New Vision—or what?"

"It's true that having the Single Eye seems a lot more powerful than the New Vision," said Janus.

"Yes, but how much more powerful?" continued Jacob. "And even if it is more powerful, does that make the requirement 0.1% or maybe even 0.01% of the Earth's population?"

"I don't suppose we can just call up the Three E Masters and ask them?" said Janus.

"I don't think the Three E Masters are on Earth anymore," I said, shaking my head. "Now that they've given us what they were supposed to give us, the rest is up to us."

"Then how are we going to find out?" asked Janus.

No one answered.

In the distance, the sun dipped behind the tallest peaks as rain-filled clouds gathered around the mountaintops. A cold wind was blowing. We sat there in silence as each of us pondered everything we'd learned from the Masters—the old ones as well as the new—in the last couple of days and hours.

"In a situation as critical as this, we can't rely on speculation," said Jacob finally. "Therefore as far as I'm concerned, we have no choice but to base our actions on the original critical mass percentage which was one percent."

"One percent?" sighed Janus. "You mean we are going to need 60 million people with the Single Eye by Friday?"

"Well," answered Jacob, "in a situation like this there's no room for miscalculation. We're talking about the fate of the world."

"Jacob is right," I said. "Since we don't know how many people are required, we should assume that the critical mass requires the highest possible percentage, which is one percent."

"So just let me ask…how are we going to get 60 million people with the Single Eye by Friday guys?" said Janus. "We're talking about a complete impossibility and besides I'm not even sure I even understand what the Single Eye is—to be completely honest!"

"Well whether you understand it or not, you did all right when you jumped into the canyon," said Jacob and gave Janus a friendly shove.

"Yippiekayai!" laughed Janus and slapped Jacob five.

"Okay guys, let's concentrate," I said. "So if we agree that we need to get 60 million people to have the Single Eye and focus on the Good by Friday, the question is now: How do we get 60 million people to do that?"

"Easy," said Jacob. "All we have to do is get in contact with the whole world and tell them."

"Tell them what?" said Janus. "Don't you realize that millions of people on Earth already believe the Ashtar Command is hostile and behind all the devastating Earth changes."

"That might be true, but at least as many people believe the Ashtar Command is friendly and comes in peace," I said. "Remember what Rebecca and Elmar told me. The thought of STARDAY has given millions of people new hope. Those are the people we have to get in touch with. We have to tell them that a new era of peace and enlightenment is now within reach—and that to achieve it, all they have to do is raise their consciousness and focus on the One Force, the Good, which is the True Nature of Reality."

"All they have to do..." mumbled Janus and shook his head.

I looked over at Ben. He was sitting with his head bowed as if deep in thought.

"Starbrow is right," said Jacob. "The time is now ripe. But the question is still, how do we get into contact with all these hopeful people and get 60 million of them to have the Single Eye at the same time?"

Janus shook his head in despair. "It can't be done guys. In order to do that we'd have to be able to talk to everyone on Planet Earth—with the entire population—like Ashtar did when he talked to all humanity on all the TV channels on all the TV sets in the world."

It did look pretty bleak. "And only the Force knows what kind of super-advanced technology the Ashtar Command used to pull off a stunt like that."

When I said that, Ben raised his head and looked at me.

"What did you just say?" he asked, suddenly seeming very eager.

"I said that only the Force knows what kind of super-advanced technology the Ashtar Command used to talk on all the world's TV channels and TV sets."

"That's not true," said Ben.

"What do you mean?"

"I know what kind of advanced technology the Ashtar Command used to talk to the whole world."

We all looked at him in surprise. "You do?"

"Yes. The Ashtar Command sent their transmission to all the world's TV sets from a high-vibrational-frequency-sender."

"A high what?" said Janus.

"A high-vibrational-frequency-sender. I never told you about it because it didn't seem relevant until now. But the way DETI was able to intercept Ashtar's first transmission to you and the other 600 volunteers was via a high-vibrational-frequency-receiver that two astronomers from a research institute called SETI built."

"A high-vibrational-frequency-receiver?" said Jacob.

"Yes," said Ben. "The SETI astronomers have a theory that intelligent life in the universe operates on higher vibrational frequencies, which harmonizes very well with everything you have told me about the Ashtar Command and the 5th dimension. Some years ago, these SETI astronomers constructed a high-vibrational-frequency-receiver, which they call 'an interdimensional radio'. This interdimensional radio can pick up messages from higher vibrational frequencies—and that's exactly what it did. It picked up the Ashtar Command's transmission to the 600 volunteers. That was how we were able to track you guys down."

"An interdimensional radio!" I said. "Sounds like you know some pretty intelligent astronomers!"

"And you're saying the Ashtar Command used the same technology as the astronomers' interdimensional radio when they sent their second transmission to all the world's TV sets and TV channels?" asked Jacob.

"Yes that's right."

"How do you know it's the same technology?"

"Well for one, I remember the SETI astronomers' high-vibrational-frequency-receiver emitted the very same high-pitched ringing tones that the Ashtar Command's transmission did," said Ben.

"I remember those high-pitched tones!" I said. "It was the same sound that came from my TV set back home in Copenhagen."

Jacob and Janus nodded affirmatively. They too had heard the same tones.

"Very interesting," said Jacob. "Was the astronomers' interdimensional radio only able to receive messages?"

"Naturally, that was one of the first things I asked them," said Ben. "And the answer was yes, their machine could only receive messages. *But*... and here's the but... the machine that the astronomers based their invention on *was* able to both *send and receive* messages."

"The machine that they based their interdimensional radio on?"

"Yes," said Ben. "According to the astronomers they didn't invent the high-vibrational-frequency-receiver. They based their invention on some now deceased Scottish professor's invention. And it was a machine that could both receive and send messages."

"Just hold it for a second, Ben," I said. "Are you saying that if we could get a hold of this Scottish professor's high-vibrational-frequency-receiver-sender we could send a message about the Single Eye to all the TVs and TV channels in the world?"

"I'm not saying anything yet," replied Ben. "You were the one who said that only the Force knows how the Ashtar Command was able to talk to the whole world. All I am saying is that there is this Scottish professor who apparently also knew how to do it."

"But if the Scottish professor's machine could both send and receive messages, how come the SETI astronomers' machine could only receive messages?" asked Jacob.

"According to the astronomers, it took them three years to construct the receiver," replied Ben, "and they said it would probably take them another three years to construct a sender."

"Three years!" cried Janus. "And we only have until Friday. So I guess we can forget about using their machine for anything."

"But what about the Scottish professor's machine?" asked Jacob, "If it really can do what you say—both send and receive signals, why isn't his invention world famous? Why hasn't it revolutionized the world's technology?"

"I don't know. The professor is dead."

"When did he die?" I asked.

"A long time ago, I think."

Ben took a worn notebook out from his inside jacket pocket and leafed through the pages.

"Let's see... I wrote it down here somewhere. Here it is. Professor Jonathan McAlister. Died 1940."

"1940? Why that's more than 60 years ago," I said.

"I still don't get it," said Jacob. "Even if it was 60 years ago, why didn't his invention revolutionize science?"

Ben shook his head. "Unfortunately I didn't have time to investigate it any further. The SETI astronomers' observatory was demolished by an earthquake and after that I was busy hunting you three."

"But how did the SETI astronomers discover the professor's invention in the first place?" I asked.

"I did have time to ask them about that," said Ben. "Some years ago they took part in a science and astronomy convention at the University of Edinburgh in Scotland. While they were there, they accidentally stumbled on the professor's papers while they were doing some research in the archives. Apparently there was a description of his invention in his papers, which they copied and took back with them. Their work is based on his discoveries."

"So you mean to say they built this high-vibrational-frequency receiver and it actually worked!" I laughed.

"So it seems."

"But I still don't understand why the professor's machine didn't become world-famous and revolutionize world history way back then," said Jacob.

"Well maybe because back then nobody had a television anyway," I guessed.

"Which only makes this whole thing even more mysterious," said Jacob, "I mean think about it...some Scottish professor inventing such a machine in 1940, it just doesn't make sense!"

We were all quiet for a while as we pondered Ben's mysterious story. Was it just a coincidence that Ben remembered all this just now or what?

I got up and walked back to the entrance of the mine. The sun had now vanished behind the mountains and darkness was beginning to fall over the valley. Far away I could hear the sound of birds crying as they circled the mountaintops.

The others were talking quietly, but I wasn't listening. The point between my eyebrows had begun to pulsate and suddenly the birds circling above became... white seagulls... white seagulls flying by the shores of the great sea... and on the shore six shining figures were standing... wind in their hair... greeting the new day...

I turned back to Ben. "Where is the professor's high-vibrational-frequency receiver and sender now?"

"Where?" Ben leafed through his notebook. "I wrote it down here... according to my notes, Professor McAlister's machine should still be in his laboratory which is located... yes, here it is. Callanish."

"Callanish?"

"Yes. Callanish is a village on the Isle of Lewis."

"Isle of Lewis? Where is that?"

"The Isle of Lewis is one of a group of remote islands off the northwestern coast of Scotland called the Outer Hebrides."

"The Outer Hebrides!" whistled Janus. "Just the name sounds far out!"

"Callanish," I said again, "savoring the sound of the name. "It sounds like its Celtic or Gaelic."

Jacob, Janus and I looked at each other.

"Where have we heard that name before?" asked Jacob.

"In our past life in England," said Janus.

"In our past life?"

"Yes!" said Janus, "Don't you guys remember? The Callanish stone circle was one of the Power Spots Merlin asked the volunteers to activate."

"The Callanish stone circle? That's right I remember it now," I said. "Callanish is a big stone circle—I think it's a bit like Stonehenge if I remember correctly..."

342

"Now that's interesting," said Jacob. "We've got this Scottish Professor who invents an interdimensional radio and now it turns out he lived by one of the Earth's important Power Spots. I wonder if there's a connection or if it's all just a coincidence?"

Again we were all silent.

I looked out at the wild mountain landscape. The pulsating sensation in my Third Eye had disappeared again—as did the vision of the six shining figures standing by the great ocean. Once again I could hear the birds above and feel the cold wind. And there was still no sign of our pursuers; but how long did we have before they tracked us down again?

"Not long," said Ben, as if in answer to my silent question. "Sooner or later they will search this valley too."

I sat down again and tried to collect my thoughts. "Okay," I said, "so we agree that we need to find a way to talk to the whole world because we must get 60 million people to simultaneously focus on the Force, the Good, by Friday. And since there's not much chance the US government will allow us to talk on Larry King Live, the Scottish Professor's high-vibrational-frequency-sender is our best bet so far."

"That is assuming the whole thing isn't just something these two astronomical wizards dreamt up," said Janus.

"It can't be Janus," said Jacob. "Because their machine worked. Remember what Ben said—their high-vibrational-frequency receiver actually picked up Ashtar's first transmission."

"And if it did, we must assume the machine they based their invention on was also able to send out messages—just like the Ashtar Command did when it sent the second transmission to all the TV sets in the world," I added.

"Okay I hear you," said Janus. "But how on Earth are we going to get ourselves from this remote wilderness spot in the middle of the Appalachian Mountains to some even more remote island off the coast of northern Scotland? I mean we can't even get to the nearest town without being caught by Ben's former employer! And who's to say we can find this miracle machine even if we should succeed in getting to Scotland in the next day or two?"

"One step at a time as the Masters say," I replied. "And let's take first things first. And first, it seems to me, we have to decide if that's what we intend to do."

"Well before we make that decision," said Jacob, "it might be a good idea to try and figure out if talking to people on TV—if we can do it—

343

would actually reach enough people to create a critical mass of one percent."

"Well one percent of the world's population must be watching TV these days," replied Janus.

"Yes, under normal circumstances. But you forget that because of the Earth changes, most of the world's population is without electricity."

"Good point, Jacob, I'd almost forgotten that," I said.

"So how do we find out how much of the world's population can actually see TV?" said Janus.

"According to the CIA's latest estimates approximately 75% of the world's population is currently without electricity," said Ben.

"75%?" said Jacob.

"Yes. And that should be a pretty accurate estimate."

"Which means that 25% still have electricity," I said. "So now the question is how many of this 25% have TV sets—and are watching them."

"I can tell you that as well," said Ben. "This is something the CIA has focused a lot of attention on since Ashtar's transmission. Of course, the differences vary greatly from continent to continent and from country to country. As you know, most people in North America and Europe have TVs whereas people in places like Africa and Asia have very few. But all in all, according to the latest estimates, there are about 1.5 billion TVs in the world—or there were before the Earth catastrophes."

"1.5 billion TV receivers," I said. "Out of a population of 6 billion. This means that 25% of the world's population have TV."

"Yes. So if 25% of those 25% still have both electricity and TVs," calculated Jacob, "it means that currently approximately 6% of the world's population have a TV set that works."

"And 6% out of six billion people," I calculated. "Is how many…?"

"… 360 million people," replied Jacob.

"360 million," I repeated. "So if only half or a quarter of these 360 million are watching TV when we send out our message we should have a chance."

"And don't forget that probably more people than usual will be watching those TV sets that do work because everyone will be wanting to hear the latest news about the Ashtar Command and the Earth changes," said Jacob.

"Good point," I said. "So even if there are fewer TVs around that are working than we estimate there still should be enough people watching TV to create a critical mass of one percent."

"But whether or not we have a high-vibrational-frequency sender, the question still remains, "said Janus, "how are we going to get 60 million people to have the Single Eye and focus on the Good?"

No one answered. Ben stood up and looked out over the darkened valley.

"The first thing we'd have to tell everyone is that the starships are not gone," I said. "We'd have to tell them that the starships are still floating above the Earth's major cities, but because the collective consciousness of humanity has fallen so low, we human beings can no longer see them. Then we'd have to tell them that the Ashtar Command is friendly and only wants to help humanity. And then we would have to explain that we have been in contact with them and that they've given us a formula that all of humanity must focus on if we want to raise the collective consciousness high enough again to make sure that STARDAY is not cancelled."

"You mean the formula that the Three E Masters gave us?" said Jacob.

I nodded.

"Always the optimist, Starbrow!" laughed Janus. "Why should people believe us? I mean won't they just think that we are a bunch of gullible dudes who've read too many New Age books?"

"Well maybe, but maybe not," I replied. "But you have to remember what's been happening on Planet Earth during the last few days Janus. I mean we're not just talking about huge Earth changes and incredible havoc all around the world; we're also talking about a worldwide transmission by Ashtar, which everyone on Planet Earth saw and about hundreds of starships floating above the world's major cities that everyone also saw. So it's not like we're making all this stuff up out of thin air. I mean everyone has seen what's going on and experienced what's going on. And everyone knows that nothing will ever be the way it was before. Ever. Just think about Special Agent Ben Nevis for one. If he can wake up, the rest of humanity can too."

My passionate little speech really seemed to shut Janus up.

"I agree with Starbrow," said Jacob. "Humanity is ready for the next step, it has to be! I mean what other options do people have right now. And if there's even the smallest chance that we can help humanity make that step, we've got to do everything we can—everything within our power to make it happen."

"Okay, okay, I give up. You guys have convinced me." Janus turned towards Ben. "What do you say to all this, Starwarrior?"

Ben took out his sword and held it up in the darkness. The light from Starwarrior's interdimensional weapon cast long shadows back into the tunnel.

"As far as I am concerned, I made my decision a long time ago," he replied slowly. "From the moment that I freed you guys from your cells, my decision was made. I will go wherever Starbrow leads me."

2

Through the Net

"So now the question is how do we get from here to Scotland?" said Janus.

"Well to do that, we need to get a hold of an airplane," said Ben as he carefully surveyed the landscape.

"But who's going to fly it?"

"I am."

Ben was quiet for a while. Then he said, "If we can get a hold of a small private jet, we should be able to make it all the way to Scotland with just three or four stops—for fuel. I guess we can manage to tank up somewhere in New York, then in Canada and in Iceland—and from there straight to Scotland. I once flew to Iceland that way myself. It shouldn't take us more than 24 hours."

"But how are we going to get a hold of a private jet?" asked Jacob. "It's not exactly like there's a lot of them parked up here in the mountains."

Ben started pacing back and forth. "If my memory is correct there's a small private air field near Westernport where the local billionaire usually has a Lear Jet or two parked. If we could get to the air strip and get a hold of a plane..."

"How far away is Westernport?" I asked.

"Pretty far. About 30 miles."

"30 miles?" said Jacob. "That will take us days in this kind of terrain."

"It's the best I can come up with at the moment," said Ben. "And no matter what we decide, it will soon be time for us to move anyway."

"Okay," said Janus. "So let's go to Westernport."

"But it's completely dark," said Jacob. "How are we going to get down the mountain in the dark?"

"True it will be slow going," said Ben, "but at least there will be much less chance of our being discovered. And we have my sword."

We all stood for a moment and gazed out into the night sky.

"OK," I said, "Let's do it. But before we go I think we should meditate on the Good. If we're going to try to get the whole world to have the Single Eye, we have to begin with ourselves."

Jacob nodded. "It's high time we start using all the techniques the Masters gave us."

The four of us walked back into the mine and sat down with our backs to the walls right near the entrance. Jacob and Janus on the one side, Ben and I on the other. We closed our eyes and took turns summarizing the teachings we'd received from the Masters—both the ones in the higher dimensions and the Three E Masters in this dimension. As each of us spoke, the other three—including Ben—repeated the words. This was the first time Ben ever joined one of our meditations.

I was first and began talking about the Nature of Reality. That which never changes. God. The Force. The Spirit. Omnipresent, Omnipotent, Omniscient. Birthless, Deathless, Eternal and Unchanging. The One and Only Reality. There was and is nothing else. In me, in you, in everyone.

Next Jacob took over. He talked about how the Nature of God, the One Unchanging Force or Spirit, is Perfect Good. The Perfect Good that everyone is seeking. Perfect Life, Perfect Intelligence, Perfect Love. There was and is nothing else. In me, in you, in everyone.

Then Janus spoke about how God, the One Force or Spirit, is Pure Consciousness, Pure Mind. And how the natural radiance of Mind is thought. And how thoughts are cause and experiences are effect. Which means that all experience, the entire universe, is but a thought.

Lastly we all vowed to have the Single Eye, to focus on and think about the True Nature of Reality, which is God, the Good.

Then each of us sat in silence for a while and let our minds wander the Infinite Pathways of the Force and dwell upon the Perfect Harmony of Being. As we sat there, we experienced more and more strongly—both together and each on his own—our unbreakable Oneness with the Force, the Good.

After a while I opened my eyes.

As I turned my gaze to my three friends, the Force within me turned Its gaze upon my three friends. And I saw how they shone as if lit from within by a Divine Radiant Light.

The Force.

348

The Good.

Individualized in each of my three friends.

The True Self.

The Perfect Being.

Moncler, Telperion and Starwarrior.

My three friends from the beginning.

Moncler and Telperion's eyes were still closed, but their faces looked blissful.

But Starwarrior's eyes—Ben's eyes—were open. He was looking out the entrance at the stars and the mountains. The light in his eyes was so strong that I realized he was now seeing everything the way the Force sees it.

With the Single Eye of the Force.

And so Starwarrior and I sat in silence, in perfect understanding, gazing at the beauty of the world outside. High above, countless stars were shimmering and one of them, a large golden star, shone brighter than the others.

And as we watched that large golden star, I suddenly knew with complete certainty that Starwarrior also knew that this was not the first time the two of us had sat like this. Had sat together and looked up at that golden star. We had done this before, a long time ago... before this lifetime... before our lifetimes as Dana and Gavin... the two of us had sat like this... gazing up at this very same golden star...

I slowly turned towards Starwarrior. It seemed to me that his body was just a thin layer, a transparent veil. Underneath it an inner light was shining. A light that was in his face, his eyes, and especially the point between his brows...

I looked down at myself. And for a moment I felt as if a fresh, cool fire was surging through me... and gathering itself in me... I felt a fierce determination and courage flare up in my heart.

I stood up.

"We're ready for action," I said in a commanding voice. "Let's get a move on."

The race was on. The Force was with us. And the Good was with us, in us, and everywhere around us. In the mountains, in the valleys, in the stars, in every blade of grass, in every stone. The Good was in Starbrow,

Starwarrior, Moncler and Telperion who ran as if on winged feet down the steep mountainside. With our entire focus on the Force—on the Good—we ran, leaped, raced, jumped, soared, thundered, and flew downwards and onwards, over stock and stone, down the mountainside, through the ravines, across the dells and streams, darting in and out of trees, between rocks and boulders, as the Force in Starwarrior—with his sword and unswerving determination—led us onwards towards our goal, the airstrip outside Westernport. The large golden star shone down upon us, the fine healing wind of the Force caressed us, and a cool fire surged through us, as we ran faster and faster, as the Force in us ran faster and faster. No one said a word for no words were needed. The Force in us knew everything we needed to know; the Force in us knew where we came from and where we were going. Those few inhabitants of the night—the beavers, bears, and birds—who noticed our passing must have wondered if for a moment four shining stars had fallen to earth. Four shining shooting stars racing down the mountain on their way to distant lands and dreams beyond knowing...

"Are you thinking about going through here?" asked Janus.

For the first time in many hours, Ben had stopped. The trail we were following had split in two. One way led into the narrow pass Ben was now studying. It looked as if the pass cut its way through the rocky sides of two mountains.

"I don't know this pass," said Ben, "I can't remember it, but if it cuts through the mountains, it would save us quite a bit of time. But it's also more risky."

We stood for a while, studying the pass. The only sound up here was the sound of the wind in the trees and the rhythm of our breathing.

"What does the Force, the Good, say?" I asked. "Will this pass lead us to the Highest Good for All?"

Ben turned towards me. "The Highest Good for All?"

"Yes," I said. "Ask your heart."

Ben looked at me for a moment then turned towards the pass and stood in silence. After a few seconds he nodded and said. "Yes, this pass will lead us to the Highest Good for All."

"Then this is the way for us!" I said.

As if we were one, the four of us ran swiftly forward, without hesitation, into the opening between the mountains.

At first the pass was very narrow and for a while Ben still seemed to be in doubt about whether he had chosen correctly or not.

Then after running through the pass for almost half an hour we suddenly came out of the pass and into a great clearing. In the dark, we couldn't judge how big the clearing was, but the four of us stopped at the same moment.

In the middle of the clearing stood a military helicopter.

Its motor and all its lights were turned off.

"Major Nevis?" called a voice from our left.

We turned towards the voice.

A dark figure emerged from the trees. At first we couldn't see who it was. But then we knew.

It was Agent Sorvino!

In a split second Ben whipped out his machine gun.

At the same moment, another dark figure emerged from the trees to our right.

Agent Jackson!

I turned around and looked back.

Behind us stood the big, broad-shouldered Agent Hama.

We were surrounded by DETI agents.

It looked like Ben's intuition was wrong.

Ben had his machine gun aimed straight at Agent Sorvino and I wondered what he would do. Would he really shoot his own people?

"Major Nevis, don't shoot!" cried Sorvino.

"Don't make me do something I'll regret!" answered Ben.

"Don't shoot, Major," Sorvino said again. "We just want to talk to you!"

"Talk?"

"Yes!"

Sorvino put his hands in the air. He looked as if he was unarmed. Jackson and Hama put their hands in the air too.

Ben looked doubtfully at his former unit.

"You want to do what?"

"Just what I said, we want to talk."

"About what?"

"It's just the three of us, Major," said Jackson. "Your old unit. We don't want to make trouble—we just want to know what's going on. We just want to know why you ran off with the three prisoners?"

Ben motioned to us. "Check and see if they are armed."

We ran over and checked them. They weren't armed.

"Check the helicopter."

Jacob and I ran over to the helicopter. Everything was turned off and there was no sign of any other agents or soldiers anywhere.

"Where are the other units?" asked Ben.

"Far from here," answered Jackson. "Nobody knows we're here."

"Then how'd you find us?"

"It was Sorvino who led us here," she said.

"Sorvino?"

Ben turned towards his former right hand.

"How did you know we'd be here?"

"I... I honestly don't know," said Sorvino. "Something told me you'd try to escape through this mountain pass and come out here. And you did."

Ben raised his eyebrows.

"Something told you?"

"Oh come on boss, we just want to talk, OK?" said Sorvino again. "Just tell us what's going on?"

"Well in case you haven't noticed, Ron, the whole world's about to go bust."

"But I thought these three guys were at least partly responsible for all the chaos?"

"No Ron, it's not their fault."

"Then whose fault is it, boss?"

"It's my fault."

Jacob, Janus and I looked at each other in surprise but said nothing.

"Your fault? What are you talking about boss?"

"I was the one who blew up the Power Spots Ron. It was me who gave the order and because of this the collective consciousness of humanity fell drastically—and now STARDAY will most probably be cancelled. So it looks pretty bad and if we don't do something drastic right away to raise the collective consciousness again, STARDAY will most certainly be cancelled and Planet Earth will be in real trouble."

"The collective consciousness? STARDAY? What are you talking about...? Are you actually telling me that you believe everything the Ashtar Command has been saying?"

"Yes I do, Ron."

"But what made you change your mind, boss? You must know something we don't know."

Ben looked over at the helicopter. As far as we could tell, it was just us and the three of them. There was no sign of anyone else.

"Go ahead Ben," I said, "Tell them."

"First I want to know why you three came here unarmed and just walked right over to us?" asked Ben.

"We know you're not stupid, Major," said Jackson. "So we figure you must have a pretty good reason for what you're doing."

"And what do you intend to do if it turns out that I do have a pretty good reason for what I'm doing?"

"Do what we always do, Major," she said. "Obey your orders."

The faint hint of a smile appeared on Ben's lips.

I looked at Jacob and Janus.

Maybe Starwarrior's intuition hadn't been wrong after all.

The three DETI agents who hunted us all the way from the US to England and back again now sat in a half-circle around Ben while he, with machine gun in hand, told them everything he'd experienced in the last few days. Jacob, Janus and I sat a couple of feet from Ben and his former unit and listened to their conversation.

The three agents, Sorvino, Jackson and Hama, still had traces of the burns and other injuries they got when Glastonbury Tor exploded. As I studied their faces, I realized that none of us any longer had any trace of our wounds or burns. It seemed that our focus on the Good had most definitely brought forth Perfect Health and Wholeness. I could tell by the way the agents were looking at us that they too had noticed our "miraculous" healing.

Like the military man he was, Ben quickly and matter-of-factly told them about his experiences. Actually it was quite interesting to hear his version of the last few days, especially since he'd never been in the Ashtar Command Mothership or in Shamballa as we had been. But nevertheless, he still gave a surprisingly clear and scientific explanation of

353

consciousness levels, vibrational frequencies and the dimensions. He even did an excellent job of explaining what it was going to take to raise the collective consciousness enough to prevent STARDAY from being cancelled. As he spoke, I realized that Ben understood far more of what we'd told him in the last couple of days than we'd thought.

Ben unzipped his long black bag and drew out Starwarrior's sword. He held the sword up before the three agents.

"Can you see what I'm holding in my hand?" he asked.

Sorvino shook his head. "No sir, I don't see anything."

Hama shook his head too. "Me neither."

Ben looked at Jackson. "What about you?"

The woman nodded slowly. "I see a sword, sir. I have seen the shining sword ever since you found it in England."

"What?" cried Sorvino. "Why didn't you say anything about this before?"

"Until now, I didn't know whether I was hallucinating or not!" she said quietly.

"When did you first see the sword?" asked Ben looking quite surprised too.

"After the explosion at Glastonbury Tor, when I went to visit you in the hospital to see how you were doing. You were still unconscious so I sat down beside your bed and prayed for you. After I'd finished, I looked up and there was a sword—this sword—lying right next to you in the bed."

Sorvino and Hama stared skeptically at Ben's hand. "How come Hama and I can't see the sword?" asked Sorvino.

"Interdimensional weapons vibrate on a 4-dimensional or higher frequency," said Jacob. "So only human beings in whom the Sight is activated are able to see them. Apparently Agent Jackson here has the Sight too."

Ben continued his story. When he came to the part about our past life, Sorvino's eyes were as big as teacups. "The two of you were twins in a past life! Talk about far out!"

Jackson smiled, "Didn't you ever notice the resemblance between the two of them?"

"Don't tell me you believe in reincarnation?" Sorvino asked Jackson in surprise.

"Well of course I do," she replied.

"Just hold it right there! We've served together for almost 10 years now and you never said anything about reincarnation!"

"Well you never asked me!"

354

The rest of us laughed.

"Nice to see such enlightened CIA agents!" I chuckled.

Ben continued his story in military fashion to the astonishment of the agents. After he briefly told them about the Three E Masters and the Lost Teaching of the Single Eye, he told them we were planning on sending a message to the whole world as fast as we could so people would raise their consciousness and STARDAY could take place as planned. The only thing he didn't tell them was that we were on our way to Scotland to find the professor's high-vibrational-frequency receiver and sender.

"But how are you going to send a message like that out to the whole world?" asked Sorvino.

Ben smiled. "I have no intention of telling you until you tell me what you are going to do now that I have told you what's really going on."

No one said anything for a couple of minutes.

It was Jackson who broke the silence. "When I ask my heart, I know that I've known all along that the Ashtar Command has come in peace. I will do whatever I can to help you with your mission, boss."

Jackson and Ben's eyes met briefly. Ben nodded. He then turned to the other two.

"I've got to admit boss that I'm not sure I understand all this stuff about collective consciousness levels and the Single Eye," said Hama. "But one thing I know for sure is that you saved my life in the earthquake out there in New Mexico. I owe you my life and that's reason enough for me. I'll do whatever I can to help you with your mission."

Ben nodded to Hama. Then he turned to Sorvino.

"What about you, Ron?"

"If anybody had told me two weeks ago that I would be having this discussion with you, I would have said they were stark raving mad. And yet I can't deny what I've seen during the last couple of days. I mean it's incredible—earthquakes everywhere and golden pyramids in the sky— it's hard to believe. And now my very own captain comes to me with this far-fetched story about the Single Eye and all the good it's going to bring humanity. I can't help it boss, but to me it all sounds just a bit too far out. I just don't see how—by thinking good thoughts as you say—we can change the whole world in the twinkling of an eye. It's just too farfetched. I mean it sounds crazy to me. Oh I don't know boss, I'm just so confused I don't know what to say... all I know is I've got a bad feeling about all this. I mean what if you've been deceived or something?"

Sorvino stared hard at the ground.

I started to say something, but Ben stopped me. "Just give him some time to think, Starbrow," Ben said. "Remember if he decides to help us, it's the end of his old life—there will be no way back."

"I'm not sure there's anything to go back to anyway," mumbled Sorvino. "The whole world is going down the tube. Even back at headquarters, everything was chaos after you escaped with the prisoners."

Then Sorvino went silent again.

Finally he sighed and said, "Okay boss, I'm with you. But I sure as hell hope your plan is going to work—because if it don't we're in deep shit!"

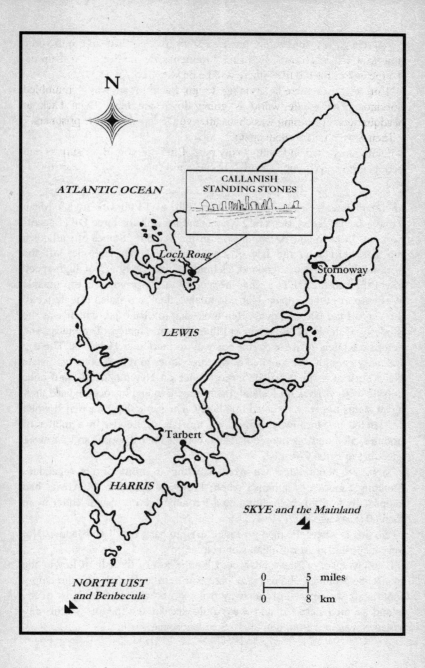

N

ATLANTIC OCEAN

CALLANISH
STANDING STONES

Loch Roag

Stornoway

LEWIS

Tarbert

HARRIS

SKYE and the Mainland

NORTH UIST
and Benbecula

0   5 miles

0   8 km

3

Callanish

28 hours later—on Wednesday, April 8th, at 13:00 Greenwich Mean Time—Jacob, Janus, Ben and I were standing with the three DETI agents Sorvino, Jackson and Hama, in front of the Standing Stones of Callanish, the stone circle on the Isle of Lewis in the Outer Hebrides off the northwestern coast of Scotland. Behind us was 28 hours of high-speed travel, first in the DETI agents' helicopter to the private airstrip outside Westernport in the Appalachian Mountains, then in a stolen private jet all the way to the Isle of Lewis. Ben took charge of the jet, which was the property of the local Westernport billionaire, in a matter of minutes. And before we knew it, we were on our way to the Outer Hebrides. The trip was easy enough. We touched down three times to refuel, once in upstate New York at a small private airport, once on Newfoundland, and once outside of Reykjavik on Iceland. Each time, Ben and his people used their agent status to get us refueled in a hurry. The same thing happened when we landed at Stornoway Airport on the Isle of Lewis. In a matter of minutes, Ben and his people had two cars at their disposal and we were speeding towards Callanish.

Now, 28 hours later, we were standing in front of the legendary Standing Stones of Callanish where Professor Jonathan McAlister had supposedly built his high-vibrational-frequency receiver and sender more than 60 years ago.

"So this is where the mad professor used to hang out?" said Janus. "Not very inspiring, apart from that stone circle."

I slowly surveyed the landscape. Like the rest of the Isle of Lewis, the landscape around Callanish was bare and desolate, much like the empty moorlands we crossed on our way from Stornoway. In fact, most of the island seemed deserted and we'd only seen a few people in the tiny villages scattered around in the rugged landscape.

358

But Janus was right, the Standing Stones of Callanish were more inspiring to behold. The great stone circle stood on a ridge near the shores of Loch Roag, a bay on the island's northwestern coast—and for some reason, the area around the stone circle seemed greener than the rest of the island we'd just raced through.

The dark silhouettes of the Standing Stones had a strange magnetic power. And they were huge. Many were more than 10 feet high, almost the size of the great standing stones at Stonehenge. But even if they weren't quite a big as Stonehenge, there were many more of them and they were spread over a much larger area. The thirteen main stones in the middle formed a large circle with a diameter of about 40 feet. In the center of the circle there was one great stone, the main stone, which must have been more than 15 feet high and almost twice the height of many of the other stones in the circle. From this center circle, four long rows of standing stones led away from the central ring—to the east, west, south and a longer one to the north. The longer row to the north had stones on each side so it seemed like an avenue. One of the agents quickly determined that the monument stretched more than 400 feet from one end to the other. Even though some of the stones were obviously missing and many were damaged, the Standing Stones of Callanish were a very impressive sight indeed, as Janus said.

To the north where the longest avenue of stones ended were the few houses that made up the tiny village of Callanish.

"It shouldn't be too hard to find the professor's house," said Sorvino, motioning to the few houses.

Jacob, Janus and I waited by the car while Ben and his agents ran up to the first house and knocked on the door. After a quick conversation, they came running back.

"There are three families with the name McAlister here in Callanish," said Ben. "One at the farm over there on the other side of the stone circle. One on the other side of the village—and one right here in the village itself. Jacob and Janus you go talk to the family in the village. Sorvino, Jackson and Hama you take the family at the other side of the village. Starbrow and I will take the farm. We meet back here by the Standing Stones in 15 minutes. Now go."

Ben and I knocked on the front door of the farm on the other side of the ridge, not far from Loch Roag bay.

A dark-haired woman with a tired face opened the door. Two children, a boy and a girl around the ages of five or six, were tugging at her skirt and staring at us curiously.

"Hello madam," said Ben, flashing his agent badge. "I am Special Agent Ben Nevis from the CIA in the United States."

"The CIA?" said the woman, obviously surprised.

"We are looking for professor Jonathan McAlister—or should I say his family and descendants."

"Jonathan?"

"Did you know the late professor Jonathan McAlister?"

She shook her head in confusion.

A heavy-set man with a beard appeared in the hallway behind her.

"Mary! Who is it?"

"It's some people from the United States of America, Eamonn," she said with a strong Scottish lilt. "From... from the CIA I think!"

The woman moved to let her husband pass. He eyed us suspiciously.

Ben introduced himself again.

"The CIA you say?"

"Yes. Well we work for DETI, which is a division of the CIA. We are looking for the family of the late professor Jonathan McAlister."

"Jonathan?"

"Yes. Are you by any chance related to him?"

Eamonn shook his head slowly.

Ben continued, "The professor died in 1940 and according to our information he had his laboratory or workshop somewhere here in Callanish."

"His workshop..." said Eamonn as he scratched his beard. "Yes, wait, it's coming back to me. As far as I recall, my great-grandfather, Joseph McAlister, had a brother who was a professor. But both brothers died some 60-70 years ago. "

"Some very important papers by Professor McAlister have been uncovered at the University of Edinburgh. American and British intelligence believe that his work may reveal significant information relating to the many Earth changes and catastrophes that have been wreaking havoc around the globe in the last week."

"Earth changes?" Now the couple was both staring at us as if to say what in God's name are these people doing here?

"Mum," said the little girl from behind her mother, "Why do those two men look so much alike? Are they twins?"

"Shh, darling," the woman said. "Mum is talking."

"I'm afraid that I can't help you," said Eamonn. "That was long before my time."

"What about grandmother?" the woman said to her husband.

"Helen? Well..."

"Who is Helen?" I asked.

"Helen is my grandmother," said Eamonn. "She's the daughter of Joseph McAlister, the professor's brother. Maybe she can tell you something about my great-uncle. At least you can try and ask her. She's lived on this farm her whole life, all 98 years of it."

"Take us to her at once," said Ben.

98-year-old Helen McAlister was as old and wrinkled as the landscape around Callanish. When Eamonn and Mary led us into her room, she was sitting in a rocking chair by her bed, dozing. But the moment we entered the room, she seemed to wake up. She didn't say anything but looked at us with great interest.

"Directorate of Extra Television Intelligence did you say?" the old lady asked in her squeaky little voice. "Well couldn't you do something about our television? Ever since the storm, we haven't been able to see anything!"

"We hope you can give us some useful information about your deceased uncle—and if you do, we will make sure your television set goes back on," said Ben and smiled.

"That sounds good," she said. "I really miss 'Top of the Pops'!"

"Your uncle, professor Jonathan McAlister, used to live here?" asked Ben.

"Aye, aye," replied the old lady. "But he couldna' take the quiet life out here on the islands so he went to Edinburgh to study at the University."

My heart sank. Edinburgh? Did that mean our coming all the way out here to the end of the world was nothing more than a wild-goose chase?

"... but then one day he suddenly decided to move back to the farm..." she continued in her squeaky voice.

"Really? He moved back?"

"Yes, I don't recall exactly when it was. I was in my early twenties, so it must have been around 1927 or 28."

"Why did he move back?"

"He said he needed some peace and quiet for his research."

"What kind of research did he do?"

"I never really found out. He had this whole room full of all sorts of strange machines and instruments."

"You don't by any chance have any of the professor's old instruments or machines?" I asked hopefully.

"No, no, no. They're all gone a very long time ago..." The old lady coughed.

"What about documents, diaries, papers?" asked Ben.

"Papers? No, no..."

"Nothing at all?" I asked.

Helen was quiet for a moment as if she was thinking.

"Well... there is the old wooden chest in the attic."

"Old wooden chest?"

"Yes. You see my father, Joseph McAlister, died just 14 days after my Uncle Jonathan McAlister. Odd isn't it? That was in 1940. After they died, I put some of their pictures and papers and other personal belongings in a wooden chest—it's up in the attic somewhere. You might just find something in there. It hasn't been opened for more than 50 years. Mary and Eamonn can show you where the chest is."

"Thank you, Mrs. McAlister."

As we walked out the room, the old lady took Ben's hand.

"Ben Nevis?" she smiled and looked up at him.

"Yes?" he said.

"That is a beautiful name you bear."

"Thank you."

"Do you know what 'Nevis' means in Gaelic?"

"No."

"It means 'heavenly'."

We gathered the whole team together and then followed Mary and Eamonn up to the McAlister family's dusty attic. It took him a few minutes, but Eamonn finally located the chest and pulled it out from the tangle of old furniture and boxes that was piled up in the attic.

Mary wiped the dust off the top of the old wooden chest. "Sorry about all the dust, we don't come up here that often."

"It's quite okay Mrs. McAlister," said Ben. "You've done more than enough. Now why don't you and your husband just go downstairs? We might be a while."

Mary and Eamonn gave us another look and left the attic.

Sorvino and Hama carried the chest over to the window and we all gathered around it. The old chest was heavy, but not locked.

I lifted the heavy wooden lid.

Inside, the chest was filled with pictures, black and white photographs, yellowing documents and worn-out notebooks.

Jackson and Hama systematically emptied the chest and we leafed through everything—all the notebooks and papers. There was even an old black and white portrait of the professor—a solemn-looking gentleman with a full beard and a good head of hair.

There was nothing about a high-vibrational-frequency receiver and sender.

At the very bottom of the chest was an old worn-out notebook.

Jacob began to leaf through its yellowing pages and said, "I think this must be one of the professor's diaries—or what's left of it."

Half of the pages of the diary had been ripped out.

"Yes it is... With dates and years... and here are drawings and sketches of some kind of machine..."

Ben stopped and looked over Jacob's shoulder.

"Bull's eye!" cried Ben. "Here it is! The high-vibrational-frequency-sender."

We all gathered around them and looked at the faded drawings in the notebook, which depicted a machine that looked as if it was made of crystals or some kind of shiny stones.

"These drawings are almost identical to the machine the two SETI astronomers used to pick up Ashtar's transmission," cried Sorvino triumphantly. "We saw it at the Very Large Array in New Mexico."

"The professor calls his machine the 'Crystal Machine'," said Jacob.

"The Crystal Machine?" said Janus. "So now the only question is where the machine is now?"

Ben kept turning the pages.

"More sketches and diagrams... The professor was really occupied with his invention... There's also some kind of list of important developments... Let's see... It looks like it starts here. Jacob you read it for us," said Ben, handing the diary to Jacob.

363

Jacob read out loud:

"April 14th, 1927: I decided to visit Joseph at the family farm in Callanish to investigate my brother's find. It is unusual for me to go home so early in the year, but for some reason my brother's description of his mysterious find in the peat fills me with a strange feeling of expectation..."

"His mysterious find?" said Janus.

"Is there more?" I asked.

"Let me see... The next entry:

"May 7th, 1927: This evening Joseph finally showed me what he had found buried beneath the peat. He had not dug out the mysterious glinting object completely because he was afraid of it. So we spent the entire night digging it out..."

"Wait a moment," I said.

I felt a chill run down my back.

"Are you saying that the professor did not invent the high-frequency-transmitter—but that he found it buried in the peat?"

"Sounds like it," said Jacob.

"He found it?" said Janus. "But what on Earth was a machine that sends signals on higher vibrational frequencies doing buried under the peat on the Outer Hebrides in 1927?"

4

The Yellow Pages

We all stared in wonder at the yellowing pages of the diary.

"The professor's brother found the machine buried under the peat," said Janus again slowly. "Now this is really beginning to get far out!"

"Does it say anything about what they did with the machine?" I asked.

Jacob turned a few more pages.

"Let me see... Yes, there's more here...

"... After we dug up the mysterious object, we carefully removed all the peat and discovered that it was beautiful to behold. Beautiful indeed. Whatever it was, it appeared to be made of clear quartz crystals. It was fascinating to look at. Apparently its stay underneath the peat had not affected it in any way because it had no stains upon it. My brother and I wondered how many years this mysterious object had lain hidden there in the peat? Decades? Centuries? Or maybe even millennia? And who created this magnificent object? God? The Devil? Man? Or perhaps some other race, a long forgotten and extinct race..."

"Millennia?" said Janus. "This is getting more and more mysterious."

"He goes on," said Jacob:

"... Joseph wanted us to summon the parish priest immediately, but I was adamantly against this. How would the servants of the Church with their blind faith react to this fantastic find? I knew the Church and was afraid that they would destroy our fantastic find just as they had for centuries tried to block and burn all the inevitable advances of science and enlightenment. No I was adamant. This find belonged to science and not to the church. But Joseph was afraid and refused to keep it on his land. I also deemed it the wisest course for us to remove it and take it somewhere it could not be seen by superstitious souls.

So under the cover of night, we transported it to a place where I could examine it in peace—without suspicious eyes prying into my work. And although it was much lighter than we expected, it still took a team of oxen to move it from Joseph's land. We worked all through the night and finally managed to transport it out to a safe hiding place on the coast..."

"Four oxen to pull the machine?" I said. "I didn't think it was that large?"

"The SETI astronomers' machine wasn't that big," said Ben.

"No, as far as I remember it was about three feet high and three feet wide," said Sorvino.

"It sounds like this machine was a lot bigger and heavier," I said.

"They said it could both send and receive messages," said Jacob. "So maybe that's why it's bigger."

Jacob leafed on through the diary. "After that, there are a lot of pages that have been ripped out. I wonder why."

"Does it say anything about where they transported the machine?" asked Ben.

"Let's see. The next entry is May 9th, 1927," said Jacob.

"... Today I constructed a pulley so we could hoist the 'crystal machine'—as we now call it—into one of the remote caves along the coast. Once hidden in the cave, there will no longer be any danger that the 'crystal machine' will be seen by anyone else so I can examine it at my leisure..."

"That's all for that day," said Jacob turning the page.

"Does it say where the cave is?" asked Sorvino.

"More missing pages..." said Jacob. "And after that... nothing but drawings of the machine and descriptions of it... clear crystals... clear crystals... Here is the next date: October 1st, 1927:

"... I think about the mysterious 'crystal machine' all the time. Its shining, otherworldly beauty is in my thoughts day and night. I am no longer able to concentrate on my research here in Edinburgh so I have decided to move back to the farm and devote myself to studying our find. Who knows what enormous advances for science it might bring..."

"What happened next?" I asked impatiently. "Doesn't it say anything at all about where he hid it?"

"No. Nothing. The next pages are nothing but drawings and sketches and diagrams... page after page... But not a word about where he hid it."

"I guess that was the whole point," said Sorvino. "He obviously didn't want anyone else to know about its existence."

"Here is the last entry in the diary," said Jacob. "August 19th, 1940:

"... For more than 13 years I have studied the 'crystal machine' and I must confess that I know almost as little about it now as I did when I first laid eyes on it. Have all my years of work been in vain? Perhaps my

366

brother was right, we should have told the world about its existence. I do not honestly know. All I know is that something tells me this will be my last summer on Lewis—my last summer here or anywhere else on Earth. Therefore I have asked my brother Joseph to send my final dissertation about the 'crystal machine' to the University of Edinburgh if I should suddenly depart, so that my findings can be preserved for posterity..."

Jacob stopped.

"That's the last entry in the diary."

The last yellow pages of the diary had also been ripped out.

No one said a word.

I walked over to the tiny window. The McAlister family's farm lay less than a hundred yards from the shores of Loch Roag. Swarms of birds were flying above the loch.

"The professor's premonition was right," said Ben. "He died the same year."

"And so did his brother," I said. "According to Helen, just 14 days later."

"Yet his brother must have had time to send his dissertation to the University of Edinburgh before he died," said Ben. "Because the SETI astronomers found it three years ago in the University archives."

"Do you think the professor mentioned where he had hid the machine in his dissertation?" asked Hama.

"I doubt it," said Ben shaking his head. "If the professor's fear of being discovered is any indication, it's not very likely."

Jacob shut the diary.

Janus sat down on an old rickety chair and sighed. "If both brothers are dead and there's no written record of where the high-vibrational-frequency transmitter is, it means that no human being alive today knows where it is."

We went back to old Helen McAlister's room to question her again. Eamonn and Mary McAlister stood in the doorway and watched.

"We found the Professor's diary," said Ben, "and in it, he mentions what he calls a 'crystal machine'—we think it was some kind of invention he was working on. Do you know anything about this machine?"

"A 'crystal machine'?"

367

The old lady seemed to enjoy suddenly being the center of attention.

Ben showed her some of the drawings from the professor's old diary. "It looks like this. You see we're trying to locate the machine."

Helen adjusted her glasses and studied the drawings. "Hmm. No, I don't remember ever seeing a machine like that. But Jonathan used to have so many different strange contraptions and instruments in his laboratory. What's so special about this one?"

"In his diary, the Professor wrote that he and your father had a secret place by the coast that he used for experiments," I said. "You don't happen to know anything about this place?"

Helen leaned back in her rocking chair. "Hmm. That is quite right young man. Jonathan did have a place where he went to work. Once he moved back to the farm, he went there almost every day—and often my father accompanied him. But they never showed me where it was."

A collective sigh of disappointment seemed to pass through the room. We were hoping the old lady would know where it was.

"By the coast you say?" said Jackson, not ready to give up. "Do you have any idea where along the coast this place could be located?"

"No, not really. All I can tell you is that my father and uncle usually sailed out there in our little boat."

"By the coast?" said Janus impatiently. "The coastline goes on for miles and miles. Can't you remember anything more specific? Your uncle wrote in his diary that he'd hidden the 'crystal machine' in a secret cave."

"In a secret cave? Oh dear!" said Helen and smiled. "That does sound exciting. I guess you will just have to go on a treasure hunt and find it!"

"We'll never find it!" said Sorvino despondently.

The seven of us were standing on the edge of Loch Roag bay, depressed and tired. We'd searched all night for the secret cave—and though we'd found several caves, none of them contained the 'crystal machine'. Now it was nearly six o'clock Thursday morning. Dawn was fast approaching and we still weren't one step closer to finding the Professor's high-vibrational-frequency transmitter.

And time was running out—fast.

Sorvino kicked the grass in frustration. "That cave could be anywhere—on any one of those islands out there, on the other side of the bay, or even further out by the Atlantic Ocean. It could take us weeks to find that bloody machine—if it's there at all."

"Yeah," said Janus bleakly, "and we only have 18 hours left before STARDAY is cancelled for good."

No one said anything, but we all knew we couldn't give up the hunt—not yet anyway.

As if we were all plugged into the same source, Ben, Jacob, Janus and I turned and headed towards the Standing Stones of Callanish. If anyone knew where the 'crystal machine' was, the Omniscient Force did. In one flash of insight, we knew it was time to ask the Force for guidance.

As if they understood, Ben's agents followed us—not in the least surprised because they'd already discovered how powerful Ben's intuition had become.

"So who do you think constructed the crystal machine and buried it long ago?" asked Janus as we headed towards the Standing Stones. "Do you think it was aliens? I mean are we looking for the 'Roswell' site of Scotland?"

"Maybe," said Jacob. "Or maybe it was human beings who built the machine."

"You mean human beings here on Earth?" I said.

"Yes," answered Jacob. "Remember back in the Crystal Cave, when Merlin channeled Sananda, and he told us about the Light Grid?"

Janus and I nodded.

"Remember he told us that survivors from Atlantis had traveled to all four corners of the world and built new temples and stone circles on the various Power Spots?"

"You think it might be descendants of Atlantis who built the Standing Stones of Callanish?" I said. "The same people who built Stonehenge and the other stone circles in ancient Avalon?"

"It's possible," said Jacob. "And if they were the ones who built this stone circle, maybe they were also the ones who built the crystal machine."

"But why would they bury the machine?"

"You're forgetting that this stone circle was built 5,000 years ago. Back then, I doubt if there was any peat down here at all. I remember from my studies of the Stone Age that the climate was much warmer up north in places like this so probably there was dry land and forests where the peat is today," continued Jacob.

As we approached the Standing Stones, the twilight cast an eerie glow over the ancient stone circle—and I noticed tiny white and yellow flowers peeking up from the grass in and around the old stones.

The moment we entered the stone circle, it was as if we'd stepped into another world.

5

The Shining Stones

The difference between the energy in and outside the stone circle was striking.

Outside the world seemed gray and dismal and the fierce loneliness of the island was almost oppressive. But inside the circle of Standing Stones, it was like standing on a hill of light. The air felt milder and more comforting, almost warm. Even the grass seemed taller and greener. And in and around the great stones grew the small flowers we had not seen anywhere else on the island.

"It feels like Avalon," mumbled Janus.

I nodded.

Standing in the circle felt exactly like being on Glastonbury Tor.

"It must be the energy of the Power Spot we're feeling," said Jacob.

I put my hand on one of the great stones and it tingled.

Ben and the agents followed us into the circle of stones and I could see from the look on their faces that they too felt the energy of the Power Spot.

"Let us sit down in a circle," I said, "with our backs to the stones."

We each chose one of the Standing Stones and sat down with our backs to it. The tall gray stone behind me felt almost warm. In the center of the circle stood the 16-foot high megalith as the locals called this great stone. For some reason I felt that it was important to keep my eyes open.

Jacob began to talk about the Force, the Good, which is the One and Only Reality. The rest of us—including the three DETI agents—repeated the words after him. It was the first time the three agents joined our meditation. We were now seven who were meditating on the Force and I felt a definite increase in the focus and power of our meditation. Before long, we were all deeply focused on and anchored in the Nature of Reality. The Good. The Good that was thinking about the Good, the

Good that was meditating on the Good, the Good that was looking at the Good... the Single Eye.

The moment I began to have the Single Eye, there was a change in the stone circle. It was as if a veil had been removed from my eyes; the great stones around and behind us began to shine as if lit from within—like sleeping giants who were gradually brought to life by our focus on the Force, the Good. The landscape around us, and the sky above us, also seemed brighter as if an invisible sun had begun to shine.

The faces of the agents and my dear friends also seemed clearer, stronger, and more alive than ever before. Their eyes glowed like stars radiating out from the six shining stones where they sat.

A cool breeze caressed the stones and our faces.

The fine healing wind of the Force, the Good.

Suddenly I felt an irresistible urge to move to the middle of the circle and sit with my back against the great megalith in the center. It was as if an invisible hand was pushing me from behind.

So I got up and walked over to the megalith. Just as I was about to sit down, I realized that another one of the six had the exact same impulse and was about to sit down on the other side of the central stone.

It was Ben.

Starwarrior.

Our eyes met for a brief moment.

Then we sat down, back-to-back, with the great megalith between us.

Immediately my mind was filled with light.

Everything was filled with light.

The point between my brows began to pulsate—and once again I felt that fierce determination flare in my heart. But I paid these sensations no heed. Instead I looked up.

Straight up at the sky above the stone circle, which had now opened.

In actual fact, it was as if there was a hole in the thick gray rain clouds that completely covered the sky—a gaping hole that was right above the Standing Stones. And through the hole stars still twinkled faintly in the night sky as dawn approached.

The moment I saw the stars, I knew.

Because the Force in me knew.

"They came from the stars," I said in a loud clear voice.

But I was not speaking alone.

At the exact same moment, Ben said the exact same words.

Because Ben also knew.

Because the Force in Ben knew.

372

For a moment all was still in the circle. Not a wind moved among the stones.

The dark hole in the clouds above us remained right where it was, right above the stone circle.

Jacob was the first to break the silence.

"Who came from the stars?" he asked.

"The ones who built the machine that we seek..." I said slowly, the Force in me said slowly, as the Infinite Wisdom and Knowledge of the Force spoke through me.

"Why did they come?" asked Janus.

"To create peace and harmony on Earth..." said Ben slowly, said the Force in Ben slowly, as the Infinite Wisdom and Knowledge of the Force spoke through him.

"When did they come?" asked Jacob.

"12,000 years ago..." I said with the Infinite Wisdom and Knowledge of the Force in me. "After the downfall of Atlantis..."

"Atlantis?" said Jacob.

"Yes..." I answered. "This place was the north-eastern border of Atlantis..."

"How did they come to this place?" asked Jacob.

"The Starseeds... entered the Earth's vibrational field through this Power Spot..." said Ben, said the Infinite Wisdom and Knowledge of the Force in Ben.

"How did they do it?"

"This Power Spot is an interdimensional opening... Connected to a larger interdimensional Power Spot in this galaxy... a Stargate..."

"A Stargate?"

"Yes..."

For a few seconds no one spoke as our listeners digested this new piece of information. But I didn't think about it. As a matter fact I didn't think at all, I just let the Infinite Wisdom and Knowledge of the Force think through me...

"But why would the Starseeds go to such a cold and barren place?" asked Janus.

"This place was not always like this..." said Ben. "What today is so desolate was once a fair and fertile land..."

"How so?"

"The climate was different and the weather was warm and mild... the sky was clear and blue... the land was covered by great forests of birch and hazel..."

373

"So how did it become this bleak and desolate island?"

"The collective consciousness fell more and more..." I said.

In my mind's eye I began to see visions of events long past.

"This place went from being heaven on Earth to being... part of the Shadow Earth..." I said. "Only the Power Spot retained something of its former glory... Which was also the reason why the descendants of those who sailed from Atlantis built the stone circle on this place..."

"What happened to the Starseeds?" asked Jacob.

"After they landed, they hid the machine near a lake in a grove of birch trees that grew at the foot of this very ridge..." I said.

"Do you mean the area just below us by the loch which is now covered with peat?"

"Yes... The Starseeds thought that their mission to create peace and enlightenment on Earth would quickly be over... but the years and the incarnations went by... and slowly they forgot all about their true selves, their true mission..."

A deep silence fell upon the stone circle.

All around us the land was shrouded in mist, but above the Standing Stones, the sky was still clear.

"What about this Power Spot?" said Jacob after a while, "The Force is very strong here. Can we use this Power Spot to raise the collective consciousness enough to prevent STARDAY from being cancelled?"

"No." said Ben slowly but emphatically.

"Why not?"

"The time of the Power Spots is past..." continued Ben. "The time of the old Light Grid is over... Now there is a new Grid..."

"What Grid?"

"The Internet..." I said.

"The Internet?"

"Yes... The World Wide Web, e-mail, mobile phones, all of humanity connected in cyberspace..."

"Are we supposed to use the Internet to raise the collective consciousness?" asked Jacob.

"No. Neither the old Grid nor the new can be used to improve life on Planet Earth without..." I said slowly.

"Without what?"

"Without spiritual understanding..." said Ben, "... That was what the cataclysm of Atlantis taught us... That is what the Internet is teaching us... Without understanding the Nature of Reality, all the technological advances of humanity are worth nothing..."

374

"The Nature of Reality?" said Jacob. "You mean…?"

"Yes... The Force is All..."

"... and the Force is Good..." I said.

"It always was..." said Ben.

"It is so now..." I said.

"And It will ever be so," said Ben and I with one voice.

Once again silence fell upon the stone circle.

Somewhere on the edge of my consciousness, I heard a rooster crow. In the east, the sun was about to rise. The twilight hour before dawn was ending. The opening in the sky above the Standing Stones began to close again. Suddenly I was aware of my body as if I was losing the powerful sense of Oneness with the Omniscient Force.

Jacob sensed what was happening and he said in a loud voice, "I have one last question. You say that the Starseeds buried their high-vibrational-frequency transmitter below the ridge where the peat now covers the land. Were the McAlister brothers the first ones to find the high-vibrational-frequency transmitter?"

Although I was about to lose my connection with the Omniscient Force I could still sense the answer in the Omniscient Mind of the Force. But before I could speak, from the other side of the stone Ben said, "Yes."

"Where is the machine now?" asked Jacob.

"In a cave by the coast..." said Ben.

"Where exactly?" said Sorvino unable to contain himself any longer.

The clouds above us had now completely covered the hole above the Standing Stones again. With one last great effort, Ben and I said in one voice:

"... on this side of Loch Roag... Approximately three miles from the McAlister farm... right across from the smaller second island in the Loch..."

The first rays of the morning sun fell upon the Standing Stones. The night was over. A new day had begun. The last day for us and our mission.

6

Treasure Hunt

In the first light of the morning, we ran down to Loch Roag. Halfway between the ridge and the bay, Ben suddenly stopped in his tracks.

"What is it, boss?" asked Sorvino.

A few yards from us deep furrows had been dug in the ground. Several bales of peat lay stacked in piles.

Ben pointed towards the furrows. "Do you see what I see, Starbrow?"

I focused on the furrows. For a moment, I saw in my mind's eye a vision of sun on a clear lake. Slender birch trees swaying in the wind...

"I see it too, Ben," I said. "This is where the Starseeds buried the crystal machine—the lake was right here!"

"And this is where, 12,000 years later, the McAlister brothers found the machine," said Ben.

Everyone stared at him in amazement.

Janus patted him on the back. "The Agent with the Sight! Pretty soon you're going to outshine Starbrow!"

We laughed and ran on towards the loch and began to run along the top of the cliffs. From where we ran, there was a drop of about 3-4 yards down to the water, which crashed up on the large rocks and boulders that lined the shore. Green and brown seaweed was everywhere. Seagulls, startled by our arrival, took off and shrieked in the wind.

We climbed over a crumbling stone wall and ran on.

After we'd run for about two miles, a large island came into view.

"That must be the first island," cried Jacob.

A little further ahead was another, smaller island.

"The second island!" shouted Janus eagerly.

We increased our speed. I thought I could see the shimmering blue of the Atlantic Ocean in the distance. And for a brief second, in my mind's eye I saw those radiant shining figures that so often haunted my dreams.

Standing not far from here on a majestic promontory overlooking the great ocean as it crashed upon the shore...

"Hold it!" cried Sorvino. "This must be it."

We stopped right across from the second island. From the cliff where we stood, it was about 4-5 yards down to the water. The strong stench of rotting seaweed hit our nostrils, coming up to us from the huge, seaweed-covered rocks and boulders that extended down from the cliff for about eight or nine yards down to the water's edge. Several old fishing nets were trapped in the pools of water between the rocks and boulders.

We scrambled down the slippery seaweed-covered rocks.

Once at the bottom Janus cried out, "There's a cave over here!"

We gathered around him eagerly and saw the opening in the rock he was pointing to. It wasn't very wide... only about half a yard or so. Sorvino turned on his flashlight and tried to squeeze through the opening. But Ben touched the point between his eyebrows and shook his head.

"It's not in there," he said.

"You're right boss," said Sorvino after surveying the cave with his flashlight, "There's nothing in there."

"It's too small anyway," said Jacob. "The Professor would have chosen some place a bit more spacious if he was going to work there."

We continued along the rocky shore. About fifty yards further ahead, the rocks were piled up in a wide half circle down by the water's edge. It almost looked like human hands had built it.

We all half crawled, half climbed up the stones towards the cliff, which extended out like a little roof, sheltering the space underneath. There were big rocks everywhere. Piled high, but no cave.

Again we started out along the rocky shoreline.

Everyone except Ben, he remained standing in front of the place where the cliff extended out over the stones.

I stopped and looked back.

Ben touched the point between his eyebrows.

"What do you see, Starwarrior?" I yelled and started walking back.

Ben pointed towards the great pile of stones.

"There is something behind the stones, Starbrow," said Ben pointing towards the stones.

I climbed up the pile of stones and pushed away the top stone—and the next and the next. I knew the Sight was strong in Ben.

The others turned back and joined us. In just a few seconds, we managed to uncover a large, gaping hole behind the pile of stones. Peering in through the hole, I could see the entrance to a cavern. The

377

entrance was large—about six to seven yards wide and almost four yards high.

"Jackpot!" I cried.

"Give the man a cigar!" laughed Janus, slapping Ben on the back.

Everyone got to work removing the stones. Soon we could crawl into the cave. Inside, we were greeted by the smell of seaweed.

The agents turned on their flashlights. Inside, the cave was much bigger than we expected. It extended about 10-15 yards into the solid rock.

In the middle of the cave, there was a large object—the mysterious structure the Professor and his brother had found under the peat almost a hundred years ago.

But it was not the crystal machine we expected to find.

It was a large pyramid.

We all stood and stared at this unexpected sight. The pyramid must have been at least nine feet tall and all of five yards wide—and it was covered with stinking, rotten seaweed.

Immediately we began removing the slimy seaweed from the sides of the pyramid with our bare hands.

Underneath the slime, the surface of the pyramid was completely smooth and shiny. Once we removed all the seaweed and slime, the sides of the pyramid glittered in the light of our flashlights as if it was completely new.

It looked like it was made of a very hard, clear crystal-like material. On one side, which we took to be the front side, there was an ellipse-shaped opening or entrance, which was just big enough for a human being to pass through it.

The clear crystal sides of the pyramid were transparent so we could see through them. Inside, we discovered there were six deep indentations in the floor of the pyramid. As we looked more closely, we realized that each indentation was made in the shape of a human body. It was as if the six indentations were some kind of beds or resting places, sunk into the floor of the pyramid. And all six of these indentations or beds were pointing head first towards the center of the pyramid.

"That's radical," said Janus, "It's like a six-pointed star or something."

And in the very middle, at the exact point where all six heads met, there was a computer-like object made of shining stones.

"There it is!" I cried. "The crystal machine!"

And it was true. Right there in the very middle of the pyramid was the mysterious machine Professor McAlister had described so meticulously in his diary. The very same machine the two SETI astronomers had based their own high-vibrational-frequency-receiver on. The very same machine that picked up Ashtar's first transmission.

Ashtar...!

Suddenly I realized where I'd seen a pyramid like this before.

The pyramid was a starship!

A starship exactly like the many starships or 'Light Bodies' I'd seen soaring around and through the Ashtar Command's Mothership and above the towers of beautiful Shamballa.

"A starship..." said Janus enthralled.

"Yes, the starship the Starseeds used to travel to Earth 12,000 years ago," said Jacob slowly.

And it was true. This was indeed the starship the Starseeds had used to travel through space, time and the dimensions to come to Planet Earth. This was the starship the Starseeds used to travel through the interdimensional portal at Callanish. This was the very starship they'd buried by the lake at the foot of the ridge, and slowly forgotten with the passing of each millennium.

I looked down at the six submerged beds in the base of the pyramid.

Six beds.

Six Starseeds.

And then I remembered.

Suddenly I understood.

Suddenly I understood the vision I had seen so many times in my mind's eye during the past week. The vision I'd had at Rebecca Randall's house in Glastonbury. The vision I'd had when I sat before the Crystal Cave waiting for the tide to go down. The vision I'd seen in my dreams several times on my way to America and again at the deserted mine in the Appalachian Mountains...

I let my eyes pass over the six intricately carved beds at the base of the crystal pyramid.

Six beds for six Starseeds!

Six beds for the six shining figures who had stood together on the windswept shores of Planet Earth.

Six shining figures with the wind in their hair.

Six radiant beings who together greeted a new world and a new day.

Six shining souls who had known each other since the very beginning.

379

And suddenly it was all clear to me.

I burst out laughing.

The others turned towards me.

"I know who the six Starseeds are," I said.

"What are you talking about?" said Janus. "What Starseeds?"

"The six Starseeds who belong to the six beds inside the starship," I said with a big grin on my face.

My friends gave me a puzzled look.

"Can't you see?" I laughed. "We are the six Starseeds!"

"Us?"

"Yes," I laughed. "We've found our own starship!"

7

The Petrified Ship

Jacob, Janus and Ben stared at the starship. The moment I said the starship was ours, they knew in their hearts I was right.

Janus was the first laugh—then Jacob and finally Ben.

The three DETI agents looked at us as if we'd totally lost it.

After a moment, Sorvino said, "You know what I think, this contraption looks like a pint-sized version of those huge pyramids that were floating over all the cities just a couple of days ago!"

"But this baby isn't one of the Ashtar Command's starships!" said Janus still laughing, "This baby is ours!"

"Do you believe it guys," I said, still chuckling, "… after all the mystery and this long treasure hunt—it turns out to be our own frigging ship!"

"But how come the Professor didn't write anything it? About the crystal machine being inside this big crystal pyramid?" asked Janus. "I mean there weren't even any drawings in his diary of the ship."

"Maybe that's what the missing pages in his diary were all about," said Jacob, walking over to the ellipse-shaped opening in one side of the pyramid.

"But why on earth would he tear them out?"

"I don't know. Maybe he was afraid of what would happen if people found out. It certainly didn't sound like he lived in the most tolerant of times."

Jacob knocked on the door. Immediately the clear door panel slid to the side with a soft swish.

"Hey presto! Enter friends!"

One by one we stepped into the pyramid. For some reason I expected I would feel a powerful heightening of the energy the moment we entered the crystal structure, but to my surprise there was no noticeable change.

Then I decided to lie down on one of the six submerged 'beds'. I immediately knew which one was mine.

The bed opposite mine was Ben's, Starwarrior's.

The beds to my right and left were Moncler and Telperion's, but what about the other two beds? Who did they belong to?

I looked at the three DETI agents standing outside the pyramid watching us explore the starship. No, the beds definitely didn't belong to them.

I closed my eyes. I could now see the past as clearly as the clear crystal walls of our starship. After the catastrophic downfall of Atlantis 12,000 years ago, the Ascended Masters of the Great White Brotherhood asked the Intergalactic Council for help. When discussing how to assist Earth, the Council decided that the Earth's population was too small to send an entire fleet. Instead, the Council decided to send starships with Starseed volunteers to assist humanity in raising its consciousness—and as a consciousness training exercise for the Starseeds themselves. Each group of volunteers entered the Earth's vibrational field through portals at the Earth's Power Spots. And the portal our starship had entered through was obviously the Power Spot at Callanish.

I wondered why we did not enter through the Power Spot at Avalon in England since we six Starseeds had such a close connection to it?

As if in answer to my question, Ben said slowly as he let his hand run over the clear crystal of the pyramid in fascination. "Avalon was too densely populated back then for us to risk a landing there. Therefore we decided to enter the Earth's vibrational field at another less populated Power Spot—Callanish. And back then, Callanish was just as beautiful and harmonious a place as Avalon..."

I nodded to my friend, my friend who had been with me since the beginning. Then I also let my hand glide across the sides of the pyramid and I knew that the starship hadn't always consisted of crystals...

And the crystal machine?

I turned towards the shining object in the center of the starship. It seemed to grow right out of the floor of the pyramid.

Jacob was already bending over it in fascination.

"Back then we called it a 'quantum transmitter'," he said as he studied the machine. "Not just an intergalactic, but also an interdimensional transmitter. This wonderful companion could do many things for us... it was able to transmit our thoughts over great distances and of course send and receive all types of 3rd and 4th dimensional signals—both audio and visual."

"So now the only question is how do we get this baby to work," said Janus.

382

"Well," said Jacob, running his hand over the machine, "I don't see any on/off switch."

"Finding the switch should be a piece of cake for you O Wizard of Wisdom," I said. "It's only 12,000 years since you used it last!"

"Hey, Moncler?" I asked some time later. "So what's the story?"

Janus, Ben, Agent Jackson and I were sitting by the entrance to the cave waiting impatiently while Jacob studied and fiddled with the 'quantum transmitter'. Ben had sent Sorvino and Hama back to the McAlister farm for torches and oil lamps since our flashlights soon would be dead—and also for food and water.

It was a little past noon and Jacob still hadn't found out how to operate the quantum transmitter or the starship—for that matter.

As our wise wizard explored the transmitter's crystals, something told me that the whole pyramid was turned off, dead, lifeless—and that there was no on/off switch.

"I think the ship is locked," said Jacob finally.

"What do you mean?" asked Janus.

"Deactivated."

"Please be more specific, O Wise Wizard."

"Before the starship landed on Earth, I think it was made of light energy—not the crystals we see before us now."

"Really," said Janus, "so what happened? Is the ship petrified or something?"

"Well not quite," laughed Jacob, "but almost. I guess you could say that in order to enter into the Earth's vibrational field and perform our mission, we had to lower our own and the starship's vibrational frequency to the level of the 3rd dimension. And when we did that, the starship's substance—light energy—turned to this crystal-like material—petrified if you like. When we left the starship and buried it beside the lake, I think we deactivated it and all its functions so that no outsider could use it or any of its highly advanced technology. I think this is why the professor, despite all his years of research, never discovered anything about the ship's purpose and functions. He simply couldn't activate it."

"But if we deactivated the ship," said Ben, "then we must be able to reactivate it again too."

"Yes," said Jacob, "Back then we must have known how to since we were planning on using it again when it was time for us to return to the stars."

"Well that means we should be able to do it now too," said Janus.

"Yes," replied Jacob slowly, caressing the crystals, "We should—but the question is how?"

"What if we lie down in the beds?" asked Janus.

"You can try."

Janus lay down in the bed to the left of mine.

The sunken bed fit his body perfectly, as if it was made for it.

"Aahh!" he said. "I bet it's really neat to meditate in this thing."

But despite the fact that the bed fit Janus so perfectly, nothing happened. The ship was completely dead.

"Maybe there's some kind of password that we have to say?" I said. "You know like Open Sesame or something!"

"Or a pin code," joked Janus from his bed, "with 199 interdimensional digits."

"It's probably something like that," said Jacob. "But who can remember a 12,000 year old pin code?"

Sorvino and Hama arrived back with more light—oil lamps, another flashlight, and some fuel and torches.

When we told Sorvino that we still hadn't made any progress, to our surprise he suggested we ask the Force for guidance.

"Why not?" he said. "The last time you meditated on the Force inside the stone circle you got help."

Jacob looked anxiously at his watch. "Sorvino is right. Asking for Guidance is a lot quicker than me spending all day trying to figure this thing out. And time is running out."

Sorvino and Hama lit the two oil lamps and set them at opposite ends of the cave. Then the seven of us sat down in a circle around the starship. The crystal pyramid was so clear and transparent that we could see each other right through the pyramid.

"So how do we do this?" asked Janus. "Do we just meditate on the Goodness of the Force until one of us gets guidance as to how to activate the starship?"

"That might take a long time," said Jacob. "And we certainly don't have all day. Maybe there is a quicker and more effective way of doing it."

"Like what?" asked Janus.

Jacob did not answer. Instead he stared at the quantum transmitter inside the pyramid. All was quiet.

I was just about to break the silence when Ben said, "If the Force is the One and Only Reality... and the Force is Unlimited Intelligence, Unlimited Knowledge... then the Force must also know everything there is to know about the starship."

"Yes that must be true," I said. "What are you getting at?"

"If there is only One Mind, the Mind of the Force, that must mean that the One Mind of the Force is really our minds."

"So?" I asked, still not quite sure where Ben was going with this.

"Well, if the One Mind of the Force knows everything about the starship," he said, "then since our minds are one with the Mind of the Force, we must in reality also know everything about the starship."

"Therefore we must also know everything about the starship..." Jacob mumbled to himself. "Therefore we also know everything about the starship... Of course!"

Jacob almost jumped out of his meditation pose. "Of course, Ben!" he cried. "Good thinking! Because the Mind of the Force knows everything about the starship, we must also know everything about the starship. Because our minds are one with the Mind of the Force! That must be the quickest and most effective way to get the answer to our question!"

Janus and I nodded. "Good thinking, Ben," said Janus.

The three agents obviously didn't know what we were talking about.

"We don't have time to go into detail right now," said Jacob. "Just follow our lead."

"All right," I said and smiled at Ben. "Let's do it. Ben, do you want to lead us?"

Ben was silent for a moment. Then he nodded. "OK I'll give it a try."

For a moment, we all looked at the quantum transmitter in the center of the pyramid. Then we closed our eyes.

Ben started to talk about the Nature of Reality. First about the One Force, which is here, there and everywhere, which is everyone and everything. Eternal and Unchanging. Then he talked about the Nature of the One Force, which is Perfect Good. Perfect Life, Perfect Intelligence, Perfect Love. The six of us repeated everything he said.

Then Ben said: "The Force is Pure Consciousness, Pure Mind... The Force is Unlimited Intelligence and Knowledge... The Force knows all there is to know about our starship... and because our minds are one with the Mind of the Force, we too know all there is to know about our starship..."

The minute I really realized and believed that Ben was speaking the Truth about the starship and about us, a torrent of images and information began to rush before my mind's eye at lightning speed...

Fiery letters and shimmering symbols... molecules and atoms...subatomic particles dancing in ecstasy... intricate geometrical forms vibrating at higher frequencies set in motion by thought and intention... high-pitched ringing tones and energetic spirals... nature and technology in perfect harmony... nature as technology... and technology as nature... nature and technology as one unified expression of the Infinite Intelligence and Organizing Power of Mind...

And as these living, dancing images and information passed before my mind's eye, I realized I was actually seeing real, live, living information about our starship.

Ben said aloud what we all saw in our mind's eye:

"A soul whose consciousness level and vibrational frequency is 5th dimensional or higher operates in a Light Body, also called a Merkabah... The Light Body is an interdimensional transport vehicle, which is able to travel through space, time and the dimensions... A Light Body can, for example, take the shape of a pyramid of light..."

At the thought of the 5th dimensional Light Body, every single cell and atom in my body, every single spiral of energy that made up my so-called physical being, began to vibrate faster and faster. Until soon, I was approaching the speed of light, the point where space and time ceased to exist—the point where the Light Body manifests itself...

"... Then when two or more souls unite their Light Bodies they become a new and larger unit called a starship..." continued Ben. "... That means a starship is a joint interdimensional transport vehicle that can travel across time, space and the dimensions... once formed, a starship accelerates immediately and travels at the speed of light... a starship can take on many different forms such as a golden pyramid of light... or a star... and when many starships come together they form a new and even larger unit often called a Mothership..."

There was silence for a few more seconds as we each experienced the fantastic technology of the higher dimensions in our mind's eye.

Then Jacob took over:

"In order for us, the six Starseeds, to carry out our mission on Test Zone Earth, we joined our Light Bodies together to form this starship... When we came to Earth, we entered the Earth's vibrational field and then followed the spiral movement of the Callanish Power Spot... downwards and downwards... and as we did so, we lowered the ship's vibrational frequency first to 4th and then to 3rd dimensional frequencies... and then we deactivated the ship by..."

Jacob stopped.

The fantastic images that were passing before my mind's eye came to an abrupt halt. All was silent in the cave.

The cool fire within me now flowed out to the point between my eyebrows. This feeling of heightened energy was both familiar and pleasant, and I felt the power of my fierce determination to carry out our mission grow even stronger.

I waited for Jacob to say more but he didn't.

The minutes passed and I slowly became aware of my physical surroundings again. Outside the cave, I could hear gulls crying and waves crashing onto the rocks outside the cave.

I opened my eyes.

Jacob was next to me, his hands caressing a long staff. The staff was made of massive oak. Intricately carved runes and symbols ran up and down the staff.

It was Moncler's magic staff!

Janus' eyes were still closed but a long two-handed sword lay across his knees. The hilt of the sword shone with jewels and gems.

It was Telperion's mighty sword!

Across Ben's knees there was also a shining light. At one end of the light a great star twinkled.

It was Starwarrior's sword!

The other agents were still sitting with their eyes closed. Sorvino was snoring.

Jacob looked up. "Our interdimensional keys have returned," he said.

I touched my forehead. The powerful feeling of concentrated light energy spread out through my whole body.

Yes.

My star, Starbrow's star had returned.

"Good to see you again, baby," said Janus, his eyes now open. He picked up his sword and kissed the hilt.

Ben, Jackson and Hama opened their eyes. Hama nudged Sorvino who was still snoring.

Jacob looked at the starship in our middle. I followed his gaze.

Nothing seemed to have changed—it was still dead.

Ben looked at our weapons. "I see a staff, a sword and... a star," he said, looking at the star on my brow with fascination.

"I see them too," said Jackson.

Hama and Sorvino looked puzzled. "What are you talking about?" asked Sorvino.

"Our interdimensional keys," said Jacob. "They have been gone since the explosion at Glastonbury Tor."

"But why do you think they have come back now," said Janus, raising his sword to the ceiling. "Not that I'm not happy to see our weapons again..." He was joyously swinging his sword back and forth. "We were meditating to find out how to activate the quantum transmitter—and what happens—our interdimensional weapons return!"

"Why did you suddenly stop, Jacob?" I said. "I was waiting for you to tell us something more but all of a sudden you just stopped."

"I stopped because I had the distinct feeling that the Force had given us the answer. It had told us how to activate the starship and the quantum transmitter..." Jacob got up and placed his hands on the pyramid.

It was still completely lifeless.

We all got up and gathered around the starship. Hama and Sorvino held up the torches so we could better study the pyramid.

"It doesn't look like there's any change in the starship," said Janus.

"I had the distinct feeling that the Force had given us the answer..." said Jacob as he again entered the pyramid. "... A distinct feeling that the Force had shown us the answer... If only I could..."

Jacob ran Moncler's magic staff over the quantum transmitter.

Nothing happened.

Then he waved his staff over the sides of the pyramid.

Still nothing happened.

"I know the Force just gave me the answer..." mumbled Jacob. "I know... I know..."

Again he began to examine the quantum transmitter.

"So what have you discovered Moncler?" I asked.

"Shh! Let me think. I've almost got it..."

When there was no sign that Jacob was going to let us in on what he'd almost found out, the rest of us walked over to the entrance of the cave and sat down.

I touched the star on my brow. It felt good to have my interdimensional weapon back.

"So how about some lunch while the genius is at work?" said Janus. "I'm absolutely starved."

Sorvino took out a bag of sandwiches. "Mrs. McAlister was a big help," he said and soon we were all busy munching away while Jacob, sandwich in hand, slowly circled the ship.

"The key to activating the ship is not the quantum transmitter," he mumbled. "... It must have something to do with the beds... or?"

"I sure hope he's soon going to find out," Janus whispered to me, "It's almost five o'clock."

Inside the pyramid Janus was pacing back and forth, swinging his sword and getting more and more irritated as each minute passed. It was almost six in the evening and nothing had happened. Outside the cave, the sun was beginning to set and Jacob was still sitting in front of the crystals with his eyes closed, mumbling to himself.

"This is really getting frustrating!" grumbled Janus. "Here we are with our own personal Star Trek starship and the technology to talk to the whole world... But the bloody machine is so sophisticated we can't get it to work!"

"Will you be quiet, so I can think!" cried Jacob.

"But we've only got six hours left, Jacob! Six hours!"

Janus was so pissed that in disgust he threw his sword into his submerged 'star bed'.

The moment the sword hit the bed, the starship blinked.

The sound of a high-pitched tone vibrated through the starship.

Jacob leapt to his feet. "What did you do?" he cried. "What did you do Janus?"

"I don't know man," Janus said, staring at his sword in surprise. "I just threw my sword down in disgust."

"No you didn't!" cried Jacob, "You did more than that! You threw your sword down onto your bed. Pick it up and do it again!"

Janus picked up his sword and threw it down on his bed again.

Once more the pyramid flashed with golden light and emitted a high-pitched ringing tone.

"Well, I'll be..."

Jacob grabbed his wooden staff and put it down on his bed.

The same thing happened.

The high-pitched tone pulsated throughout the pyramid and the sides of the pyramid glowed.

"Starbrow!" cried Jacob. "Come in here and lie down in your bed."

I came in and got into my bed.

The same thing happened again.

389

The pyramid flashed and we heard the high-pitched tone sound throughout the ship.

Ben came in and put his sword in his bed.

Same thing happened again.

"Of course..." said Jacob, obviously greatly satisfied with our discovery. "Our interdimensional keys are literally the 'keys' we need to activate our starship. Just like when we activated the Power Spot at Avalon! It's so obvious. And of course that's why our interdimensional keys suddenly appeared when we asked the Force for advice. It was so simple we just didn't get it!"

The four of us got into our beds with our interdimensional weapons.

The ship came to life, the pyramid flashed and the high-pitched tone rang, but then it went dead again. The starship was still lifeless.

"It's because we're only four," said Jacob. "To activate the starship and the quantum transmitter, we obviously need the other two Starseeds and their interdimensional weapons."

"But who are the two others?" asked Janus. "We don't even know who the other two are?" He scratched his head and pointed to the three DETI agents. "Do you think it's Jackson and Hama—or what about Sorvino?"

I was just about to answer, but Ben beat me to it. "No," he said. "They are not the missing Starseeds."

"But who are they then?" asked Janus sitting up in his bed. "If Jackson and Hama and Sorvino aren't the other Starseeds, then who are they? We haven't got a clue—and without the other two how will we ever get the starship activated?"

"We can't," said Jacob. "There's simply no way. Not without the other two Starseeds' interdimensional keys."

"But what if the other two Starseeds are on the other side of the planet right now, eating shrimp fried rice in China or something?"

Jacob bowed his head in despair.

"Then we're really in deep shit."

8

A Voice in the Mist

Daylight was fading fast as I stood upon the cliff above the cave and surveyed Loch Roag, thinking about our desperate plight. We had less than six hours left to raise the collective consciousness of humanity and if we didn't, STARDAY would be cancelled. But in order to raise the collective consciousness, we had to send a message out to all of humanity so people could understand what was going on and join us in raising their consciousness and focusing on the Good. Only in that way would it be possible to achieve the critical mass needed to lift the collective consciousness.

But to send out a message like this—and reach enough people—we needed a transmitter like the one in our starship. And now we discovered we couldn't activate the quantum transmitter or our starship without the two missing Starseeds and their interdimensional keys. Unfortunately, we had no idea who or where the two missing Starseeds were.

After all we'd been through, it was almost too much to bear.

To think we'd traveled so far—only to fail so close to the finish line.

Down below in the cave, my friends were still fiddling around with the starship, hoping against hope to find some way to activate it and the quantum transmitters without the presence of the other two Starseeds. The other two Starseeds who had come with us some 12,000 years ago… to this desolate and empty place… the two who had journeyed so far to Callanish… Callanish.

Although I could not see the Standing Stones in the distance, I still sensed their powerful presence—and felt myself drawn, as if by some unseen force, towards them.

But I knew our mission was no longer there with the stones. It was here and so I turned my eyes away from the direction where they stood and slowly began my way back down to the cave.

That was when I heard someone call my name.

391

I stopped in my tracks and turned and looked back. But there was no one there.

I was just about to continue when I heard it again, someone calling *Starbrow*.

I looked again, but there was no one in sight. Not a soul. The place was completely deserted.

But I could have sworn someone called my name.

I stood completely still, waiting, but nothing happened.

The seconds ticked by but there was no sound, so I turned back towards the cave again, thinking it was just my imagination. Down below, I could hear the sound of my friends' voices, echoing up in the cave.

Starbrow...

There it was again.

Someone *was* calling my name! And not from the cave. No, the call had come from the opposite direction, from the direction of the Standing Stones. I turned back in the direction of the stone circle.

But who could be calling my name out here? Calling *Starbrow*...because besides my friends down in the cave, who in the whole wide world even knew my cosmic name?

I gazed in the direction of the Standing Stones, but couldn't see a thing. Not a living soul anywhere.

Starbrow...

There it was again.

Like a faint whisper coming from the direction of the Power Spot as if the Standing Stones were calling me.

I closed my eyes and focused my attention on the star on my brow. Starbrow's star, my interdimensional key was back—and with it I could see many worlds. And so I did... and the moment I did, it was if the star was pulling me towards the Standing Stones in the distance.

Starbrow... I am here...

This time the voice was much clearer and not quite so far away. And then I realized that the voice was calling me from the inner plane—not from the outer.

Someone was trying to contact me on the inner plane... in meditation. I was sure of it. But who?

I opened my eyes and started to walk as fast as I could in the direction of the Standing Stones. In just a few seconds, the cave was far behind me and I was walking over the mist-covered fields. I pulled out my flashlight but didn't turn it on. Starbrow's star shining on my brow, the Sight in me, was leading me on with absolute certainty.

Starbrow... I am here...

The voice in my inner was becoming clearer, the call more insistent.

I hear you, I answered within. *I hear you...*

I climbed over a low stone wall and once on the other side, I could faintly make out the Standing Stones in the distance. Standing tall and silent with a mysterious, otherworldly sheen about them. Truly they were the entrance—or exit—to another world.

I began walking faster, almost running over the wet grass.

Starbrow... I am here... Elantha is here...

I stopped.

Elantha?

Who is Elantha?

The star on my brow pulsated even stronger, as if in answer to the mysterious caller who knew my cosmic soul name.

"Elantha..." I whispered, gently tasting the name.

Elantha.

Yes.

I ran faster towards the stone circle, filled with sudden expectation and hope, like one who had unexpectedly been told that a loved one whom he thought to be far away, had suddenly returned after a long journey.

Starbrow... I am here... Elantha is here...

A few minutes later I was at the foot of the raised ground where the Standing Stone stood. I climbed over another stone wall and began walking up towards the stone circle. When I came to the first long aisle of standing stones extending down from the center stones, I stopped.

It looked as if someone was sitting inside the stone circle.

I walked quickly and quietly forward to get a closer look.

Yes. Someone was sitting with his or her back to the huge central megalith, just as Ben and I had done when we meditated here at dawn. In the fading light, it was impossible to see who the person was.

I kept walking along the long stone avenue with the tall stones towering around me like silent sentinels. And again, I felt the heightened energy of the place, just as we had done earlier this morning.

Starbrow... I am here... Elantha is here...

There was no doubt now that the voice calling me on the inner plane was coming from the person sitting in the center of the circle against the great megalith.

I wasn't more than 15 yards from the megalith when I realized that a faint golden light surrounded whoever was sitting there, deep in meditation. As I approached, a cold gust of wind suddenly blew through the circle dispersing the mist around the center making it much easier to see the golden light surrounding the mysterious caller.

I held my breath, enthralled by what I saw.

The meditating figure was a woman.

A beautiful woman—beautiful beyond words. And though she sat, I knew she was tall and slender, and very graceful. As I got closer, I drank in her beauty. And even though her eyes were closed, with the Sight that was given me I knew her eyes were blue, deep blue—like the immeasurable Atlantic Ocean not far from us. A great power and love flowed from this majestic woman with the golden hair who was like a princess in a fairy tale or an elven princess from the Lord of the Rings.

I stood for a while gazing in awe at her finely chiseled face—and as I did, I realized that her outer beauty was but a reflection of her inner beauty. A beauty that came from deep within, from the deep wisdom and love that was her nature. A wisdom and a love that I knew and had experienced before. A wisdom and a love that could only be....

Elantha's!

The fifth member of the starship!

My dear friend since the beginning.

I stepped into the stone circle.

"Elantha..." I whispered softly.

The meditating woman opened her eyes.

Our eyes met. She remained sitting without moving.

We held each other's gaze without blinking.

Eye to eye, soul to soul.

And I knew that Elantha also saw me, my True Self, as I really was, and as I had been since the beginning.

Elantha smiled. Her smile was like the warm, intoxicating light of the sun on a perfect midsummer's day.

She stood up. Spread her arms wide.

I took a step forward. Elantha took a step forward.

Then we lovingly embraced each other. Like we had done so many times before...

"Elantha..." I whispered.

At that very moment, two dark figures leapt out from the great stones standing at the other end of the central circle.

"Freeze!" cried one of them. In his hands glinted the cold steel of a gun.

"Hands behind your heads!" shouted the other. He too pointed his gun straight at us.

394

The sudden attack of the dark figures abruptly ended the magical moment between Elantha and me. The light around Elantha disappeared and the energy around us came crashing down. Frightened, Elantha pressed herself towards me.

"Starbrow..." she said.

Confused, I looked back and forth between Elantha and the threatening dark figures. Without the clear light around her, Elantha suddenly seemed older, her face more wrinkled, her body heavier. Without the loving light, her long hair was no longer golden but silvery gray...

"Rebecca?" I cried in surprise. "Rebecca Randall?"

"Hands behind your heads!" shouted one of the two men again as they approached us. I was still staring at the woman at my side. Now that the golden light was gone, I could see that the love of my grandfather Elmar's life was not wearing the garb of an elven princess, but ordinary dark blue rain gear. Her sturdy walking boots were covered in mud as if she had traveled far and long.

"Hands behind your heads or we'll shoot!" the man shouted again, snapping me to attention. They were right next to us now, pointing their guns straight at us. I knew they were agents.

The bigger of the two pulled out a pair of handcuffs. "Turn around!" he ordered. "And keep your hands behind your heads."

Rebecca and I looked at each other.

"Are you hard of hearing or what?" the other man cried threateningly.

Rebecca and I slowly placed our hands behind our heads.

"Turn around!"

As we slowly turned around, a million thoughts raced through my mind. Somehow I had found Rebecca Randall—Elantha—the fifth member of our starship! But at the same time these two agents had found us!

"Give me your hands!" cried the agent as he prepared to cuff me.

Slowly I began to lower my hands, the thoughts racing through my head. What on earth was I going to do? If the agents captured us now we would be unable to activate the starship and send out the message. Our mission would be over, terminated—after all that we'd been through.

No! I felt the strength and fierce determination of the warrior surge up in me again. Should I resist and fight? During the last couple of days, I learned I had the strength and courage to fight these men. Maybe I could even win and render them 'non-operational' as Ben would say. Then Rebecca and I could escape.

The agent roughly yanked both my hands behind my back. This was my very last chance, the very last moment. In another minute the chance would be gone. Over. Done with. Forever. It was now or never—my last chance to show my courage and fight! But the Masters said that *violence ceases not with violence*! Oh what was I to do? I felt our mission was hanging in the balance, on a very thin thread. Hanging on the wisdom of my decision and there was only a fraction of a second left to decide before the handcuffs were locked around my wrists.

At that very moment, a voice pierced through the mist, "Drop it!"

The agents froze.

Immediately I recognized the voice.

It was Ben!

I sighed with relief.

Rebecca gasped in horror when she saw Ben approaching. She looked as if she'd seen a ghost.

"It's OK Rebecca!" I said softly, "It's OK."

The two agents looked at Ben in surprise and slowly dropped their guns.

"Now," said Ben, "just give me those handcuffs, real nice and easy. Throw them down on the grass right over here."

The agents did as Ben said and threw the handcuffs down. Then Ben slowly picked them up without taking his eyes off them.

When he was standing up again he said, "OK, now turn around real slow—hands behind your backs."

Cuffs in hand, Ben approached the two as they began to turn around.

"Starbrow," he started to say, but before I knew what was happening, the bigger man swung round, kicking Ben ferociously in the gut and knocking the gun right out of his hand. They both tumbled to the ground, but the agent was no match for Ben. Before the other agent and I could react, Ben had knocked the big agent out cold. Then the smaller man tried to pick up his gun, but again Ben was faster. With his lightning-like reflexes, he swept the other agent's feet out from beneath him and knocked him out with a well-aimed blow to the side of his head.

Both agents were lying unconscious on the grass. Non-operational.

Rebecca just stood there, stunned.

"It's OK Rebecca, " I said slowly. "Ben is on our side now."

"On our side?" she repeated after me, obviously not comprehending a word of what she was saying.

"Yes," I said. "He's decided to help us."

"Help us?" Rebecca stuttered in disbelief, "But I thought that..."

"Trust me, Rebecca," I said. "I'll explain it all later..."

Ben was already examining the two unconscious men.

Suddenly I felt Rebecca reel at my side.

"It's okay, Rebecca," I said and held her. "You're safe now."

Rebecca took a deep breath and leaned against one of the stones.

I joined Ben who was pulling a wallet from one of the agent's pockets.

"Who are they?" I asked.

"MI6 agents," he said. "They must have followed Rebecca, hoping she would lead them to you and your friends."

"MI6 agents?" said Rebecca weakly. She was now sitting by the stone, her hands trembling. She looked very frail and tired.

"Yes," said Ben and took out the other agent's wallet.

Rebecca shook her head. "But why would they follow me?"

Ben stood up and looked around in the stone circle. "Because I ordered them to."

"You?" I looked at Ben in surprise. "What do you mean?"

"Before I left Glastonbury, I gave MI6 orders to follow Rebecca's every move." Ben smiled ruefully. "Already back then, I had a strong feeling that Rebecca was somehow connected to you, Starbrow. Unfortunately I didn't have time to recall the order after I captured you."

I looked out at the darkening landscape around us. "Do you think there are more agents here?" I said.

Ben surveyed the stone circle and the village a little further away. "When Commander Holm sends agents on surveillance, he usually sends them in pairs, two and two, it's standard procedure. So we better move in case there are more around. And besides, time is running out. It's almost seven o'clock."

I turned to Rebecca. "How did you find us?"

Rebecca looked at me and Ben and the unconscious agents as if she still didn't quite believe that Ben and I were now on the same side.

"It was Elmar who told me to come here," she said.

"Elmar?"

"Yes, Elmar," said Rebecca, taking a deep breath. "Three days ago in deep meditation, Elmar contacted me from the other side. He showed me six shining figures standing on the shores of Planet Earth—six Starseeds who came to Earth in their starship many thousands of years ago."

I nodded. "I've had the same vision several times during the last couple of days."

"Me too," said Ben.

Now I was surprised.

"You had the vision, too?" Rebecca and I said in unison.

"Yes."

Rebecca and Ben looked at each other with intense interest.

"What else did you see in your vision?" said Ben.

"I saw how the six Starseeds in their starship came to Earth," said Rebecca. "Through the portal at the Callanish Power Spot. That was many, many thousands of years ago."

"Did you see who the six Starseeds were?" I asked.

"Yes," answered Rebecca. "I was one of them."

I smiled at her. "Elantha."

Now that she'd calmed down a bit, I could again see the beautiful elven princess in her... the elven princess who sat deep in meditation with her back to the great megalith.

Rebecca continued. "Yes, Starbrow," she said, smiling. "You too were one of the six Starseeds—as were your friends, Moncler and Telperion."

I nodded. "And the two other Starseeds?"

"The fifth member of the starship was Starkeeper," she said.

"Starkeeper?" asked Ben. "Who is that?"

Rebecca turned her gaze from us and looked up at the night sky. I could see in her eyes that she was recalling the beloved face of our companion.

"Who is Starkeeper?" asked Ben again. "Do you know him—or her?"

Rebecca nodded.

"Who is it?"

Rebecca was just about to answer when I said, "Elmar,"

"Yes, Elmar is Starkeeper," said Rebecca, "the fifth member of the starship."

Ben turned towards me. "Your grandfather?"

"Yes," I said. "He left his physical body last week and is now in the higher dimensions in Shamballa."

"The City of Light?"

"Yes."

All three of us were silent for a while. The sun was now completely gone and dusk had turned into night.

"And the sixth member of the starship?" I asked. "Did you see who it was?"

Rebecca shook her head. "I couldn't really see who the sixth member was. Although there was also something very familiar about his face."

Ben and I looked at each other and smiled.

"Do you know who the sixth member of the starship is?" Rebecca asked.

"Yes," I said. "The sixth member of the starship is Starwarrior."

"Starwarrior?"

"Yes. The Warrior from the Stars."

398

"And who is that?"

I nodded towards Ben. "Ben is Starwarrior."

Rebecca again looked at Agent Nevis in surprise. "You?"

Ben nodded.

"You are Starwarrior?" she said in wonder.

"Yes!" I said, laughing at the surprised look on her face.

"You are the sixth member of the starship?" she said.

"Show her your sword, Ben," I said.

Ben opened his shoulder bag and a clear light flowed from it. Then Ben held up the shining sword. Rebecca put her hand on the weapon. Now it was her turn to smile.

"Starwarrior's sword..." she said in fascination. "Starwarrior's sword..." Then she started to laugh. "Well I never! Special Agent Ben Nevis, the man who was hunting Starbrow over stock and stone, is Starwarrior, the Warrior from the Stars! Truly it must be said that even the very Wise cannot see the end of all things—or the beginning for that matter!"

Then she said slowly. "This also explains why I always felt there was this mysterious connection between the two of you... as if there was some kind of invisible link pulling you together."

"Yes Rebecca and there's more," I said thinking of our past life when Ben and I were twins and she was our mother.

"But there's very little time for stories," said Ben, putting his sword back in the bag. "It's quarter to seven and we have only five hours to raise the entire collective consciousness before STARDAY is cancelled."

I looked at my watch. Ben was right. I'd been so occupied with meeting Rebecca and the two MI6 agents that for a moment I'd forgotten all about our mission.

"Raise the collective consciousness before STARDAY is cancelled?" said Rebecca. "What are you talking about?"

Ben looked back at the two unconscious MI6 agents. "We'll explain in a minute Rebecca. But first we need to get rid of these two—and then back to the starship before it's too late."

9

The Ring and the Stone

It didn't take long for former Special Agent Ben Nevis to deal with the two MI6 agents. Once he'd found their car in the parking lot nearby, he gagged and bound them both and put them in the back seat. Then he took everything they owned—their guns, keys, wallets, mobile phones and laptop and shoved it all in his backpack. As soon as he was done, we ran back to Rebecca who was waiting for us by the Standing Stones, flashlight in hand.

"Where to now?" asked Rebecca.

"To our starship," I said. "We found it earlier today. Follow me."

"We? You mean you and Ben?"

"And Jacob and Janus," I said.

"Jacob and Janus? But I thought they were..."

"... dead? Yeah, so did I. But it turned out that they too survived the explosion of Glastonbury Tor. But we must hurry Rebecca, we have very little time."

As we rushed back to the starship, I briefly told Rebecca what had happened since she last saw me at Chalice Well. When I told her that Ben and I had been twins in our past life and that she had been our mother, she stopped in surprise.

"I was your mother in a past life?"

"Yes," I said. "Ben and I were twins—Gavin and Dana. We were your son and daughter."

Rebecca stared at us in disbelief. "Twins?"

"Well it's a long story, 'Mom'," I laughed, grabbed her hand and started walking again. "But now we've got to get back."

Rebecca followed, laughing quietly to herself. "This is getting more and more fantastic! At any rate, it certainly explains why the two of you look so much alike..."

I told her the rest of the story very quickly. How we found the quantum transmitter and the starship and discovered it was our own ship—the starship we used when we came to Earth 12,000 years ago. Then I explained to her that we couldn't carry out our mission because we couldn't activate the starship without the six Starseeds' interdimensional keys."

When I said this Rebecca came to an abrupt halt.

"Then I better understand why Elmar told me in my meditation that it was of the utmost importance that I went to Callanish and gave you this, Starbrow."

Rebecca held out her hand. On her finger was a solid golden ring. The golden ring I'd seen glinting on her hand not long ago when I awoke in her house in Glastonbury. Back then I'd only faintly glimpsed the ring. Now I could see it clearly.

"The ring is my interdimensional key," said Rebecca.

I took Rebecca's hand and touched the ring. A cool but powerful energy flowed from it. The light from the ring lit up her face and for a moment she was again the beautiful elven princess I'd seen back at the Standing Stones.

"Keep the ring, blessed Elantha," I said reverently. "Now that you are here, you can put the ring in its rightful place in the starship yourself."

Rebecca smiled. We continued across the heath at a fast pace.

"You said before it was Elmar who told you where we were," said Ben. "How did you get here?"

"After Elmar showed me a vision of us—the six Starseeds—he told me that Starbrow was on his way to Callanish," explained Rebecca. "Then he said it was of the utmost importance that I went to Callanish and gave my ring to Starbrow. So I left immediately."

"But how did you get here?" asked Ben again.

"It wasn't easy, I can tell you that," said Rebecca. "All the airports are closed because of the Earth changes so I had to drive the whole way."

Ben looked at Rebecca with respect. Although she was almost out of breath, she was forcing herself to keep up with Ben and me. She must have been around 70, yet she moved and acted like someone 20 years younger. Just like Elmar.

"But how did you get out here to the Outer Hebrides?" asked Ben.

"All the ferry connections were cancelled too. Fortunately, one of my old friends lives on the west coast of Scotland, so he sailed me out here in one of his boats."

"And at no point did you realize that the two agents were following you?"

"No. I didn't suspect anything. And I honestly don't understand how they found me. I sailed alone with my friend in his tiny boat all the way to the Outer Hebrides. The two of us must have been alone in that boat for almost 24 hours. And the only other person who knows I'd gone to Callanish is my daughter Gail—and she'd never tell anyone."

Ben did not answer—but he looked very thoughtful.

"As soon as I came to the Isle of Lewis I hitchhiked to Callanish," continued Rebecca. "And the minute I got to the Standing Stones, I sat down to meditate."

"Yes, I heard you call me on the inner plane," I said, "So I followed the call to where you sat in the stone circle. How about you, Ben? How did you know where I had gone?"

Ben answered as if he was thinking about something else. "I left the cave to have a word with you," he said. "When you weren't there, I started looking for you and saw your footprints in the wet grass. I was following them towards the Standing Stones when I heard voices coming from the circle. That's when I started running towards the Standing Stones—and the rest you know."

We climbed over another stone wall and could see three beams of light up ahead.

"That must be the others looking for us," said Ben.

We hurried towards the beams of light—and heard the three DETI agents calling our names. They too must have seen the light from our flashlights because suddenly all three of them started running towards us.

"Major Nevis!" cried a voice. It was Sorvino.

"We're here, Ron!" cried Ben.

Ben's stocky Lieutenant joined us followed by Jackson and Hama.

"What's going on boss?" asked Sorvino when we reached each other. He and the other agents looked at Rebecca in surprise.

"We've found the 5th member of the starship," said Ben. "Rebecca Randall. You probably remember her from Glastonbury."

The agents looked at Rebecca. "How on earth did you find us?" said Sorvino.

"Rebecca's not the only one who's found us," said Ben. "Two of Commander Holm's MI6 agents followed her."

"MI6 agents? What happened?"

"I rendered them non-operational. Right now they're cuffed and gagged in their own car."

402

"That doesn't sound good, boss," said Sorvino. "Do you think the two agents are the only ones out there?"

"We didn't run into any others," answered Ben. "For jobs like this Holm usually only sends out one team, so there's probably no one else in the area right now."

"But whether or not there's another team out there, MI6 will discover something's up when these two don't report back," said Hama.

"Yeah, that's true," said Ben, "But chances are they won't begin to get suspicious until tomorrow. And by then we'll either have accomplished our mission and sent our message out to the world or nothing much will matter anyway."

We headed for the cave again.

"It's not so much the two agents I'm worried about," continued Ben. "What worries me is how the agents were able to follow Rebecca all the long way from Glastonbury to Callanish without her discovering they were on her tail."

"What do you mean?" asked Jackson.

"Rebecca says she sailed to the island on a tiny boat and she was alone on the boat with a friend of hers for almost 24 hours."

We reached the cave and I entered first. Jacob and Janus were still inside the pyramid. When they saw me, they came out of the ship and over to us.

"So what's going on?" asked Janus. "Where were you Starbrow? "

"I've been over by the Standing Stones where I found one of the missing crew members," I said.

At that moment, Rebecca and Ben joined me. "Allow me to introduce you to Rebecca Randall," I said, "also known as Elantha."

Rebecca smiled at my two friends. "Greetings, Moncler. Greetings, Telperion," she said. "It's been a long time."

Jacob and Janus looked curiously at this mysterious woman. Although she was dressed in rain gear and looked very tired after her long journey, she still emanated a majestic beauty.

"Greetings, Rebecca." Janus walked over to shake her hand, but instead of shaking his hand, Rebecca embraced him warmly. She did the same with Jacob.

"Elantha?" said Jacob. "Is that your..."

"Elantha is my... true name, my original name," said Rebecca. "Just as your cosmic name is Moncler."

"And you're the fifth member of the starship?" asked Janus.

Rebecca nodded.

403

"But how did you find us?" asked Jacob.

Rebecca looked curiously at the crystal pyramid, which still showed no sign of life. "The sixth member of the starship lead me to you."

"The sixth member?" said Janus. "And who may I ask is the sixth member?"

"Starkeeper."

"Starkeeper? Who is Starkeeper?"

"Elmar."

"Elmar!" laughed Janus and turned to me. "It seems to me your old granddad is here, there and everywhere!"

"You arrived in the nick of time, Rebecca," said Jacob. "If we want STARDAY to happen as planned, we only have five hours to raise the entire collective consciousness."

"Yes, I've heard!" said Rebecca, getting closer to the crystal pyramid. "Starbrow told me of your plan to try to get one percent of the Earth's population to focus on the Good at the same time."

Jacob followed her. "We know that the quantum transmitter inside our starship can broadcast on every channel on all the world's TV sets," he said. "Just like Ashtar did when he sent his STARDAY transmission out almost a week ago. Our plan is to talk to all of humanity via the quantum transmitter and explain the situation to them and ask them to join us in seeing the Force, the Good, as the One and Only Reality."

"But we have a small problem," said Janus. "The starship and the quantum transmitter are locked—deactivated. But we're pretty sure we can reactivate it by placing all six crew members' interdimensional keys in their beds inside the ship."

Rebecca put her hands on the translucent sides of the starship. Then she turned towards us and stretched forth her right hand. Elantha's golden ring cast its light on her and the starship.

"That is why Elmar sent me here," she said. "To give you my interdimensional key."

"Excellent!" said Jacob and clapped his hands. "Now all we need is Elmar and his key."

"Elmar didn't by any chance give you his key?" asked Janus.

"No," said Rebecca. "Many many years ago, Elmar received his interdimensional key—a perfect, ellipse-shaped stone—from the Ascended Master Djwal Khul in the Himalayas. Djwal Khul also gave Elmar my interdimensional key—this ring—and told him to give it to me when he first came to Glastonbury more than 50 years ago. When Elmar left his physical body some days ago I think he took his interdimensional key with him to Shamballa where he is now."

"But if Elmar and his key are on the other side in the higher dimensions in Shamballa, how are we going to get his key?" asked Janus.

"When we were in Shamballa, remember Elmar said that all we had to do was call him if we needed him," I said.

"Starbrow is right," said Rebecca. "In spirit Elmar is right here, right now. It is time for us to meditate and call upon him. It's time for the Brotherhood to be reunited once again."

We gathered around the pyramid. I noticed that Ben looked worried.

"What's wrong, Ben?"

"There's something about the arrival of the two MI6 agents that doesn't feel right."

"What do you mean?"

Ben turned towards Rebecca.

"You say while you were on your way to the Isle of Lewis with your friend you never saw any other boats? No one was following you?"

"That's right, there was no one around," said Rebecca. "I still don't understand how anyone could have followed me. I was all alone with my friend on the boat for 24 hours."

"And yet they were right on your heels all the time," said Ben. "The moment Starbrow showed himself to you, they came out of hiding?"

"Yes," I said. "The two were there immediately. As if they were just waiting for me to show up."

Ben walked over to the cave entrance and looked out.

"What are you thinking, boss?" said Sorvino.

"There's something about this whole story that... unless..."

Ben ran over to Rebecca. "Give me your purse."

"My purse?"

"Yes."

Rebecca looked surprised but put her hand in her inside pocket and handed him a thin worn, leather purse.

Ben quickly opened it and emptied the contents onto the floor.

Some pound notes, coins, a couple of credit cards and a driver's license.

Ben pulled out his pocketknife and said, "When MI6 questioned you, they searched all your belongings...?"

405

"Well yes… they did…" replied Rebecca.

With a quick stroke, he cut the lining of Rebecca's purse. A tiny round piece of metal fell out and landed on the floor.

"… and had this put into the lining of your purse!"

We all stared at the tiny piece of metal. It was as thin as a button and no bigger than a thumbnail.

Ben drove his knife into the round piece of metal, which first bent and then broke into several pieces.

"What is it?" I asked.

"A tracker," said Sorvino, furrowing his brow.

Ben took off his backpack and emptied the contents onto the floor—the stuff he collected from the two agents—their weapons, ammunition, mobile phones and laptop computer.

"What's a tracker?" asked Janus.

"A long-distance tracking device," said Jackson.

Rebecca looked afraid. "That means they tracked me all the way here?"

Jackson nodded. "The only question now is what kind of tracking device they used."

She looked at Ben. He had turned on the agents' laptop and was staring at the screen intently. "Come on, come on…" he mumbled, clenching his fist as the laptop started up.

"Major?" asked Jackson. "You don't think they used…"

"Shh!" he said and motioned for us to be quiet. We all gathered around the laptop as the computer's menu appeared on the screen. Ben's fingers flew across the keyboard.

A picture appeared on the screen. It looked like an infrared picture—an infrared picture of a darkened landscape taken from the air. Water and rocks covered with seaweed. Plus rocks piled up in a kind of stone barrier or wall between the water and the cliff. Under the cliff, a faint light seemed to seep out from the rocks. In the middle of the picture, there were big red capital letters, which read:

NO CONNECTION WITH TRACKING DEVICE.

The MI6 agents' laptop showed an infrared picture, taken from the air, of the shoreline right where our cave was!

"Damn!" cried Ben and turned off the computer.

"What was that?" asked Janus.

"Satellite tracking," said Ben. "Why the hell didn't I think of it?"

"Satellite tracking?" said Rebecca.

"You mean like in the movies when the intelligence people can hear and see everything you do via satellite?" said Jacob.

"Something like that," said Ben, looking at the other agents and shaking his head.

"Is that how they tracked me all the way here?" asked Rebecca.

"Yup," said Ben. "But not only that, they also heard every single word you said while your purse was in your possession."

"Then they know we're in this cave?" I said.

"Yes."

"And they know who we are?"

"Yes."

Janus looked around like a trapped wild animal. "What does that mean? Is there a whole battalion of soldiers waiting outside?"

Ben walked over to the cave exit. "I don't think so. If I know Commander Holm, he only sent the two agents who followed Rebecca. But via the tracker they now know our exact location and exactly who we are." Ben looked at the other agents. "Commander Holm and General Hecht's next move will be to send a large task force after us. The only question is, how long will it take for them to get here. Sorvino, don't you have a map of these islands?"

Sorvino pulled out a map and spread it out on the stone floor.

I looked at my watch. It was twelve minutes past seven. Less than five hours to STARDAY.

"Let's see..." said Ben. "The nearest military base on these islands is... the Benbecula base on North Uist... approximately 75 miles from here... and they have an air base... damn! Commander Holm will most certainly order the base to send troops here."

"How long will it take for the troops to get here?" I asked.

"Since the base is only 75 miles from here, it won't take them long to fly here. It really depends on how long it takes for them to round up their troops. One hour, maybe two, it's hard to say."

"Then we better get started!" I said.

"The sooner the better," said Ben. He signaled to the other agents. "Hama, you climb up the cliff and keep watch on our land side. Sorvino and Jackson, you guard the cave. See if you can use some of the rocks and boulders to reinforce the wall of stones that is protecting the entrance. If those troops arrive before we've finished our transmission, you must keep them at bay at all costs!"

10

Guardians of the Earth

Jacob, Janus, Rebecca, Ben and I gathered around the starship. The pyramid's four crystal sides glowed dimly in the light from the oil lamps.

We stepped into the pyramid one by one and lay down in our beds.

Five times the pyramid blinked and emitted a high-pitched ringing tone.

Five times—for Moncler, Telperion, Elantha, Starwarrior and Starbrow.

Only the sixth bed, Starkeeper's bed, was empty.

I made myself comfortable in my bed. It wasn't hard since the bed was made for me and fit perfectly.

I closed my eyes—and began to focus on the Force, the Good.

Like I had done countless times before, here, in our shimmering starship.

No one guided the meditation, no one followed, for we were all One. In the One Mind of the Force.

After we had dwelt on the Nature of Reality for a few minutes, the five of us said in unison:

"With the Force as our witness we now call upon Starkeeper!"

The moment we said this, my mind went completely blank.

The boundaries between my four dear friends and myself disappeared.

Time stood still.

Space disappeared.

In the Eternal Now.

In the Eternal Now where the Force, the Good, is the One and Only Reality.

Slowly a Light, a Divine Light that had neither beginning nor end, began to grow out of Eternity. Like an everlasting shining sun of Love and Grace that showered its blessed Light on everything and everyone... on this and countless other worlds.

Countless worlds, one of which was Planet Earth, where we six Starseeds had landed millennia ago, from another Divine World, blessed with the same Divine Sun's Love and Grace.

The Great Sea stretched out in all directions, without beginning, without end.

And there we stood.

Six shining figures with the wind in our hair.

Six shining souls watching the waves crash on the windswept shores of Planet Earth.

Six sparks of the Great Central Sun, sent to bear witness to and enjoy Its Glory on this beautiful, blue-white planet at the edge of the Milky Way Galaxy.

Moncler, Telperion, Elantha, Starwarrior... and Starkeeper.

My five dear friends since the beginning.

In my mind's eye, I looked long upon each of my five dear friends, inhaled and memorized every feature of their unique Divine Beings.

Moncler, Telperion, Elantha, Starwarrior, Starkeeper... and myself, Starbrow.

Each one of us the Perfect Being.

Each one of us the Force, the Good, individualized.

The Higher Self.

Greater than anything I had ever dreamt of. All-knowing, all-loving beyond anything I had ever imagined when I thought that this earthly life was all there was.

And I saw how my present lifetime, my lifetime as a young Dane in Copenhagen, was but a drop in the ocean compared to my Higher Self, a microscopic grain of sand on the infinite beach of my Soul's journey. I saw how all my lifetimes together on Planet Earth were but the briefest blink of an eye in Eternity.

All my lifetimes, all my roles, all my many entrances and exits...

But always, in all my lifetimes, together with my five dear friends.

With the eyes of my Higher Self I now saw at lightning speed my soul's entire history on Planet Earth... from our arrival 12,000 years ago on Test Zone Earth... in the aftermath of the third and final cataclysm of Atlantis... I saw how we, the Starseeds and other initiates, worked ceaselessly throughout the centuries to create Peace and Enlightenment on Earth... Cities of Light were built... enlightened civilizations arose and fell...

I saw how the Ascended Masters of the Great White Brotherhood gathered the Starseeds and sent them all over the world in an attempt to reactivate the Light Grid and anchor a positive New Vision in the collective consciousness of humanity... and I saw how each of us, Starbrow, Starwarrior, Moncler, Telperion, Starkeeper and Elantha, had incarnated at the same time to contribute to this work... in 5th century Britain... But the mission failed... and the Prophecy of Starwarrior remained unfulfilled...

The centuries and incarnations passed... followed by new attempts to raise the collective consciousness... and gradually the consciousness of humanity began to rise... At the same time Mother Earth at the end of the 20th century began Her ascension into the 5th dimension... and once more the Force, the Good, brought these six Starseeds together, each to play their role in the Great Game... Elmar and Rebecca... Djwal Khul and Shamballa... Ben and the Three E Masters... Jacob and Janus and myself...

I saw the critical 48 hours when 600 of the Starseeds, including Moncler, Telperion and Starbrow, were reunited with their brothers and sisters from the stars in the Ashtar Command's Mothership... at the very moment when the threat of an axis shift that would annihilate all life on Earth loomed on the horizon... I saw the 600 Starseeds' crash course in ascension and desperate race against time... their anchoring of the positive New Vision in humanity's collective consciousness... the suspension of the axis shift... and the activation of STARDAY...

I saw the American intelligence agency's destruction of the Power Spots and the Light Grid... and how the collective consciousness fell drastically... and how the amazing offer of STARDAY seemed to be withdrawn...

But the Force, the Good, kept bringing these six friends together... Starwarrior, Starbrow, Moncler, Telperion learned about the Lost Teaching of the Single Eye... A Teaching that could raise the entire collective consciousness of humanity back to quantum level 5... and release STARDAY... a new era of Peace and Enlightenment... exactly what these six Starseeds had so untiringly worked for during the last 12,000 years...

And now we were here again... back where it all started... back in Callanish... the place where we six had entered the Earth's vibrational field in our starship 12,000 years ago...

Then my mind went blank again as past, present and future blended together and became one.

In the Eternal Now where we are all One.

The Divine Light showered its blessed rays upon us, the six Starseeds.

Then in my mind's eye I turned my gaze towards my five friends and slowly savored the Goodness and beauty of every feature of these beloved

410

souls. Starwarrior, the Warrior from the Stars. Moncler, my wise and loyal friend. Telperion, my strong and fearless companion. Elantha, the unwavering light. And Starkeeper...

As with one movement I felt the five of us turning towards him.

Towards Aran.

Elmar.

Starkeeper.

Our eternal friend and companion with his undying smile.

He walked towards us with that characteristic glint in his eye.

Aran.

Elmar.

Starkeeper.

As he had been from the beginning.

As he was now.

And as he always would be.

"Dear friends..." said Starkeeper and motioned to the windswept shore where we stood. "Here we arrived. Here we began our adventure some 12,000 years ago. Here we started yet another one of our mind-boggling adventures through the Infinite Creation of the Force. And here, 12,000 years ago, we forgot, for a little while, for a few brief lifetimes, who we really are and what we came here to do."

For a moment our many incarnations on Earth again began to flicker past us, but Starkeeper raised his hand and pulled our attention back to the Eternal Now.

"But no matter how much we forgot," he continued, "no matter how many misunderstandings and so-called mistakes each one of us made... The Force, the Good, our Higher Self, knew that sooner or later we would again remember who we are."

Starkeeper looked up at the Omnipresent Light above us.

"Yes..." he said. "The Force, the Good, has foreseen everything and provided for everything. And even though we, in our earthly bodies with our earthly personalities, seem to forget, the Force never forgets. But now, by the Grace of the Single Eye, we were able to return to where it all started. Now we once again remember who we are. Now we once again remember that we are the dearest of companions. Truly we have come full circle—to be reunited again with our starship and each other."

Starkeeper looked down from the Omnipresent Light and smiled at us.

"And now oh dearest of companions, before we leave this beautiful planet and continue on our journey onward, let us do everything in our power to help our brothers and sisters here on Earth remember who they

411

really are. After countless long years, the opportunity we have been waiting for has finally arrived. All roads are coming to an end and everything, and I mean everything, is now coming to fruition. That is what STARDAY is all about—the fruition of countless long years of struggle and dedication. So dear ones, let us make one final effort to ensure that we succeed in our mission this time so that all our brothers and sisters on Planet Earth can now experience the same joy of recognition that we have experienced. And let them understand, once and for all, their Eternal Oneness with the Force, the Good."

As if in answer to Starkeeper's words, Elantha stretched forth her hand with the golden ring. Moncler beat his staff into the ground. Telperion drew his long two-handed sword. Starwarrior raised his shining sword up to the heavens. The star on my brow began to pulsate and send out rays of light.

And in one swift movement—the six of us remembered—as if with one thought, One Mind, the Oath we had taken together more than 12,000 years ago when we first embarked on our mission to Planet Earth. The very same Oath we took more than 1,500 years ago in Merlin's Crystal Cave—the very same Oath we six were now called upon to fulfill in this lifetime.

The Oath of the Guardian.

With one voice we said together:

> "WITH THE FORCE AS MY WITNESS
> I NOW CLAIM
> MY RIGHTFUL PLACE
> AS GUARDIAN OF THE EARTH!"

And so it was.

We were all ready.

Ready for the last lap, the final stretch of our long mission.

Starkeeper stretched his hand out towards us.

As he opened his hand, we saw something in his palm.

And at that very moment, a strong golden light surrounded us—a light that had the shape of a four-sided pyramid. And we heard that familiar high-pitched ringing tone.

The windswept shoreline around us disappeared. We were back in our starship.

But this time the crystal pyramid kept glowing and the ringing tone continued.

412

The shining crystals in the quantum transmitter began to pulsate.

As if with one movement, the five of us opened our eyes and sat up in our beds.

We looked over at Elmar's bed, half expecting him to be there.

But no—in his bed lay a stone.

A smooth, ellipse-shaped stone that was slightly smaller than the palm of his hand.

Starkeeper's stone.

Elmar's interdimensional key.

The circle was complete.

The starship was activated.

11

The Storm Is Upon Us

Now that the starship was activated, Jacob and Ben were trying to get the quantum transmitter to work. It was already 9:45 in the evening and for the last half hour, the two of them had been trying to figure out how this highly advanced piece of equipment actually worked. It seemed a difficult task, even for our wise wizard friend. While they were working, Janus and I were preparing our "full blanket" speech to humanity. Rebecca was sitting at the other end of the cave with her eyes half closed, studying the starship. The three DETI agents were keeping watch outside. So far we hadn't heard or seen anything of Rebecca's pursuers.

"Hey Moncler!" I yelled, turning to the pyramid. "What's going on? We're running out of time!"

"Shh!" motioned Ben back. "I think he's almost there."

Janus and I tiptoed into the pyramid. Its translucent sides shone with a faint golden light. At the edge of one's hearing there was that faint, but pleasant high-pitched ringing tone. Inside the pyramid, the air was electric.

Jacob stood in front of the quantum transmitter with his eyes closed, waving his hands over the machine's clear crystals.

"What's he doing?" whispered Janus.

"He says that the quantum transmitter is controlled telepathically," replied Ben in a whisper. "So he's trying to tune into the machine."

"A computer that is controlled by telepathy? Far out!"

Now we realized that we were hearing other tones, which seemed to be coming from the quantum transmitter itself. As we listened, we realized that these sounds were moving up and down as if they were following Jacob's movements—or thoughts.

"If this transmitter is controlled by thought transference how were the SETI astronomers able to connect their machine to the observatory's antennas?" I asked.

"The SETI astronomers' machine was child's play compared to this baby..." said Jacob slowly, eyes still closed. "A primitive attempt to duplicate something way beyond their understanding... something totally out of their league... But this baby... this baby has knowledge and functions that far surpass anything I've ever seen or imagined... it's like being plugged into the Cosmic Computer Itself..."

"That's all well and good, Moncler," I said. "But right now we need to send out our message to the whole world, don't forget that okay."

"I haven't forgotten..." said Jacob. "But the problem is that this machine is so advanced... asking it to send TV signals out on a 3rd dimensional vibrational frequency is like asking an entire symphony orchestra to make one little fart."

"Jacob! It's almost midnight for crying out loud!" said Janus. "Saving the whole world at the last minute is getting to be a very bad habit."

"Shh... Be quiet will you so I can concentrate..."

"Is there anything we can do to help?" I asked.

Jacob didn't seem to hear us anymore. "If only I can find the frequency lines and tune them..." he mumbled. Tiny beads of sweat were beginning to appear on his forehead. That's when I noticed his hands were shaking. "3rd and 4th dimensional... Test Zone Earth... TV signal... Specific? No... Full blanket coverage? Yes..."

Jacob's concentration was suddenly interrupted.

Agent Jackson came running into the cave shouting, "Major they're here! Eight Thunder helicopters are on their way in from the south!"

"Eight?" cried Ben, emerging from the pyramid. "Commander Holm is really sending in the cavalry!" He turned back to the pyramid and said to Jacob. "Stay here Jacob and get this thing working on the double. In the meantime we'll just have to keep them occupied!"

Ben ran out of the cave, machine gun in hand. In the distance, we could hear the sound of the approaching choppers.

"All hell is about to break loose!" cried Janus.

"Damn!" said Jacob, wiping the sweat off his brow. "There goes my concentration. Now I have to start all over again."

"You can do it, Jacob," I said as calmly as I could. "The Force is with you."

Jacob took a deep breath and started moving his hands over the quantum transmitter again.

Janus and I ran out of the pyramid and motioned to Rebecca to go and support Jacob inside the pyramid. We ran out of the cave to find that the agents had been busy while we were inside. They'd reinforced the semicircle wall of rocks and boulders that stood in front of the cave, making it higher and wider. Now the entrance of the cave was pretty well protected. Jackson and Sorvino were already in position behind the barrier, machine guns in hand. Ben was standing on top of the barrier staring into the darkness.

Loch Roag might have been covered by the mist and fog, but there was no doubt about what was happening. The sound of helicopters came thundering across the bay.

We could see the choppers' searchlights scanning the mist and darkness. Jackson was right, there were eight of them. And now they were almost over us. The exact same type of choppers that Ben had used when he'd hunted us down in England—only now Ben was the one being hunted. He jumped down from the barrier.

The helicopters roared overhead as we pressed ourselves against the rocks that were piled up before us. The noisy choppers disappeared into the darkened landscape behind the cave. Ben began to climb up to have a look.

Sorvino grabbed his arm. "Better let me go, boss. It's important that nothing happens to you in case you're needed inside the starship."

Ben looked at his Lieutenant for a moment. Then he nodded and climbed back down to let Sorvino pass.

"Wait!" I cried. "Don't you go killing anyone now Lieutenant Sorvino!"

The stocky Lieutenant turned around. "This is reality boys—we're not talking no fantasy role-playing anymore!" he said. "If you boys want to buy enough time to send your message out to the whole world, it's probably going to cost lives."

"But we're not supposed to use violence on our mission," I protested.

Sorvino shook his head and looked over at Ben.

"Do as he says, Ron," said Ben slowly. "It's their mission. No killing."

"But how the hell do you expect us to keep them back if we can't use violence?"

"Use your imagination, Ron," said Ben. "Shoot 'em in the knees or something."

"Aye aye captain," grumbled Sorvino and began to crawl up. He was soon out of sight. Less than a minute later, he was back, shouting down at us, "Four of the choppers are about to land, Major!"

"Tell Hama to get back down here right away!" cried Ben. "It's too dangerous for him to be scouting around up there anymore!"

Sorvino disappeared from sight.

I looked at my watch. It was now eight minutes past ten. We had less than two hours to STARDAY.

Four more choppers flew over us again, focusing their powerful searchlights down on us as we tried to hide. They were so close I could see the faces of the men staring down at us from one of the choppers. After they passed overhead, the four choppers spread out. Two of them veered to the right towards the landmass that jutted out into the bay to our right about a hundred yards away. The other two headed straight for the island out in the bay that was also about a hundred yards away. Behind us, we heard the sound of the other four choppers landing.

"They're closing in on us!" cried Jackson.

The two choppers that veered right now landed on the promontory to our right. From where they were, their powerful searchlights reached us and illuminated the barrier we were hiding behind. Through the mist, we caught glimpses of 10-15 soldiers in army-green uniforms jumping out of each helicopter and begin running towards us, machine guns in hands.

The other two choppers landed across from us on the island and immediately directed their searchlights in our direction. Over there we could see men jumping out too and bringing all kinds of gear and equipment with them as they took up their positions along the shore of the island facing us.

"Paratroopers!" cried Ben. "Looks like the storm is upon us. What the hell is Jacob doing?"

Ben and the other agents began to pile up their weapons and ammunition on the rocks. Ben unzipped his black bag and placed Starwarrior's sword next to the ammunition. The sword gave off a faint glow in the mist.

"Are they going to kill us?" asked Janus.

"I sure hope Commander Holm gave them orders to bring us in alive— but you never know," said Ben as he loaded two more machine guns and took out some handguns. "If he was in London when he got the news of our whereabouts, which he probably was, he can't have gotten here yet. And that means if we begin to shoot at these men, they will definitely shoot back."

I looked back into the cave. In the glow of the oil lamps I could see Jacob, still standing inside the pyramid with his hands over the quantum transmitter. Rebecca stood by his side, her eyes closed.

Suddenly I heard the sound of gunfire. Ben and Jackson were in position, their machine guns raised, Ben aiming at the soldiers on the island across from us, Jackson aiming at the soldiers on the promontory to our right. But neither of them was firing. The sound of machine gun fire I was hearing was coming from behind us and seemed to be increasing. Sorvino and Hama were still out there somewhere. The glare from the searchlights was almost blinding.

Two soldiers appeared up on the cliff behind us to our left. One of them let out a cry—shot in the leg by someone behind him. He grabbed his leg in pain and fell over the edge, plunging down towards the hard rocks below. The other soldier disappeared from sight.

On our right, soldiers were approaching through the mist from the choppers on the promontory. There must have been at least 20 of them and they were moving rapidly in our direction. Jackson fired a warning volley at them. They ran for cover behind some boulders and fired back at us.

"Get down!" cried Ben.

We pressed ourselves behind the stone barrier as the bullets whizzed over our heads, hitting the rocks behind us with loud pinging sounds. More soldiers appeared above and to our left. They also began to fire at us. We were being attacked from all sides.

Ben swung around and fired a sharp volley at the soldiers to our left while Jackson kept firing to our right.

Suddenly two figures appeared on the cliff directly above us, obviously running as fast as they could.

It was Sorvino and Hama.

A torrent of machine gun fire followed them. Sorvino threw himself over the edge and tumbled down towards us.

Hama stumbled and got up, but was hit by several shots in the back.

"Hama!"

Ben leapt up onto the rocks and began to crawl up towards the fallen Hama.

With a giant effort, Hama got to his feet again.

In the blinding chopper light, we could see that Hama was badly wounded. He was covered with blood. He took a step forward, but was riddled with more bullets.

Hama tumbled forward and fell off the cliff. He landed lifelessly on the rocks below.

"Damn!" cried Ben as he hurled himself behind the barrier.

"Are you hit, Major?" asked Sorvino.

"No, it's nothing, the bullet just grazed me."

Ben ripped the empty cartridge from his machine gun and reloaded. "What the hell is taking Jacob so long?"

418

Jackson and the soldiers to our right began exchanging fire again.

At the same moment, Rebecca appeared in the entrance of the cave, shouting, "Starbrow, Telperion! You've got to get in here now and help Jacob. We must focus on the Force."

"Go ahead boys," hollered Ben.

"But we can't use violence Ben," I cried as the gunfire raged around us.

"You get yourself into that cave right now Starbrow, all I'm trying to do is buy you some time!"

There was nothing else to do, so Janus and I dashed into the cave as bullets whizzed around us.

Inside, Jacob was still standing in front of the quantum transmitter with his eyes closed. Sweat was pouring down his face and his whole body was trembling.

"Is he still trying to get that thing to work?" whispered Janus to me. "And even if he does... are we going to be able to talk to the whole world while being shot at from all sides?"

The battle outside had intensified. Suddenly there was a loud boom. I looked back and realized that a well-aimed mortar had just made a huge hole in the middle section of our stone barrier. Ben and Sorvino were frantically throwing rocks back into the gapping hole.

"They need help!" I cried.

"We need you more here, Starbrow!" cried Rebecca in return. "If we don't focus on the Force now, all will be lost!"

Suddenly two projectiles came hurtling straight through the hole in the barrier and landed with a hollow thud right in the entrance to the cave.

By the way the projectiles smoked, I knew they were tear gas.

Ben and Sorvino ran from the barriers and grabbed the grenades and threw them out towards the bay.

Shots hammered through the opening in the barrier. Sorvino was hit in the head and fell to the ground.

"Ron!" cried Ben.

Janus and I ran back to the entrance.

Ben held Sorvino in his arms. The side of his face was covered in blood. Agent Sorvino was no longer in this world.

"This is crazy!" cried Janus. "We're all going to be killed!"

I looked back at Rebecca and Jacob who were still inside the pyramid. Jacob's eyes were closed. Rebecca looked at me as if to say that more than anything in the world Janus and I were needed inside the pyramid.

I looked back and forth between Jacob and Rebecca and the agents battling outside.

My eyes met Ben's.

"Do it!" he cried. "Do what you have to do! Without the Force nothing matters anyway!"

I turned and ran back towards the pyramid. At that very moment, another projectile flew through the barrier and into the cave, landing right in front of the pyramid.

Rebecca stared at the smoking tear gas grenade in horror.

I plunged for the grenade and grabbed it. It was a lot heavier than I expected. I picked it up—the gas already pricking my eyes.

I held my breath and ran back to the cave opening. Then I hurled myself to the right of the barrier and threw the grenade into the water with all my might. It landed with a splash far out in the bay.

The next few seconds passed as if in slow motion.

Under the cover of darkness, more soldiers had crept up behind the stone barrier. Now one of them was towering right up in front of me.

"Starbrow!" cried Ben.

With one swift movement, Ben grabbed his sword and leapt towards me. The moment he grabbed Starwarrior's sword it began to shine brightly, like a torch that had suddenly burst into flames.

The soldier fired.

But the bullets never reached me.

Instead they hit Starwarrior's flaming sword, which Ben had swung right in front of me.

CACHIIING!

The machine gun bullets glanced off the sword's shiny surface—just like that!

The soldier fell back in amazement.

But Starwarrior's sword was not the only thing that was illuminating the mist around us. The moment Ben grabbed hold of his sword, a bright silvery star began to glow on my forehead.

The star of Starbrow.

The star of the One with the Sight.

"Starwarrior! To your right!" I cried.

With one mighty stroke, Ben swung Starwarrior's sword to the right.

A torrent of bullets came flying towards him from the right, but the shining sword blocked them all.

CACHING! CACHING! CACHING!

"To your left!" I cried.

Ben turned left and blocked another barrage of bullets.

CACHING! CACHING! CACHING!

420

"In front of you!"

Two soldiers appeared in the gaping hole in the barrier.

With matchless precision, Ben swung Starwarrior's sword in a wide arch towards the soldiers.

The sword cut through their machine guns as if they were made of butter.

"Left!" I cried. "Right! Front!"

Ben jumped back and forth between the stones, blocking one volley of bullets after another.

It was more like a dance than anything else.

The star on my brow was the fine-tuned radar that registered every single projectile that came charging towards us. The sword in Ben's hands was the impenetrable shield that blocked and neutralized everything the star picked up. Starwarrior revealed in all his might.

The seconds ticked by and still Ben and I wove our intricate dance among the stones.

The star and the sword.

Starbrow and Starwarrior.

The One with the Sight and the Warrior from the Stars.

It all happened so quickly—and was so perfectly synchronized—that I no longer had any sense of who was looking through the star and of who was swinging the sword... of who was Starbrow and of who was Starwarrior.

Then the machine gun fire stopped.

All was silent.

The attacking soldiers had retreated back behind the rocks and boulders in stunned amazement. Obviously they'd never seen anything like this before. They must have thought we had strange magical powers.

And they were not the only ones.

Janus and Jackson were also staring at us in surprise.

"You two are..." began Janus.

"... amazing...," cried Jackson.

I smiled at my friends. Slowly Ben lowered Starwarrior's sword, breathing hard.

At that very moment, several things happened.

A soldier, who apparently had been hiding behind the barrier, jumped up behind me as I turned my back to the barrier.

I didn't see him but saw Ben crying "No!" as he hurled himself towards me.

As if in slow motion, I heard the soldier fire and felt Ben slam into me, pushing me aside just enough so that the bullets didn't hit me.

But they hit Ben instead.

"Major!" cried Jackson.

She fired a round at the soldier, who quickly disappeared behind the rocks.

Ben and I landed hard on the ground.

I rolled to one side and turned to look at my rescuer.

Ben didn't move.

He'd taken the bullets that were meant for me.

12

Blood and Gray Mist

I pulled Ben back towards the entrance of the cave and turned him over. His chest was covered in blood. He opened his eyes.

"Star... brow?" he groaned.

"Ben!"

Blood began to trickle down one side of his mouth.

Again the soldiers began firing from all sides. Jackson fired back as Janus desperately tried to block the gaping hole in the barrier by throwing huge rocks into it.

I no longer paid any attention to the frantic battle around me. I bent down over my bleeding rescuer.

"Were you... hit?" gasped Ben, heaving after air.

"No, no... lie still and I'll..."

"It's too late now."

"But you saved my life, Ben!"

"That is... as it should be," he gasped. "I took your life in England... and now... I repay the debt."

"No, Ben!" I cried in a choked voice. "You and I have only just started. We still have so much to do together. We're going to experience STARDAY together, we're going to..."

Ben coughed as the blood seeped from the sides of his mouth.

"Ben!"

Desperately, I tried to stop the bleeding but there was blood everywhere.

"Stay with me, Ben! The Force is with you! The Good is with you!"

"No, no... it's too late now..." he whispered.

"Don't say that!"

I gripped his bloody hand and clenched it tightly.

It felt strangely cold and lifeless.

Ben started to get a faraway look in his eyes.

"No, Ben, no…"

Then a light began to glow in Ben's eyes, as if he suddenly saw something immensely beautiful. His eyes shone like they did when we were in the mountains looking up at the large golden star… like they did when we sat on the windswept shores of Planet Earth and looked up at the Great Divine Light...

"No, Ben..." I whispered, clenching his hand tightly. "Not yet, not yet..."

Ben's body trembled slightly.

"Ben!"

Starwarrior let out a deep sigh and went limp.

"No Ben! No!"

I gripped his shoulders and shook him.

"Ben! No! Not yet!"

But he didn't move. Instead he lay lifeless, staring up at the sky as if he was looking at some invisible heaven.

Ben was no longer in his physical body.

Ben was... above me because I saw a great shining etheric form lift itself from his body. A soft breeze wafted over me.

I released Ben's lifeless body and placed him gently on the cold ground.

For a moment, the shining form floated before me.

Ben's shining soul.

Starwarrior.

Tears welled up in my eyes.

Starwarrior.

My eternal friend.

My eternal brother.

For a brief moment, it felt as if Ben's shining soul was smiling at me. Then the breeze took Starwarrior's soul and I watched as it floated away from the entrance to the cave and into the gray mist and fog of Callanish.

"Ben..." I whispered slowly.

The shining form became a solitary point of light in the mist, like a solitary star in the darkest night. A few seconds later, the point of light disappeared. All that was left was the gray mist.

"Ben..."

I bowed my head and felt hot tears on my cheeks.

My hands and clothes were covered with blood.

All that was left was blood and gray mist.

Around me I heard the sounds of a battle raging.

More killing, more dying, more death and destruction.

So much death.

Death everywhere.

Death.

Ben's death, Sorvino's death, Hama's death, the death of so many brave volunteers. It was all so meaningless. The death of all the good people who had fought so bravely to create peace and harmony on Earth.

It was so meaningless!

Meaningless!

Absolutely meaningless!

And now they were all gone! Done for. Dead. Finished. Over.

It was such an incredible waste.

Just like our deaths would be. Because in all probability, it wouldn't be long before Janus, Jacob, Rebecca, Jackson and I would also be killed by the troops that were rapidly closing in on us. And then it would be over. All over. And we'd be gone too.

Just like Ben.

And all that would be left would be blood and gray mist, death and destruction.

The harsh sound of death and destruction was upon us, creeping ever closer. Machine gun fire raged on all sides. Grenades, machine gun fire, gun fire. Fire everywhere. Fire in the soldiers, fire in Jackson and Janus. And fire in me. Burning, burning…

I too was on fire. Burning like everyone else.

No! I thought to myself.

No!

I will not let them die in vain.

I will not let my brave friends die in vain!

No!

I took Starwarrior's shining sword from Ben's bloody hand and leapt to my feet. The moment I grabbed the sword, I felt a tremendous sense of strength and determination flood through me like an enormous power. It was the same feeling I'd felt more than once during the past few days— and each time it seemed to grow stronger in me. Now I knew it for what it was, the indomitable strength and fierce determination of a warrior!

But I had no time to think because righteous anger welled up in me and consumed me. I was on fire. On fire for Ben, on fire for Sorvino and Hama, on fire for all those who had been killed because they were trying to create peace on Earth. On fire for all those meaningless deaths! On fire…!

I turned around, the rage consuming me. Gunfire was pounding us from all sides and our stone barrier was almost blown completely to bits. Janus was desperately trying to hurl stones back in the hole while Jackson was panting hard, her shoulder red with blood.

I clenched Starwarrior's sword firmly with both hands and then with a mighty shout I charged forward, straight into the midst of the battle.

Two soldiers had crept right up to the remains of the barrier and were now aiming their machine guns at Janus. I could see that my friend, exhausted as he was from the intense battle, would not have time to leap for cover.

The soldiers fired but the bullets never hit my friend.

In one mighty leap, I was at Janus' side.

CACHING!

The machine gun bullets glanced off on the sword's shiny surface.

The astonished soldiers fired another round at us, and again I deflected every bullet with Starwarrior's sword guided by the star, the faultless radar on my brow—just as Ben had done earlier.

CACHING! CACHING!

With every sword stroke, Starwarrior's weapon shone more and more brightly. Like a torch bursting into flames. The sword in my hands was on fire, the star on my brow was on fire, the attacking soldiers approaching me were on fire, my friends were on fire, I was on fire, everything was on fire, the whole world was on fire…

An inferno of fire!

Death and destruction!

Blood and gray mist!

A group of soldiers to our right fired at us, but again the star on my brow anticipated the attack.

CACHING! CACHING! CACHING!

And Starwarrior's sword deflected the onslaught with effortless ease.

Machine gun fire continued to rain over us from all sides, but without knowing how, I deflected every bullet with Starwarrior's sword. Encouraged by this unexpected turn of events, Jackson, although wounded, began to return our attackers' fire. Janus picked up Ben's machine gun and began firing at the attackers to our right.

CACHING! CACHING! CACHING!

The battle now waxed furiously on all sides, but the soldiers were unable to penetrate the invincible shield of Starwarrior's sword that I was swinging up and down, right and left, with skillful strokes.

And with every mighty stroke, I felt the fire within me grow stronger and stronger... burning, burning... I was burning with rage at the senseless death and destruction all around me...

So fierce and skillful was my dance with Starwarrior's sword—and so precise was Janus and Jackson's machine gun fire that slowly the elite soldiers began to retreat even though they greatly outnumbered us. Slowly, slowly they faded back towards the promontory to our right.

And then suddenly all was quiet.

The machine gun fire stopped and all the soldiers had faded from view. Each and every one of them—except one—a big, burly fellow who had been lying behind one of the boulders in front of me. I had known he was there all along, but since he wasn't carrying a machine gun, I took little heed of him, focused as I was on deflecting bullets with Starwarrior's sword.

Now suddenly he lunged towards me with a big knife in his hand. But I was too quick for him. With a well-aimed kick worthy of Ben Nevis himself, I knocked the knife right out of his hand. Then he turned to run, but I had no intention of letting him go. I was on fire, on fire...and everything I touched was going to burn too.

I raised Starwarrior's sword and was ready to plunge it into the soldier with all my might when a loud voice cried from behind me, "No Starbrow! Don't do it!"

I stopped in mid-air and froze.

I was so surprised by the voice I heard that I dropped Starwarrior's sword on the wet rocks with a loud clang. The burly soldier disappeared into the mist.

The voice was Ben's!

I turned around.

Ben was still lying on the cold ground, his face and body covered with blood. But his eyes were wide open and he was looking straight at me.

"Don't do it, Starbrow," he said, struggling to speak. "Don't set the wheel of more death and destruction in motion..."

13

The Spiritual Warrior

I stared at Ben wide-eyed.

I thought he was dead and gone!

But there he was, my dear friend, looking straight at me with his eyes wide open.

"Ben!" I cried rushing over to him in amazement. "You're alive! You've come back!"

"Yes," he said hoarsely as if he was trying to regain the use of his voice. "But only for a moment."

"Ben!" I exclaimed, kneeling by his side, more surprised than I'd ever been in my whole life. Janus and Jackson were also staring in wonder at our friend who had miraculously returned from the dead.

"Ben!" I cried. "This is fantastic. You're back!"

"Only for a moment," he said slowly. "So listen carefully!"

"Ben, what are you talking about?"

"I'm not waiting another 1,500 years to do this again. Not a third time!"

"It's a miracle!" I whispered, not understanding what was going on. "I thought that you were…"

Ben clutched my hand tightly and pulled me very close to him. "Starbrow, I only have a moment," he said with great effort. "So listen!"

I looked at him uncomprehendingly. Jackson and Janus were still lying at each end of the remains of the barrier, machine guns in hand. There was no sign of the soldiers who had retreated into the mist. All was silent around us.

"Listen, Starbrow!" Ben said fiercely. "Just now when I left my physical body I soared up a great tunnel of Light."

"A tunnel of Light?"

"Yes! And when I did, my whole life flashed before my eyes. My whole life in the blink of an eye. And in that blink of an eye, I saw and remembered everything!"

I just stared at him.

"Everything, do you understand?" he said in an intense voice. "I saw and remembered everything! Including the last crucial part of the Lost Teaching of the Single Eye... the part about putting the Single Eye into practice."

"Into practice?" I said, suddenly remembering what happened on that fateful day when we were unexpectedly interrupted... just as The Three E Masters were about to tell us about putting the Single Eye into practice. But we never heard the last part of the teaching because of the bloodhounds...

For a moment Ben looked up at the night sky above us. The light in his eyes blazed fiercely. Then he looked at me and said resolutely, "Listen, Starbrow and listen well. The last thing the Three E Masters were about to tell us about the Single Eye was that to fulfill the Prophecy of Starwarrior two things are crucial. The first is that we must have the Single Eye and focus all our attention on the Truth, on the Force, which is Good—all the time. The second is that we must put this Truth into action, that we must practice this Truth every moment of every day."

"Put this Truth into action?" I said. "But isn't that what we have been doing all along?"

"No," said Ben, "unfortunately not."

"But..." I started to reply.

Ben cut me off as if time was running out. "It's true that a lot of the time we focused on the Truth, on the One Force, on the Good. But that isn't enough to really influence the course of human events. To really make a difference, we must act according to the Truth we have learned. And that means putting it into practice—in our every action. In other words, we must live the Truth and breathe it. We must become it and be it. You must understand Starbrow, it won't be good enough until our every thought, word and deed reflects the Truth. Until our every thought, word and deed is an expression of the Good. Until our every thought, word and deed is the purest expression of love and compassion that we are capable of. And all this translates into non-violence."

"Non-violence?" I looked down at my hands. They were still shaking from my fierce encounter with the soldiers.

"Yes!" said Ben sternly. "Non-violence. Because love and compassion in action are non-violence. Love and compassion in action mean not harming a single living creature. Ever. Not in any situation, at any time, under any circumstance, no matter what!"

"No matter what?"

429

"Yes," said Ben, "That's what non-violence means. It means never harming another living creature, ever. No matter what."

"Even in self-defense?"

"Yes, even in self-defense," he replied, his body twitching violently. For a moment, I thought he was leaving me again but he struggled hard and forced himself to stay. He moved his face closer to mine. "Now listen carefully!" he said, speaking as fast as he could, "There are two reasons, Starbrow, why you must never harm any living creature. The first is because of our essential Oneness. When you understand the Truth of Being, you understand that we are all One Being. We are all One with the Force. So if you harm someone else, you are really harming yourself."

He clutched my hand tightly. "And the second reason, Starbrow, is the Great Law of Cause and Effect, which the Masters also call Karma. Whatever you do to another is going to come back to you. That's the Law! Your every thought, word and deed will, sooner or later, in this life or in the next, come back to you. Do you understand?"

"Come back to me..." I said slowly, trying to engrave Ben's every word on my memory.

"Yes!" cried Ben. "Sooner or later, in this life or in the next, it's all going to come back to you. Thought for thought, word for word, deed for deed. That's what I just saw when I had my life review! All the pain and suffering, all the death and destruction I caused others in my past life as Gavin, I experienced with mathematical precision in this life as Ben."

"But you just gave your life for me..." I exclaimed.

"Listen, Starbrow, I'm not done," he said, fighting desperately to stay in his body. "The reason I returned just now is because you were about to make the same mistake that I—and all of humanity—have been making for thousands and thousands of years! You were forgetting the Truth of Being and giving in to rage and reckless anger! And by doing so, you were setting the wheel of Karma in motion again, planting new seeds of pain and suffering—planting new seeds of death and destruction. By giving into anger, you are creating more suffering."

He was breathing hard but he continued, "And that's not what our mission is about, Starbrow!" he said with all his might. "Our mission is about putting an end to suffering, death and destruction! Our mission is about creating peace and harmony on Earth by raising the collective consciousness. And you can't do this by using violence!"

I looked down at my bloody hands again.

Ben was silent for a moment and then he said very slowly, "Starbrow, you must lay down your weapons immediately. You must stop fighting and choose love and compassion instead. No matter what the cost. Even if it means that our mission fails, you must do it right now. Because… there is no violent way to peace."

Ben coughed hard. There was blood everywhere.

"Remember what I am saying Starbrow… there is no violent way to peace. Peace is the way. This means that if you want peace, you have to be peace. You have to embody love and compassion—every step of the way—in your every thought, word and deed. This is the only way we can create peace, by being peace. This is the only chance for peace. This is the only way to fulfill the Prophecy of Starwarrior."

"Peace… is the way…?" I repeated after him.

Ben smiled. "Yes, Starbrow. *There is no violent way to peace. Peace is the way—every step of the way.*"

Then he continued, "But Starbrow, it won't be easy. In fact, choosing love and compassion every step of the way, in your every thought, word and deed, will be the hardest thing you've ever done in your life and it will require immense strength and courage—the strength and courage of a warrior. Don't you see how nicely it all fits together?"

"What do you mean? I said, shaking my head.

"Just now when my whole life flashed before my eyes," continued Ben with great effort, "I suddenly understood why the Three E Masters chose me, of all people, to receive the Lost Teaching of the Single Eye. For who better to put the Single Eye into practice than me, Starwarrior? A warrior full of strength and courage, someone who was ready to give his life for the Common Good? Only I forgot that the true warrior, the true Spiritual Warrior, does not use violence in his attempt to achieve the Good. Does not cause pain and suffering for his brothers and sisters. On the contrary, the true warrior, the true Spiritual Warrior, has the Single Eye and uses all his strength, courage and determination to see God, the Good, as the One and Only Reality behind all changing outer appearances. And the Spiritual Warrior puts this Truth into practice. The Spiritual Warrior lets his or her every thought, word and deed be an expression of the Good—an expression of love and compassion, an expression of our oneness. This is true peace."

Ben looked over at Janus. He was still clutching a smoking machine gun in his hands. "Remember what the Masters taught you, Telperion," cried Ben. "Thoughts, words and actions are the cause and all our outer experiences are the effect. If your thoughts, words and actions are violent, although you do it for a good cause, a just cause, the end result will still be death and destruction, not the peace and harmony you seek. Because cause and effect are the same. The seed and the plant are the same."

Ben closed his eyes. I could feel it was taking a superhuman effort for him to remain in his physical body.

Then he opened his eyes again and motioned first to Janus and Jackson, then to me. "You must stop the fighting now," he said firmly. "You must lay down your weapons. You must stop seeing and treating these soldiers as your enemies. You must see and treat them as they really are, as living expressions of the Force, the Good. No matter what they do to you. Do you understand?"

"But if we lay down our weapons, they'll kill us," protested Janus from where he lay. "Look what they've done to Sorvino and Hama!"

"If that is the price you must pay, so be it," said Ben. "Remember that the true Spiritual Warrior sees only the Good and acts accordingly—no matter what the outer appearances. This means that even if the outer appearance is violent, even if the outer appearance is one of pain, suffering and even death, the Spiritual Warrior still sees only God, the Good. This is the only way we can break the vicious cycle of violence on Earth. Because *there is no violent way to peace. Peace is the way.*"

I looked back into the cave. Jacob was still standing by the quantum transmitter, Rebecca by his side. His eyes were closed and so were Rebecca's.

"But we're so close to sending out our message, Ben!" I cried desperately. "If we lay down our weapons now, the soldiers will capture us and prevent us from sending out the message. Then all will be lost. All our efforts will be in vain. STARDAY will be cancelled."

"So be it," said Ben. "Remember the teaching of the Masters. *There is no violent way to a peaceful end.* It is impossible to send out a message of love and peace while acting violently! Don't you see Starbrow, if you are acting violently, your own consciousness will not be high enough to send out such a message. And even if you do manage to send out the message, the energy charge behind the message will be too low, so people won't feel the Truth of what you are saying and you will fail anyway!"

"But..."

"No buts," said Ben. "Our mission is to raise the collective consciousness of humanity. And as you yourself have said countless times, we can only do this by raising our own consciousness. And we can only raise our own consciousness by thinking, speaking and acting peace."

"But..."

"No buts Starbrow," said Ben again. "Remember that it is your intention that counts. It is your intention that creates the energy charge

432

behind everything you do. That is all that matters. The end result is in the hands of the Force!"

I realized that the fire that had burned so violently inside me just a few minutes ago had cooled down.

"Do it now," said Ben motioning towards Starwarrior's sword. It was lying among the rocks, still shining faintly. "The sword of Starwarrior now belongs to you, Starbrow. It may be too late for me to put the Single Eye into practice this time around, but it's not too late for you. You are a Spiritual Warrior now. And a Spiritual Warrior knows that *there is no violent way to peace. Peace is the way, the only way. Every step of the way.*"

Ben smiled at me and then looked up at the night sky and sighed. For just a second, the light in his eyes grew, but then it dimmed. And a gust of wind, which this time I knew was from Ben, touched me.

"Ben!"

His body went limp.

"Ben…"

He moved no more. And then for the second time I saw that radiant light soar up from his body and I knew that Ben was dead—again.

But this time I did not shake him or beg him to come back because I knew there would be no coming back this time around. With the immense force of his will, Ben had returned to tell me the true meaning of the name Starwarrior.

The sword of Starwarrior now belongs to you.

You are the Spiritual Warrior.

And the Spiritual Warrior knows that there is no violent way to peace.

Peace is the way.

Every step of the way.

I gently closed Ben's eyes. Then I turned towards Janus and Jackson. Janus was looking at me intensely, but Jackson was staring into the mist. "They're getting ready for another attack, Starbrow," she said. "What do you want us to do?"

14

Peace Is the Way

Janus and Jackson were both looking at me. Somehow it had fallen on me to make the decision whether to continue fighting or not.

I looked out into the midnight mist of Callanish. Jackson was right. Our attackers had regrouped and were slowly approaching, getting ready for another round.

Ben's last words echoed in my ears.

You must stop seeing and treating these soldiers as your enemies.

You must see and treat them as they really are, as living expressions of the Force, the Good.

With each passing moment, the soldiers were getting closer. As they slowly advanced, machine guns in hand, I found myself looking at the face of one of the soldiers in the front line. For a moment, the mist parted and the pale moonlight shone on his face. He must be very young, I thought as I looked at him. Younger than me. Probably in his early twenties. Then I realized that the expression on his face was not really one of hostility. No, it was fear. Pure fear.

My heart went out to him. My so-called enemy was afraid, just like me.

And with that thought, it was as if I saw right past the tough-guy exterior straight into his soul. Underneath it all, he was just a young guy, a kid like me and Janus and Jacob. Maybe from London, Newcastle, or Glasgow. Trying to live his life, trying to make a living, trying to make sense of it all. Just like Janus and Jacob and me were doing back in Copenhagen.

Just like me.

A regular guy.

An ordinary human being.

Just like me.

Seeking the Good.

Seeking Peace, Happiness, Love.

Now sent to this desolate place, to this God-forsaken island in the Outer Hebrides, and thrown into battle with a strange enemy with seemingly magical powers. Seeing his friends get shot and wounded, one by one. Desperately trying not to get killed. Desperately trying to stay alive. Wanting to go home. Wanting some peace. Just a little peace.

How could I ever fight him?

How could I ever hurt him?

My own brother.

I looked down at Ben's lifeless body. Although his face was covered with blood, there was still a faint smile on his lips. As if he'd found peace, even if his last moments on Earth had been in very violent surroundings. Inside, his smile said, he had found peace.

I walked over to Starwarrior's sword. The weapon was still glowing faintly. Janus and Jackson followed me with their eyes.

I picked up the sword and held it up before me. Immediately the sword grew brighter and inside me, I once again felt that strange power stirring. That feeling of strength, courage and determination that were now mine.

The sword of Starwarrior now belongs to you, Starbrow.

You are the Spiritual Warrior.

Ben was right. It was just as the Prophecy of Starwarrior said.

Starbrow, the One with the Sight, was not just me. And Starwarrior, the Warrior from the Stars, was not just Ben. The One with the Sight and the Warrior from the Stars were fully present in both Ben and me. That was why in his past life as Gavin and in his present life, Ben had experienced such powerful stirrings of the Sight. Because Starbrow, the One with the Sight, was also a part of him. And that was why I had experienced such a strong awakening of the strength and courage of the warrior during the past few days. Because Starwarrior, the Warrior from the Stars, was also a part of me.

The sword of Starwarrior now belongs to you, Starbrow.

You are the Spiritual Warrior.

The soldiers were getting closer and closer. I gripped the sword firmly with both my hands.

Strength. Courage. Determination.

I knew that I could resist and fight bravely. I knew if I did, I would truly be a force to be reckoned with.

But was that really what the strength and courage of the Spiritual Warrior was meant for?

Ben's words raced through my head:

435

The true warrior, the true Spiritual Warrior, does not use violence in his attempt to achieve the Good. Does not cause pain and suffering for his brothers and sisters.

The true warrior, the true Spiritual Warrior, has the Single Eye and uses all his strength, courage and determination to see God, the Good, as the One and Only Reality behind all changing outer appearances.

And the Spiritual Warrior puts this Truth into practice.

The Spiritual Warrior lets his or her every thought, word and deed be an expression of the Good—an expression of love and compassion, an expression of our oneness. This is true peace.

Because there is no violent way to peace.

Peace is the way.

Every step of the way.

Slowly I lowered Starwarrior's mighty sword. Then I turned and walked back to Ben. Janus and Jackson were still watching me intently.

I knelt beside Ben's body and put Starwarrior's sword in his hand and closed his fingers around the shining weapon.

"Okay, Starwarrior," I said softly. "I get it now."

Then I stood up, turned around and faced the mist and the soldiers. Janus and Jackson remained as if turned to stone. Then Jackson said slowly, "Without that sword to defend us, we'll be dead meat in no time."

I didn't answer her. Instead I gazed out at the soldiers. More and more were approaching, getting ready for the next wave of attack. In the pale moonlight, I could see their cold weapons and their young, frightened faces. Any moment now, one of them would raise his weapon and fire at us.

I felt a wave of fear wash over me. But I tried not to focus on it. Instead I tried to focus on my breathing, just as the Masters had taught us. I tried to focus on the air flowing in and out of my lungs, calming the pounding of my heart, calming the sense of panic that shook me, calming the flames that had burned so violently within me just a few minutes before.

At the same time, I really tried to see the faces of the soldiers approaching us through the mist and fog. And as I did, I saw that each and every one of them was just like the young man I had focused on before. Each one was young, insecure, confused, and frightened. Each one was a stranger in a strange land just like myself, trying to make sense of it all, trying to stay alive, dreaming of peace...

And even though it now seemed very far away and long ago, I realized the profound Truth of what dear sweet Emma said as we stood on the Sea of Glass—we are all seeking the exact same things. We are all seeking

Peace, Freedom, Love, Life and Happiness. We are all seeking the Good. All of us—without exception. The soldiers, the agents, Ben, Janus, Jacob, Rebecca, Jackson, me… And because of our lack of understanding of our essential oneness with the Good, we were all—each in our own way—suffering and creating more suffering because of our own ignorance of the true Nature of Reality.

"Starbrow!" cried Jackson. "The soldiers are within range now. If you don't get down, you'll get yourself killed!"

I paid her no heed. Instead I slowly began to repeat the Three E Masters' formula.

"IN THE BEGINNING: THE GOOD…"

"What are you doing?" hissed Jackson. "Have you gone mad?"

Janus, who was still staring at me, took a deep breath. Then he laid down his machine gun and stood up next to me. Looking out at the approaching soldiers we began to repeat the Masters' formula:

"IN THE BEGINNING: THE GOOD
HERE AND NOW: THE GOOD
AT THE END OF THE END: THE GOOD
HERE, THERE, EVERYWHERE: THE GOOD
FROM ALPHA TO OMEGA: THE GOOD
IN HEAVEN, UPON EARTH: THE GOOD
IN THE GREATEST, IN THE SMALLEST: THE GOOD
IN FIRE, IN WATER, IN EARTH, IN AIR: THE GOOD
IN ME, IN YOU, IN EVERYONE: THE GOOD
ABOVE ME, BELOW ME, AROUND ME: THE GOOD
IN ME, THROUGH ME, FROM ME: THE GOOD
IN MY THOUGHTS, IN MY WORDS,
IN MY ACTIONS: THE GOOD
THE GOOD IS ALL IN ALL
ALL LIFE, ALL INTELLIGENCE, ALL LOVE
THE GOOD IS THE ONE AND ONLY REALITY
AND SO IT IS!"

As we spoke these words, slowly and clearly, the soldiers kept advancing from all sides. But despite the fact that they were now within shooting range, not one of them fired a shot. Whether it was because we had laid down our weapons or because they had received orders to take us alive or for some other reason all together, it was hard to say. But it mattered not. All my attention was on the Three E Masters' formula. And as Janus and I slowly repeated each word of the formula, Jackson put down her gun too and stood up and joined us. As we spoke the words, I tried to recall everything the Three E Masters had said about the True Nature of Reality. About the Good that everyone is seeking... About the Perfect, Unlimited Life, Love, Peace, Happiness, Freedom that everyone is seeking... About the Nature of Reality that is this Good... About God, the One Force, Spirit, Life, Presence, Mind... in me, in you, in everyone... here, there, everywhere... and as I remembered their words... slowly slowly I began to experience what lay behind the words we were repeating... just as I had done when I stood in the presence of the Great Masters...

Because their words were merely signposts.

Gateways.

Gateways that led to the actual, living, breathing Presence itself.

The Radiant Spirit.

The One Force.

God.

The Good.

The more I thought about God, the One Unchanging Reality behind all physical appearances, the more the bodies of the soldiers coming towards us seemed like a veil to me... a very thin veil... that was covering the Radiant Light within... the Radiant Light that was the Light of the Force, the Light of God, the Good... pure natural Goodness... with no limits... no boundaries... no borders... with nothing blocking it... with nothing between me and the soldiers... with nothing between me and Janus and Jackson... with nothing between me and Emma and Emmet and Ernest... in the Light of this pure natural Goodness, we were all One... One Life, One Love... our bodies but passing ripples on the One Great Ocean of Life and Love...

And with this realization came a heightened awareness of our indestructible Oneness and I felt a great wave of love and compassion arise in my heart... and a soft breeze, a gentle wind, caressed my face...

The fine healing wind of the Force, the Good.

And I knew that I was not the only one out here on Callanish who was feeling the fine healing wind of the Force, the Good... I knew that I was not the only one whose heart was now overflowing with love and compassion...

Because out there in the mist, walking right next to the soldiers, were many more beings of pure natural Goodness, showering each and every soldier with their boundless love and compassion...

Yes.

I could see it now.

We were not alone out here in the mist.

The star on my brow pulsated strongly and with the Sight that was given me, I could see a great Being of Love and Light walking next to each soldier, regarding each soldier with such infinite love and compassion that I felt as if my heart would burst.

Yes, they were all here.

They had always been here.

And they would always be right here.

The Masters.

Walking next to the foremost of the soldiers was dear sweet Emma... with that look in her eyes, that smile of perfect contentment on her lips... because she knew, as I now knew, the True Nature of that soldier... And walking next to the soldier beside him was Sir Emmet... And dear Ernest was walking next to the soldier on the other side... Yes... And next to each one of the other soldiers walked another one of the Masters... Sananda, the Most Radiant One, who was once known as Jesus the Christ... and his beloved disciple, Saint John the Divine, now known as Master Kuthumi... And there was Master Serapis Bey... and Saint Germain, once known as Merlin, with his Violet Flame... and El Morya, once known as King Arthur... and Djwal Khul, the Tibetan... and many more of the Enlightened Masters that Jacob, Janus and I had seen on our way to Shamballa... in the Ascended Masters' Hall of Fame... the Ascended Masters of the Great White Brotherhood... the Masters who had gone before us... the Masters who had walked the same path of love and compassion... They were all there... Buddha, the Awakened One... Mahatma Gandhi, the Great Soul... Krishna, the Lord of Love... Master Moses... Mother Mary... Saint Francis... the Tibetan Buddhist masters... the Hindu gurus... the great Christian saints... the Muslim mystics... countless Buddhas, Christs, Starbrows and Starwarriors... and many other Masters from both East and West that I had heard of but never seen before... the Spiritual Warriors of humanity...

They were all here.

The power of their love and compassion was so great that the tears were streaming down my cheeks.

And I knew that they would always be with me.

And with each one of the soldiers, always whispering in our ears, whispering those sweet words of love and compassion—no matter what. Whispering, whispering—hoping one day we would stop and hear.

"And so it is," I said softly as I stopped and heard.

I took a deep breath and wiped away my tears.

Then I looked down at my watch.

23:42:18 Greenwich Mean Time.

Less than twenty minutes to STARDAY.

I turned away from the soldiers and the vision of the Masters and began walking towards the cave.

"Let's go," I said to Janus and Jackson. "It's time for us to give Moncler and Elantha all our support."

The moment the three of us turned our backs to the soldiers, many came leaping over the remains of our barrier.

"Don't move! Hands above your heads!" they shouted.

A wall of machine guns was pointed at us. Soldiers came charging in from all sides. We were brutally pinned down under the crushing weight of the many men bearing down upon us.

The next moment we heard a loud, high-pitched ringing tone coming from the heart of the cave. A bright golden light blazed forth from the cave, illuminating us all.

"Greetings, brothers and sisters in the Light!" I heard a familiar voice say inside my head. "I AM Moncler."

15

Calling All Humanity

As the soldiers pinned Janus, Jackson and me to the ground, dozens of other soldiers charged into the cave, which was now illuminated by a bright golden light.

The bright light was coming from our starship, which was not only glowing radiantly, but also sending out a continuous pleasant high-pitched tone, as if all of the ship's technology was now operating. From the corner of my eye, I could see Rebecca standing outside the pyramid, intensely watching Jacob who was standing in the middle of the ship with all his attention on the glowing quantum transmitter. His focus was so intense that he didn't seem to notice the soldiers who were charging into the cave. Rather he was looking straight at the transmitter as if it was some kind of TV camera.

And I knew why.

Jacob had finally gotten the transmitter to work!

Although his lips were not moving, I could clearly hear every word he was speaking into the quantum transmitter inside my head.

Jacob was talking to all of humanity on all the world's TV channels and being beamed out to every TV set in the world.

Good old Moncler!

Three soldiers ran over to Rebecca and grabbed her too. The others surrounded the pyramid and aimed their guns straight at it.

Jacob paid no attention to them. Within me I could hear every word he was saying. The quantum transmitter glowed and hummed as Jacob spoke, "... Less than two weeks ago my friends and family called me Jacob—and I was a graduate student at the Niels Bohr Institute in Copenhagen. But now, since my visit to the Mothership and the Ashtar Command with my two friends—Starbrow and Telperion—I am known as Moncler. During our visit to the Mothership and in our meetings with the Ashtar Command, we learned that all the things Commander Ashtar told you about in his 'full planet' global transmission a week ago are true. The members of the Ashtar Command are really representatives of the

Intergalactic Federation and they really have come here as our brothers and sisters in the vast multi-planetary, multi-dimensional universe that is our home. And as Ashtar said, they really have come in the true spirit of peace, love and brother-sisterhood to welcome the inhabitants of Planet Earth to the greater universe..."

The soldiers pulled us to our feet and shoved us into the cave. At the same time, the leader of the soldiers was shouting at Jacob inside the pyramid, "Put your hands above your head—and exit the pyramid slowly—now!"

Jacob paid no attention to him and kept on talking into the quantum transmitter. "... The reason the starships are no longer visible to the inhabitants of Planet Earth is not because they have disappeared. On the contrary, they are still here. But you cannot see them because the collective consciousness of humanity has once again fallen to a very low level due to the fearful and highly charged atmosphere on Earth and because of our separation thinking.

"By separation thinking I mean when we human beings think of other beings as different from us, as possible enemies... as 'them' in opposition to 'us'. This is separation thinking; this is the 'them' versus 'us' thought. We have been indulging in this type of thinking for far too long here on Planet Earth and many of us are doing this right now when we think about our brothers and sisters from the Ashtar Command. The moment we regard these representatives of the Intergalactic Federation as 'separate' from us, we become afraid of them because we think they might harm 'us' or do something to 'us'. This type of thinking is one of the main reasons why we can no longer see the starships. Unfortunately this type of separation thinking is a sign that we have forgotten the true fellowship of all beings, forgotten that we are all one family in the vast multi-planetary, multi-dimensional universe that is our home.

"But even though we've forgotten the truth, the starships are still here, waiting and hoping for STARDAY, which is scheduled to begin in just a few minutes time! But STARDAY will only happen if we human beings can again raise our consciousness to the high level we achieved when the New Vision was released almost exactly seven days ago. If you remember, together we experienced a higher level of consciousness that was characterized by the feeling of universal love and good will and by a deep understanding that we are all One—all members of the same family. Surely we can all remember the peace we felt in our hearts on that wonderful day.

"If we can raise our consciousness to the same high level again, we will then be able to see the starships because they are operating on a higher

442

frequency level—on the level of love and peace. By raising our consciousness to this level, together we will be able to trigger the release of STARDAY on Planet Earth. And for all of us, this will mean a new era of peace, love and enlightenment—a new era of limitless opportunity for all of humankind. If we do not succeed in raising the collective consciousness of humanity in the next few minutes, STARDAY will be cancelled and the Ashtar Command will leave Planet Earth. If this happens, we can realistically expect that hundreds of years will probably go by until humanity once again gets the opportunity to join the fellowship of the universe that is our home…"

The captain kept yelling at Jacob to stop and come out of the pyramid, but his words fell on deaf ears. He motioned to two of the soldiers. "Get him out of there fast! And be careful. We don't know what this thing is capable of doing!"

The two soldiers walked up to the entrance of the pyramid, machine guns cocked. "Please, my friends," I said as calmly as I could in a loud voice. "You must not interrupt him…" I tried to free myself from the soldiers, but they held me tightly.

"Please!" I said again. "He is talking to all humanity, asking them to focus on the brotherhood of man, on peace and universal love, so we can all experience STARDAY in a few minutes time…"

Their captain motioned for the soldiers to proceed.

"Just give him a few more minutes!" cried Janus. "Then you can do whatever you want with us!"

Since the pyramid was shut, the two soldiers banged on the door with the tip of their machine guns, but nothing happened. They then tried to pry it open with their hands, but since there was nothing to hold onto on the pyramid's smooth surface, they failed.

For just a moment I felt a flash of fear, maybe the soldiers would blast open the door and stop Jacob before he completed the transmission.

"Please don't interrupt him!" I cried. "The future of humanity is at stake!"

The soldiers kept trying to find a way to open the door to the starship, but it was no use. Suddenly I realized why. Once the starship was activated only someone with an interdimensional key could enter the ship!

I took a deep breath and returned my focus to Jacob's telepathic message to the world.

"… So dear brothers and sisters, we can only experience STARDAY in a few minutes time," continued Jacob, "if we join together now and raise our consciousness, each and every one of us. It is as the Ashtar Command

443

has told us... It is as all the great spiritual scriptures of Planet Earth teach us... our focus determines our experience. Your individual focus determines your individual experience. And humanity's collective focus determines humanity's collective experience. And since every human being's individual focus is a part of humanity's collective focus, all you need to do right now and in the next few minutes is raise your own consciousness and focus your attention on love and compassion, on the universal brother and sisterhood of humanity, and on peace.

"To help us do this, we have been given a formula or scientific prayer for you to repeat and meditate on during the next minutes. The purpose of this scientific formula or prayer is to help you focus your attention on the True Nature of Reality—by whatever name you call it—be it the Great Spirit, God, the Goddess, the Quantum Field, your Buddha Nature, your Christ Nature, Tao, Brahman, the Self, Jehovah, Allah, Brahman—or any other name. The most important thing is to realize that whatever you call the Absolute Unchanging Reality behind all changing physical appearances—Its Nature is Good. Its Nature is Perfect, Unlimited Love, Intelligence, Life, Peace, Harmony..."

Suddenly I heard the sound of a gun being fired. Since the soldiers couldn't open the door, their captain was now trying to blast the door open.

CACHING! CACHING!

The pyramid reacted just like Starwarrior's sword—the etheric substance deflected the bullets. Everyone ducked as the bullets ricocheted back into the cave. Miraculously, no one got hit.

But Jacob was shaken out of his trance-like state and was looking at us all in surprise.

"Put your hands above your head!" shouted the captain. "And exit the pyramid slowly."

I shook my head, trying to signal Jacob to continue his speech.

"Don't stop, Moncler!" cried Janus.

Jacob looked back into the quantum transmitter.

"Dammit!" cried the captain. "Get out of there now!"

I took a deep breath and focused on Moncler's words again.

"... The words of the formula will now appear on all your television screens," continued Jacob. "Watch your screens and keep repeating the formula over and over again, dwelling deeply on the meaning of the words for the next minutes. We must keep doing this until the collective consciousness has been raised to a higher level of love and the starships appear and make ready to land. You will not be in doubt when this happens.

I, Moncler, greet you in Peace and in Love, on behalf of all human beings on Planet Earth. Adonai, brothers and sisters in the Light! The Force is with you!"

In my mind's eye, I could see the words of the Three E Masters' formula now appearing on every single television screen around the world.

IN THE BEGINNING: THE GOOD
HERE AND NOW: THE GOOD
AT THE END OF THE END: THE GOOD
HERE, THERE, EVERYWHERE: THE GOOD
FROM ALPHA TO OMEGA: THE GOOD
IN HEAVEN, UPON EARTH: THE GOOD
IN THE GREATEST, IN THE SMALLEST: THE GOOD
IN FIRE, IN WATER, IN EARTH, IN AIR: THE GOOD
IN ME, IN YOU, IN EVERYONE: THE GOOD
ABOVE ME, BELOW ME, AROUND ME: THE GOOD
IN ME, THROUGH ME, FROM ME: THE GOOD
IN MY THOUGHTS, IN MY WORDS,
IN MY ACTIONS: THE GOOD
THE GOOD IS ALL IN ALL
ALL LIFE, ALL INTELLIGENCE, ALL LOVE
THE GOOD IS THE ONE AND ONLY REALITY
AND SO IT IS!

I was focusing on the words of the formula when the captain grabbed me roughly and pressed his gun to my head. "Tell me how to get into that thing or I'll blow your head off!"

"There's no need," a voice behind him said.

The captain looked around. It was Jacob standing in the open door of the pyramid. "It is done," he said. "I have asked all humanity to dwell on the Masters' formula, to use the Single Eye and see the Force, the Good, as the One and Only Reality, now and in the next few minutes until 00:00:00 Greenwich Mean Time. The rest is up to the Force."

In two seconds flat, the soldiers had handcuffed Jacob, Janus, Rebecca, Jackson and me—and taken us out of the cave and up to the cliff above the cave. They ordered us to sit down in the grass not far from the waiting helicopters and posted soldiers all around us. The bodies of Ben, Sorvino and Hama were brought up from the cave below on stretchers and placed on the grass next to us. There were several wounded soldiers—most of them seemed to have been shot in the legs—who were now being treated, but there were no dead among them.

At the same time, two new choppers approached from the south and landed next to the others. About a dozen men dressed in civilian clothes jumped out of the choppers led by MI6 Commander Holm. The captain quickly briefed Holm who regarded us coldly and shook his head when he saw Ben and the other dead agents. Then he turned and ran down to the cave to see the unusual find.

I looked at my watch.

Only five minutes to midnight.

"Only five minutes to go," I said to my friends. "Time for us to focus on the Good."

"Let's hope enough people were watching TV just now and are willing to answer the call," said Janus.

"Whether they do or not, we still have our bit to do friends," I said.

Before I could say more, the captain returned with Commander Holm and his agents. They surrounded us.

"Quiet" said the captain. "I don't want any talking here, understand!" Then he looked at his men. "Split them up." The soldiers immediately separated us.

I turned my head. "Remember all that you have learned!" I cried to my friends. "And *fight like a Spiritual Warrior*."

My friends nodded back at me.

"For Ben," said Janus.

"Yes," I said. "For Ben."

16

00:00:00 Greenwich Mean Time

The soldiers separated us so we couldn't talk to each other, but it didn't matter. We all knew what to do. Now we just had to do it.

I closed my eyes and began to repeat the Three E Masters' formula in my head. But I'd only finished the first sentence when someone hit me quite hard in the face. I opened my eyes and found myself looking straight into Commander Holm's steely gray eyes. Two of his agents grabbed hold of me.

"Now you better talk to me and talk quick!" he said. "What is going to happen at midnight?"

Out of the corner of my eye, I could see my friends were also being questioned.

"Talk to me!" said the Commander. "What is going to happen at midnight?"

"Hopefully STARDAY will be released," I answered. "We have asked all of humanity to focus their attention on peace and love. And if everyone does that, we will have STARDAY on Earth."

"Don't give me any of that New Age crap!" roared the Commander. "We all know just how loving and peaceful the Ashtar Command is! Tell me the truth! Have you been in contact with the Ashtar Command in that pyramid thing? Are they going to start an invasion at midnight?"

I tried to remain calm. "It's like I said. If everyone focuses their attention on peace and love, the collective consciousness of humanity will rise and we will have STARDAY on Earth."

"Don't give me that bull! What's really going to happen at midnight?"

"Hopefully the starships will land as planned and humanity will have its first contact with the intergalactic community. But now you must excuse me because I want to join my brothers and sisters and focus all my attention on peace and love too." I looked at the agents and said, "For the sake of all humanity, I ask you to join us too."

The Commander grabbed me by the collar. "You will do nothing of the kind my young friend!" he bellowed and shook me violently. "You will talk to me, do you understand and you'll do it now! What does that damn thing in the cave do?"

I closed my eyes again and took a deep breath. "IN THE BEGINNING..." I said inside myself.

The Commander shook me roughly and hit me in the face again. This time I felt the blood trickling from my nose. Fear and anger welled up inside me but I reminded myself of Ben's last words.

There is no violent way to peace.

Peace is the way.

Every step of the way.

"Talk to me I said!" roared the Commander. "What is going to happen at midnight?"

The Commander was interrupted by a group of soldiers who came rushing up from the cave. "Captain!" they cried. "The pyramid has gone haywire! It's blinking like crazy and making all kinds of weird sounds."

I looked over at Jacob and Janus who were getting the same rough treatment as me.

The captain and the Commander exchanged looks.

The Commander pushed me away in disgust and cried to the captain, "Better get all your men out of there! We don't know if it's some kind of bomb!" He looked down at his watch. "Dammit, less than two minutes to midnight. Tell everyone to get away from that cave now! If there's another explosion like the one we had at Glastonbury Tor, we'll all be blown to kingdom come!"

The soldiers started running away in a panic. Four agents grabbed me and began dragging me away. I fell but they just continued dragging me along the ground. My friends were being dragged away too.

Less than two minutes to go! I thought!

Suddenly I was gripped by a terrible fear—what if we were too late? What if we didn't have time to repeat the whole formula again? Midnight was less than two minutes away!

I closed my eyes and tried to focus on the formula. I got as far as the first sentence when suddenly I felt something.

Despite all the shouting, confusion and rushing about, I felt something.

Something very subtle yet unmistakably clear.

Something that was stronger than all the chaos and confusion around me.

Yes.

There was no mistaking it.

I could feel it caressing my face.

Something so infinitely tender.

448

Something so fine.

Something that came from within—and from without.

And from all directions.

That wind.

Indeed that wind.

That fine healing wind!

The fine healing wind of the Force, the Good.

The fine healing wind that caressed my face the first time I looked at Emma and the other E Masters.

There was no mistaking it.

And now it was here.

Here on the cold, windswept cliffs of Callanish!

Here!

The agents deposited me and my friends behind one of the helicopters, a good distance from the cave.

I looked at Janus, Jacob and Rebecca and cried. "Can you feel it?"

"Feel what?" they replied.

"Feel that wind!" I cried joyously. "That fine healing wind!"

I laughed and breathed deeply. There was no mistaking it.

Jacob stared at me. "You mean…"

"Yes!" I said. "It's here… there… and everywhere!"

I could see that my friends were feeling it too because the grim expressions on their faces were replaced by looks of delight. Yes they were feeling it too! Feeling the infinitely tender caresses of the fine healing wind that was now coming from here, there, and everywhere…

Yes indeed, from everywhere.

The fine healing wind of the Force, the Good.

And then, as if it was awakened by the tender caresses of the fine healing wind, the star on my brow began first to tingle, then to pulsate, then to throb, with light and clarity… and then my friends, the agents, the soldiers, and all my surroundings seemed to fade… as my inner vision grew… and grew and expanded until I could see all of Callanish, all of the Isle of Lewis, all of Britain, all of Planet Earth… until I could see all of humanity… every man, woman and child on Earth… and I saw them all as sparks of Light and Consciousness… as billions of sparks of Light and Consciousness… all over the planet… everywhere… in every country, in every city, all over the world… millions of people all repeating the Three E Masters' formula… focusing their attention on the Force, the Good… millions of people… lighting up like light bulbs… in London, in Glastonbury, in Copenhagen, in Washington DC, in Moscow, in Rome, in Cairo, in Johannesburg, in Los Angeles, in Jerusalem, in

Mexico City, in Santiago, in Beijing, in Tokyo, in Delhi, in Katmandu...
in cities great and small, in towns and villages...in home upon home...
millions of people... each in their own way focusing on the Force... some
calling it God or the Christ... some calling it Mind or the Buddha... some
calling it Brahman or the Self... some calling it Allah, some Jehovah,
some Tao, some the Goddess, some the Spirit... but all of them,
regardless of the name they used for the Unchanging Reality behind all
changing outer appearances... were realizing that Its True Nature is
Good... is Perfect Life, Perfect Intelligence, Perfect Love... and all of
them were repeating the Three E Masters' formula ...

IN THE BEGINNING: THE GOOD
HERE AND NOW: THE GOOD
AT THE END OF THE END: THE GOOD
HERE, THERE, EVERYWHERE: THE GOOD
FROM ALPHA TO OMEGA: THE GOOD
IN HEAVEN, UPON EARTH: THE GOOD
IN THE GREATEST, IN THE SMALLEST: THE GOOD
IN FIRE, IN WATER, IN EARTH, IN AIR: THE GOOD
IN ME, IN YOU, IN EVERYONE: THE GOOD
ABOVE ME, BELOW ME, AROUND ME: THE GOOD
IN ME, THROUGH ME, FROM ME: THE GOOD
IN MY THOUGHTS, IN MY WORDS,
IN MY ACTIONS: THE GOOD
THE GOOD IS ALL IN ALL
ALL LIFE, ALL INTELLIGENCE, ALL LOVE
THE GOOD IS THE ONE AND ONLY REALITY
AND SO IT IS!

And as they did so, more and more people began to have the Single
Eye... more and more people began to realize and acknowledge that they
themselves... and their families... and friends... and neighbors... and
communities... and countries... that all of humanity... every race, every
nation, every religion... was and is the Force... the Good... the living
expression of Perfect Life, Perfect Intelligence, Perfect Love... and with
that realization came the fine healing wind of the Force, the Good...
revealing what will come to pass... revealing everything as it truly is... as
it always was and ever will be... One Glorious Garden of Goodness...
One Heavenly Hymn of Harmony... One Blissful Blessing of Beauty...
One Law of Life and Love... One Wonderful Wealth of Wisdom... One
Rainbow River of Riches... One Celestial Song of Sweetness... One

Perfect and Profound Peace... One Living, Loving, Laughing Life... on Magnificent, Magical Mother Earth... Our Heavenly Home in the Universe...

The Perfect World.

The dark storm clouds that had shrouded the planet in darkness the last few days disappeared, revealing the great, wondrous manifestations of the Goodness of the Force that were floating ever so silently and gracefully over Planet Earth.

And now everyone could see them, could see over each of the world's capitals and major cities the huge golden pyramids of light that were floating in the sky. Indeed the golden starships had been there all along, but now they were again visible to the human eye.

And yes, they were here; they had arrived. Our intergalactic brothers and sisters! Representatives of the billions of individualizations of the Force, the Good, that were strewn across the galaxies and the Universes—who had now come to celebrate the all-embracing Oneness and Goodness of All with us today.

On this, the Day of the Stars!

And then I heard it.

That clear, pleasant sound of high-pitched ringing tones coming from the golden starships that were floating above all our cities, all around the globe.

And in that moment I knew that the time must be 00:00:00 Greenwich Mean Time. And that it was Friday, the 10th of April here on Planet Earth.

STARDAY had begun.

17

Not Without My Brother

The capitals and cities of the Earth were not the only places where the starships suddenly appeared at 00:00:00 Greenwich Mean Time.

At the very same moment that the Ashtar Command's golden pyramids became visible over all the world's major cities, a large luminous starship also appeared in the sky above the Callanish Standing Stones. Like a small sun it was, in the night sky that was now clear and dotted with innumerable stars.

The pleasant sound of high-pitched tones emanated from the starship for a moment and then it began to move in our direction. A few seconds later, it was over us, lowering itself down to the open plain right next to us.

Whether it was because of the sudden appearance of the great starship, or because of the fine healing wind and the elevation of the collective consciousness or both, not a single soldier or agent fired a shot at the starship. A few fled in fear, but most just stood there, rooted to the ground with a look of complete wonder on their faces.

The great pyramid landed not far from us and the door opened. Jacob, Janus, Rebecca and I watched the opening in silent satisfaction, knowing that our friends were waiting for us to come on board.

"Boy am I glad to see that starship," said Janus. "I don't know about you guys, but for a moment there, I didn't think we were going to make it in time!"

"Yeah, I know what you mean," I said smiling in relief. "Commander Holm was so busy bugging me that I never really got a chance to repeat the formula at all."

"Do you realize what that means friends?" smiled Jacob.

"No professor," said Janus, "what does it mean?"

"Well it means that this time it wasn't just us and a couple of hundred volunteers who raised the collective consciousness. This time we weren't alone."

"No we weren't," joined in Rebecca. "And isn't that wonderful! This time it was a large part of humanity focusing on the Good—all at the

452

same time—that did it! Jacob your message really reached them—and made people join together and focus on the Good. I'm so proud of you my boy!"

"Yeah," laughed Janus, "It's truly amazing. This time humanity was actually saved by humanity!"

Jacob chuckled, obviously pleased that his superhuman efforts to master the quantum transmitter were not in vain. "Yes," he said and sighed. "I really can feel it. Can't you? The huge collective focus on the Force… on the Good… that is all around us right now?"

And with that, my three friends started to walk towards the golden pyramid.

But I didn't move.

They stopped and looked back at me questioningly.

I motioned over to the stretcher where Ben's body lay.

"Not without my brother," I said.

I walked over to the agent who had cuffed me and held up my hands. He looked at me for a moment and then took out some keys and unlocked my handcuffs.

I turned and went over to Ben. My friends did the same and joined me. A moment later, Jackson was with us too.

We all stood still for a few moments, looking down at Ben. There was still a faint smile on his lips—as if he was truly at peace.

"The Prophecy of Starwarrior has now been fulfilled," I said slowly, "thanks to you, Ben. You showed us the true meaning of being a Spiritual Warrior."

And with that, we lifted up the stretcher—Jacob and I on one side, Janus, Jackson and Rebecca on the other—and headed for the entrance of the starship. As we made our way, the silent soldiers stepped aside in respect, making way for Ben.

Making way for the one who had shown us all the true meaning of being a warrior.

There is no violent way to peace.

Peace is the way.

Every step of the way.

As we made our way towards the starship, we stopped, put Ben's stretcher down, and took one last look at Callanish—the wild and mysterious place where our strange adventure had unfolded. The very same place where we six Starseeds first began our mission on Earth some 12,000 years ago. The very same windswept corner of Planet Earth where the six of us were reunited again some 12,000 years later.

"What a trip," said Janus.

"Yes," I said sighing. "It sure was."

"Now don't you two go getting any wild ideas about interdimensional holidays or anything like that," said Jacob.

"What do you mean?" said Janus.

"Well we might have just released a STARDAY and removed the threat of an axis shift," replied Jacob. "But don't forget that all of humanity still has to ascend into the 5th dimension with Mother Earth."

"Hmm, you're right, Jacob," I said laughing. "Well I guess that means we can forget all about having an interdimensional day or two off?"

Janus shook his head, "And just when I was thinking we could enjoy a bit of breakfast and some well-earned chill time!"

With that, we all broke out laughing and gave each other our secret Dungeons & Dragons handshake.

And as we did, a fresh breeze from the Western Sea blew in over us.

And it was a fine breeze indeed. A fine healing wind that now caressed the face of every human being on Planet Earth as wave upon wave of people flocked to the capitals and city centers to welcome our intergalactic brothers and sisters. It was as if, right where we stood, we could hear all the pleasant high-pitched ringing tones that were emanating from all the golden starships all around the globe.

"Do you hear that amazing sound?" asked Janus.

"Yes," I said, "I do. And it reminds me of what was foretold in the Prophecy of Starwarrior. *From the Single Eye will come the Perfect World... and then the Angels sing.* That's what that sound coming from the starships must be—the sound of angels singing!"

Then we laughed again, picked up Ben's stretcher, and walked with our brother, the great Spiritual Warrior, into the starship.

3 X THANK YOU

I would like to extend a special thanks to the Three E Masters for everything they have taught me about the Nature of Reality. Their full names are:

Emma Curtis Hopkins
Emmet Fox
Ernest Holmes

I highly recommend their many wonderful books to everyone who wants to know more about the Nature of Reality and the Lost Teaching of the Single Eye.

I would also like to thank all the many other spiritual teachers and Masters, East and West, past and present, who ceaselessly enlighten, inspire, comfort, guide and bless us on the Great Spiritual Adventure.

- Tim Ray -